Mariner's Wake

by

ADAM MARSH

Brick Cave Media
brickcavebooks.com

Brick Cave Media
brickcavebooks.com

❀ ❀ ❀

To everyone who knows that
a story can be so much more than just a story.

Mariner's Wake

by

ADAM MARSH

Brick Cave Media
brickcavebooks.com

Chapter One:
Trespassers

"It seems so outlandish now. A fever-dream with no chance of success. Only a handful of us had ever set foot on a ship, much less operated one. That, more than anything, will tell you how desperate we were when we started the slow journey from the Cottonwood camp to San Diego."
James Keeling, Reborn at Sea: Mariner History 2041-2063

A thick silence filled the bridge of the Penitent. Not a large bridge, to be sure, with only enough room for the captain, his first officer, the navigator, and the comms chief. Normally it would be lively enough inside the tin and plastic box, with comm chatter and arguments and laughter. At this moment, however, the absence of all that sound pervaded everything.

The deck below Captain Grayson's feet rolled gently. "Still nothing?"

Chief Fen met the captain's gaze. He shook his shaved head. "No, Skipper. No response on any channel or app."

Captain Grayson stood. He ran a hand over his own stubbled scalp. Everyone on the ship wore the same haircut, the fallout from a passenger a week ago who had brought them a case of lice as well as paid cargo haul.

"Let's see them again," Grayson said.

Chief Fen brought the video feed back up on the bridge's central monitor. Crystal clear, but moving along with the roll and swell of the ocean, the fishing vessel grew as they approached. She had a rust-red belly topped with grimy white. Five fishing lines trailed from her starboard and port sides, net lines dragging off her stern. The bastards were fishing, all right. Even worse than that...

"Sons of bitches are stealing our crop, too. Bold as brass," Commander Orozco said. Something about his first officer always put Grayson in mind of the kind of cur you saw roaming the docks year after year. Dingy, wiry, teeth permanently bared. "Orders, Skipper? We could ready the flashbangs and clappers."

That earned a couple of affirmative noises from the bridge crew.

"No," Captain Grayson said. When Orozco looked to object, the Skipper lightly brushed the eagle tattoo on his left cheek. Orozco quieted.

"How many times is this? Just this season alone?" Grayson asked softly.

Bilby, the navigator, piped up. "For us? Three. For the Mariner commonwealth, this is twelve."

"Twelve." Captain Grayson stood taller, clasping his hands behind his back. His pistol belt weighed heavy on his hips. "Twelve. Twelve times. How many times have we sailed in, made noises, and caused a fuss, politely asking these thieving bastards to leave our waters? Twelve. Every year they grow more bold. And why?"

Clearly, the bridge crew felt this question to be rhetorical.

"Because," Grayson continued, "we don't make them pay anymore. Not in property. Not in riches. Not in blood. Our peace and freedom came at a cost, gentlemen. When we don't pay it, the vultures start circling again. We're done talking. Commander Orozco, order the deckmaster to prepare for a critical removal. Chief Fen, jam their comms. Nothing in or out. Instruct helm control to bring us alongside our trespassers."

"Sir," Orozco said. "Our orders from command…"

"Are being followed to the letter, Commander," Grayson said smoothly. "You have your orders. We need everyone in position in five."

"Aye, Skipper," Orozco said.

The bridge burst into action. Grayson took a yellow bullhorn from its place by the entryway hatch. Trotting down the steps to the deck, he found the organized chaos of a well-oiled crew moving into action.

"Set the bumpers!" The deckmaster yelled. Deckhands scrambled to place the thick rubber pads over the port side of the ship, readying them for a hard jolt if they came in too fast against the fishing vessel.

The Penitent shifted to starboard, the ship's port side moving toward the rust-bellied fishing vessel. Closer and closer they drew together in the intervening seconds. She wasn't a large fishing ship, maybe thirty meters stem to stern. The Penitent was larger and sat a couple meters taller than her. Rather than be intimidated, though, the ship stayed put.

Out in front of the fishing vessel sat her dinghy. A tiny thing with a single motor. Two of the fishing crew leaned over its sides, bundling the kelp and sea-wheat growing from the Mariner's floating platforms. They barely looked up as the ship approached.

"Bold as brass." Orzco spit over the portside

railing.

"Let's do something about it then, shall we?" Grayson said.

Orozco gave him a wicked a grin. He rolled his bare shoulders back, his light vest blowing in the wind, revealing sparrow tattoos beneath. The commander put one hand on the machete at the left side his belt, and the other on the pistol at his right.

Captain Grayson let out a high-pitched whistle. The silence from the bridge rolled out on to the deck. The distance between them closed. The men in the dinghy looked up. One shaded his eyes.

Grayson put the bullhorn to his lips. His voice boomed across the deck and over to the other ship. "This is Captain Grayson of the Mariner Vessel, Penitent. You have one chance to cut your lines and leave our water. You have one minute to signal your compliance."

From the deck of the fishing vessel, three people emerged from the small bridge and walked out to view the Mariners, who were almost on top of them. Orozco passed Grayson his binoculars.

Looking through the glass, range data scrolled across the top of his vision. He could clearly see one man in an orange jump suit. He stood with arms crossed over chest, smirking.

And what's so damn funny? Grayson thought. *Is it us you're laughing at? Having a chuckle at the shipsies?*

Off to either of the orange man's sides, some of the reason for his confidence came clear. Two men, obviously professional mercenaries, clad in gray and black body armor stood with sub-machine guns in hand.

"What do you reckon?" Grayson dropped the binoculars. The Penitent was only moments from contacting the ship.

"Augmented," Orozco said. "Targeting, reflexes, strength. Standard Milo Merc bilge, I'd wager."

"Agreed." Grayson took a deep breath. "I'd say we have our answer, eh, Commander?"

"Aye, Skipper."

Captain Grayson looked over his right shoulder at the deckmaster. The deckmaster gave a single nod, then ran down to the weapons locker. Grayson raised his right hand skyward, paused, then flattened it in the direction of the dinghy. Lifted it, then pointed it again to the men on the bridge.

He whistled.

Shots rang out from behind the captain. Reports from bullets pierced the air, echoing across the deck of the Penitent. Two trails of fire spiraled across the deck, leaving a hot wake billowing over the captain and his commander.

The dinghy exploded. One of the men, burned and trailing blood from a missing arm, flopped down onto the nearest kelp platform and screamed. He wriggled across the slimy seaweed, blood billowing into the seawater.

On the deck of the fishing vessel, the second rocket struck the deck wide from its mark. It knocked the men from their feet, but they looked more or less uninjured. One of the fishing masts groaned and toppled into the water.

Grayson kept his footing steady as the Penitent made contact. Metal squealed as bumpers took most of the impact. Immediately, the deckhands threw their grapplers over the side and fixed to the fishing vessel.

"Rifles, on me!" Grayson shouted. "Board!"

The Mariners screamed a blood-curdling war cry. Dozens of men and women bearing gun and blade poured over the deck railing of the Penitent and dropped two meters down to the fishing ship.

Grayson and Orozco followed.

In seconds, Mariners opened the ship's hatch and poured below decks. Screams rang out from below. Mariners swarmed the fishing equipment, breaking it apart and throwing it overboard.

Grayson marched his way to the ship's captain, guns drawn.

Unfortunately, the mercenaries looked to be recovering from the blast. The larger of the two moved inhumanly fast to pick up his weapon. It could've been the end of Grayson, but fire burst from Grayson's left, opening small craters of blood along the man's face and neck.

"Good work, Mariners," Grayson said. From his right, two Mariners walked sideways, holding their fully auto rifles trained on the last mercenary. Not content to surrender, the armored man made to charge, pushing forward almost too fast for Grayson to track.

His Mariners held strong. Before the merc could cover a meter, he fell mechanically onto his knees, his skull split wide open in the back. Blood poured freely down his neck before the mercenary's body gave way and hit the deck.

"What did you do?" The ship's captain, down on his ass, looked at his mercenaries, then back to Grayson's crew.

"I'm asking you politely to leave," Grayson said.

Flecks of fleshy pink debris mingled with the puddles of blood and saltwater.

The fishing captain's face went white. "I'll go. I swear. I'll turn around right now. I'm sorry. I didn't know!"

"Didn't know what? That we could fight back?" Grayson smiled. He took a knee in front of the orange-clad man. Seawater and blood seeped into the fabric of his trousers where they touched the deck. Screams faded. The battle was all but over. "Haven't you heard it's bad luck to fish Mariner water? Haven't you heard it's bad luck to cross the shipsies?"

"I... didn't mean..."

"You thought you could take what's ours, is what you mean. See, it's bad luck to interfere with Mariners, because ships that leave port with that intent, rarely return. Over the years, some folks might have noticed."

Grayson gave him a toothy smile. Mariners gathered from across the deck. Their faces lit by flame, ink scrawled across their bare skin.

"Below decks are clear," Orozco said. "Five dead, two laid down arms."

Grayson nodded. "Treat them fairly. I'll be in to see them once we're under way."

"M-me, too!" The fishing vessel's captain rushed out the words. "I surrender, I'm not armed."

"Oh, not you." Grayson's eye twitched. "You had your chance. A captain must stand by his orders. You opted for a fight. A captain's words are as much a weapon as a blade or bomb."

Grayson lifted his right hand, holding the gun to the other captain's forehead. "At least you had the minerals to stand by your crew when it came time to fight. I can't abide a coward who calls themself a captain. There's some honor in that for you."

He fired.

Chapter Two:
Under Truce

"Having a code of honor means you follow it,
even when it's the most difficult thing
you've ever had to do."
Ethan Shan, Engine Mate, M.V. Water Lily

Kara scowled over the starboard railing. A Mariner couldn't have asked for better conditions. Blessedly calm waters and clouds just thick enough to take the sting out of the sun without hiding it completely. Overhead, the sun sails held firm to the masts, the black wings drinking in more than enough energy to keep them moving. Voyager's deck rolled gently under her feet as they made way to port. Absolutely ideal.

Why couldn't she have this? The beautiful day at the end of a successful mission? One hand rested on her hip, the other on her sidearm. Her pistol belt cinched down the waist of her loose shirt, ensuring it wouldn't get in the way if she had to move. The whole crew had already armored up, woven plastic and Kevlar plates secured in and on their clothes. Everyone wore different pieces, different sets, depending on their shape and how they fought. Would it come to that? Her frown deepened.

"Think you're gonna scare them away like that?"

Kara gave a small start. She hadn't heard the captain walk up to her side. In her defense the deck crew was making a hell of a racket behind her.

"No, Skipper," she said. "Just wishing they'd drink dirt, is all."

Captain Ansari stood silent for a few seconds, hands clasped behind his back, gazing out in the same direction, looking every bit the ship's captain.

Kara glanced his way, wondering. How did he do that? The man exuded confidence and authority. Even after Kara's first successful mission as a senior officer she barely felt deserving of her post. She shook it off. There'd be time to reflect later. Right now, the Voyager had bigger concerns. She and the captain watched from afar as the white-uniformed crew scrambled over the deck of their yacht, the distance reducing them to match heads. Their narrow ship cut through waves on a parallel course, more blade than boat; Kara had to admit there was a certain loping grace about her. But what was that ship doing in their waters?

Everything about them felt off. Foreign. Their clean uniforms covered in patches and badges. She looked down at her own sun-bleached clothing and the blue ink on her shoulders and hands. Sparrows to show the knots she'd sailed. A compass on the webbing of her left hand to prove her skills as a navigator. How could you show commitment with something you could shrug off like a shirt? Those people had no true loyalty to anything but greed and consumption.

As if reading her mind, Captain Ansari spoke. "They're flying a flag of truce. We're honor bound to respect that."

"Aye," Kara said. "It's the jack underneath the white that worries me."

"You're not the only one, Lieutenant. Come on. You've had your look. We're needed on the bridge."

Deck hands called to each other behind them, making ready for port. Tension thickened the air between them as the Mariners all kept a wary eye on the other vessel. They sang the port songs as they readied lines to trim the sun sails, but the notes carried none of the joy a homecoming normally did. Tension buzzed beneath their lifted voices.

None of the deckhands worked barefoot. Weapons lockers stood open, rifles bared in rows like predator's teeth. Chief Lambros, the deckmaster, stood ramrod straight, calling orders as she stepped around working deckhands.

Beneath her feet, the Voyager hummed a little softer as the engines slowed. Captain Ansari stepped through the hatch to the bridge, but Kara paused. She looked over her shoulder once more at the yacht across the water. A white flag of truce flew from her prow. Just beneath it, the stars and stripes of their bastard neighbors to the east.

"They've been instructed to moor on the east end of the pier, Captain." Ensign Martin didn't look up from his monitor, but he had everyone's attention. "Admiral Kim sent a company of Mariners from Vish Central to wait for them."

Captain Ansari's eyes held a tightness that normally wasn't there. "Inform Control that every Mariner on this ship is at the ready as well."

Martin relayed the message. Without the engine hum it was eerily quiet on the bridge. Even the deck crew kept it down. They'd finished mooring already. True to the captain's words, they all stood on deck, weapons ready. Over at Chief Atwood's helm station, all four of his monitors showed video feed focused on the American yacht. Outside the bridge, Voyager's deck stood eerily quiet. Every Mariner held themselves like tightly wound coils, ready to spring at the slightest touch. The ship's cat, Chief Rocket, who normally prowled the decks was nowhere to be found.

"Captain," Martin said. He paused a moment longer to listen to the radio. "You're being requested to accompany the, uh, the American officers. Admiral Kim is insistent that you understand this is a diplomatic escort."

Martin's cheeks flushed. He stared at his monitor as if sacred text spilled across it. Kara couldn't blame him. No junior officer would want to be in the middle of that pissing match.

"Tell him I copy. Commander Satry, you have the bridge."

The first officer frowned. Which was more or less the default expression on his long, jowly face. "I'll see the crew off and get her ready for maintenance. Just don't turn your back on those bastards, Skipper."

Captain Ansari barked out a laugh then motioned to Kara. "Consider it done. Lieutenant, you're with me. Remember, we're being diplomatic."

Don't shoot until they do, got it.

"Make sure you've got a phone with you," he added. "Last thing we need is to be out of communication if something happens."

The rest of the bridge crew got back to work while Kara grabbed one of the ship's phones—a sleek, flexible little number she'd won for them down

Okinawa way. It wasn't as fast and didn't have the storage of other phones. An acceptable tradeoff in her opinion. Not like she'd be watching video on it. Being concealable and waterproof made it gold as far as she was concerned.

Ensign Martin typed some notes while listening to whatever was going on. Satry scooted to the intercom, calling stations while tracing a slender finger down one of his infamous checklists. With nowhere to go, Chief Atwood left the helm to be with the deckhands and the rest of the crew, ready to blow that yacht to chum if the Americans tried anything stupid, as they were wont to do.

Mariners pressed fists to hearts as Kara and her captain crossed to the gangway. The salutes were for the captain, Kara knew. Their eyes held true respect for the man. A Mariner would always recognize another Mariner's command. But there was no force that could demand a Mariner's respect. Only competence could do that.

Wind from the ocean picked up. This time of year it could get strong enough to send a person doubled over against it, ebbing only with nightfall. The gentle breeze from earlier was now long gone. Deeper into the island, past the jagged windbreaks on the perimeter, it wouldn't be bad. From second-hand stories her mother had told her, the wind hadn't always been so severe. But that was just another one of those tales the elders liked to tell. Maybe things were better. Maybe they weren't. Either way, that time was gone.

As her boots clopped against the laminate planks on the pier, Kara looked out to the double column of Mariners now watching the yacht. It's pristine, white hull looked sterile compared to Voyager, with her running mural of dolphins cresting floating platforms of wheat and rice in gold, purple, and blue paint. Mariner ships celebrated their way of life.

This close she could make out the American ship's name emblazoned on her port side: The Gallant. Kara snorted.

"She's a sleek one, no?" Captain Ansari said.

Kara cleared her throat. "Doesn't make sense, sir. Why are they here in a civilian craft? This screams trouble. It's some kind of American trickery, I swear it."

White uniformed figures made their way off The Gallant and onto the pier. The mariners didn't greet them, exactly, but one at the front of their formation did start talking.

"If I were an optimist," the captain said, "I'd say they didn't come in a military craft to show goodwill and peaceful intent."

"Are you an optimist, sir?"

The delegation moved en masse toward Kara and her captain. A clutch of white-clad sailors stood completely surrounded by armed Mariners.

"I'm a realist, Lieutenant. Let's not disrespect our ways. They came here under truce."

"Aye," Kara said.

"I'm also a realist who was a deckhand the last time they tried to invade us," the skipper added. "I haven't forgotten. They make one false move, and you start killing everyone wearing white."

Her neck tensed. "Aye."

"They're a small group and not noticeably armed," Ansari went on. "But they could be enhanced with God knows what, or even spliced. Let's treat it like walking into any territory that's not ours."

"Smiles on lips," Kara recited. "Guns on hips."

Word spread quickly, but that couldn't be helped. Vish wasn't a huge settlement in mainland terms, but it was the second largest the Mariner's had. Only Gane was larger, but Vish was the original and held a special place in all Mariners' hearts. Their tiny empire consisted of five small settlements, flung over a swath of the Pacific on ignored islands and abandoned oil platforms. They'd turned rejected places into homes, either placing or restoring life as needed. Every meter of land was special and had to be protected. Primarily from the very people Kara now escorted down the Homefront Path.

True to her promise, she kept her hand close to her sidearm. She wasn't the only one. Along each side of the winding path, lined with citrus trees, the Mariner's walked with hands on rifles and eyes on the Americans. Only one of their group made any attempt at conversation; a man of unremarkable height and build, topped with dark hair and eyes holding up thick brows. He had an easy smile. Kara couldn't decide if it was because he was stupid or smug, but either way she wanted to slap it right off his face. Unlike the taller blond with the pencil mustache, the smiling man had a plain uniform. No badges or patches. The beanpole had more decorations than a Christmas tree and looked at the Mariners like they were stinking puddles of bilge. Clearly, he was in charge.

Captain Ansari had given them a quick greeting, but had only spoken since then to provide directions while they walked.

"Just around the corner," he said.

Past the edge of the orchards a corrugated steel entry gate barred their way, flanked by guard towers. Captain Ansari gave a nod to the tower guards, who signaled for the Mariners below to open up.

"Funny," Beanpole said. "We didn't know you were so well defended this far in. Couldn't be hiding anything, could you?"

Captain Ansari returned Beanpole's look with interest. "You didn't know, because your forces never made it this far. And never will. Keep in mind where you are right now, Captain. I'd recommend diplomacy."

Beanpole tried to look down at Ansari. He wasn't quite tall enough to pull it off but attempted it anyway. "Don't forget we're here under truce and at the invitation of your Admiral, Captain."

The gate rolled open to each side. Mariners holding rifles beckoned the group in.

"Oh, I haven't forgotten. Thing about truces, Captain," Ansari said, "is that they aren't one-sided. Both parties need to maintain peaceful intent. Without that..."

Beanpole gave him a small nod.

Condescending prick.

The steel gates marked the border between the town proper and the orchards that faced the southern port. As soon as Kara crossed over and her feet touched the paving stones leading to Vish Central, she found her people waiting.

Mariners of all stripes openly watched the procession. They stood in front of their homes and shops, made from shipping containers, or simple brick, or poured cement. Farmers stood with hands on hips, their light clothing hanging loose on their frames. Even the normally irrepressible children stopped their ceaseless games of chasing the local dogs and chickens to watch. Some of the Vish Mariners were armed with a knife, or a spear, or staff. Guns wouldn't be brought into action yet. This was simply posturing. Yes, we're tradespeople, yes we're farmers, and yes, we won't hesitate to tuck you in if you act up.

The small thoroughfare leading through Vish Central funneled them to the Square, which had never been square, but that was part of the charm. Overhead, shade canopies of solar sailcloth snapped in the wind. Hot plastic, salt air, chicken crap, peppers and citrus, it seasoned the air and smelled like home. One of Beanpole's subordinates wrinkled his nose while his buddy laughed. A sudden, violent urge to deck the bastard ran through Kara like a stomach flu. Before she could ruminate on it, something else about the prick caught her eye.

Gloves. No one else in their group wore them and it certainly wasn't close to cold outside. These weren't cotton dress gloves, either. Some kind of other faux leather material. This guy had to be hiding fingertip contacts. Forgetting about the man's earlier insult, Kara watched him unabashedly. If this locust thought he was going to get anywhere close to a device on their network, then his brain was fry-junked. She'd see him bled dry first.

Captain Ansari cleared his throat with a pointed look at Kara.

She made a quick hand sign for "glove." He caught on immediately, giving her a look as if to say, *as you were.*

Not all Mariners were adept with hand signs, but for Kara, a Navigator, having the ability to signal to other Mariners in the company of strangers was vital. She caught the eye of a Chief walking just behind the foreigners. Kara hadn't met him, but the two knotted ropes inked on his wrist could only mean one thing. She couldn't be sure if he completely understood her hand signs, but he must have caught the gist, as he sent a trio of Mariners to stand uncomfortably close to the gloved man.

The crowd thickened as they entered the Square and neared its most defining feature, the Bowl. Depending on who was telling the story, the reason for the spending precious resources on the amphitheater in those early days of Vish's settlement varied. Aravind Krishnamurty wrote that any who spoke on the amphitheater's stage had to look up at the people listening. A Mariner leader was then forced to always keep in mind that they served their people, not the other way around.

According to James Keeling, the Bowl was already half dug when they got to the island—the result of bomb testing a century before. His histories tended to be less romantic than Aravind's. That didn't change the fact that Aravind was right. At least in Kara's mind. Mariner leaders were still Mariners. Keeping those in power accountable is what separated Mariners from the nation they had left a few generations ago.

The same nation whose emissaries trailed into the Bowl.

Kara followed, now unsure if she should go all the way to the circular stage with Captain Ansari, or if she should find a place to stand nearby. Mariners from all over Vish filled the rows of curved benches that lined each terrace down to the bottom. Most stood, gawking at the Americans and talking to one another. She hadn't seen the whole town turn up like this in ages. It looked like she was going to end up standing next to her captain whether she wanted to or not. There was nowhere else to go.

On the stage stood the full spectrum of Vish's decision makers. Eight members of the Vish Island Council, plus their two visiting representatives from the Mariner Council. They'd prepared themselves well, considering the short notice of the Gallant's arrival. All representatives stood with their loose, sleeveless clothing, baring their tattoos to show their experience and service. Some had ornaments of bone and shell in their hair. All but two wore weapons, whether they were blunt, blade, or gun. In the foreground stood Peter Shostakovich, Vish's

Elect. Hard to believe he was on the third of his five-year term already but, according to Kara's mother, time had a way of speeding up as you got older.

Shostakovich had been a Navigator, once. Kara felt a point of pride that she had the same compass tattoo on her hand as their Elect. If the stories were true, he had been one of the best, which made him ideal for this spectacle. A navigator who couldn't negotiate wouldn't keep their job for long. Whatever was about to happen, they needed a shrewd representative on their side. She could already see Shostakovich's hand in this. The display of overwhelming numbers contrasted by a ceremonial welcome; the way he stood proudly with hands clasped behind his back with just a hint of a smile. Nothing too much. Nothing too soon.

To the Elect's left were Admiral Kim and Spark Hannigan. Both of them watched the Americans, Kim with more unease than Hannigan. At least Kara wasn't alone in feeling iffy about all of this business. Admiral Kim had been the captain of the Water Lily, the first ship Kara had been assigned to as a junior navigator. If he looked worried, then there was something to worry about.

Kara took a breath. If nothing else, she'd ensure that American sailor with the gloves on wouldn't go anywhere away from the road that took him back to their ship. That could be her small contribution. Was she imagining it, or did he look a little disappointed that they ended up here instead of some headquarters building filled with computers ripe for the plucking?

Silence settled over the Mariners in waves. Great triangular canopies snapped overhead. Knots of coltish teens scrambled barefoot up the poles holding the solar canopies and reeled them in for the night. It was good training for climbing masts and working aloft. Watching them usually brought a smile to her lips, it reminded Kara of her own youth. But her face remained impassive tonight. As the kids shouted and the canopies furled, the great sheet of stars lay above them. Her guides.

Elect Shostakovich bid a greeting to the Americans, then asked Spark Hannigan to lead them in a moment of contemplation. Hannigan kept it simple, asking only that they slow down and reflect on their intentions, always questioning if they were truly working to end suffering or if they were creating it.

Kara normally took the teachings of the Core of Being seriously. It called to her more than religion, even her mother's, ever had. But she excused herself from this meditation to keep her eyes open and on the Americans. As seconds ticked away in that moment of silence, strands of lights crisscrossing the Bowl and the surrounding Square winked to life. They cast a warm, orange glow on all assembled.

Sweat ran down her back. Kara watched as faces slowly raised. Spark Hannigan thanked them and stepped into the background.

Beanpole stepped forward and doffed his cap. The decorated sailor squinted around, clearly confused by the number of people watching. He must have considered his visit something of a secret. But the Mariners' leadership didn't keep secrets from them. Not if they could help it, anyway.

"Thank you for receiving us under the flag of truce." The man's voice was high and rough. "My name is Captain Marcus Falkner. My crew and I, we come in the name of Hunter Victor Gilligan and under the terms of the Great Calm."

Captain Falkner paused, obviously for some great effect, but was met with only confused whispers.

"What in the new spooky hell is he talking about?" Kara whispered.

"Maybe he got off on the wrong island." A Mariner behind her sniggered.

If Falkner noticed how his words were received, he didn't show it. The man next to Falkner, the only one with a plain, unadorned uniform, eyed the crowd with, what? Worry? Suspicion? It was hard to tell. And if Kara couldn't tell, that was saying something. Part of her job was shaking out intelligence from strangers. A few years of having her crew's safety rest on her diligence gave Kara an almost superhuman bilge detector.

Elect Shostakovich raised a broad hand. His thick, silver hair grew damp along his brow. Silence settled over the Mariners. "We respect the flag of truce and are ready to listen. Please, be welcome as guests and speak."

Calling them guests was a bit of a stretch but, as Captain Ansari said, the white flag must be respected. She noticed Shostakovich hadn't said anything about the whole Great Calm business, whatever that was. But their Elect was adept that way. Embarrassing the mainlanders would be counterproductive.

For some reason, despite Elect Shostakovich's welcome, worry lines deepened across the forehead of the plain-uniformed man next to Captain Falkner. His eyes darted from the Elect to Admiral Kim and back to the crowd. It looked for a moment as though he might interrupt his Captain.

Falkner stood straighter. "We are here to invoke the terms of our sovereignty under the treaty of the Great Calm. We have come to invoke command of your fleet for a most necessary purpose."

This time, silence gripped the crowd. Kara could almost hear the muscles tensing in Admiral Kim's jaw. Every Mariner in the Bowl glared at him.

Elect Shostakovich's face turned to stone. "You dare? You dare to claim command of our fleet? To claim any power over us? A free people?"

Captain Falkner's face reddened. At his side, his companion looked positively desperate. Most of their crew tried to retain composure, but surrounded and outnumbered as they were, Kara could imagine they wanted nothing more than for their Captain to shut his trap.

A wish he had no intention of granting. "So, you will violate the terms of our treaty? You would risk open war with the United States?"

"We risk nothing in a war with you," Admiral Kim spoke through gritted teeth. "We bought our freedom with your blood once, and we'll gladly pay that price again."

Kim's sentiment echoed through the Mariners, including a throaty, "Arr," from the marine behind Kara. She didn't know what the mainlanders had thought would happen here, but this was clearly getting out of their hands.

Finally, Falkner's companion raised both his hands and stepped in front of the Captain. When the Captain looked to overtake him, the man stared daggers at Falkner until he stood down. Kara watched with interest. Perhaps the American's chain of command wasn't as she had thought.

"Please, Elect Shostakovich, Admiral Kim, everyone," he said. Unlike Faulkner, this one spoke with the fluid grace of one used to persuasion and negotiation. "Please, can we start over?"

By the muscle pulsing in Admiral Kim's jaw and the unflinching stare on the Elect's face, Kara didn't think starting over would be quite that easy. Still, they let him speak.

"Let's forget about the treaty for a minute. It's not the point."

"There is no treaty," Kim interjected.

"I don't disagree," he said, "Let's set that aside for

now, please. We have a misunderstanding there, and honestly, it doesn't matter. It's beside the point. My name is Arnold Drummond. I'm a congressman from the United States here on a diplomatic mission. A mission that is incredibly, terribly important to both our people. I'm here to ask for your help."

Chapter Three:
Terms and Conditions

"Treaty? Contract? Sure, let's sign a treaty with a country that's never honored one."
Lizzy Hernandez, Sail Apprentice, Gane Island

Weeks of hard work and diligence had led to this moment. Tren did his best not to focus on the obvious. Which, first and foremost, was that this crucial moment wasn't simply disappointing, it was downright depressing.

In times not long passed, Tren would have launched a new project proposal as part of a team. Product demos, slick graphics, a pristine meeting with catering and drinks. Perhaps in the terraced garden of Easy Maggies, the finest steakhouse in Detroit. Only the best.

Now? No team. No demos. Maybe this place served food, but from the number of cockroaches that had brazenly charged him already, Tren decided it wouldn't be the best idea to sample the menu. Unlike the soothing electronica guaranteed to stimulate the necessary theta waves to get his audience receptive to their new product pitch, Tren had to endure an almost assaulting volume of C-Pop music relentlessly pounding out of the bar's jukebox.

As much as he tried to fight it, to tell himself that times were changing, Tren couldn't let himself believe it. Because this bar was terrible, the music was terrible, and Tren's life had become, most definitely, terrible. Still, as his father used to say, nothing worth doing was easy. Generally, that advice preceded a request for some type of menial chore that Tren found himself unsuited to finish to the man's standard, but the spirit of the expression remained. Right?

Tren made himself sit up straighter in front of his potential client. No slouching. He was never good at this sort of thing. This was what product and sales people did, not engineers. Still. This is what he had to work with. Tren had qualifications and a fantastic business plan. That would be enough.

He tried to speak loud enough to be heard over the blaring pop music. One good thing about the garish pink and blue lighting in the bar, Big Madrid wouldn't notice the stains on Tren's shirt.

"So, uh, you see"—Tren tried to finish his rehearsed pitch strong—"in conclusion, I am the best bet you have for your job. My resume speaks for itself. I've done many of these types of decryption jobs in the past and I can get yours done, too. My services can be yours, completed in no time at all, for the low price of five thousand."

Tren waited for a response. The song changed. He shot a nervous glance toward a nearby table, where his two mercenaries waited. Over at the bar a couple of women wearing heavy eye makeup and little else showed him a modicum of interest.

Oh, wait. Are they?

Tren blushed.

Big Madrid picked at his metal teeth. He sat calmly, fake fox fur stole around his bulging shoulders, eye lines darkened with micro-tattoos. Across the chipped plastic table and its layers of creative graffiti, the bald man regarded Tren like something caught in a reclamation filter. Violent pulses of purple and neon-pink circled around the bar's LED system. It gave the place a rushed, dreamy sort of feel.

"Thing is," Madrid said softly, "five large would be a standard price, wouldn't it? But you can't exactly charge a going rate, can you? Or a friend rate? Or a sweet nothings-in-my-ear rate, either? Cause you're out, Trenny-Tren-Tren. Out like a pocket-picker in forty-two. You've got no standing now, sonny. Not exactly"—Madrid leaned in, hand by mouth in a stage whisper—"legal."

"W-w-wait," Tren stammered. "Party blacklists don't apply here. This is a free zone. I'm free to offer my services at fair market value. Perfectly legal. Five thousand is far less than you'd pay on the mainland. That isn't conjecture. I've brought a prospectus, and I can show you a table of rates, which accounts for my experience and the necessary skills for the job required. This is a fair price, Mister Madrid."

"Oh dear, oh dear." Big Madrid chuckled and put a hand to his cheek in mock anguish. "Dear me, poor lad, you do over estimate your position here, don't you?"

What did that mean?

Why did people have to be so obtuse? Tren stuck shaking fingers in his shirt pocket and pulled out a poker chip. Just a precaution. Keeping it in his hand made him feel that much safer. He might not have been the best at reading people, but after a childhood of Tren being, well, Tren, he had learned to tell when danger lurked around the corner.

"Listen, Mister Madrid, I really need this job." *Idiot!* Tren winced. *You're not supposed to say stuff like that!* "What I mean is, I want to do this job and, and, and build my reputation here. Yes. That's it. So, I can bring down the price to two thousand and five hundred. Final offer, sir."

Big Madrid showed him a wide, chrome-filled grin. "Oh, playing hard ball now. And who, my love, is going to stop me from reaching over this table, grabbing you by that scrawny neck, and beating the ever-loving excrement out of you until you agree to do the job for free, eh? You have no standing, my son. None. No one to speak for your interests, shall we say. An unfortunate position to find yourself in, given this barbaric world of ours."

"You can't threaten me. I've brought backup!" Tren flipped over the chip, and touched his thumb to an indentation in the center.

One table over, Tren's pair of hired mercenaries stood. They were incredibly intimidating, Tren had seen to that. Like tough guys in movies. An unfortunate side effect of doing business in a place like this, but Tren had done his analysis right and predicted the need. He'd done well, if he said so himself. Gill only stood five and a half feet, but with her sharpened teeth and dual pistol bandoleers, people cleared well out of her way. Her towering partner, Gary, didn't have a single muscle un-enhanced, and not a scrap of his bald scalp un-inked. His poly-pigment tattoos glittered deep red and gold.

Their boot heels thudded over the weak flooring. Tren tried to shove backward in the booth, as far out of Big Madrid's reach as possible. On second thought, considering the lice and bedbugs that lurked in the cushions...He leaned forward again.

Gill and Gary arrived.

"Gill, Gary. Please explain to Big Madrid that I am under your protection," Tren said.

Except...

Tren blinked. Did it seem like his team was standing a little closer to Big Madrid than him? And not in a confrontational way? It almost, and he could be wrong, but it almost seemed like their backs were turned a bit toward his opponent. Not exactly offensive posturing.

Tren cleared his throat. "Gill, Gary. You mind, uh, explaining to Mister Madrid why accosting me would be a bad idea and why are you making those faces? What's going on here? How come you're both...Oh, come on, guys!"

Gill at least had the courtesy to look embarrassed. For a few seconds. Then she went back to her normal surly self.

Gary shrugged. "We're mercenaries, Tren."

"For God's sake, I thought you had some kind of code, at least? What the hell, you two? I thought we were in this together, like a, like a, family? Like a crime family?"

Gill made a noncommittal noise.

"Guys, how is this long-term thinking? I showed you my business plan. We had a future. My projections are solid." Tren couldn't help the rising pitch of his voice. His poker chip clattered down onto the table. "How are you going save for retirement now, Gill? How?"

"Be fair, Trenny," Madrid chided. He flicked an end of his faux-fur stole toward Gill. "Those enhancements? Her lifestyle? You really think retirement's in the cards, do you?"

Gill didn't bother to look affronted.

"It's your fault more than theirs, really. You didn't check to see if they were already indentured before you tried to hire them? Tut, tut. That's just amateurish, Tren."

Tren bit his tongue. That was actually a fair point.

"You'll do the job for free, my love."

"One thousand," Tren said.

An annoyed flutter passed over Big Madrid. He motioned with two fingers to Gary, who had Tren by the collar and out of the booth in a blink. Choking and coughing, Tren pawed uselessly at Gary's thick wrists while blood thickened in his skull. C-Pop blasted his ears. Was he already in hell? Was that it?

Big made a meal of getting up from his seat, dusting himself off, and readjusting his stole, all while Tren struggled for air. Stopping with his face centimeters from Tren's, he patted his cheek.

"Free, my little lamb," Big said. "Free."

Tren gasped. If he could've talked, he would've lobbed back a real burner.

"And if you do a very good job, bring Daddy back home his bacon nice and neat, maybe, I'll even allow you the dubious privilege of continuing to breathe. G and G, let's get him back home, shall we? Easy does it. Tren won't cause us a fuss, now will he?"

Defeated, Tren shook his head.

Perhaps, Kara thought, in the mind of Arnold Drummond the scene should have played out differently. The earnestness in his plea came through well enough. Shouldn't that have cut through the earlier tension? That change of subject from mystery treaty to plain request? It may have worked on a different audience.

Admiral Kim swelled. Drummond took a half step backward, his eyes wide.

"Help? Help you?" Kim said. "Two invasions,

years of skirmishes, lives lost, and you ask us for help? I don't give a sail's flap what you need, the answer is—"

Elect Shostakovich held up a hand, cutting off the Admiral in the midst of his tirade. Even with that gesture, the Elect didn't appear much more willing to discuss the subject than the Admiral.

So, probably not what the young American congressman had hoped for.

"I assume," Elect Shostakovich said, "that you can summarize what this request is?"

"Elect," Admiral Kim said, "even listening to this is insane. It's obviously some kind of ploy."

"They came under truce," Shostakovich said. "We'll let them say what they came here to say. To do otherwise steals our honor. You know this."

Kara knew that look all to well. The set of the jaw, the quick nod. Admiral Kim wasn't exactly sailing on sunshine.

Drummond, finally given leave to speak, collected himself. To his credit, he recovered quickly. Standing up straighter and ensuring that all the Mariners assembled could hear him, he spoke. "Thank you for hearing me out. I'll get right to it. There's a threat to our nation and yours at this very moment. It's difficult to explain in a way that makes sense. So I'll back up. Before the war, the United States naval power was much greater than it is today."

This comment earned a pointed throat clearing from Captain Faulkner.

"It's true," Drummond said directly to Faulkner. "We're not supposed to admit it—ever—much like many other inconvenient facts, but there it is. Before the war, the U.S. military had hidden weapons storage facilities in remote locations. As you can imagine, only weapons of mass destruction would warrant this kind of security. That is, nuclear, biological, and chemical. Unfortunately, as a result of the war and the, uh, instability that followed, our government lost track of some of these facilities."

Scattered groans and swearing came from the Mariner council. But, Kara noticed, Drummond did have their attention.

"These facilities were already layered in secrecy, even from some of the highest ranking officials in the pre-war government. During the war, as some of these key secret-keepers were killed, or government buildings destroyed, we lost what little accountability we had. The truth about some of these secret facilities was completely lost. I'm telling you this embarrassing truth, because the Mariners know better than anyone that we in the United States government have made a lot of mistakes. This is turning out to be one of the bigger ones. We recently received an intelligence report that one of these pre-war storage facilities has been discovered. Not by us. By a third party who, we believe, doesn't realize the extent of what they've stumbled upon."

"Explain," the Elect said.

"In short, a passing cargo ship picked up an acoustic transmission from a facility on the ocean floor. Deep in your territory. We're just not sure where. They haven't said, because they want to sell that location to the highest bidder. We believe that the vessel and sailors who picked up this short-range transmission haven't been able to decrypt it, and are unaware of what it contains. They've provided portions of it to potential buyers to validate that it's authentic, but there's no indication that they've cracked it. From what we understand, they believe they've found an old and valuable shipwreck."

"I'm not hearing the urgency, Congressman." The Elect folded his wiry arms over his chest. "In fact, it seems like it may be a good idea to keep your people as far away from this little honeypot as possible."

Drummond took in a sharp breath. "The urgency, Elect, is what that snippet of the broadcast contains. It's an encrypted message that contains error and warning codes. The weapons containment in the facility, the systems—which keep the nuclear, chemical, and biological weapons within stable—are failing. If allowed to fail, you could have a nuclear meltdown or a detonation of unknown power in your waters, irradiating the ecosystem I know your people have been trying to nurse back to health. There could be unknown viruses released into the waters. We honestly have no idea what could be down there. What we do know, is that we don't have a lot of time to stop it. And we can't do this without your help."

Every stitch of Kara's being told her not to trust this man. The only clue to the contrary she couldn't ignore was Faulkner. If the man grew any more red his head would burst. Even in the dim glow of the string lights she could see him holding on to his temper with all he had. The very idea of admitting such weaknesses to their enemies must have been eroding him from within, physically paining the man.

Every cloud did have a sliver lining after all.

That didn't change the seriousness of the claim, though. Kara surveyed the Vish Council. Every head bent low, whispering to one another. Could they be taking this seriously? She squinted at the congressman. It was too early to tell. So far all he had was a story. What was he going to ask for? That was the question. Because buried somewhere in that piece of information would be what it was he wanted.

Elect Shostakovich took a sharp breath in. "Are you looking for permission to bring your fleet into our waters to deal with this...threat? More importantly, do you even have the capability to deal with it? It sounds like there is an awful lot of information you don't have."

Faulkner looked like a mosquito about to pop.

Drummond took the question. "No, I'm afraid it's not as simple as that. Most of our fleet is supporting the EU blockade."

"Ah," Admiral Kim sighed dramatically. "Can't say no when Mother Russia calls, eh?"

"We have a long-held strategic partnership with Russia that has made America stronger than ever," Faulkner spat. Apparently, his resolve had finally weakened.

"Captain, please," Drummond said. "Yes, our forces are supporting the Russian Federation's blockade. As you can imagine, that puts most of our ships very far away from this problem. More importantly, the ships uniquely equipped to deal with this, the ships with submersibles, are too far away. We can't risk waiting. We need permission to take the Gallant into your waters, but, we also need your help getting to the underwater facility. We know you have craft capable of it. And, we may also need help locating the freelancers who are selling the location."

Drummond finished a bit weakly, all his cards now on the table. The Elect took his time, watching both Captain Faulkner and the congressman.

"Anything else you need us for?" Shostakovich asked lightly. "Sounds like all we need to do is completely solve your problem. Do you plan on participating at all in this little adventure? Or would you like us to come back with your weapons of mass destruction once we've found them?"

Surprisingly, Drummond returned the barb with a half-smile. "I deserve that," he said. "In fact, you're taking this better than I thought you would. I'd like to say that if the positions were reversed, my government would be as willing to hear you out. To be frank, I don't know if that's true."

"Then why come at all?" Shostakovich said.

"Because this"—he gestured to the space between their groups—"has to change. We've been at each other's throats for decades, and what has it gained either of us? If there's going to be change, real change, in the relationship between our people, it has to start somewhere. It has to start with some trust. That trust has to be built on something new, and fate is forcing our hand."

Spark Hannigan's voice cut in, "Do you believe in fate, Congressman?"

Drummond blinked, taken aback. He considered Spark for a moment, then turned up his palms. "I think I could fill volumes with what I don't know. Fate, blind chance, act of God, it all amounts to me standing here, asking for help."

"Well said." Spark tilted his head, asking for Drummond to continue.

"We have a chance to work together. Of course you can turn us down, or ignore us, or let us go it on our own in your territory without your help. Lots of options. Our best shot, our only real shot, at stopping a tragedy is to work together. But I can't stress enough the danger we face if we don't take this seriously."

Drummond paused, but if he was expecting some response from the Elect or Admiral Kim, they didn't oblige him.

"Look." Seized by inspiration, Drummond stepped to the side and motioned toward Captain Faulkner. "Does he look happy about any of this? Does this look like a man who's getting what he wants? No. Frankly, he looks five seconds away from a stroke."

That earned a couple of chuckles from some of the Mariners watching from the benches.

"If there is one thing my countrymen are known for, it is our inexhaustible supply of pride. For some people in my government, the idea of coming here, admitting our failures, and asking for help was less preferable than waiting to see what would happen with these unknown WMDs. If you think this is some kind of trap or ploy, then, ask yourself what the end game is here. You know our navy is too far away to support us. You know we won't use drones or air support against you and risk another round of sanctions. Why would we choose open warfare now? The last thing we need is more enemies."

Kara watched, waiting for the sweet moment when the Elect would shoot down Drummond's request and send the American's packing. But for some reason, the moment didn't come.

"We have to discuss this. Myself, the council, and the Admiral," the Elect said. "You understand that you will need to wait on your ship, where you will be under guard."

"We understand," Drummond said before Faulkner could protest. "Thank you for giving this thought. While you talk, please keep in mind that we're working against the clock. If you have any questions, well, you know where we'll be."

With that, the excitement in the amphitheater ebbed away. Kara stood in disbelief while the American delegation was taken back to their yacht. Why was the Elect even considering their ridiculous request? Mariners filed out of the benches, except for the diehards who wanted to hear the council's deliberations. They made their way closer to the stage as seats on the stone benches freed.

Captain Ansari said her name, snapping her from her thoughts.

"Sir?" she said.

"It occurs to me that before all this excitement

happened, you would've been planning something else tonight."

"Oh." Her cheeks flushed. "This is more important."

He gave her a rare smile. A small thing, but sincere. "It is important. But it's under control. You've earned this, Navigator. I'm sorry the rest of the bridge crew won't be there with you. Under the circumstances, it'll have to be a small group. In fact, I think someone's coming your way to make sure it gets done."

Captain Grayson and Lieutenant Bilby stood on the deck of the Penitent, just after midday. Most of the crew still wore their long sleeves, but jackets and coats weren't necessary in the summer. Even this far north. One ship mate hung off the side by rope to touch up Penitent's bright red and gold mural of Mariners cleaning plastic from the ocean. Other deckhands busied themselves with cleaning and rigging. Both on the Penitent and her neighbor. Grayson watched the empty deck of the fishing vessel next to them, now moored securely with line and a gangway.

"Aye. Could do it, Skipper. Of course," Lieutenant Bilby said.

"But?" Grayson gave his navigator a wry smile. He knew the man's mannerisms too well. The slight hesitance, the hand on the back of his neck. It added up to the navigator saying yes but wanting to say no. Bilby had earned his second set of compass points years ago and was among the best navigators. His only weakness was a tendency to manipulate conversations rather than speaking up. Grayson was his captain, not some damn fence shifting stolen goods at the docks that needed to be finessed.

"But," Bilby said, "my gut's yelling at me not to, sir. We've swept four times and found two dormant trackers. Broke them, of course. Saved the diamond batteries; those things are dead useful. Wish I could say that was the end of it, but who knows? There could be one buried inside her girders for all I know. We don't have the tools on board to do that kind of search. If we tell Chief Fen to drop the jamming signal now, any passive beacons left in that ship will light up like a Sailing Day party. Then we'll have all manner of unwanted attention."

Captain Grayson leaned his bulky frame against the railing, looking out at the fishing vessel. "I understand. If your instincts are telling you no, we should trust that. Still, we need to open comms back up soon. There's too much going on that we need to be aware of. For all we know the RF and EU are best friends now and we'll be knee deep in cruise ships and fishers tomorrow. They'll steal and fish and dump and pump until the ocean is black and the Mariners are homeless again."

"I'm with you, Skipper." Bilby didn't offer much more in the way of commentary, though. Together the men stood and watched the deckhands moving signal detectors across the fishing vessel's deck.

"She's got good bones, Bilby. Seems more than a waste to scuttle her." Captain Grayson rubbed at the stubble where his beard used to be.

"Then let's not. It's a bit of a slog, but we can keep up the jam and escort her to Cora. The breakers there will make short work of her. We'll have to deal with a couple more days of blackout."

Grayson sighed. Why couldn't the man just make his suggestions to begin with? "And we get a new ship to add to the fleet. Seems a fair trade to me. Talk to Commander Orozco. He can lead a skeleton crew over there to pilot her back. Speaking of crews, how are the two prisoners?"

"Ah." Bilby wagged a finger. "I've been to see them. Got the reports from Deckmaster Thomas. They've been model guests so far. No escape attempts. They answer questions honestly; appreciative of the food and company. Thomas says they even make their bunks. You could argue it's fear driving them. We did put on quite a show when we took their ship."

"That all?" Grayson said.

"No." Bilby's hand went to his neck again. "They're very interested in us. How we find work, split profits, that sort of thing. Deckmaster Thomas tried to explain some of our ways. They had trouble understanding it. I believe they think we're having them on. Regardless, they've both asked The Question."

That gave Grayson something to think about. He shifted on the rail and looked out toward the kelp and sea-wheat platforms floating on the waves. Was this really the time for such things? But why wouldn't it be? When facing a larger threat, wouldn't they need larger numbers? Could this be connected?

Of course it is. Everything is connected.

"What of their attachments?" Grayson asked.

"Worley, the elder, has no one. A girl in Skatch who gives him a discount and shows him some kindness. Antony, the younger, claims to support a mother and younger brother."

"I'll go down to the brig and talk to them. If it feels right, we'll need to arrange chaperones from the crew for their first trial." Grayson pushed himself off the rails, ready to move on.

"One more thing, sir. Worley gave me some information. Probably a peace offering. He caught wind of a possible job. I think it could be more lucrative than he realizes."

"What are the details?"

"Non-existent. We have to get them. Down Skatch way. But, if we're going to be sailing to Cora, that's not too much farther..."

Captain Grayson couldn't help but chuckle. "Masterfully done, Bilby."

"Sir?" At least Bilby had the good grace to look confused.

"How many years have we sailed together? If you felt a trip to Skatch worthwhile, you only needed to say so. No need to nudge the tiller."

A half smile touched Bilby's face. "Honestly, sometimes I don't realize I'm doing it."

Maybe all wasn't lost. Grayson considered the possibilities as he made way down to the brig. Could this be guidance, of a sort? People wanted to join them. Resources became available to them. It was as if the path had been lit a few steps ahead of him and the way became clearer. For all of his worry about losing their home, was there a solution waiting for him to find? One that could empower them to be masters of their own destiny? Mariners could no more change the laws of other nations than they could will away storms. But they could stand up for themselves.

And just as the captain of their captured fishing vessel had found, when Mariners stood, they were strong.

Chapter Four: Preparations

"You wouldn't believe what it took to get those first ships. Those overpriced, leaky tubs were worth every cent. Every drop of blood."

Aisha Warner, Founding Mariner

Finally, the last members of the U.S. delegation crested the steps at the top of the Bowl. The same company of Mariners that escorted them in moved to see them back to their ship, where the Americans would wait for the council's ruling. With the evening's excitement near an end, most of the islanders followed the group out, keeping a wary eye on their visitors. As much as Kara wanted to allow herself some relief at seeing those same unwanted guests leave, she knew this wasn't nearly the end of their troubles with the Americans.

Kara felt a tap on her shoulder. She turned to Captain Ansari, who pointed to their left. Kara's mother caught her eye from across the walkway nearest the Bowl's stage. She must have been on the other side of the amphitheater during the meeting. Her mother walked, no, glided, over to them. Grace was simply built into the woman. Try as Kara might while growing up, she never could get the knack of it. Her mother's loose, sleeveless dress billowed artfully around her willowy frame, the natural cotton fibers contrasting with her dark chocolate skin. When her eyes met Kara's, her face bloomed into a wide smile.

"Congratulations, Master Navigator." She touched Kara's shoulders with both hands and kissed her daughter's cheek. The traces of South Africa still peeked out of her accent. "Your first tour as a senior officer. You don't know how proud I am."

Captain Ansari inclined his head. "Iminathi. It is a joy to see you again."

Kara declined to comment, she was far too used to the effect her mother had on men.

"It is a joy to be seen, Captain," her mother said. "Did you hear about that squall we had last week? Lucky to make it back at all in that old tub of mine."

"Lose your haul?" he said.

"Bet your life I kept my haul. Who do you think I am? Some mainland amateur?" She laughed easily and put an arm around Kara's shoulders. "Come, my heart. We have somewhere to be, yes?"

Kara bid farewell to her captain, and walked with her mother out of the amphitheater and into Vish Central. Mariners coming from the Bowl returned to their usual spots at the markets and on the streets where bright chains of string lights draped above them. Citrus and spice from the food stalls rolled over Kara, sending a gurgle through her stomach.

As they strolled, her mother filled her in on the details of the storm, the damage to her ship and Vish and how everyone on the island was coping. There was such comfort in her mother's soothing words.

Enough to make her feel somewhat childlike, which was odd considering they were walking to the inker. She loved her mother dearly, but her shadow had been hard to escape. She knew her mother never intended it, but it didn't take much for Kara to feel like some kind of outgrowth of Iminathi, rather than her own person.

"Ah, I almost forgot. Old Jesk finally retired," Iminathi said. "Made good on his threats and moved down Cora way."

Kara perked up. "Then who's running the inker?"

"His name is Omar. Just came from Ordinal. He was Jesk's apprentice some years back. The old man requested Omar replace him, anyway. Very solid. Don't worry. I've seen his work. It is beauty."

Kara grunted. "Yes, but does he have Jesk's sparkling personality?"

Iminathi barked out a laugh. "That old timer was bitching about his arthritis back when I earned my first sparrow."

"Jesk knew his craft. It's still bright and clean." Kara pointed to her mother's bare shoulder, where a sparrow, no worse for wear, sat inked in white over Iminathi's dark skin. All of her mother's tattoos popped brilliantly in the same way. When Kara earned her first, the Mariner Fleet anchor, it was almost disappointing how the dark ink looked on her milky skin.

Three deckhands from Voyager stood outside the door to the inker, passing a bottle of canni-tea. The loudest of the three, Goldi, had the two men roaring with laughter at something she said. Kara waved to the three of them, getting a polite greeting in response.

As soon as Kara stopped to chat, a hot wave of embarrassment flushed her cheeks. She couldn't remember the men's names. She had to get better about that. She might be new to Voyager, but she was a senior officer now. She had to know her crew.

All three sported a freshly inked monkey leaping a barrel on the back of their triceps. Kara made sure to congratulate them before heading in. They'd done well in the last squall and had more than earned the marks. The hold was fastened perfectly. When the ship rolled they were back right-side up in no time at all.

Hearing the story, Iminathi also commended them.

"Thank you, Emeritus," Goldi said in her clipped, Russian tones. "Better than getting out and flipping her back over, no?"

The air inside the inker smelled cleaner than outside, carrying hints of alcohol and menthol. Disinfectants were everywhere to keep the place as clean as possible. A fresh tattoo was essentially an open wound, after all. In the dim waiting room, three candles burned beside a stick of incense. Bright light pushed through a bead curtain leading into the parlor. Behind it, a low electric hum played under Korean reggae-dub.

Kara smirked. "Definitely not Jesk's music."

"I can't think of a tattoo without hearing sad banjos," Iminathi said.

"Is that the Emeritus and the Navigator?" came a voice from behind the curtain. "Be welcome, be welcome. Reflect and enter."

Kara and her mother paused in front of the candle and closed their eyes. Kara used the moment to find her breath and stillness. She reflected on her new position and the responsibility that came with it. She wondered if her mother would be praying to her Christian god, instead. Kara always found more of a connection to the Core of Being, than she did to any religion.

The contrast in the light was so great, Kara squinted for a moment when she brushed aside the clattering strings of beads and entered the parlor. Already waiting by his chair, the inker himself deftly loaded inks in thimble-sized cups.

"Ah, Iminathi, excellent. And you must be her daughter, the newly minted Master Navigator."

Kara bowed her head and touched her right fist to her heart. Outside of their community, she was used to the occasional confusion as to her relation with Iminathi, as they were so biologically different. Kara with her hazel eyes and straight red hair. Mariners didn't dwell on such things, though.

"Omar." He saluted in return. "Looks like we'll be seeing a lot more of each other, now that Vish is where I call home."

He motioned to the chair with a slender hand. Like most inkers, very few spots on Omar's skin remained untouched. Kara slid into the adjustable seat and placed her arm on the rest.

"Word came down with your crew. Looks like you've earned a new set of points on your compass and an embellishment of your choice. What will it be?"

"Polaris," Kara said. "Behind the compass."

"Our north star it is." Omar pushed a pedal with his foot and raised the chair a few centimeters. "Ready?"

Kara nodded. Omar's hand remained steady as the machine buzzed into her flesh. The first bite made her jump a little. It always did. At least she kept her hand still. Omar started chatting, the way inkers do to keep your mind from the discomfort.

"I heard Voyager missed the big squall, thankfully. When it hit, I was on The Ram, ported off Skatch way. You know the port well?"

"Of course," Kara said.

"That's where I found my heart." Iminathi touched Kara's free elbow.

"Ah!" Omar gave them both a broad smile. "I knew I felt a kinship with you, Navigator. Dock rat, too, eh? Old Jesk found me when I was twelve. Norwin docks, about to take the beating of my life for an amusing, if unflattering, illustration I had spray painted of a local security boss. Jesk bribed the cop and took me in. Said he liked the quality of my line work, but that I needed discipline. What about you?"

"I found her trying to defend a kitten from a pack of kids twice her age. Skinny as a twig and riddled with lice. Felt the pull in my soul and I knew," Iminathi answered.

Kara reached out and gripped her mother's hand.

"Best day of my life when Jesk took me in. Mind you, he was never one for hand-holding." Omar laughed. "So what's the latest from the Bowl, eh? Americans, here on Vish! I suppose you saw it all?"

Thankfully, Iminathi filled Omar in. Kara always had a hard time talking while being tattooed.

"Hmm." Omar lifted his machine for a moment to change the ink. "You know, there might be something to this."

"You don't believe that bilge," Kara said.

Omar finished cleaning his needle and loaded a measure of blue on the tip. "Stranger things and all that. Like I said, on my way here we ported at Skatch Harbor. You know how it goes when you're waiting out a storm. Well, scuttlebutt at one of the finer establishments was that a crew fresh from some disreputable skim was looking to sell a bit of intel about a job in the deeps."

Kara sat up. "Get anything else?"

"Sadly, no." Omar motioned for her to relax her hand. "Only heard a name. Ionova. Don't know if that's first, last, or otherwise."

Omar went back to work. Kara hardly noticed the needle this time.

"There's a flat hauler called Ionova," Kara said. "Busted old container ship. She sails the strait sometimes. I've seen her at port during storm season. Never met her crew, though."

"Well," said Omar. "I'm no navigator. Even if it wasn't jam packed out there, I can't tell you exactly who was at port when we were. A small container ship would've fit right in, though."

"What about their navigator? I mean the ship you sailed to Skatch on?"

"The Ram." Omar shook his head. "I was the only passenger to stay on Vish. Rest of the crew got underway two days ago. You could call them, I suppose."

Kara met her mother's eyes. She held back the sigh that wanted to escape. She had to tell Captain Ansari. She was the ship's Navigator. Intelligence gathering was her duty. Even if she didn't like what that intelligence pointed to.

Kara only wished that doing her duty could be a little less nerve-wracking. Working over a dock boss trying to squeeze extra fees out of her? Fine. Extracting intel from junkies and street toughs? Doable. But something about dealing with the Mariner Council set her teeth on edge.

Her mother accompanied her back to the Bowl, where Kara had tried to get a quick word with Captain Ansari, away from the rest of the council. It lasted all of twenty seconds before Emeritus Mayer, a sharp-eyed crone who appeared to be evolving into a turtle as she aged, snapped her fingers and demanded Kara tell the rest of them what she'd been reporting to her captain.

Captain Ansari gave Kara a kind of resigned wave, telling her she may as well get on with it.

Her eyes darted around the space. String lights dotted the space high above them. Only the brightest of the stars' light made it through the net of lights. A few, but not many, Mariners sat on the stone benches around them. Mostly elders and those who took the people's business seriously. A dry tickle in the back of her throat suddenly robbed Kara of the ability to speak. It didn't help matters that she stood at the base of the steps that led to the stage and had to stare up at all of her people's leaders—Elect Shostakovich, the Council, Admiral Kim—all with their eyes locked onto Kara and her captain with varying degrees of expectation and impatience.

The fresh tattoo on her hand burned. Kara flexed and relaxed her fingers. Off to her left, she caught her mother's profile in the corner of her eye. Iminathi gave her daughter the slightest of nods.

Clearing her throat, Kara repeated what she had learned from Omar in what she hoped was a confident voice.

Elect Shostakovich held her gaze for a moment once Kara had finished. "You're certain about this?"

"It's shaky, but it fits. Omar readily admits he only heard rumors, but I can't deny that it lines up with what the Americans are saying. It's either the truth, or a very well thought out ploy."

"Which means exactly nothing." Emeritus Mayer shook her head. Bits of shell ornaments tinkled together in her silver and black hair. "All that proves is that the Americans have done some prep work to support their lies, or are basing some fabrication on a fragment of truth. These people cannot be trusted and this new information doesn't change that. Have we learned nothing from our history? My grandparents nearly starved to death trying to escape that wretched country. Even then, these people still weren't content to let us live in peace."

"No one has forgotten anything, Emeritus." Elect Shostakovich kept his voice on the line between firm and commanding. "Every one of the original Mariners sacrificed to get us here. We know very well why. Their wisdom should be considered, but this is a new problem facing those of us who are here today."

"Well said," Spark Hannigan added in his calm tones. "The only thing constant is change. Our problems are not our ancestor's problems. We must consider that they cannot be solved the same way."

Mayer snorted. "A very insightful way to be completely unhelpful, Spark. Of course we have to solve this problem our own way, which is exactly what I'm trying to get you all to do. We need to send these Americans packing and we need to do it now."

Kara opened her mouth, urging herself to speak up. They had to consider all angles of this situation. "Wait. The man who spoke earlier, Drummond. Something he said keeps coming back to mind. If this is some elaborate scheme, what would be the point? We won't send more than a ship or two. There's no way we'd leave any island undefended. On the off chance they want one of our ships to sail into an ambush, there's no way that would work out well for them. They must know this, no matter how arrogant they are. Logically, there must be some truth to their request."

"Siding with the mainlanders?" Emeritus Mayer said with a cold stare.

Kara's cheeks flushed. "Of course not, Emeritus. I'm only being rational. There's something else going on here. There has to be. However, that doesn't mean their request isn't real. I hate this, Captain. I do. But, I think there's enough truth to what they're saying that we should look into this. I've thought about it. We can try and get the intelligence on our own, without the Americans."

"Oho," Mayer said. "The Navigator with her second set of points still bleeding thinks her dotard elders didn't consider this already?"

A thick, invisible band tightened around Kara's chest. Her fists balled as fiery words jammed themselves together in her mind.

Before she could erupt, Admiral Kim interjected. "We've been discussing options, Lieutenant. That's come up already. If we go this alone, what happens when we find this undersea bunker of theirs? We have no idea what automated defenses are waiting, or how to stabilize the containment systems. Even if we did, do we really want to be in possession of WMDs, anyway? That would be just the excuse the U.S. would need to invade us again. This time with international support. No, if we decide to do this, we have to do it with them."

"Bah!" Mayer spat at the admiral. "I've heard enough of this. Trespassers at our doorsteps, threatening to overrun us at any moment, and this is what we spend our time debating?"

"Fortunately," Elect Shostakovich said, "this decision isn't yours alone to make. This is serious, Emeritus. If their story is even half true, we could be looking at an ecological catastrophe that would destroy our people, not to mention the damage it would do to the ocean and the world. If you're so concerned about what our ancestors would have done, do you really think they'd let a threat like this go by without at least investigating it?"

Admiral Kim joined his voice into the debate again and Kara realized she'd been thoroughly dismissed. None of the council or the other leaders seemed to remember she was standing there at the base of the steps, barely containing her anger at the turtle-faced old fool who wouldn't give her the time of day.

Kara almost jumped as fingers gently touched her shoulder. Her mother met her gaze, then motioned with her head for them to go. Sighing, Kara agreed. Obviously, she wasn't going to do any more good here. Time was running out and her people needed to reach a decision, quick.

But as she turned back to look at the heated debate raging behind them, Kara wondered if they could reach a decision at all, much less a fast one. Unfortunately, she'd found that in situations like this, where the clock ticked loud and fast, the longer you waited to act, the fewer options you had.

"It's not the price which concerns me, lovey-bruvy." Big Madrid admired his reflection in the darkened glare of a scratched shop window. Gary and Gill lingered a few steps out of reach, giving Madrid a chance to speak with the sellers. Obvious muscle had a way of making negotiations more tense then they needed to be.

Captain Dillon grunted. His partner, Marsden, chuckled as a trio of sailors vomited their way out of the nearby drinker, arm in arm, a mass of stumbling, bad decisions. These were the back streets, far from the neon glow of the tourist traps on the piers. No amateurs would be drinking away their pay back here.

"What's your problem, then?" Dillion said. He hocked a thick wad of phlegm into a nearby puddle.

"Integrity, my darling. Integrity." Big ran a finger over his fox fur. "You sell me some succulent secrets, but what's to say you haven't previously vended a bite of this particular apple, eh?"

"Christ," Marsden grumbled. "You prattle on like an emo-whore. Same deal as usual, Madrid. Nav data stored in a lock drive. Look at the damn audit trail yourself. No one else has read it. Buy it and it's all yours. What's the problem?"

"Not stricken from that lovely head of yours, though, is it, Marsden?" Big Madrid stepped to the side of the narrow alley and proceeded to piss on the brick wall. A curl of steam rose from the growing trail.

"What else you want, Madrid?" Dillon pulled a vape from his coat and took a hit. "You think one stretch of the ocean looks any different from another? These ain't ancient days. We ain't navigating by stars and compasses, are we? Ship sails itself. One of us just stays sober in case we gotta get the guns up."

"Sure we could guess," Marsden said.

Dillon's look could cut glass.

"But any guess would be dead useless," Marsden backpedaled. "I could say two days out from whereever, but that don't tell you near enough. Be searching the rest of your life and still never find it. We wouldn't even have found it, if the Ionova hadn't gone around that squall."

"Besides," he added, "we cross you and we don't get our final cut, right? Then you tell everyone in Skatch Harbor we can't be trusted, and it's nothing but trouble for us. Don't overthink it, Big."

"All right, all right." Big Madrid hiked up his trousers and zipped up. "No need to get worked up, my lovelies. It's just business, is all. I need to protect my investments. This is a rather large investment."

"So we're on?" Dillon said. "Thirty-five big?"

Big Madrid gave the men a wide, metal-toothed grin. "It's a deal. Gentlemen, let's get our accounts straight, shall we?"

Dillon's shoulders visibly relaxed. He pulled

out his phone, as did Big Madrid. After a moment of tapping, both Dillon and Marsden looked considerably happier. They weren't shouting with joy and punching each other just yet, they had enough professionalism to wait until later. Dillon plunged a hand deep into that voluminous coat of his and came back with a thin, slate gray stick a few centimeters long. On one side, a thin, monochrome display glowed a gentle blue.

"A pleasure doing business, gentlemen. Many happy returns." Big Madrid took the lock drive, then tipped an imaginary hat. Dillion rapped Marsden on the shoulder and the men left, Dillion's filthy coat waving like a flag. As they rounded the corner, Marsden let out a peal of laughter.

Gill made her way to Madrid's side.

"What about them?" Gill slurred. She didn't look at Madrid. Her eyes stayed fixed on the end of the alley the men had disappeared around.

"Dear, oh, dear." Big Madrid clicked his tongue. "Tut, tut, and all of that bollocks. I have a feeling that the value of my purchase may have been diluted. Be a lamb and keep a very close eye on these children, Gill. Should they begin to whisper sweet nothings to persons outside of our covenant, I believe corrective actions will be in order."

Gary frowned at them from across the alley. "Huh?"

Big Madrid let out a dramatic sigh. "Do fill him in, Gill. Come on, we need to check on our guest. You may have to remind him why hard work is a virtue. I think I could do with a little more information about our lovely shipwreck. Am I right, or am I right?"

Chapter Five: Contracts

"The only thing certain is uncertainty. Start by accepting this. Life gets a little easier if you do."

Alan Schwab, *The Tao of the Core*

Two black paws found their way onto Kara's knee. Reaching over, she gave the graying cat some attention. "Come on up, Scratchy."

"You may want to pick him up. His arthritis has been bothering him." Iminathi and Kara sat on wicker chairs in front of their family home, a converted shipping container on the edges of Vish Central. Bamboo poles, silvered with age, held up the sun sail canopy that had been flapping overhead for as long as Kara could remember.

"Ah, poor old man." Kara gently lifted the aged cat into her lap. He accepted the transport without question, and immediately settled into a familiar, curled position.

For a moment they sat, listening to the night and the sound of Scratcher's rough purr. Thick leaves rustled, a neighbor's wind chimes tinkled and night birds chirped.

"The ships have been getting closer," Iminathi said.

Kara took a sip of her tea. The fresh tattooing on her hand burned a little as the skin stretched. "We heard the same out west. Fishers are getting ballsy. Up north, the Penitent had a scrape while we were underway."

"What happened?"

Kara bobbed her head. "About what you'd expect. That's Captain Grayson's command. He told them to go, they got violent, Grayson's crew wiped them out."

Her mother didn't comment.

"It's probably that damned trade agreement. Got all these thieves and scavengers thinking it's open season on the Mariners."

Iminathi pursed her lips. "That's what tonight's meeting was supposed to be about before the locusts showed up. We need a plan. The EU and RF are going to come to some terms soon. Fishing and ocean conservation are of little concern to them. That proposition may as well be a done deal."

"How can they give rights to waters that aren't theirs to begin with?" Kara fumed. "Even if they don't recognize us as a nation, they can't pretend we don't exist. All of those proposed shipping lanes go right through our waters, and let's not even talk about fishing, salvage, and dumping. That's like me selling someone else rights to a building in Paris that I don't own. How can this possibly be legal?"

"That's the thing about power." Iminathi stared out into the dense collection of homes and tropical greenery. "Ultimately, it comes down to who takes it. Laws only matter when people obey them. Does the

EU or the RF really need permission to do what they want?"

"We've stopped them before. We've been doing it for decades."

"Be reasonable, daughter."

Kara tensed. "What's unreasonable about standing our ground? We've fought before. We've won before."

Iminathi shook her head. "That's a rosy view of the past. Our people have fought, true. We've fought well. But what saved us, what kept us free even more than blades and guns, is our story."

Kara snorted. "What kind of sentimental crap is that? Who cares about our story? So the last time the Americans tried to storm Vish, we storied them off our coast?"

"Don't be ridiculous. What else happened at the time of that battle? Go on."

"You mean that thing with Dietrich and the U.N.? Who cares?"

"Us," Iminathi said. "That's who cares. The Americans could have kept sending ships until the end of time, chipping away at us until we broke. Don't look at me like that. It's the truth. Yes, every Mariner fought like ten of theirs. But they had us by sheer numbers alone. What saved us was Dietrich's appeal to the U.N. and getting the media on our side. His charisma, the story he created about our struggle and refuge from the U.S., got enough pressure put on the Americans to make them leave us be or face international sanctions. That saved us more than any gunship."

"What's your point?"

"That we can't think with our guns all the time, Kara. Our ancestors knew this better than anyone. This trade agreement could send scores of fishing and shipping vessels into our waters, killing the ecosystem we've tried so hard to save. Not to mention what it would do to our way of life. We can't sink them all."

Oblivious to the growing tension, Scratchy dug his claws into Kara's thighs, eliciting a wince, and she gently lifted his front paws.

"Why not?" Kara said. "Why do we hide our strength?"

"Because of our story. The moment the world sees us warriors rather than survivors, it will be over for us. Especially if this treaty is signed. We will go from people who deserve to be helped to people who must be stopped the second they realize what we can do."

"Sure, once the EU and the RF aren't at each other's throats, they'll have more time to pick on us. I get that. What I'm saying is that we need to be ready to stand up for ourselves."

"Hmm." Iminathi settled back into her chair. Insects chirped and chittered around them. "There are many ways to stand up for ourselves. It doesn't always have to be violence. In fact, when facing overwhelming odds, violence is rarely the path to victory. The first Mariners knew this. That's why we're still here."

Footsteps clopped across the laminated bamboo boardwalk leading up to their home. Iminathi leaned forward in her chair.

"Emeritus Nkosi?" A familiar voice said. "You still up? Kara, that you?"

"Teacher!" Iminathi glowed. She rose and greeted the deckmaster. Chief Lambros took Iminathi's hand in both of hers and showed a crooked smile. Kara rolled her eyes.

"Come, sit and have some tea. I'm hoping you'll be at the community center while you're back? I always miss your talks when you're gone. No one teaches the Core like you," Iminathi said.

"Hey, Chief," Kara interrupted. "What brings you out this way?"

"Looking for you." Lambros leaned a hip against the bamboo post that supported the porch's awning. Something of Lambros's figure reminded Kara of the women in renaissance era paintings. Strong, curvy, maternal. Not that Kara would ever say that to her.

"Word came down from the Skipper," Lambros said. "Looks like we'll have to delve into universal mystery another time, Iminathi. Leave's been cancelled. We're underway again tomorrow at midday, Kara. Looks like we're the lucky ship that's going to escort the Americans."

Kara sighed. "Of course we are."

"I don't like this, Kara." Worry lines creased the skin by Iminathi's eyes. "It doesn't feel right. This isn't just a mother's worry. Something is very wrong. Do you feel it, Teacher?"

Chief Lambros made a non-committal noise. "It's difficult. I feel it, too, but I don't know if this is my own fear or if it's deeper than that. Beyond my fear, I know that we have to go. There is a pull we can't ignore. We are being brought into this one way or another. That I know to be true."

Kara tilted her head. "Did you See something?"

"No." Chief Lambros smiled. "Didn't have to See anything. Skipper said we're going, so we can't really ignore that, can we?"

Tren toggled his retina display on long enough to check the time. Fifteen minutes. He bit his thumbnail and looked around the shabby room. Corrugated plastiboard walls, decorated tastefully with latest in rat and cockroach chew holes. His "workstation" was little more than a turned over bucket with a thin cushion on top. But, if he slid it next to the wall he had a backrest. At least until the bugs got too curious and started crawling over him.

Saddest part about the place? The room he'd been kidnapped into was actually nicer than the room he'd been renting. At least here, everyone was so terrified of Big Madrid they gave the place a wide berth. At least here, he had a bucket with a cushion.

Was this Stockholm syndrome?

No, he thought. Checking his mental inventory he verified that he still held an irrational hate for every molecule that comprised the man named Big Madrid. So, no, this didn't fit the definition at all.

Speaking of which, it had now been sixteen minutes since Big left and took the Traitorous Duo with him. He flipped his inner-eye display on again, to check the state of his decryption cracker. Still running. Funny. He'd been brute forcing all the known decryption algorithms from that age but so far had nothing. Considering the significantly advanced power in his servers it should have been done already. Maybe Big's intel was wrong and this signal was coming from a newer source?

No! Tren shook his head, flipped the retinal display inside his eye off and stood up. This was no time to get sucked into the problem. What was he doing? He had to leave. He was a prisoner, a literal victim of kidnapping, like in some Korean melodrama. This was not a situation he should get comfortable with. His jailers had been gone for a quarter of an hour. If Tren's guess was right, they'd be gone for another hour or two if they were meeting up with whoever Big was buying the shipwreck data from.

It might be his only chance. An image flashed through his mind, Tren turning over the decrypted data just to have Gary crush Tren's skull in one strength-enhanced hand.

They'd taken him up three flights of steps to bring him to the room, so jumping out of a window was out of the question. Plus, there was no window.

Tren ran to the front door. Depending on the lock he might have to get fancy, like pulling off the plate and taking his best guess as to which wiring would give him I/O on the main control unit. Nothing showed up on his wireless listing, so it might be an offline lock. Could even be a purely mechanical thing. Those could be even harder to break. He squatted down by the grimy door, eye level with the lock unit. Gently, he tapped the metal knob.

Nothing. Okay, no electrified defense. Point, Tren! If he could just find out what kind of door lock he was dealing with, that would be at least a place to start. Flipping his display back on, he opened a browser and searched for basic lock identification methods. One thread on a locksmithing forum said to look at how the knob was attached to the base of the lock. Great. Step one, done.

Twenty minutes since Big left. Hurry it up, Tren!

That image of his head getting squished like an over-ripe grape pushed its way back into his mind.

Desperate, Tren twisted the knob.

The door popped ajar. It creaked slowly open onto a dim hallway.

"What in the simulated hell?" Tren said to no one.

They left it open? What was this? Some kind of trap?

Tren ducked back into the room. That would be just like Big Madrid, wouldn't it?

Or would it?

Big could be cunning in his own way, obviously. Why would he waste time toying around with Tren, though? Wouldn't it be more important to keep Tren working on the damn decryption then by baiting him to escape? That was a level of psychological warfare that seemed a bit beyond the reach of Skatch Harbor's chief thug and fence.

No, Tren decided with his thumbnail clamped between his teeth, this was a simple case of Gill or Gary being an idiot and not locking the door. The two of them were so fried from their enhancements they basically shared a brain cell. Too stupid to see a good thing even when it was dangling right in front them, certainly.

"Hello, darling. How goes the work?"

Tren nearly jumped out of his skin. Big Madrid suddenly appeared in the doorway, Gary at his heels. "What's all this? Not planning on taking a stroll, I hope? And here I thought our relationship was rock solid."

"It wasn't locked," Tren sputtered. He did his best to not look shifty. His best wasn't that great.

"Tut, tut." Big Madrid gave him a coy smile, full of metal teeth. "Before we get on with the excuses, lovey, let's get absolutely crystal on a couple of points. First, I know the door wasn't locked. I don't lock it. I don't, because I don't need to. No one will tempt a tangle with Big Madrid. I have not a worry for the meager possessions inside this charming abode. Not so long as I draw breath."

Big stepped closer to Tren, who backed against a grimy wall.

"As for your escape, my sweet digital virtuoso, where would you like to go? Back to Anchorage? Detroit, where you once worked? New York, which you once called home? How very far they are from Skatch, are they not? Will you be taking that trip by foot or imagination, darling? Perhaps you fancied yourself hitching a ride with the shipsies and sailing to adventure?"

Tren winced as Big Madrid jabbed a finger hard into his chest.

"You're black listed, Tren. Unwanted. Unpaid. Unfriended. Broke. Your one pathetic gamble to get back on your feet has landed you here with me. Think you can do better than this? Well, go. Go, my dear. Take your chances on the street. Let's see how long you last with your liver and kidneys intact. Here you've got a roof over your head. Fed from my generosity. Protected by my good name. Run if you will, then. But you better think as long and hard as my aroused member about where you hope to get to. Because from where I'm standing, Trenny-Tren-Tren, the situation in front of you is astoundingly dire."

Tren's fingers trembled. He looked down at the floor. Big Madrid snorted, then shoved something else toward Tren.

Tren glanced at it. "What's on this lock drive?"

"Coordinates," Big Madrid said. "But that's not what I need you for. Verify if that data is as pristine and virgin as my dog-ugly sister. I suspect I'm being played for a fool."

Tren nodded.

"And how's that sodding decryption coming?"

"Almost there," Tren said softly. Holding the lock drive, he shambled back to his bucket.

At least it had a cushion.

Gulls cried and wheeled overhead while waves beat against the rocky harbor. Kara stood with her mother by the docks, watching the steady flow of Mariners boarding and debarking Voyager. While the crew took their places, harried service technicians and suppliers rushed to complete their work. Iminathi raised a hand to block the rising sun as she surveyed the scene, worry wrinkling her eyes.

As a navigator herself, her mother knew better than anyone the risks of a life at sea. Which made her concern even more remarkable.

"Stop." Kara gently laid a hand on her mother's wrist. "I've done this a hundred times by now."

"Not like this, you haven't. Not with them." Iminathi inclined her head to the American vessel and looked her daughter in the eye. "Don't take this for granted. You've earned all eight of your compass points, but don't get complacent. This mission of yours is anything but normal. You know what we say about the sea."

"It changes everyday, I know." Kara grimaced. "I don't trust these locusts any farther than I can throw them. You don't have to worry about me falling asleep on watch. My guns are staying warm."

"No, no! You can't do that, either."

"Well," Kara let out a bitter laugh. "What do you want, mom? Trust them or don't trust them?"

"That's the wrong question. You can't take any of this for granted, Kara. You can't make up your mind now. You have to keep your eyes open. All of them." She touched Kara's forehead.

Kara reached up and took her mother's hand. "I know you're worried. I promise I will stay alert. I will watch everything that happens with open eyes."

"And an open mind," Iminathi said.

"Sure." Kara let go of her mother's hand. "You need to trust me."

"I trust you." At Kara's flat stare she went on, "Of course I do. Yes, I worry, you're my child. This is deeper than that, Kara. Something is very wrong. Something big. Many of us have felt it. Just ask Chief Lambros."

"If I want cryptic warnings with absolutely no useful information attached to them, then, yeah, I'll go talk to the Chief."

Iminathi frowned. "For someone who takes the Core seriously, there are some elements of it you completely ignore."

"Does it honestly matter? Seriously. Let's say you're right. Something strange, out of the ordinary, and probably terrible is happening. I already know that."

"What I have felt, in my meditations, is that you need to stay aware and open. Things are not what they seem. There is real danger. And I need you to take this seriously."

A whistle blew from the deck of the Voyager. Kara pulled her mother in for a hug.

"I promise. Open. Alert."

When they pulled apart, worry still lined Iminathi's face. She nodded and stood up straighter. "Calm waters and peaceful passage, my heart, my little cat wrangler."

"Calm shores and plentiful harvest. I'll be back soon. Then we can argue more about the Core."

They shared a smile before Kara joined the group walking to the Voyager.

As she ascended the gangway and made her way to the bridge, Kara couldn't shake the feeling that followed her after her parting with her mother. What was it? A sense of unease? No, it was just her mother's paranoia poisoning Kara's mind. Yes, the Core emphasized the connectedness of all, and sometimes people did See. Sometimes they had insight. That didn't mean she needed to run scared every time something new came her way. Of course her mother was on edge. They all were.

Five deckhands worked the gantry, it's motor humming and straps from its long arm lowering an A-Type submersible vehicle from the water onto the deck. For some reason Kara didn't understand, everyone called them A-divers. Regardless, they were nimble little things that could get reasonably deep underwater. It'd be needed soon enough, assuming the Americans weren't completely full of it.

Every Mariner walked to their duty station with a sense of preoccupation. They hadn't expected to be back on board for two weeks. Now, after a single night with their families, friends, and lovers, they were setting sail again. At the behest of their sworn enemies.

Naturally, they'd be tense. As they should be. But that didn't mean they were doomed. A Mariner crew was a force in itself. All they had to do was stay together, stay alert, and stay on top of anything that came their way.

"What in the new spooky hell is he doing here?" Kara couldn't stop herself from blurting out the words as soon as she stepped foot on the bridge. She pointed in between Captain Ansari and Admiral Kim, to the American congressman who had pulled them into this mess.

Congressman Drummond wore an awkward grimace. Captain Ansari, on the other hand, didn't take the outburst so gracefully.

"Lieutenant. Outside. Now."

Kara closed her eyes.

That could've gone better.

Breathing deep, she walked right back outside, and stood at attention, waiting for the Captain to come take her to task.

He didn't disappoint. "You will never," he began, "show such blatant disrespect on my bridge again, do you understand, Lieutenant?"

She nodded. "Yes, sir."

"Do we need to have this conversation again? Are you so eager to lose a posting you've worked your whole career for?"

Ansari didn't yell. He didn't need to. The matter-of-fact way he dug into the heart of the matter was enough to make Kara curse herself twenty times over.

"No, sir. I'm sorry, sir."

"Don't be sorry, Navigator. Be better." Ansari dismissed her with a nod and ducked back inside.

Before Kara could follow, Admiral Kim made his way out of the hatch. Kara forced herself back to attention. Kim must have come for his pound of flesh as well.

Well, Kara thought. *It wasn't as though I didn't earn it.*

"At ease," the Admiral said.

Kara clasped her hands behind her back. Oddly, the Admiral didn't carry the same kind of tension as her captain. He leaned over the portside railing and motioned for her to follow.

"You need to be more careful, Kara."

"I know, sir. That was disrespectful. I don't know what came over me."

Kim snorted. The sun struck the flat planes of his face, casting his eyes in shadow. "You saw a filthy American locust on your bridge is what happened."

Kara wasn't sure if she should laugh or not.

He saved her the trouble of responding. "You're the Navigator. Responsible for guiding the ship and her people, yes?"

"Yes, sir."

"You're one of our best, Kara. It's true. I recommended you for this post because of it. Don't stumble now. I know how you feel about the Americans. Trust me. But think about this. How would you ever get intel at port if you pissed off every low-life you actually can't stand, hmm?"

She swallowed. "I understand, sir. But, why are we even allowing one of them on our ship? On our bridge, of all places?"

"You don't have to like it, or him. You don't even have to pretend to like it, or him. You do have to look out for your ship and crew and mission. This"—he waved a hand at the bridge—"situation is part of the deal we made with the Americans. One of theirs stays with us, to discourage any skullduggery. They won't torpedo your ship if their congressman is on board, will they?"

"Like a medieval hostage exchange," Kara said.

"Exactly. Now he's on board. It is done. Do you want deep intel on the Americans no Navigator before you has managed to get? Here's your chance. Don't blow it on the first day."

"Aye, sir," Kara said.

She left the railing and faced the bridge. Before she could walk in, the Admiral stopped her.

"And Kara," he said. "I don't think I need to say it, but, something here stinks. Be careful."

Chapter Six:
Unscheduled Visitation

"Why lend aid and relief at sea when so many are hostile toward us? Because compassion is crucial to human survival. We know that better than most."
James Keeling, Reborn at Sea: Mariner History 2041-2063

Tren could be patient when he needed to be. True, he loved a good shortcut as much as the next human, but some things just took time. Trouble was, although he could be patient, it didn't mean he was any good at it.

His knee bounced up and down as he hunched forward on his bucket seat, staring at the display tacked against the damp plastiboard wall. After a bit of whining on his part, Big Madrid caved and got Tren the monitor. Sure, he could have kept using his in-eye retinal display, but the resolution wasn't that great and it wasn't really meant for this kind of large volume work. Want to see a quick display of your incoming messages? Fine, great. Writing a few thousand lines of code? No thanks.

Maybe his childhood was to blame. Isn't that what people did? Took things from their past and held it responsible for their terrible behaviors? Problems like this—math, programming (math in drag), logic, puzzles—these weren't hard for him. Ever. So when one did stump him, his wiry body filled with impotent rage at the universal injustice of it all.

The metal pads of his two contacted fingers stayed planted on the I/O pads of the slender CPU deck resting on his thigh. Text scrolled, halted, scrolled, and halted over the screen.

"This isn't right," Tren mumbled. The thumbnail of his free hand found its way between his teeth again.

"What are you babbling about over there, sweetness?" Big Madrid's voice made Tren jump in his seat. He hadn't realized the man was in the room.

Tren didn't have time to dismiss Big's statement before the man stomped his faux-fur clad self over to Tren.

"Have you sorted out that lock drive yet, darling? Or do I need to incentivize the situation?"

"The what?"

Big's eyes burned.

"Oh, that!" Tren waved as if brushing away a fly. He toggled his screen to a different window. "I've been running an audit on the distributed ledgering mechanism used to secure the chain of custody on the data. Takes a little while to complete because of their security, which is pathetic, by the way. Anywhoozle, your seller is lying to you. There's a falsified hash where the data deletion step is entered. Whatever he's selling you was never removed from it's origin. That's not the interesting thing. It's the encryption on this message, when I, hey!"

Big Madrid had Tren's collar bunched in one

powerful hand. He jerked him upright quickly enough to send him into a coughing fit. Big shoved his fist, and Tren's collar, higher still, forcing Tren to his tip-toes to keep breathing.

"Interesting?" Big Madrid screamed. "That's not what's interesting? You tell me I've been hoodwinked? Bamboozled and cheated? But that's not what's bloody interesting? You'd better get your priorities straight, love!"

Big dropped him. Tren stumbled back, tripped over his bucket and fell to the floor. Massaging his neck and hacking, Tren scrambled back as far against the wall as possible without going through it.

Plastic scraped against cement as Big Madrid slid Tren's bucket. He made a show of dusting off the cushion before seating himself in front of Tren. He leaned forward until the breath that moved over his metal teeth washed hot on Tren's face.

"Now, darling, let's start over, shall we? How did the bad man cheat daddy?"

Words caught in Tren's throat, sending little knives of pain into his larynx. He rubbed at the dull ache in his neck and tried again. "The way safe ledgering works with lock drives..."

Big Madrid tilted his head.

Tren started over. The only way to stop the stinging was to speak in a low rasp. "There's supposed to an entry for each step taken with the data. An entry when it's created, read, copied, deleted. That sort of thing. The entry made when your seller was supposed to delete the data is fake. You have no proof he deleted it. He could still have it."

"You're absolutely sure of this? Cross your heart, hope to die, needles in your eye and all that?"

In Tren's mind, there was no doubt these would become literal needles in his actual eye if he misled

Big Madrid in any way.

"Absolutely." Tren took a painful swallow.

For a handful of extremely long seconds, Big Madrid continued to stare at Tren. At last, he stood, tapped his watch and spoke. "Gary, be a lamb and meet me by the kebab shop on pier twelve. I have some very pointed questions for the owners of the Ionova."

Tren went back to massaging his throat. Was being strangled supposed to hurt this bad after the fact? Was something broken? He made a note to look his symptoms up. As Big strolled across to the door, Tren slid his bucket back into place.

"What are you doing?" Madrid said from the doorway.

"The decryption..." Tren said weakly.

"You're not mucking about with that, pet. You're coming with me to have a look-see at a certain ship's computer."

Tren swallowed again. Still hurt.

The worst part about their "guest" was that the man seemed to exist absolutely everywhere at once. When Kara reported for duty on the bridge, there he was, making chit-chat with Ensign Martin or posing asinine questions to Commander Satry or Captain Ansari.

What's the longest you've been at sea? Did you train to sail as children? How is the Elect chosen? Who gets to sit on Mariner councils? Do you keep data on ocean ecology in your waters?

It never ended. Kara knew she shouldn't have been so glad that he gave her space (probably as a result of her outburst his first day on board), but she was. Yes, she should be using the opportunity to get more intelligence on the Americans. She couldn't bring herself to do it, though. No matter how good her intentions at the beginning of her shift, once she reported for duty she'd see his stupid, gormless face, and her only desire would be to punch it.

The most infuriating part of the witless wonder's campaign to ingratiate himself with the crew was that it seemed to be working. At least a little. Ninety percent of the crew had enough sense to stay clear of the man, but others may have taken the Admiral's guidance a little too seriously. Martin and Drummond now had a thing where they'd try to find a joke the other one hadn't heard before. Martin seemed to be winning. Spending your life traveling from port to port filled with sailors will do that. Just this morning, as she reported for duty, Commander Satry took Drummond to the starboard railing and pointed out a pod of their humpbacks.

When she went to the galley, he was there.

When she went on deck for some air, he was there.

His pasty, unmarked skin seemed to preempt her every move, sticking out in the sea of Mariner faces aboard the Voyager. She couldn't accuse the man of following her, since he was always at her destinations first, but that didn't make it any less annoying. At least, Kara was sure, there was one place on the ship she wouldn't run into the American congressman.

At 1700 hours Kara looked up from her workstation. She'd been compiling all of her existing intelligence together with what the Mariner's had centrally to get a better picture of who would be associated with the Ionova and where they'd be found at Skatch Harbor. Normally, there would be a junior navigator to relieve her and work the night shift on this kind of mission. Voyager was one short, however. That Mariner wasn't due into Vish for another week. Voyager's early departure meant that

Kara was doing both jobs.

She stood and stretched, looking at the bridge's front view display. Something about the still water, the thick gray sky nagged her. Kara took a quick look outside, felt the air and returned to her workstation.

"Everything okay, Navigator?" Ensign Martin watched her return.

She shook her head. "Could be nothing. I'm setting a barometer warning before I head out."

"You think we got a squall on the way?" Martin said.

"I'm not psychic, Ensign," she snapped. "Just tell the Commander we need to be ready."

"Aye," Martin looked slightly affronted. "I'll log it and message the Commander."

On her way below decks Kara wondered if she'd been too short with Martin. She was relatively new to the Voyager, true, but she'd been getting along with him well until now. Could she be unfairly taking out her frustrations on the communications officer? After all, by working with Drummond, he was only doing what they'd been ordered to. Something Kara had yet to accomplish.

Guilt swirled into the anger that floated so close to the surface these days. As she walked through the interior, junior crew members made way for her to pass. She thanked them and found the large multipurpose room just off the galley.

Space on a ship, even a larger ship like Voyager, always came at a premium. For lifelong sailors like Kara, the cramped cabins were hardly noteworthy. The idea that a room had multiple purposes was a given. Anything else would be a waste of precious meters. Tables in their central dining room folded up into the walls and latched to make room for any other community function. Games, trivia nights, book clubs, live music, the occasional dance, religious services of all stripes, and Kara's favorite refuge, Core meetings.

About twenty Mariners had already seated themselves and a few more, including Kara, were grabbing cushions and finding a spot on the floor. Already the room held enough people that Kara had to take careful steps around those already sitting to avoid bumping or stumbling into them. As she moved to the back of the room, she passed a few familiar faces, including Goldi. A nod passed between them.

Thoughts of nosy mainlanders and unpredictable weather still poked the inside of her skull. She settled down into a full-lotus on the flat cushion and took herself through some simple breathing. Slowly, the flames inside began to cool.

"So it's meant to be a kind of supplemental religion, a shared addition to existing beliefs? Like how Esperanto was meant to be a common, second language?" Drummond's voice echoed in from the passageway.

The flames rose.

"I wouldn't discourage the analogy if it helps," Chief Lambros said. "It may be thinking too formally, though. The Core isn't a religion. It doesn't ask you to believe. It is a way of asking questions, a way of experiencing ourselves."

No, Kara thought. *No way. Not here. Not him.*

"I don't want to intrude," Drummond said.

"The Core is open to all. Please, grab a cushion and find a seat." Chief Lambros closed the hatch behind her and gestured to an empty spot in the front. Somewhat sheepishly, Drummond grabbed a seat and sat in a stiff cross-legged position. Judging by the reactions of some in the room, Kara wasn't alone in her feelings about this intrusion.

What the hell was Chief Lambros playing at?

Chief Lambros dimmed the lights, set the oil

warmer down, and took her own seat on a straight back chair so she could see everyone. She leaned forward slightly, her elbows resting on her knees.

"Welcome to *satsang*," she said to the group. "As you no doubt heard, we have a visitor with us today. As the Core teaches us, we are all interconnected, and in a way, we are all visitors. Let us bid welcome to each other."

Kara clenched her jaw shut.

Others in the room murmured greetings to each other. Kara's nearest neighbors, perhaps on seeing her expression, decided to forgo that part.

"It's important, on occasion, to revisit the fundamentals of the Core. As we have a new seeker with us today, this is a perfect opportunity. The Core of Being could be considered a loose set of philosophies, but at it's heart it is a way of examining our existence and opening ourselves to the mysteries that have been with humans since our beginning. Alan Schwab, one of the original Mariners, was a student of many belief systems. Vedanta, Buddhism, Taoism, Sufism, Christianity, to name a few. Dogma and doctrine aside, he found common threads between them, which are stillness, reflection, and openness. This was the beginning of what would become the Core. Early Mariners found Alan's teachings beneficial. As refugees in their own nation, they were constantly beset by hunger, poverty, and struggle. As these people were from all beliefs and walks of life, the Core became something they could share. A commonality with a purpose. By using the meditative practices Alan taught, they found a way to better manage their reactions to a life filled with trouble and pain. So when we have *satsang*, a Sanskrit word that means associating with true people, we first discuss these teachings before practicing...Yes, Kara?"

Her blood had reached the boiling point. Kara hadn't noticed her hand raised, it was as though it had lifted on its own accord. Even her voice began to sound on its own.

"Could you explain to our visitor, Chief, just who it was that made these refugees starve and die in droves? Who it was they were seeking refuge from? Maybe our visitor should know what country it was that did that to their own citizens. To our ancestors."

Chief Lambros blinked and grimaced. "We cannot change the past, Kara. Do we gain anything by—"

"It's all right, Chief." Drummond stood and replaced his cushion. "It's understandable. Lieutenant Nkosi, I know very well that the first Mariners were American refugees. I will not hide from those crimes. But I see that this was a step too far on my part, so I apologize."

Drummond thanked the Chief and quietly left.

Good, Kara thought. *Now we can get back to it.*

But they didn't. Chief Lambros simply sat, staring at Kara. Seconds ticked by, one after another.

"What?" Kara turned her palms up. "Chief, I only asked a question."

"Kara," Lambros said softly. "What is the first essence of the Core of Being?"

Her cheeks flushed. Knowing that the chief wouldn't be satisfied until she said it, Kara conceded.

"The Core of Being is accessible to all," she mumbled.

Chief Lambros raised her eyebrows.

"All right!" Kara stood, took her cushion and replaced it on her way out. "I was being an asshole. I'm sorry."

"Am I the one you should be saying that to?" Lambros said.

"I'm going." Dejected, Kara opened the hatch and followed Drummond.

Naturally, he was topside, looking over the forward railing on the bow. Because that's where Kara would have gone had she wanted a minute of peace. She took a moment before approaching, willing herself into a better frame of mind. The Admiral's words came back to her. She didn't have to like him. She did have to work with him. At least for this mission. Maybe her anger was justified. That didn't mean she hadn't been petulant. How did a feud with this man serve the crew, the ship, or the mission?

The sun hung low, firing the thick cloud cover in orange and pink. That electric prickle from earlier still hung in the air. Wind ruffled the collar of Drummond's shirt. Behind them, a couple of deckhands secured equipment to the deck with tie down straps.

"Congressman." Kara stepped to his side. "I would like to apologize for my actions. I spoke out of turn."

Drummond turned, his dark eyes examining her. "I appreciate that. We're good. If I have questions about the Core, I'll see if I can talk to Chief Lambros away from your meetings."

"No, it's not..." Kara searched for the right words. A sharp, chill gust blew around her, flapping her sleeveless shirt and pebbling her flesh.

"You should go back. Or go to the next one," she said. "Chief Lambros reminded me that the Core is for everyone. That's kind of its whole deal, I guess. Anyway, she's right."

"Look, I wish I could say that I understand how you feel about me, or us. Americans, I mean. I can't say that with any honesty, though. I'm not you, I'm not a Mariner, so, I really don't know. All I can do is try to empathize. That's why all the..." Drummond rapidly opened and closed his hand like a chattering mouth. "I know you probably think I'm gathering intelligence, spying, but it's not like that. Either way,

I know it drives you crazy."

"No," Kara said. "Well, yes. I kind of hate it."

He smirked. Another blast of wind hit them. This time from the port side. Kara instinctively moved her legs with the accompanying roll of the deck. Drummond, however, gave a little start and held his arms out for balance.

Kara gave him a pitying look. "Keep your legs loose. Try to move with it."

Drummond nodded, although his face had gone pale.

"If you want to understand how we feel, it's going to take more than our history with your people. There's plenty happening now. Do you know what your naval captains act like out here?"

"Like petty warlords?"

That took Kara back for a second. "Yes. I've personally had a couple of scrapes with your navy. Out in our waters, where they shouldn't be, escorting privateers who want to steal from us, or dump waste where they think no one is looking. Those whales you saw? They're only alive because of us. Because we stand up to your people. Maybe you're being straight with me when you say you're trying to build bridges. To be honest, I don't know if you can build one long enough."

"Did you know," Drummond spoke up against the strengthening wind. "In our navy, the pay difference between a commander and a captain is fifteen percent? But the difference in net worth between the average commander and captain is over three hundred percent?"

Kara bobbed her head. "They have to get that money from somewhere, is that what you're saying?"

"That's what anyone with half a brain would say. And yet, everyone in our government refuses to implement any real oversight. All they want to do is repeat the mantra that we have the greatest military on earth. It's all corrupt," he said with real bitterness in his voice. "Top to bottom."

"Don't take this the wrong way," Kara said. "But, how did you get elected?"

"Actually," Drummond began, but the rest of his words were smothered by a shrill whistle.

Kara's pulse leapt. She turned around, searching the horizon. There, off the port side she saw it. A column of swirling gray and black, half obscured by the darkening sky. A squall.

Tren finished counting off five minutes. He killed the clock on his in-eye display and tried to steady himself. Liquid rushed through pipes that ran along the painted metal interior of the Ionova, further crowding the claustrophobic passageways. God, did he hate boats. The constant rocking and getting tossed around on the waves. And the water? Don't get him started on the water. All you needed to know about the ocean was that it was the world's toilet. A toilet teeming with disease and sharp-toothed creatures whose only goal in life was to eat whatever swam in front of them.

Time to go.

The noise down the corridor had quieted down like Big said it would. Noise. What a polite way to describe feral grunting, screams, and the ring of metal on metal. He took a deep, shaking breath, sending a jab of pain through his throat.

When did he get so filthy, anyway? The cuffs of his once pristine blue checked shirt were now stained in brown and yellow. Unidentified smudges filled the creases on his palms.

Is this what life is now? When did this happen?

Dirty hands pushed open a dirty metal door with the word "Bridge" painted in block letters.

"Ah," Big Madrid said. "Here comes our expert. Ready to do some sleuthing, darling?"

Tren froze halfway over the threshold.

Blood. Spattered on the floor, running down the walls, even dripping from the ceiling. It filled the room with a sickly copper and meat smell. Crumpled in a heap on the floor was what must have been the source of most of the blood. He wore all the standard merc attire, black and gray armor, fake leathers, but all of it torn, disheveled. Tren couldn't help but stare, open mouthed. Below a bald scalp, where a face should be it was like...like someone had punched a bowl of ground beef over and again. Were those shards of bone?

Tren's stomach gave a lurch and, strangely, his bowels loosened, letting out a squeak of a fart before he got a hold of himself.

Two men who could've been brothers for how similar they looked sat stiffly in metal chairs surrounding a table that folded out from the wall. The leaner one, who wore a heavy coat, sweated freely. Both gave him bemused looks.

"Man up, lovey." Big Madrid had placed himself in a chair directly opposite the two men, where he absently stroked his faux-fur stole. Without looking at Tren, he pointed to the bridge's central computer. "Chop, chop."

Tren walked as lightly as possible. He passed Gill, who sulked in a corner of the room, tending to a deep cut on her right shoulder. Gary had a medkit open and busied himself with stapling her flesh back together. More blood blossomed from his knuckles. Torn skin exposed metallic bone underneath. How augmented were these two?

His heel slipped on a glob of the fresh blood,

sending Tren sliding forward until he crashed into the fixed metal desk that held the ship's computer.

"I'm fine," he said.

No one responded. Gary kept on stapling Gill. Madrid kept staring down the brothers.

Tren eased himself into the seat by the desk and found the contact pads by the keyboard. They'd been used recently. A surreptitious glance showed him that neither brother had contacts. If they were augmented it wasn't with a machine interface. Someone else must have been plugged in here. The metal pads on his first two fingertips rattled against the contact plates. Try as he might, Tren couldn't keep his fingers from shaking.

Big Madrid slowly turned his way. Another whiff of blood filled Tren's nose.

Quickly, he brought his left hand over and physically held down his fingers on the contacts until the magnetic locks engaged. The workstation monitor flickered on, as did Tren's inner-eye display. Immediately, he got to work scanning the user accounts and running cracking programs.

"That's more like it," Big Madrid said. "Now we shall see what we see, eh?"

The brother with the lighter hair, the one without a coat (Marsden? Was that his name?) stared right back Big Madrid.

"You're making the biggest goddamn mistake of your life, Madrid," he said.

Big treated him to a toothy smile. "Am I? Because from here, my sweet, everything's looking a bit rosy. Not so good on that side of the table though, is it?"

"We didn't cheat you," Dillon, the one in the coat, said. "What's the problem, Big? You got the ledger, you got the lock drive. We had a clean deal."

"But did we?" Madrid pursed his lips. "You see, a very knowledgeable source has informed me that your ledger is, in fact, dirtier than a dock cop's dick."

"Who says?" Marsden might have leapt to his feet at the insult, if he didn't have a credible fear for his life.

Lazily, Madrid placed both hands on one knee, then tipped his head back toward Tren.

The brothers' eyes could have bored holes straight into Tren's soul. He swallowed, winced, and focused back on his work. It wasn't possible to hide completely behind the workstation, but that didn't stop Tren from trying.

"Let's all just calm down," Dillon said. "We can fix this. Your man made a mistake, is all. Now, you shoulda just said so, Madrid."

"But, Dillon, darling"—Madrid's eyes narrowed—"chances for conversation were becoming ever slimmer, what with you readying to leave port and all. And so soon after relieving me of my hard earned money. One might even call it suspicious."

"That's cause," Marsden made an irritated sound, "that's cause we got a whole damn storm system heading our way, Big. We got us a haul to hitch down south and we can't afford to wait it out or we'll lose the job."

"Just let me get on that computer." Dillon looked more encouraged by the second. "I can show you anything you want to see, okay? Now, we just had a top tech in here not too long ago making sure Ionova got her security upgraded. There's no way your black hat there is going to beat his way in. We can give you all the proof you want, I swear it."

"Is that true?" Big tossed the question back to Tren. "Are you being prevented from the few meager tasks you contribute to this operation, Trenny-Tren?"

"Hmm?" Tren said, still looking at the display. "Oh, no, I've been in for ages. I'm tracking down the data."

The brothers blanched.

"Bullshit," Marsden said. "He's full of it."

Tren grimaced. With a few thoughts he opened three files. Tren swiveled the display toward their group. "This your porn, Marsden?"

No response.

Swiveling the display back toward himself, Tren resumed his work. He closed the windows in question. They'd served their purpose and Marsden had some very specific—if not disturbing—tastes that Tren didn't share. At all.

"F-fine," Dillon said. "Either way. Your guy hacks in or we let you in. Doesn't matter, it comes down to the same thing. We didn't cheat you."

Tren didn't exactly enjoy this type of work. There was no art to it. No nuance. When you got to it, hacking and intrusion was rote. Boring. Tedious. You tried the same kinds of exploits, did the same sort of endless sifting through the data. The only thing that raised Tren's spirits in this case was that he already knew what the data was, he only needed to locate it. Tremendously easier than investigating from scratch. It gave him confidence that he'd get the job done quickly.

Well, that, and his ever-increasing (and quite justified) fear of Big Madrid.

"Oh, but my little angel over there assures me that there's been some hanky-panky, my wayward partners." Big leaned back in his metal chair. "And little Trenny-Tren-Tren knows better than to waste my precious time."

"He's not gonna find anything." Marsden pulled a sullen face. "Then you're gonna owe us one hell of an apology, Madrid. Plus, the balance on his contract. Still had three years left. Amount we shelled out on his augments..."

Madrid followed Marsden's pointed finger to the pile of parts and blood on the floor.

"As a man of honor," he said, "I will make right any undue suffering, of course. I pay the price, gentlemen. Bear that in mind if I expect you to do the same. Because, if you have done as I am afraid you've done, then you've cost me a lot more than money. What the bloody hell are you doing staring at my angelic visage, Tren, when you've got work to be doing?"

"Oh." Tren shifted uncomfortably. "I'm done."

"Why didn't you say something, then?"

Tren's eyes went wide. "I didn't want to interrupt. It's rude."

Seeing all of Big Madrid's metal teeth bared at once, Tren threw his hands up. "Yes, yes, I found it. Yes. Right here. See? Your coordinates. They had them stored on disk, but it was outside of system partitions so you wouldn't see it if you logged in and poked around."

"Very clever." Big Madrid turned back to the brothers.

"Not really," Tren mumbled.

At once, both Dillon and Marsden shrank.

"Now, I believe, we are to speak of recompense. Reparations. And retribution." Big Madrid rose slowly from his chair. "Gill, Gary. Are you feeling up to a bit more work? I fear I'm in need of your services again."

Tren looked down at the metal desk and attempted to will himself into invisibility.

Chapter Seven: Squalls

"Most sailors with an ounce of sense don't get underway during squall season. At first, some companies tried sailing unmanned, but those ships just became pirate-bait. Mariners, however, aren't normal sailors. Weathering storms is what we do."
Schweeta Kanwal, Navigator Emeritus

Within seconds the hatch closest to Kara flung open. Chief Lambros ran onto the deck, Goldi on her heels. Gales of cold wind howled across the deck, sending the rope lines quaking. One line, unsecured, flapped and cracked like a whip from the top of the mast where it had been secured. The ship lurched both starboard and a little forward.

Kara grabbed Drummond by the arm and pulled him away from the bow. "Come on," she yelled over the wind. "It's only going to get worse. You need to get below decks and strap in."

"Wait!" Drummond said. He pointed to Chief Lambros who was waving to them. "She needs our help."

"That's not for you—" but before she could finish, Drummond was already stumbling on unsteady feet toward the chief. Kara hurried to catch up. An icy spray pelted the side of her face.

"Drummond!" Lambros belted. "Go with Goldi and help get the top up. She'll show you how. Kara, crank down the forward mast, I'll get the central."

Kara didn't need to be told twice. Over the increasing sway of the ship, she bolted back to where she'd come from. A crash of foam rocked the port side, spilling cold seawater over the deck. Automatically, she kicked off her shoes. Her bare feet would track better on the textured deck. On her way she passed the two deckhands who were now fighting to get the last of the deck equipment strapped down. One braced a hydraulic lift with his shoulder while the other fought to ratchet down its yellow straps.

The shrill whistle shot through the air again, this time twice in succession. Kara chanced a glance back at the black column, but the sky had darkened far too much to see it properly. She slid to a stop a meter from the forward mast. Reaching down to its base she popped open a white access box and pulled on the aluminum crank within, extending it out far enough to turn.

Voyager lurched again. This time she leaned steep enough that Kara had to grab on to the crank with both hands to keep from sliding toward the port side. A creaking groan came from below decks as the ship righted. She jolted down hard. Kara's feet lifted from the deck as a wall of icy water crashed against her. Spitting out sea water, Kara grabbed the crank and turned with everything she had.

Slowly, the mast began descending into the ship. It wouldn't sink all the way down, just enough to give clearance to the cover, which they desperately needed judging by the severity of the squall. Her shoulders and arms burned as she rolled the crank over and over. Out of the corner of her eye, she could see Voyager's thick cover raising from the port side. Her heart lifted as she watched the two halves of ribbed plastic and carbon fiber rise from either side of the deck. In truth it was more shell than cover, and when the two sides magnetically locked in the middle, they'd have the best protection available should the ship capsize. Just seeing it on the way up gave her courage.

Kara's stomach rose up, telling her another roll was on the way. Quickly she pulled herself to the side of the mast and clenched it with one arm, while still cranking with the other. Stopping would do no one any good. If they couldn't get the cover up and Voyager rolled too far and capsized, it would be on her head. That cover would be the difference between a clean, full roll back right side up, or taking on water and sinking.

Finally the crank jolted to a stop. Kara looked up and saw the mast had retracted as far as it would go. Automatically, she locked the crank and closed the box. But when she looked to the port side, she didn't see the cover moving. As the next lurch hit, she grabbed the mast and looked back to the others. A new blast of sea foam smacked the side of her face and stung her eyes. Wiping away the water she blinked up at the central mast.

Her breath caught.

With the howl of the wind in her ears and the cracks of thunder rolling in, Kara couldn't hear what Chief Lambros yelled to Goldi and Drummond. But she saw the problem, plain as day. Somehow— the heavy wind, she guessed—the free line she spotted earlier had gotten tangled around one of the T-handles that dotted the inner border of the cover. The line had pulled taut like a guitar string. Since one end was anchored about a third of the way down the mast, there was no way they could close the cover, or drop the mast. Neither piece was going anywhere. And they were exposed.

Kara got to her feet just as Goldi scrambled over to the central mast. Another roll sent Kara grabbing for the collapsed forward mast again. Farther down the deck, Goldi ran with the momentum of the ship's roll and jumped, using the ship's list to get her higher up the mast. Expertly, she wrapped arms and legs around the mast and found the handholds. Voyager righted herself on the waves, sending Goldi's lower half swinging like a pendulum the other way. Her ropy muscles tightened as she continued to climb toward the tangled line.

Taking advantage of the pause in between waves, Kara ran toward Chief Lambros. Partway down the deck, however, she stopped dead, her eyes glued with horror to what was happening on the central mast.

Goldi had her knife in one hand reaching out toward the line. Her legs stayed firmly wrapped around the mast, giving her some stability, but the next wave was already on top of them. A veritable wall of sea water crashed against them. Kara's feet swept out from under her. With a heavy smack she landed back first onto the deck. Before she could scramble up, Voyager's next roll sent her sliding fast toward the port side railing. With nothing to slow her down, Kara lifted both feet and pointed them toward the rails. She picked up speed, sliding faster. Below the rails the ocean churned dark and angry.

Voyager groaned. Her tilt lessened and Kara slowed, but only just. The rails slammed against her bare feet, sending bolts of pain up through her ankles and legs. But she was still on board.

"Navigator!" One of the deckhands called to her,

his voice almost lost in the storm.

Kara looked to her right as Voyager started her corrective roll. The two deckhands she spotted earlier had strapped in to the center of the deck using the emergency belts. They beckoned her to come join them.

A flash of light caught her eye. Kara snapped back to the central mast. Goldi cradled her right arm, which flopped awkwardly past the elbow. Broken. Her knife nowhere to be seen. That must have been the flash Kara saw.

Before she could react, a stout figure in a white dress shirt, soaked to the bone, scrambled up after Goldi. Drummond had her knife clamped firmly in his mouth, by the handle, not the blade. What did he think he was doing?

The deckhands called to her again, more urgently.

Drummond wasn't nearly the climber Goldi was, but he managed. Awkwardly, he grabbed at the stuck line twice before landing it. Lightning arced across the sky, lighting up the dark clouds. Thunder broke so loud it may as well have started inside Kara's skull.

He cut the line. Drummond looked to Goldi. Unsure of what to do with the knife, he chucked it away from them and slid next to her on the mast.

Voyager cried again as the next wave broke. Kara buckled down and held on to the rail with all her strength. They rolled and lurched. Water broke over her again, for a moment she felt as though she'd actually submerged. When it passed she spit the water from her mouth and tried to find Drummond and Goldi again.

They were in the same spot on the central mast. Drummond had wrapped one arm around Goldi to weather out the last roll. Now he moved slightly between her and the mast so she could wrap her good arm around his neck. Slowly, they moved down the mast. Drummond carefully gripping one handhold after another until there weren't any to grab on to.

A meter from the deck, Drummond and Goldi slid the rest of the way down. Chief Lambros waved to Kara and flashed the hand signs for help, cover, and starboard. Kara sprang away from the railing and splashed across the deck to the crank that Goldi had originally been manning. As she ran by the central mast, Lambros strapped Goldi into an emergency deck belt.

Once in place, Kara wasted no time in working the crank. As it spun, the starboard side cover rose into place. She looked over her shoulder and saw a shaky Drummond at the other crank station going through the same motions. Chief Lambros had the central mast retracted just enough to give the cover halves clearance to meet and seal. Some of the whistling ceased, but the peals of thunder were only slightly muted.

Kara's triumph was short lived, however, as the ship rolled again, harder than before. With some of the noise of the wind shut out, Kara yelled over to Drummond to come with her. He didn't need telling twice. Struggling to fight the tilt of the deck, Drummond made it far enough to grab onto the base of the central mast and wait out the roll. Voyager groaned again but held fast.

"Drummond, here." Chief Lambros, focused as ever, deftly wrapped the emergency belting around Drummond and the central mast. Kara quickly did the same after ensuring that Lambros could get herself tied in.

Drummond's ragged breaths were audible even amidst the noise of the storm. In a shaky voice he said, "Now what?"

Chief Lambros reached behind her and patted his

shoulder. "Now we wait. Just focus on your breath. Everything else is out of our hands. All you can do is breathe."

"Or puke," Goldi added in a soft voice. "You can do that, too."

Drummond let out a weak chuckle.

Morning came like a sigh of relief. Something about the hours right after a storm made everything feel renewed, reenergized. Most of the crew walked around with a sort of manic energy, full of giddy laughter and bad jokes, everyone thankful that they'd made it through. After such a squall with no loss of equipment or personnel, the win lifted everyone higher.

Kara finished sending a report on the squall to Vish command. No telling if the storm had blown itself out or if other Mariners might get caught in it. The storms were small, violent, ephemeral. In the past they might have been classified as a particularly severe type of microburst, but weather was much more stable and predictable back then.

She stepped out of the bridge hatch and out to the stern of the ship. Voyager's foamy wake trailed behind in blue-green waters, almost as if the storm had never happened. Chief Lambros might have a chestnut about how last night's squall only lives inside their minds, but Kara didn't feel philosophical at the moment. With the ship's cover down and masts back up, she only wanted to feel the breeze and watch the sun rise. From behind her, the ship's black sun sails snapped in the wind. But it was other sounds that caught her attention.

"Naturally, he proposed marriage to me afterward," Goldi said in her thick slavic tones to a group of laughing deckhands. "I told him this would not work. Our people are too different. But then he cries, so I offer him my virginity as prize, yes? When I tell him he is only sixteenth man to receive this honor, he is very pleased, I think."

Laugher rolled across the deck. Kara couldn't help but smile, too.

"All right, now you're making me regret the whole thing," Drummond said. "I should've left you up there."

"*Kotyonok*," Goldi purred. "Only thing you should regret is how you climb aloft. You look like constipated monkey up there. Do not worry, we shall fix you. First, we take care of this."

Kara turned around to watch the deckhands roaring as Goldi patted Drummond's belly with her free arm. The other was bound with a bright yellow plastic cast and held in a sling.

"Don't worry, kitten," Goldi said. "We get you in climbing shape."

Catching Kara's eye, a red-cheeked Drummond made his excuses and came her way. The deckhands jeered as he left.

"Just need to see the navigator," he said.

"What about?" Kara said when he made his way to the stern.

"Anything." Although Drummond looked in good spirits, there were shadows under his eyes and he moved more stiffly than normal.

Kara snorted. "Count yourself lucky. If the deckhands are giving you bilge, it means they like you."

"What an honor," he said with a smirk. "Seriously, I had no idea it could get that bad. I thought we were done for a while there."

Before Kara could respond, Ensign Martin poked his head out of the bridge hatch. "Lieutenant Nkosi,

I've got the Gallant on the horn."

"Squall get them, too?" Kara said.

He shook his head. "It's not that. You better get in here."

Inside the bridge, Commander Satry stood by the helm control, inputting new coordinates. Kara felt the engines shift direction and power. Captain Ansari stood by Martin's communication station. He held a headset against his ear. Upon seeing Kara, he waved her over and put the transmission on speaker.

"We're sure, Captain," the voice on the other end said. Kara couldn't identify it. It must have been Gallant's signal officer. "Our optics can zoom in on her hull. Name's painted right there. C.S. Ionova."

"On our way," Captain Ansari said. "ETA one hour, if all courses hold steady."

Once Martin terminated the call, Kara spoke to the Captain. "They found her? Out here?"

Captain Ansari didn't look as pleased as he should have. Finding the Ionova had been the first step in their plan. An uncertain step at that, given that the ship could have left port and gone anywhere since it's last sighting. Now here the Ionova was, timely as a sunny day when the ship's batteries were low. A little too perfect, really. Kara couldn't help but share the Captain's skepticism.

"It appears so," he said. "But according to the Gallant, she's not answering hails on any commercial or military radio channel. They've tried signal via satellite network as well. Nothing."

"Maybe they're trying to stay hidden?" Drummond said. "Lieutenant Nkosi said these aren't the most reputable sailors. Could they be smuggling and trying to avoid detection?"

Kara shook her head. "Doesn't fit. If you're running dark and someone notices you, the game's up. You try to act natural and give the best cover story you've got. Pretending to be invisible when someone can clearly see you wouldn't work. Something else is going on here."

"Think the storm could've knocked out their comms?" Drummond crossed his arms over his chest.

"Possible," Kara said. "Then again, the squall could've missed them entirely. They're unpredictable that way."

"Squall that got us completely missed the Gallant." Captain Ansari rubbed his chin. "They reported choppy seas and some rain, that's all. The Ionova is closer to them than us. Odds are they got missed, too."

"Maybe it's a ghost ship." Drummond laughed at his own joke. No one else joined him. "Come on, that's not really a thing. Is it?"

Captain Ansari patted Drummond's shoulder before going to see the commander. Drummond gave Kara a questioning look.

"We'll know in an hour." Kara paused for a moment. "Or if you're impatient, we could ask Chief Lambros."

Drummond raised an eyebrow.

Chief Lambros stood her post on deck. With the sun sails trimmed neatly and the equipment in perfect order, her duties shifted to readying the boarding party.

"We'll try light and semaphore signals first. If we don't get a response, we'll board," she told Drummond. Kara stood by the port side rail and looked forward. The Ionova was off their bow, but they had a few minutes yet before they would come alongside her. Floating next to the black and red container ship was the Gallant, sleek, tall and ivory.

"Ensign Martin will do the signaling, so nothing for us to do there but wait," Chief Lambros went on.

"So," Drummond asked tentatively, "Why did Lieutenant Nkosi say you could tell us more about the Ionova? Do you know the crew?"

Lambros gave him a half smile. "Because Kara, for all her love of the Core, doesn't have much time for the more esoteric parts of the practice."

"I don't understand." Drummond looked at both the women in turn.

Kara watched the Ionova and the Gallant through binoculars, but grinned all the same. "Ask her what the ink between her eyes is for."

Drummond looked to Chief Lambros, who watched them with an amused expression. She pointed to a coin-sized tattoo set just above and between her eyes. It resembled a flower surrounding a simple eye with a triangular pupil. "This is earned when you have proven Sight. I earned it when I was younger. These days, I'm not sure we should offer this as a mark of merit within the Core. All the same, that's what she means. You may not realize it, but beneath that serious exterior, our ship's navigator is quite the smartass."

"You don't mean seeing, as in..." Drummond wiggled his fingers at her. "Mystical sight, right?"

Kara laughed while the chief sighed.

"I do," Chief Lambros said. "Yes, I realize how that sounds. Before you ask, this is how it works. There are many ways to look deeply within. Even Kara will agree with this. At times, when we look deep enough, we touch upon that which connects us all. At those times, it is possible to gain insight, intuition, or even knowledge, about people and places that are seemingly separated from us by space or even time. It is possible because these separations are an illusion."

Drummond gave her an uncertain look.

"To earn the mark," she went on, "is simple enough. If you feel you have Seen, or gained such insight, you can go to a teacher of the Core, such as myself. You will record your impressions. That information is logged with the time and date. If your vision turns out to have been correct, then you have truly Seen, and earn the mark."

"But..." Drummond obviously wanted to tread lightly. "That could be falsified, couldn't it?"

"Of course it could." Chief Lambros said. "There is no lock that can't be broken, Congressman. Adding more security measures is pointless. Ultimately, what would we be protecting against? If a person, for whatever reasons, wants to fake that they have Seen and is ready to go to such lengths, then so be it. What did it gain them? As I said, sometimes I feel like offering a mark of merit for Sight is counterproductive."

"Why? I mean, if it proves that Sight is real, doesn't that help people's faith in the Core?" Drummond asked.

Kara lowered her binoculars.

"The Core isn't about faith," the Chief said. "It's about questions and experience. When people get caught up in phenomena such as the Sight, as I once did, it's ultimately a distraction from the true path. Even in ancient texts such as the Yoga Sutras, Pantanjali warns us not to be too taken by these *sidhis* as he calls them. From a practical standpoint, Seeing is unpredictable, sporadic, and too inconsistent to be relied upon."

"But you believe it is real?" Drummond said.

"Having experienced it myself, absolutely."

"It just seems so..." Drummond searched for the right word and failed. "Couldn't people simply have a vision based on data they already have? Imagining things from what they already know and established patterns? If I have a vision of my aunt getting divorced for the fourth time, it could just be prediction more than anything mystical."

"Of course it could be," Chief Lambros said. "Experience tells me otherwise, but I don't wish to debate it. As a teacher of the Core, I know Seeing does happen. I also know that it's not important, really. Kara may like to think she's getting my goat when she ribs me about things like Sight, but honestly, as a teacher I appreciate the fact that she won't get caught up in that distraction."

Kara placed the binoculars back in the case where they belonged. "No insights about what's happening on the Ionova then?"

Chief Lambros snorted. "You need Sight to tell you something bad is going on there?"

As if on cue, the deck speakers crackled to life. Ensign Martin's voice filled the air. "Boarding team, be ready in five."

Voyager's engines slowed. She coasted closer to the Ionova, on her starboard side. Gallant had already set up a gangway with the port side, although her crew held fast, waiting for Voyager before boarding. Kara commented on as much to Chief Lambros.

"They didn't say they were planning on waiting for us before boarding." Kara double checked her armor plates and sidearm while she spoke.

"Could be courtesy," Chief Lambros said lightly. "Or they want us to trip any booby traps before them."

"What?" Drummond stiffened. "Why would there be traps?"

"Not to worry, *moi horoshiy*," a voice said from behind them. Goldi gave Drummond a toothy smile and grasped his shoulder. "You will not go with first party. Much too dangerous for my special kitten, no? Stay and keep Goldi company."

Kara's chest shook with laughter. Chief Lambros gave her a light smack before calling for bumpers to be placed over the railing and hull. Deckhands scrambled to get the large rubber ship bumpers in place. Engines reversed, slowing their approach until they delicately nudged the Ionova.

Chief Lambros faced Kara and her crew of three other deckhands. "Final checks," she said.

Each member of the boarding team checked their weapons and gear. Buckles tinkled while the sound of dozens of soft pats rose and fell.

"Masks," Lambros said.

As one, they fixed gas masks over their faces and sealed them. One by one they signaled readiness with a thumbs up. Chief Lambros nodded. Her voice came from the mask, tinny and muffled. "Weapons hot. Eyes open. Let's move."

The first Mariner in line, a hook-nosed deck mate named Collin, picked up the docking ramp and secured it between the decks of the two ships. Chief Lambros took point, flashing a bright light across to the Gallant. Two flashes came back.

Chief Lambros signaled them forward.

Their boots clomped across the gangway, then onto the deck of the Ionova. As soon as Kara stepped foot on the deck, a chill sense of unease swept over her. Collin stood closest to her, so Kara signaled for him to come with her on a sweep of the deck. From the Gallant's side, she saw their sailors doing the same. Although they wore significantly better masks and each carried identical, compact assault rifles.

Ionova may have been small for a container ship,

but that meant she was still fairly large compared to a Mariner vessel. The majority of her was simple, flat deck dedicated to holding shipping containers. Of which, she only had a few empties. As Kara and Collin traveled around corners and swept the containers, all they found was caked mud and rust.

And yet. That foreboding followed Kara with every step.

At last she signaled Collin that they'd return to the rest of the group.

"If we ever let Voyager get this filthy," Collin muttered, "Chief would bring back keelhauling just for us."

Kara gave him a chuckle, but her heart wasn't in it. That sense of anxiety had worked its way into her gut. On their sweep they'd identified several hatches that led below decks. Kara relayed the info to Chief Lambros, who had a quick conference with the leader from the Gallant. They decided on a plan, divvying up the teams to each entry point. Kara and Collin were assigned the hatch that led to the bridge, which sat in a small tower above deck.

"Remember," Chief Lambros said. "Watch for traps. Use your lights and your brains. Radio back when you're clear or if you find anything. Don't assume contacts are hostile unless they show aggression."

Although the crew from the Gallant looked as though they might argue the last point, the teams divided up and waited for Lambros's signal. Kara and Collin hustled to the hatch at the base of the bridge tower. Collin wrapped his hands around the locking wheel and waited.

Kara clicked on the light at the end of her sidearm. She pointed the weapon at the deck.

Two shrill whistles pierced the air.

Collin spun the wheel and swung the hatch open. Kara darted inside.

A large fly bounced against her head on its way toward the open portal. Kara swept the floor and ceiling with her light, looking for trip lines or sensors. Nothing. Treading carefully, they rounded a corner in the narrow passageway, which led to a steep ladder.

Darkness set in around them as they climbed, the beams of their lights looking more narrow as they went on. Inside her mask, Kara's breath rolled rough and hot against her cheeks. A hint of something rank penetrated her mask. It wasn't the normal, spicy smell that came from the filter. She sniffed deeper, but it was gone.

"Lieutenant Nkosi?" Collin said behind her.

Kara nodded and stepped onward, sweeping the passage with her light. Two more flies shot toward her. She swore. They walked on. A low buzz grew ahead of them. Kara sighed. She signaled for Collin to stop.

Moving her light left to right, she could see three hatches. One in the middle hung partially open, the word "Bridge" stenciled across it. She shone her light directly into the open crack. A half dozen buzzing shapes swarmed around the beam. Using hand signs, she signaled Collin to show where they were going.

Using her foot to swing open the bridge's hatch the rest of the way, Kara stepped back and moved her light around the room.

"Grab your radio," she said. "Call this in."

From behind her, Collin gagged.

"You may want to leave your mask on," Chief Lambros told the Gallant's crewman lightly.

The blond man had just squeezed his white-uniformed frame into the bridge. "I've seen worse," he said confidently. Kara thought she recognized him. Once she spotted his white gloves, she knew. He was the one with the augmentations she'd seen on Vish.

With one hand, he stripped off his protective mask.

At the first breath he made a sour face, squinted and began hacking. One hand to his mouth, he scrambled off of the bridge.

Doc Young cackled. He leaned over one of the slumped bodies by the map table. With a jewelers eye piece in one eye and armed with a pen light and metal probe, he examined the corpses.

Kara couldn't blame the idiot from the Gallant for heaving. The bridge was beyond putrid. Kara's first order of business was to switch on the lights and get the portholes open. It didn't seem to help much, though.

"How's it going over there, doc?" Kara said.

"Oh," Doc Young said through his mask, "Just trying to determine cause of death." He tapped the bullet hole in the man's forehead and laughed again.

She shook her head. "Any idea how long they've been dead?"

"Hard to tell with Mister Pulverized over there." He gestured to the floor. "But these two? I'd say a day or two. I'm no entomologist, but the flies that were in here were probably hitchhikers. There's some larvae in the bodies that look to be close to 48 hours old."

"Aside from the maggots," an impatient voice came from the entrance, "what else do we know?"

Captain Faulkner entered with the blond man— once again masked, Kara noticed—at his heels. Faulkner stood a head shorter than his subordinate but led the man like a well-trained dog.

Doc Young looked from the Gallant's captain over

to Kara. She nodded.

"They were both executed by shady characters unknown. Not before they were subjected to a round of interrogation first."

"Interrogation?" Faulkner's eyes zeroed in on the doc. "Why do you say that?"

Lazily, the doc pointed to the floor. Specifically, to a scattering of blood-covered shapes that looked like broken shell fragments. "Fingernails pulled off. Couple of teeth yanked, too. Definitely before death, blood and swelling prove that. Whoever the doers were here, they're not squeamish."

Faulkner beckoned to the blond man and sent him to the workstation. "Grant here will check their ship's computer. Could be some clues as to what happened there."

"Or the coordinates," Kara said.

Faulkner focused on her. "Say again?"

"The coordinates of the underground bunker they found." Kara watched for Faulkner's reaction. "It could still be in their travel logs."

"Ah," Faulkner said. "Yes, of course. That goes without saying. But if we'd also like to bring their killer to justice, we must hope for some evidence."

Kara inclined her head. "Of course."

"I'm trying to break the personal accounts," Grant said. "But the logs are unprotected. Last entry is them porting in Skatch."

"No auto-logs?" Kara said.

"None," Grant answered.

Faulkner looked more than a little annoyed at Kara for questioning his sailor. "How did they get out here? Where is their killer? Is there anything there?"

"Uh, hang on, sir." Grant looked flustered. "Ship's on autopilot. Weird though, there's no autolog entry for going into autopilot. That shouldn't be possible."

"Where was the ship headed, then?" Faulkner

said.

"Here? I guess, sir?" Grant scratched his head with his free hand. "I mean, the ship stopped on its own. Still has power and no systems are down."

Kara's face fell. She turned to Chief Lambros in time to see her picking up her radio. "Everyone off this ship, now! On the double, this is a direct order! I say again, abandon the Ionova. Ensign Martin, make ready for departure."

Doc Young didn't need to be told twice. His heels were already over the threshold to the bridge before Kara could turn to Faulkner.

"What are you to yammering on about?" Faulkner said.

"Captain," Kara said. "We need to leave, now. This ship is about to get scuttled."

Even through the clear plastic shield of his gas mask, Kara could see Faulkner's sneer. "Is this some shipsy superstition?"

"No," Kara spoke fast. "It's someone getting rid of evidence. Stay or go, it's your ass."

As she spun to leave, she caught Faulkner and Grant exchanging a look.

Chief Lambros ran five paces ahead of her, yelling into her radio each step of the way. Collin caught up with them as they ran out of the bridge tower, their heels ringing against the deck plating. Down the deck, Doc Young ran across the gangway over to the Voyager. Kara picked up the pace and sprinted as fast as she could while keeping Chief Lambros and Collin in front of her.

Deckhands on the Voyager were already unlocking the gangway. Ahead of her, both Lambros and Collin fled across. Kara put a hand on the railing.

The world went sideways.

A hammer blast hit her feet from below. Kara fell backward as the Ionova listed away from the

Voyager. Her ears rang. She tried to get back up, but the world kept spinning and she couldn't regain her footing. Was the ship listing more?

Suddenly, hands had her under the armpits and at her ankles. Kara felt her weight lift off the Ionova. What direction she went then, she couldn't tell, but in moments she was being set back down. Doc Young's face spun in figure eights in front of her. He spoke, but his words were swallowed by the fierce ringing in her ears. Kara struggled to get up, but a firm hand pushed her back down.

Voyager's engines hummed beneath her, vibrating the deck. Wind rushed overhead, sending Doc Young's auburn hair flying around his weathered face.

Kara felt more than heard a second blast. Deckhands ran to the starboard side railing, probably to get a better look. When Kara tried to join them, Doc Young forced her back down and gave her a no nonsense stare.

She sighed, resigned. Looking up at the blanket of white clouds and the edges of their sun sails, Kara tried to calm herself. But she couldn't help but wonder. At this rate, would they even make it to Skatch?

Chapter Eight: Skatch Harbor

"It is clear that when it comes to business, the best action government can take is to get out of the way. Today, with the dedication of the first official Free Market Zone, America makes good on the promise of economic prosperity and opportunity for all."
Aiden Spencer, 53rd President of the United States of America

Ensign Martin had been able to set them up with a video call on the bridge. Apparently, Captain Faulkner wanted some answers.

So did Kara.

Her hearing hadn't totally returned, but Doc said that was normal. At least the dizziness had passed after a night in sick bay. He didn't think she was concussed, but he couldn't rule out some other kind of traumatic brain injury. Although he told her to take it easy, the events of the last few days told Kara that was wishful thinking.

The large display in the bridge showed what looked like a meeting room over on the Gallant. Captain Faulkner sat at narrow, polished black table along with Grant and a couple others she recognized from Vish. They must have been his senior staff. Or accomplices, depending on how you looked at it.

"Don't think we aren't thankful for the warning, Captain Ansari," Faulkner said. "What I'd like to know is why we didn't get that warning sooner."

"From what I understand, Captain," Ansari said from next to Kara, "You were made aware of the danger at the exact same time my crew was. What's the problem?"

"I can't help but feel suspicious." Faulkner rose from his chair and walked closer to the camera. "As soon as we start digging through the ship's computer your people suddenly figure out there's a bomb on board? Who placed the explosives, I wonder?"

A deathly calm settled over Captain Ansari. "If you want to accuse my crew of bombing the Ionova, have the courage to say it, man."

"Well then, if we're done mincing words. How is it possible that no one found a bomb before, unless it was placed after our crews swept the ship?"

Kara made eye contact with the Captain. He gave her a short nod.

"It's simple, Captain Faulkner. When we called in the situation in the bridge, your team had stopped sweeping below decks. I've confirmed it with our deckmaster. We were all on the same radio channel. They called in that they were coming back. She told them to finish, but they ignored her. None of us bombed the Ionova, Captain. We don't need to assume malevolent intent, there's enough incompetence to explain what happened."

"Well," Faulkner said. "That sounds very convenient, doesn't it?"

"Actually, it wasn't," Kara said. "I got caught in the first blast. Not convenient in the least. Listen, if that bomb was left as far below deck and as close to the bottom of the hull as possible, then of course it would be the last place our search teams would reach. Or in this case, ignored. Are your people always so thorough, Captain?"

Captain Ansari gently raised a hand. Kara stopped.

"Of course our communications officer was monitoring and recording all of the local radio traffic, Captain Faulkner. I'm sure we can provide copies so you can find out exactly which of your crew members stopped their search prematurely."

"Of course," Faulkner said. "How did you know there was a bomb, then?"

Well, it wasn't shipsy superstition, Kara barely stopped herself from saying.

"Navigator," Captain Ansari said.

"It's not uncommon," she told Faulkner. "It's hard to hide a stolen ship unless the thieves are very good at finding dormant tracking devices. Most aren't. When criminals attack each other and steal cargo, it's an easy way of destroying evidence. The owners of the Ionova must have crossed someone who doesn't play around. Once Grant found that even the auto-logs had been sanitized, it made sense. If the entries from the black box are there and someone comes nosing around, the crime could eventually be traced to its source. That, and the ship being sent into deep water for no apparent reason. It added up."

"Well, it's the first I've heard of such a thing," Faulkner said. "But it does make a certain amount of sense."

"Speaking of the data," Ansari said. "Did your signal officer find anything else of note?"

Faulkner leaned over the table and waved dismissively to Grant.

"Uh, yeah, Captain." Grant brushed a lock of his blond hair way from his forehead. "It wasn't so much what I found, as much as what I didn't find. Like I said, whoever this guy who deleted their autologs was, he was good. I couldn't even find stripped data in the disks to look at. He zeroed out the bits on all the memory sectors that he used. It's like your, uh, navigator, said. There wasn't even any record of the ship being set on autopilot. Only thing we have to go on are the last good log entries. They were definitely in Skatch."

"So," Faulkner said. "In summary, we're back where we were, with one less lead."

"Not necessarily," Kara said. "There are a lot of players in Skatch, but only a few that would have the minerals to pull something like this. They bribe the dock cops and the local judges to overlook a lot, but this kind of grand theft and murder? No. It'd be bad for business if too much of it went on. When we get to Skatch, we at least know what to look for. The owners of the Ionova got on someone's bad side. That kind of fire always makes smoke and leaves burns."

"Hmm." Faulkner considered her. "You could be right. Let's touch base when we make port, Captain."

"Agreed." Ansari motioned for Martin to cut the conference. "You really think we've got enough to work with here?"

Kara sputtered. "Maybe I embellished a little. I couldn't stand looking at his smug face."

"Can't blame you there," Captain Ansari said. "Reckon you've already got some suspects lined up, though?"

"Some," Kara said. "It's impossible to keep up with the black marketeers, but I've got enough to start with."

"Put a quick report together so we can get more of the crew in on the search. Maybe this time we can get a straight out victory."

No one on the bridge commented.

✦ ✦ ✦

"Why didn't we take just the Ionova?" Gill didn't often speak. When she did, there was that slur she tried to hide. She may not have always had it, Tren thought. The sort of back-alley butchers that did augmentations on the cheap and sly weren't exactly known for their clean work. Nerve damage and other unpleasant side effects were commonplace. For mercs like Gill and Gary, the risk was worth it. As much as Tren had come to rely on his own augments, he shuddered to think about what could've happened if he had gone to such a place.

"Because, Gilly darling," Big Madrid said, "that move, while beneficial immediately, would have been disastrous in the long run. One must think strategically. What good would it do to take our prize only to have the Ionova's drop-dead logic trigger the dormant beacons and report herself stolen? Any local magistrate at any port we could go to would be more than happy to seize our cargo and throw us to a firing squad."

They moved together through the crowd choking the walkways of pier eleven. Sailors and tourists mingled with the vendors selling fake native jewelry, fake meat kababs, and outdated entertainment maps. Dock rats crowded the sailors, promising to show them to the best whores and fights for a modest fee. Odors of sweat, piss, and perfume overwhelmed everything else.

A few days ago, a younger, more naive Tren, might have thought this could be the perfect opportunity for an escape. He knew better now. Big had a point: where would he go? And when they did catch up to him? The image of the pulverized mercenary on the Ionova rushed back in on him, setting a sick feeling in his stomach.

Big Madrid hadn't disclosed exactly where they were headed yet, but, he didn't often clue Tren into his plans. From the sound of it, Gill and Gary weren't exactly in the loop, either. Tren chanced a dip online and pulled some maps up on his in-eye display.

"Why couldn't he fix that?" Gill motioned toward Tren. Speaking, as usual, as though he were an irksome pet. Why did they bother feeding the dog if it didn't protect the house?

"You can't interface with those beacons over wireless," Tren made a point of addressing no one in particular. After the Ionova, he wanted no part of Gill or Gary's bad side. "We'd have to find them all first and that can take days."

Big stopped them and put a hand on his stole. "You need to trust that daddy knows best, sweetheart. Because he does. Have I not steered us to success thus far? Have I not delivered on all I've promised? Have I ever breached the terms of our contract, written or verbal?"

His stare could have melted steel. Gill looked away.

"No," she slurred.

"Then we're in unanimous agreement." Big tossed the end of the stole around his neck. "I'll keep us climbing the ladders of wealth and society, and you stay ready to make with the punchy-kicky-shooty, yes?"

Gill nodded.

Big Madrid resumed their stroll across the pier's entrance. Gary had been silent during that exchange, Tren noticed. That didn't mean much, however. The man was a tough read. Tren had previously watched him spring from complete inaction to violent explosiveness in less than a blink of an eye. Assuming Gary wasn't paying attention because of his silence and vacant expression was foolish.

They stopped shy of the entrance to the Painted Punter, a crew bar that, unlike the competition, boasted floors that were cleaned on a monthly basis. Tren could smell the skunky cannabis leavings and mildewy air of stale alcohol from outside.

"Now, my lovelies," Big Madrid addressed them. "We have several stops to make on this fine day. Your intrepid leader is going to find not just any crew, but the correct crew, to take us on our voyage. As you have no doubt realized"—he looked at Gill— "we have been unfortunately placed in a position where I must adjust my previous plans. Our former associates decided to be less than honest with the exclusivity of our purchased intelligence. In order to secure my investment, it has become necessary that I be personally involved in this little treasure hunt, subduing competition when needed. Time is of the essence. Our success is a priority. Do we all know what this means?"

Big Madrid looked to the group, clearly expecting an answer. Tren shifted nervously.

"It means," he answered for them, "that darling Tren is going to personally crack into every device our prospective seamen carry and every bit of data therein, and will report his findings. It means, that Gill and Gary are going to be on their very tippy-toes, ready to spring into action and crush the faces of any who might try to use this opportunity to simply take the data we have worked oh-so hard to attain. Are we crystal, my lovelies?"

Tren nodded. He stole a glance over at Gill and Gary. Could they possibly be as worried as him? Strangely, as much as Tren couldn't think through any escape plan that didn't ultimately lead to his painful and messy end, it felt like sticking with Big Madrid was turning out to be just as shaky a proposition.

There had to be a way to get into Big's good books. Maybe if he could come up with a way to get them a ship? That was a longshot, even for him. Tren bit his lip, thinking. After a moment, he kicked on his in-eye display, trying to keep half his attention on where they were going and the other half on his searches.

Maybe, he thought. *Maybe he could help.*

"You should go back," Kara said for the third time. Noise—not only human, but also musical and machine—filled the humid air over Skatch Harbor. As the sun set, the breeze off the harbor waters grew more chill. Kara had put on her long sleeves. The shirt covered many of her tattoos but did keep her warmer.

She blew a strand of red hair from her eyes. When they got back to the ship she'd see if someone could cut it for her. Word was that Peter in engineering had some decent barber skills.

Drummond shook his head. "I've been to worse places, I'm sure. Besides, I need to be here and we're wasting time talking about it. Captain Faulkner has his people from the Gallant already searching."

"Right, I'm sure they're giving it their best," Kara scoffed. "Faulkner sent out a token group of three. Last I heard they've been drinking all day."

"Regardless. If things go sideways like they did on the Ionova, you'll want me around as a witness."

Kara considered it. She had intended on working the pier with a deckhand. Collin, for example, had been proving reliable. When Drummond volunteered, she hadn't expected Captain Ansari to go along with it. Maybe his thoughts were in line with Drummond's.

"Come on," he said. "Chief Lambros and

Commander Satry are already out looking. We should get a move on."

"Fine." Kara jabbed a finger at Drummond. "But, if you get in trouble out here, I'm not going to be the one to explain it to Goldi."

"Was that a..." Drummond's eyebrows rose high up his forehead. "You actually do have a sense of humor. I can't believe it."

"Never mind that," Kara said. "If you're in, then you're all in. Over here."

Kara beckoned him to follow her over to the periphery of the crowds swarming Pier Nine. It was one of the most run-down piers in Skatch Harbor, which made it a favorite of the dock control's office when it came to giving Mariners a place to moor their ships. Kara knew it well.

Skatch was one of several grand experiments on the part of the United States. A territory designated as a Free Market Zone, which meant the American government collected annual duties from the land owners and essentially washed their hands of everything else. Governance and law enforcement was left mostly to the corporations that controlled the harbor. The results were interesting, to say the least. In any case, a Mariner was marginally more welcome in an FMZ than in a proper American city like Seattle or Portland.

"Are you armed?" Kara asked.

"No."

She thought for a moment, then reconsidered. "Ever had any weapons training?"

"Er, no." Drummond fidgeted. "Should I be armed? I've been to the San Diego FMZ and didn't have any problems."

"San Diego's a ghost town compared to Skatch. Still, I don't want you armed if you don't know what you're doing. Don't worry about it. As long as we don't overplay our hand, nothing today should get violent." She looked down at her pistol belt and wondered if she'd live to regret saying that. The way things had been going? Probably.

"Here's our plan," Kara said. "See that run down bar over there? It's called the Masked Mohican. Before you ask, I have no clue why. Only time I've ever heard anyone talk about the Ionova was in there. We go inside, keep a low profile, and ask around about Dillon and Marsden, those are—were—the ship's owners. All we want to know is if they were in talks to sell their intel to anyone. Stay alert. Don't let on more than we're supposed to know about them."

"Basically, you want me to shut up," Drummond said.

Kara gave him a look that said, *more or less*.

"You know, I talk to people for a living. That's what politicians do."

"And I'm sure you're very qualified." Kara started walking. "If we need to get the bartender at the Mohican to vote for us, I'll take you off the bench."

Drummond followed. "Cute. I think I liked you better before the jokes."

Neon and LED lights burned the air around them. Pinks, purples, blues, reds, they ran over the windows and signs in lines and squiggles. It put a carnival veneer over the carnal delights, which would be put on offer after dark. Advertisements and silent vids projected from the eaves of the shops lit the boardwalks and paths in front of them. Being the seedier pier, the more decadent and specialized establishments called the place home. Kara couldn't take a step without treading on the light-inscribed face of a doxy with bee-stung lips or the glittering rows of a chem-purveyor's wares. It wasn't all candy shops and brothels, either.

Drummond jerked a thumb at a window as they

passed. "What kind of place is 'Upgrade X Tours' anyway? That for people with tour guide fetishes?"

"Not that I doubt such a place exists," Kara almost laughed, "but, no. It's an augmentation broker. There are a ton of places where you can get enhancements off the books and cheap. Since they're not exactly legal, they can't advertise. So, you go to a guy like that, who claims to be a simple tour guide, but if you pass the sniff test—"

"He gets you where you need to go." Drummond kept surveying the area. "Sounds like a clean and safe way to get enhanced. Come to think of it, I haven't noticed a single Mariner who's been augmented."

Kara kept her eyes on their destination as they walked.

"Sorry," he said. "Being nosy again."

"It's fine. Most Mariners don't have any use for augmentations. It's not like we have any rules against it or anything. Many of us do feel that...It's not easy to explain. Think of it this way, have you met people who've had a lot of work done?"

"Not what you'd call a ton, no. My roommate from college got an integration set. But he was studying to be a computer engineer."

"Betting that was done by a good surgeon using the best equipment, right? Side effects get a lot worse for the people who don't have that luxury. Sad thing is, most people that get enhanced are only trying to qualify for work." Kara abruptly cut herself off.

A man and a woman wearing dark blue uniforms and hi-vis belts strolled slowly by from the opposite direction. Both carried sub machine guns at the ready and both had eyes only for Kara. She pointedly kept her gaze forward. As the dock cops passed, the larger one spit on the boardwalk between them.

"Watch yourself, shipsy."

Drummond stopped. He watched the cops, an

indignant expression on his face. Kara raised a finger to her lips and motioned him on. Once they had more distance between them, he spoke.

"Hell was that?"

"Superstition," Kara said. "Mariners are bad luck. Haven't you heard? We steal babies and give the evil eye. It makes your ships get lost at sea."

She half expected Drummond to pick up the sarcasm and run with it, but he kept a grim silence as they closed the distance to the Mohican.

They stopped in front of the bar's entrance. Above a filmy window, an LED display showed a low-res color image of a cartoon man with a multicolored Mohawk and a comic burglar's eye mask.

"Classy," Drummond deadpanned.

"This is why you aren't allowed to talk. Come on." Kara led them inside.

The carnival glow from outside seemed to follow them, only a hundred times brighter. Like many of the older buildings around Skatch Harbor, the Masked Mohican had once served as a corrugated steel warehouse. Over the years people added insulation, lighting, and the cast-off furniture from dozens of ships from around the globe.

Most of the patched and frayed furniture had occupants. Some would be sailors waiting for the more exotic brothels to open. Others were crew ready to start blowing their pay. Kara didn't shrink from the stares that came her way. In fact, she took it with a sense of pride. Never once did she hide her face or the tattoos that clearly marked her for who she was.

They snaked their way to the bar, Kara in front. She pointed out a couple of seats.

"Regular bartender is good for a word. Name's Arthur. Mariners pulled him from a shipwreck a couple decades back, so he's got a soft spot for us."

"He doesn't look like he would've been alive twenty years ago, much less sailing." Drummond motioned to the bartender, a thick-necked young man with a heavy ring through his septum. On the side of his skull an e-ink tattoo played a looped animation of a viper slowly coiling and striking. Seeing Drummond and Kara, he came their way.

"Arthur in the back?" Kara said.

"Arthur retired," the bartender said. "What can I get you?"

Drummond pulled out his phone. "I'll take a whisky, neat."

"Label?" The bartender's tone couldn't be less enthusiastic.

"Give me what you drink," Drummond said.

"I don't drink whisky. Just pick something."

Drummond kept his smile on. "Uncle Nearest, if you got it."

"Fine." The thick-necked bartender took his attitude and his nose ring in search of the bottle.

"What an engaging young man," Kara said dryly. "Listen, if you're done glad-handing the masses, let me take a shot."

"He's all yours," Drummond said.

When their sullen bartender returned with a plastic tumbler containing a scant amount of whisky, Kara got his attention.

"I'm looking for Marsden and Dillon from the Ionova. You know them?"

He gave her a non-committal shrug. "I know they ain't buying any plastic or grain. Got a ship of their own. What's a shipsy need with 'em?"

"Word is," Kara continued unabashed, "they've got some intel for sale. I'm interested in buying. Docks are pretty full and I can't find them. You point their way and there's a finders fee in it for you."

A smug half-smile spread across his round face.

"Now we're talking. Tell you what, give me that money now, and I'll see what I can do."

"No good." Kara held her eye contact. "I don't pay for see-what-I-can-dos. If you really know how I can reach them, this should be the easiest money you've made in a while."

"Let's say I do," the bartender said. "Why would I need—"

"He doesn't know bilge," a rusty voice came from behind them.

Kara snapped around, finding herself face to face with a Captain's eagle inked across the cheek of a rock-like man with a shaven head.

"That's not true," the bartender said, affronted.

"Pssh," the captain said. "I've got ass hair that's seen more of Skatch Harbor than you. Scrape off, kid. Stick to serving drinks. You're gonna cheat the wrong sailor some day. Mind you don't end up feeding the crabs in the ocean as well as the ones in your skivvies."

Both Kara and Drummond stared at the newcomer.

"Pleased to see another of my blood and heart, Navigator. Name's Grayson. Captain of the Penitent. I think we may be after the same thing."

Chapter Nine:
Culprits

"There is only one way to respond to attack: Violent aggression explosive enough to stop any thought of counter-attack from your enemy. You will immediately disengage when your attacker is incapacitated or ceases pursuit. In this way, your life and soul will both remain intact."
Mariner Fleet Training Manual, Chapter IX

"I miss Arthur," Grayson said as he led them through the cluttered space back to his table. "Good man. Hope his retirement is quiet. God knows he had his hands full with this place."

Another Mariner waited for them in the corner of the room. A short, skinny man with dark stubble on his otherwise pale scalp. Seating arrangements were simple, two couches that had seen better days sitting across from each other with a threadbare rug and stained table between them.

Before they sat, Kara held out a hand to the captain. "Where did you sail from?"

Captain Grayson took her hand. They both covered the grip with their left hands to hide it from passersby. Kara felt his finger tap her wrist twice, as she did the same.

"I sailed from trouble into calm waters," he said.

"May we all find peace," she finished.

The other Mariner inclined a hand to Kara. "Bilby. Do we need to do the..." He flapped his hand limply in her direction.

Kara smirked. To Captain Grayson she said, "I see you brought the ship's comedian."

Bilby laughed. "Guilty. And who's your guest?"

"United States Congressman Drummond," Kara said. "Long story. We're working this one together."

Drummond looked as though he might speak up, but thought better of it. Kara approved. Bilby chewed on this new development.

"Your ship?" Grayson said.

"Voyager, out from Vish way. Captain Ansari's command. We made port a couple hours ago. You Mariners looking for the Ionova, too?"

"Didn't realize anyone else was. We've been running dark the past few days." Bilby showed Kara the eight-pointed compass rose on the webbing of his left hand. "Let's compare notes, navigator to navigator. We got word the Ionova ran over choice salvage she couldn't pull, so they wanted to sell the deets off. Came as soon as we heard. Brought along our little A-Diver for some undersea rummaging. Anyway, that sound like the same story you heard?"

"That's the short of it." Kara leaned in and spoke softer. "There's a lot more, though. That salvage? Some kind of pre-war American weapons bunker. Stuffed full of WMDs. Drummond and one of his naval captains came to us because it could blow and take half the Pacific with it, apparently. My skipper will have to fill you in on the rest. As you can imagine, we're pressed for time. Forget about the Ionova, though. You aren't going to find her or her crew."

Grayson didn't seem like the type of man to give away much, but as he listened Kara watched his focus sharpen at the mention of the weapons. When she got to the Ionova, he asked, "What happened?"

"Cut and scuttled. A day out of here toward Vish. Definitely an information extraction job on the brothers. Ugly. I boarded her ghost myself. Barely made it off before the charges blew."

Grayson let out a low whistle.

"What's your plan, then?" Bilby said. "Ask around for the Ionova, see who curses their name?"

Kara grinned. "Pretty much."

"I see you're earning those fresh compass points of yours. *Mazel tov*, by the way. We're of the same mind, Lieutenant. When we heard the Ionova left port, we started looking for jilted lovers. Turns out, there were a few people making inquiries about Dillon and Marsden when they had that data for sale. One in particular caught my eye. A very unstable fence by the name Big Madrid."

A passing waitress flicked a glance at their group as she brushed by. Had she heard Bilby's mention of Big Madrid? Was it possible she heard them speaking over the din of the music and raucous laughter? Perhaps, it didn't matter. Kara wondered if she was being paranoid.

"I didn't have him shortlisted." Kara waved away a cloud of smoke drifting over to them from another group.

"Nor did I, at first," Bilby said. "He normally stays out of the watery end of business. Been looking to make a name for himself recently. This sort of job would be the perfect entry into a new source of revenue."

"Any luck finding him?" she said.

Captain Grayson groaned. "Been chasing him

all over Skatch today. Barely missing him here and there. Worse, we've got it on good authority that he's chartered a ship. A ship with deep sea salvage capabilities. That all but confirms he's the buyer."

"Still doesn't explain why he'd cut and scuttle the Ionova," Bilby said. "Maybe he decided he shouldn't have had to pay. Who knows? I think the skipper's right. All signs point to him."

Kara sank back in the couch. "Perfect. Don't suppose you know what ship he hired?"

"No. Don't lose heart, Navigator," Bilby said with a smile. "We found something just as good. Where he lives. Had a rotation of watchers moving through, keeping an eye on the place. He hasn't come home yet, so it's only a matter of time before he goes back to pack his bags. Especially if he's in the hurry it appears he's in."

"How'd you like to come with us for a visit?" Captain Grayson said.

Kara hadn't expected Big Madrid to live in a nicer part of town. In fact, she wasn't entirely sure there were nicer parts to Skatch Harbor. Tenement blocks blended one into another, the newer ones only distinguishable by their increased height. A mountain ridge at the end of this side of town marked the edge of Skatch Harbor. Just past that, the well-to-dos lived in gated communities that grew more expensive the higher up they went. No way could a fence could ever afford a place there.

It seemed telling that even a moderately successful criminal such as Big Madrid still lived in cramped squalor along with the rest of the population. True, her own house wasn't large. Size wasn't the point, though. Kara's home was clean and safe and that was what mattered. For someone like Big Madrid, who made a career of inflicting pain and misery upon others, who did so in the pursuit of material gain, what did his living situation say about the profitability of his crimes?

She crouched low in the narrow alley, her left side against a block wall. Drummond sat on a plastic crate nearby, dutifully staying quiet. A trio of barefoot, half-dressed children ran by the alley, their dirty feet slapping on the broken asphalt.

Most of her life before she met her mother was a blur now. There were the good days, but only a couple of recollections remained from then. Birthday cake baked in a shaped pan. A soft dress. After that? Just running, hunger, theft, the occasional bowl of soup from the white-haired priest whose name she couldn't recall. Half-remembered details of an apartment came back. A white plastic bag with a change of clothes. A tall man with long, vice-like fingers and eyes like dark pebbles. Running. Hiding. More running. And then...

As it turns out, I'm in need of a fine mouser. And a wrangler to handle them. You don't know where I could find such a cat wrangler, do you?

"Heartbreaking, isn't it?" Drummond whispered. Kara snapped away from her thoughts. He flicked his chin toward the children, who were turning down another road. "It's like this in every city. The FMZ's especially. Although, I didn't see anything like that on Vish, come to think of it."

Drummond's tone snagged Kara's ears. The careful hesitancy, the thoughtful, but open-ended statement.

"Jesus, Drummond, you've never been too shy to ask a question before. Don't start now."

At least he had the good grace to not act affronted. "It's...I've noticed a lot of Mariner's, like yourself, weren't born Mariners. Given what people say, I'm just curious—"

"Oh, for all the fry-junked..." Kara sucked her teeth. "You really asking me if we steal kids?"

"I've never seen any data that says Mariners are legally adopting anyone, okay? So, yeah, that's what I'm asking."

Kara gritted her teeth. "My biological mother sold me to a pimp when I was six. When I ran away he didn't bother chasing me. Probably because he knew I'd get hungry and come back. Well, the joke was on him because I was fully prepared to starve to death on the docks."

Drummond sputtered. Several half-formed sentences started and stopped before Kara brushed him off.

"My life began the day my mother found me. Adoption is a part of Mariner tradition. We don't pick up strays willy-nilly. There's a process. She made damn sure that no one claimed me first, because that's how it's done. We'd no sooner kidnap a child than we would abandon one to die underneath a pier."

A thick moment stretched between them. Drummond took a heavy swallow. "I'm sorry, Kara. I just had to know."

Taking a breath, she gave him a half-shrug. "Now you do."

"Sounds like adoption is a pretty big deal to your people. I didn't realize that."

"Well"—a dose of acid crept into her voice—"many of the founding Mariners were sterile. Adoption was the only way they could have children. It's a part of who we are."

Drummond cocked his head to one side. "Why? What happened? Was there an accident or something?"

"What happened?" Kara let out a bitter laugh. "If you don't know, go check your own government's records."

Something in her tone must have told Drummond to drop the subject. He did.

A short, high whistle floated through the night air.

"That's Grayson," Kara said. "Hang back in case it gets hot. If it does—"

"Duck back in the alley, run to the Voyager, tell them what happened. Got it." Drummond rubbed his arms. "Be careful, Kara. Okay?"

"Me? Watch your own six, Drummond. If you don't make it back, the skipper will blame me." She gave him a wry smile and left him in the alley.

Kara walked swiftly from the alley, her eyes scanning the street and buildings. Briefly, she wished she had run back to the ship for some armor plates. They wouldn't stop rounds from a rifle, but they'd be effective against a handgun or a blade, and that was better than nothing.

Grayson's profile was unmistakable as he appeared from the entrance of an adjacent building. Hair bristling off the scalp, the barrel chest and thick arms, it had to be him. To confirm, he chirped once at Kara, who returned the whistle.

An electric hum filled her chest. Kara knew the feeling of adrenaline setting in well. Her vision sharpened as she and Grayson approached the group assembled at the side of the broken road. A broad man with some kind of fake fur draped around his shoulders. Two mercenaries and a reedy looking guy who twitched at every noise.

The mercenaries worried Kara more than anyone else. One looked like he could bench press a dump truck while the other had the preternaturally calm stance of wired-reflex enhancements. That kind of speed could be almost impossible to fight. More worrying still, was the fact that the group appeared to be waiting for Kara and Grayson.

"Big Madrid, I presume." Grayson opened with a friendly countenance.

The one wearing the fake fur opened his mouth to speak. Polished metal teeth flashed in the orange and yellow street light. "You presume correctly, darling. Curse these aging eyes, but do I have the pleasure of being visited by the shipsies on this auspicious evening? Not here for the children, are you?"

Grayson didn't look needled at all. "Came with a business proposition. Word is you bought a job from the Ionova brothers. We'd like to buy it from you."

"You heard wrong, love." Big Madrid raised his chin as he spoke. "True, I entered into negotiations with the brothers Ionova, but we couldn't come to terms. Obstinate, they are. I think they found a different buyer in the end. Check with Slim at the Masked Mohican. He may know who has your data."

"Ah, in the end." Captain Grayson let the words sit between them. "The end. You are very well informed about what the brothers got up to in the end."

Kara couldn't be sure in the dim lighting, but she thought she caught the slightest pause in breath from Big Madrid. His skinny companion started bouncing slightly on the balls of his feet.

"Is there something you'd like to say plainly, sweetness?"

"The brothers don't concern me," Grayson said. "Only the data. It could be a good job for me and mine. And an easy profit for you. No sailing. No mess. From what I hear you prefer dry land anyway. Why trouble yourself when there's money to be had here and now? It's squall season out there, you know. Why risk it?"

Big Madrid gave Grayson a toothy smile. "You

overestimate the risk of my position. You want to stand there, lean over me, try to push me into giving up what I have earned through sweat and blood? No, lovey, it doesn't work that way. Big Madrid sells when he wants to sell. And he don't want to bleeding sell. Now, why don't you two piss off back to whatever raft you sailed in on. If you haven't noticed, you're a bit outgunned."

A curl set on Grayson's lip. He spoke louder, "Outgunned? What do I care about your mercs? I only have to shoot you."

Asphalt exploded by Big Madrid's feet. Kara heard the gunshot at the same time flecks of rock and tar pelted her legs.

Both Kara and Grayson dived to either side of the road. When facing augmented, trained mercenaries like the type Big Madrid ran with, a head-to-head fight never ended well. The reedy man at the end of Big's row howled with pain and fell to the ground. Bilby's shot must have gone wide. Instead of hitting Big Madrid, he must have nailed the unfortunate man now writhing on the filthy street. Gunfire erupted from Madrid's group.

Kara skidded behind a row of trash cans and a burned-out car chassis. Holding her pistol at the ready, she quickly peeked through the car's busted window. The smaller merc had Big Madrid behind her as she returned fire in both Grayson and Bilby's directions in short bursts. In the second that she had, Kara couldn't find the large mercenary. He must have gone to pull the injured man out of harm's way.

Bursts of gun fire rattled against the walls of the buildings and lit the street in fiery bursts. Kara ducked around the car, aiming her gun at the smaller, female mercenary. The merc's attention was on Grayson. It was the perfect chance for Kara to fire. Her finger pulled down on the trigger.

Stars exploded from the side of her vision. Kara didn't get the chance to shoot before her pistol clattered uselessly to the ground, her body limp with shock. Her mind reeled, trying to string a thought together. Dull heat radiated from her left ear and skull. Before Kara could recover, a steely grip wrapped around her neck, lifting her and forcing her back and up against a nearby wall. Rough cement scraped the back of her head and shoulders.

It was the big one; the other merc. He hadn't gone after the injured guy, after all. No matter how she pounded or clawed at his unnaturally thick arms, she couldn't make him budge. His reach far outstripped her own, Kara had no way of striking back at any other part of him with her hands.

She sputtered and choked. Kara's vision turned red, dark, and wobbly. His eyes reflected only dispassionate hatred. This man would kill her. With a twitch to the side of his nose, he lifted her off her feet.

Kara slammed the back of her boot heel against the wall. She felt a familiar snap and click of the blade locking in place before she kicked with all her remaining strength. Her toe-blade connected with a wet slap against his groin.

The huge merc grunted and immediately dropped Kara, both of his hands moving toward his inner thigh. She hit the ground, hard, tailbone first. Gasping for air, Kara didn't spare any concern about the pain in her throat next to the joy of breathing.

Her gun.

Kara scrambled up on all fours, intending to make a grab for it. But a thick, bloody hand plucked her weapon off the street first. She dove to the other side of the car as shots barked behind her. Not good.

Headlights washed over the street.

A narrow cargo van slid to a halt, the cargo door

sliding open at once. A tall, statuesque man dressed in form-fitting black leapt from the van, easily clearing a distance of three meters. With a handgun at the ready, he covered Big Madrid and his female body guard as they climbed inside. In the time it took Kara to blink, he loped gracefully to the other side of the burned out car and returned with Kara's attacker in a fireman's carry. He moved like that massive killer wasn't anymore bother than a sack of flour.

Then they were gone.

Only the afterimage of red lights remained where the van raced away from them.

"Kara! Bilby!" Grayson shouted. He staggered across the street, holstering his own sidearm. Footfalls thundered from the nearest building entrance. Bilby's shaved head appeared next to Grayson. They both helped Kara to her feet.

"I tried to get over to you," Grayson said. "That merc had me pinned but good. That was quick thinking with the toe knife."

Kara could only nod in return.

Bilby looked down the street, cursed. "We'll never find them!"

"Maybe we don't need to," Drummond's voice caught Kara's attention.

All three Mariners faced the congressman.

"You were supposed..." Kara's raspy voice trailed off into a hacking cough.

"Forget about that." Drummond walked into the street light, half carrying and half dragging someone else with him. It was the skinny man from Big Madrid's posse, with a strip of Drummond's shirt tied around his calf muscle in a hasty bandage.

A wide grin split Grayson's face. "Don't worry," he said to the half conscious man. "We'll get you medical aid and treat you fairly. But make no mistake. You're coming with us."

✦ ✦ ✦

"In summary, Captain," Faulkner said. "Not only did you fail to get the intelligence from this Big Madrid fellow, but he escaped and for all we know is already underway to get our prize."

Once again, Faulkner spoke from the comforts of his own conference room. Captain Ansari had offered to host everyone aboard Voyager, but Faulkner had declined.

"Sounds like a lot of blame being thrown around for a captain whose own crew contributed absolutely nothing," Captain Grayson said. He stood shoulder to shoulder with Ansari on the bridge, both men facing the large display.

"Ah, yes." Faulkner faked amusement. "Let's not forget the best part of tonight's activities; the addition of yet another Mariner ship into our little flotilla. Something which is expressly not part of the agreement we made with Admiral Kim and your Elect."

"Enough." Drummond stood off to the side, leaning up against Ensign Martin's communication station. "Captain Grayson came to us with intelligence regarding Big Madrid. Without him none of us would have turned up squat here. Can we please focus on what's happening now?"

"Which is what, exactly, Congressman?" Faulkner said. "Your prisoner? Who may be too injured to talk? From what you've sent over about this Big Madrid fellow, it's highly unlikely that any criminal in his confidence would ever wish to betray him. After what we saw on the bridge of that ship, I can see why. If Big Madrid is, in fact, the man behind the attack on the Ionova, as you think he is, what criminal in their right mind would cross him by speaking to us? If he knows anything at all!"

"You are vastly underestimating our navigator," Captain Ansari said. While Grayson may have been a blunt instrument, Ansari stayed as surgical as ever. "I have every confidence in Lieutenant Nkosi. While I understand you wish to interrogate the man, we need to use your kind of coercion—torture, to speak plainly—as a last resort. Navigators such as Kara have turned information gathering into an art. When she talks to him, every movement, every twitch of the face, every syllable of his speech will tell us what we need to know, even if his words won't. She will stay on him for as long as it takes, subtly influencing him until he reaches the breaking point. Kara will spend hours, even days if need be. She will stop at nothing until he betrays Big Madrid and talks."

"If this is my last act"—Tren breathed from the narrow surgical table in sick bay—"Then you use it to drag Big Madrid to hell! To hell, you hear me!"

Bilby clapped Kara on the shoulder. "Well, it was a tough job, Navigator. But you pulled it off in the end."

"Shush," she told Bilby.

"Last act?" Doc Young's red beard bristled as he gave Tren a disgusted look. "You're hardly grazed. The bullet barely looked at you before it scraped off somewhere else. Hell, I'm not even convinced you didn't just catch some shrapnel."

Tren sat up and blinked at the fresh bandage around his leg. Forceps clattered to Doc Young's surgical tray. A red-stained gauze pad sat among a couple of disinfectant bottles.

"What about sepsis?" Tren said. "Blood poisoning?

These are serious threats. There could have been parasites on the ground. Roundworm. Hookworm. Tapeworm. What if one got into the wound?"

"Lieutenant," Doc Young said to Kara. "Get him out of here before I give him a real injury. You're clogging up my sick bay."

"Come on, champ." Bilby patted Tren's shoulder. "Let's give the doc some space."

As they filed out of the sick bay, Kara led the way.

"So what now," Tren said. "Interrogation? Is it torture?"

"No," Kara said. She opened a hatch and walked in to the galley.

Tren poked his head inside and gave the place a suspicious once over before stepping in.

"Thought you could use something to eat. Frankly, you're in pretty rough shape. We missed dinner, but I can rustle something up for you."

"Don't suppose you could grab me something?" Bilby said.

"You?" Kara shot back. "You can get it your damn self, Mariner."

Once they had seated Tren with a bowl of miso and egg soup and a heel of bread, Kara was ready to get to business. Tren wasted no time, he immediately gorged himself on the bread and soup, making small moans of delight.

"Uh," Kara said between his vocalizations, "how is it? Good? Wait, are you crying?"

"No!" Tren quickly wiped his face with the back of his hand. "It's been an unbelievably bad week, okay?"

The tips of Tren's fingers clicked against his spoon as he ate.

"It was you," Kara said. "You wiped the data from the Ionova."

Tren paused.

"We're not the cops," Kara told him.

"I didn't have anything to do with…" He shuddered. "With what they did. That was beyond awful."

Kara made eye contact with Tren. "I'm getting the impression that's not your style. Listen, if you're afraid of crossing Big Madrid, we can look out for you. But you've got to help us help you. We're interested in what you found on that computer."

"The coordinates?" Tren said lightly.

Both Kara and Bilby looked at each other.

"You have them?" she said.

"Sure," Tren shrugged. He tapped his temple. "I backed them up in my own internal memory augment. Wasn't sure if I'd need insurance from Big, you know? Anyway, I'll give them to you."

Kara grabbed the phone from her pocket and copied down the coordinates as Tren recited them. She passed the device to Bilby, who looked ready to sprint with them all the way to the bridge.

"Tell the skipper we'll need to hurry if we're gonna beat Madrid's ship," Kara said.

Bilby started for the hatch.

Tren snorted over his soup. "Beat Big's ship, sure. Who knows if you'll get there before everyone else."

Kara froze. "What do you mean, 'everyone else?'"

Tren had his soup bowl lifted halfway to his mouth, but stopped. "Wait, you don't know?" he said. "Why do you think Big was so mad at the Ionova brothers? Did you think Big's the only person they sold this data to?"

Chapter Ten:
Open Waters

"Throughout history many voices, in many words, have admonished us about the same thing: Don't ignore the beauty of small moments."
Alan Schwab, *The Tao of the Core*

"You'll be charged for the medical assistance, of course," Mister Grint said. "As well as the unplanned extraction."

Big Madrid already couldn't stand the poncy bastard. What was worse, everywhere he went on the DCV Verne, Grint's jowly, aged face seemed to appear around every corner. At first, Big found himself liking the attention. His very own steward, a lifelong ambition coming to pass. But the first time the prick kept Big from getting on to the bridge, he realized what the score really was.

He was being handled.

Which didn't sit well with Big Madrid. No, indeed, not well at all. He put all the pieces together for this job, he extracted the data, he got the necessaries together. Which made him the Governor. Everyone else on the bloody boat were hired hands as far as he was concerned.

So when Mister Grint found Big just outside of the sick bay, fresh from visiting poor Gary, the steward did not find Big in the best of spirits. Especially, as it seemed he was being nickeled and dimed at every turn. He hadn't asked Nakamura's spliced up bed boy to hop out of the van and start interfering. Only now he was expected to pay for it.

"Put it on my tab, sweetheart," Big told Grint. "I'm sure Mister Nakamura will understand and take care of the necessaries. Cost of doing business, love. Now, if you don't mind."

Big flicked one end of his furry stole at the steward and started off to find Gill.

"You will be able to tell him yourself, sir. As he has requested a conversation. A call has been arranged in the orange meeting room. I can show you the way, if you wish."

"No, I, bloody well..." Big started, but realized that he actually had no idea where that room was. Boats were like rat's nests, full of twists and turns, and horribly claustrophobic. "Have it your way. Chop-chop, then."

Grint wore his poker face well, Big Madrid would give him that. Nothing he said to the man over the past couple of days even came close to phasing him. They clomped down metal halls, their heels ringing with each step. Oh, how the sound grated on him. After two narrow staircases, they arrived. Mister Grint turned the handle on the thin metal door and then bowed Big inside.

A long, narrow table made of veneered pressboard took most of the room. As soon as Big entered, he noticed the central display already glowing and on.

"Mister Madrid!" came a voice from the room's speakers.

Big forced on an agreeable expression and faced the display. "Mister Nakamura, a pleasure."

Nakamura wore a stylish, narrow-cut dark suit. A little plain for Big's tastes, but he approved nonetheless. The flat planes of his face and dark eyes spoke of Japanese ancestry, but his accent had to be from the Pacific Northwest of the United States. Maybe Seattle, could be Portland. Big wasn't sure how he did it, but Nakamura perfectly embodied success.

"Short notice on this one, buddy, I know." Nakamura set down a golf club he had been toying with and walked closer to the camera. The office behind him had floor to ceiling glass windows overlooking a pristine lake.

"No worries at all," Big said. "This about my message?"

"Right in one," Nakamura said. "Listen, I heard from Grinty that you needed some extra services from the Verne and my Vasco guys. I don't want you to worry about that, okay? You're my partner on this, and my partners don't worry about that kind of trivial crap. Don't let them give you a hard time. Crack open the minibar in your room if you want, all right?" He finished with an easy laugh.

"I appreciate that, sir. To be honest, I have a very good feeling about this partnership." Strangely, Big found that he meant it.

"As do I! Speaking of, let's talk about this course correction you want. So, I don't mind telling you, Big, over on my side, there's a lot of buzz about our project. My analysts took a look at your data and they think this could be a pre-war wreck, a container ship with literal tons of valuable resources aboard."

Big Madrid stood a little taller and straightened

his stole. "Truthfully, I thought so, too."

Nakamura snapped his fingers then pointed at Big through the screen. "See? You have an instinct for this stuff, my man. An instinct. That can't be taught. I'm gonna be straight with you. So, I'm thinking, if Big Madrid wants this as bad as I do (or worse, am I right?) then what's with changing the course? Talk to me, partner."

"Unpleasant business, Mister Nakamura. Unpleasant. As I wrote in my message, we had that dust up before launch."

Nakamura held up a palm. "Sorry to interrupt, partner. How is Gary? I've been worried. Frankly, everyone in the office has been."

"Lost some blood, but the doc here has him on the mend, thank you."

"Big relief." Nakamura let out a breath. "Now, please, go on."

"Well, it's like you say. Gary got injured. Not an easy thing to do. These shipsies—"

"Woah, woah," Nakamura said with a sly grin. "Mariners, Mister Madrid. They prefer to be called Mariners. Let's not with the racism."

Big Madrid chuckled. "Right you are, sir. Well, I got a sense for their determination to get to our prize. As you know, there could be other contenders. My gut's telling me they're on our heels. What I'd like to do is position us to—"

"Say no more," Nakamura cut in. "I'm reading you loud and clear, partner. It's of utmost importance that we are the sole team in control of that wreck. Here's what we do. Our Vasco support team is still under way, so we're taking lead. You, your team, my Vasco guys, and the Verne can take care of your, let's call it, clean up operation."

"My thoughts exactly, Mister Nakamura." Big showed a metal-toothed smile.

✦ ✦ ✦

"TXM International? Sure, I know them," Kara said. "Transport conglomerate. Run almost all the major shipping operations in the Pacific. They're backing him?"

Tren finished chewing another mouthful of bread. She decided to talk to him in the galley again, since the man seemed to want nothing but food, and more of them could fit in the larger room. Kara sat across from him at one end of the long fold-out tables. Chief Lambros had assigned Goldi to watch Tren, since he was still something of an unknown, and Goldi's arm would need another few days to heal, even with the bone-stim treatments Doc Young gave her. Naturally, Goldi readily accepted the assignment as it gave her ample opportunity to harass her favorite passenger.

Bilby and Grayson were back on the Penitent, which made Kara the lead regarding all things Tren.

"You know," he said. "Your ship is very nice. You wouldn't know it from the outside. Not that I don't enjoy the paintings on your hull. Those black sails you use, are they made from some kind of poly-filament solar cloth? Clever. Are they strong enough to act as regular sails? I didn't know anyone was using it that way. Then again, I'm not a boat guy, personally. I did go on a cruise once with my grandma when I was a kid. I miss her. Oh, if she could see where I am now, she'd have another heart attack, let me tell you."

"Tren, focus," Kara said. "Why would TXM care about a shipwreck? Much less deal with a guy like Big Madrid?"

It went without saying that the team hadn't told Tren where those coordinates really led. It was far too early for that kind of trust.

Tren gave her an almost pitying look. "Of course

TXM wouldn't care about a shipwreck unless it was blocking their traffic. You have to think bigger. Who owns TXM? What else does that corporation own? Those relationships are more tangled than aristocrats' family trees. Ownership does tend to be grouped by interest, though. So, the shipping company may have a sister-cousin company that deals in salvage. It was a longshot, sure, but Big was running out of choices. When I first pitched him the idea he almost had Gary punch me. He wasn't so smug after a whole day rolling snake eyes with the charter ships, I'll tell you that much."

"Wait," Kara said. "You gave him the idea?"

"Worked, too." Tren suddenly stopped, his eyes widening. "Look, I wasn't on your side then! I didn't even know you guys. I was just trying to keep my fingernails and teeth intact."

Kara waved him on. "Fine, so how did this work?

"TXM has an office at the harbor," he shrugged. "So do other, uh, water-based, businesses. What do you call that? Maritime? Anyway. My plan was a shot in the dark. We take our proposal to the local TXM rep. Ninety percent chance he tells us, 'No way.' Fine. If that guy is a good corporate drone, he still has to input the request in some internal system. Now, all I had to do was use my magic to hitch a ride on his request and make sure that any other companies under TXM's umbrella also saw that same information. It's only light network intrusion, nothing nefarious. So if there is a sister salvage company, they'd know that we had a juicy opportunity for them. Naturally, we didn't include any of the important details. We needed them to need us."

Drummond pursed his lips. "That's actually kind of brilliant."

"Thank you!" Tren said. "Couldn't get Big to

admit it. Ungrateful bastard. Is there any more of this toast? What kind of jam is that, anyway? It's marvelous."

"Allow me," Drummond said, rising. "I need to stretch my legs."

"*Kotyonok*," Goldi said. "None for you, hmm. We have climbing practice later."

Drummond rolled his eyes and headed across to the service area of the Galley where he could make Tren another piece of toast.

"Wait." Kara shook her head. "You're telling me that some unknown sister company of TXM wants this salvage so bad that they not only gave Big Madrid a charter vessel, but also gave him more mercs? That guy who came and pulled Gary into the van was no ordinary gun. I've never seen enhancements that let a person move so fast."

"Because they weren't enhancements," Tren said thickly. He swallowed his last bite of bread and eyed Drummond. "He was spliced."

Goldi blew a raspberry. Kara sucked her teeth and put slapped hands flat on the table, as if ready to stand up. "Are you seriously messing with me, Tren? I thought you wanted protection? I thought you were on our side?"

"No, no!" Tren raised both palms. "I'm serious as a heart attack."

"That's why you're telling me fish stories about spliced mercenaries working for a Skatch Harbor crotch-sniffer like Madrid? No one who can afford splicing is going to be working for a dumper like Big Madrid. That's one-percenter tech."

Tren blinked, struggling to get control of his words. "Hang on. Let's back up. You see these?"

Kara looked at the silvery contact pads on the first two fingers of his right hand. "So?"

"Top of the line. Layered alloys guaranteed not

to lose conductivity or rust. Have your doc scan the wiring. There is none. Pure nerve fibers harvested from my own stem cells, running back to a Lumenco generalized mind-machine interface. No side effects, no rejection. It'll run for three standard lifetimes. Installed ten years ago, still not available to the public."

"We are very proud of you," Goldi said. "You are still full of bilge."

"That's not the point." Tren made an impatient noise. "I'm telling you this because it's proof. I can prove that my augment isn't even available in places like Skatch Harbor. It's..."

Kara watched as Tren drifted for a moment.

He swallowed. "Up until three months ago, I had a very different life. In Detroit, where I lived and worked, I was a principal software engineer for AssureGen. You know, the genomics conglomerate. My everyday life was spent in the company of people like the man who picked up Gary like he weighed as much as a toddler and ran with him faster than you or I could sprint. I guarantee you, he did not throw out his back or strain muscle in doing so. I can assure you he is spliced. That kind of physical perfection does not come from augmentations—even the best enhancements have a point of diminishing return and can only be stacked on top of each other so much."

Kara watched Tren fidget, all interest in getting his new piece of toast gone. "If you had a position like that, then why were you even in Skatch?"

"Can we stay focused? Isn't that what you wanted?" Tren snapped. "I'm telling you that I know what I'm talking about."

"We're back to the same question." Drummond placed a small plate with a fresh slice of toast in front of Tren. "Why would those kind of resources get sent Big Madrid's way? A mercenary who's been spliced can't be cheap."

"I admit," Tren said, "I was more than surprised when I saw them show up."

"There's more than one?" Kara said.

Tren nodded. "Two that I saw. I don't know why they were sent. But I figured that any ship that could stay under water for so long and still have an active beacon would be a ship that people didn't want getting lost. Maybe a ship like that was carrying goods that could still be worth something. Could be there's a load of cobalt or lithium still sealed up and ready to sell down there. Hell, it'd be worth more now than it was back then. Even if that was the case, you're right, it does feel like these people are investing a lot in Big's score. I wasn't expecting that much buy-in."

Kara and Drummond shared a dark look. She knew he was thinking the same thing as her.

Did these people from TXM already know what was down there?

Captain Ansari took this latest development as stoically as he could. Commander Satry couldn't hide his dismay at the idea of spliced mercenaries fighting on Big Madrid's side. Up until now, that sort of possibility wasn't even on their radar. More telling was Faulkner's reaction. When they conferenced with all the captains, Faulkner couldn't even cough up a snide remark. He only said they'd have to remain even more vigilant.

A definite sense of foreboding built up on the bridge after that. When they came within satellite range, Kara used the time to pull as much data about the TXM corporate ownership chain as possible. Despite the fact that the information was supposedly public record, she found the document trails dizzying. What's more, the ownerships changed so frequently that once she thought she finally had an understanding of what the chain looked like, she'd find that the whole damn thing had shifted a month afterward.

Her worries compounded with a new message from Vish Central. According to Admiral Kim's command, the EU and RF were projected to wrap up trade talks within the day. Media outlets reported that they expected the agreement to pass with only minor adjustments. Which meant that, with the trade blockade over, Kara's people could expect fleets of ships encroaching on their territory soon after. Admiral Kim and the Mariner Council still hadn't decided on a response.

Waning sun cast red and gold streaks across the bridge. Kara stood and stretched. She needed to clear her head. Slipping through the hatch, she went to the ladder on the stern side of the opening and climbed up to the top of the bridge. Opening the clasps of a plain plastic box fixed to the decking, Kara lifted out Voyager's astrolabe and telescope. Deftly, she extended and placed their tripods as the colors of sunset faded into night.

The first of the night's stars winked into life in the blessedly cloudless sky. Kara found Polaris first, locating her by finding Ursa Major and Minor, as Iminathi had taught her to do so long ago, standing on the deck of the Wave Runner, a towel around her small shoulders, hair damp and scalp raw from the washing and delousing. Iminathi pointed to the constellations and told her stories of the sailor's favorite star. Mariners came to visit them, introducing themselves and having a chat, or simply pointing out other constellations. They brought treats and fussed over Kara and Scratches, her kitten. Her new people, welcoming her.

Her people.

What would they do the first time a corporate ship landed on one of their islands, claiming to own the place? Who would monitor phytoplankton and oxygen levels? How would they protect their platform farms of kelp and gold-wheat from tankers dumping radioactive mining slurry, or from cruise ships bulldozing their way through the last ocean sanctuary so their rich passengers could take videos of the creatures they were helping destroy leaving nothing but bilge and noise in their wake?

Would they fight? Kara's focus drifted away from the sky. That argument she had with her mother before leaving Vish haunted her. Was the answer as simple as she wanted it to be?

Footfalls clanged against the ladder leading up to the observation deck. Kara watched Drummond's head pop up over the decking as he made his way up.

"Found you," he said. "I was thinking about what Tren said and wanted to run something by you."

He summited the ladder but stopped on his way over to her. Drummond tilted his head a bit. "What's going on?"

Kara bit back an automatic retort. Yes, he was an American. But maybe he wasn't a typical locust. Hadn't he proven himself enough? Begrudgingly, she caught him up on her failure to untangle TXM's corporate structure, and the dire news of the end of the EU and RF trade dispute.

"It's funny." Drummond took a place not too far from her at the forward railing. "Back home all anyone seemed to want is an end to the trade dispute. Up until a few days ago, I was right there with them. We never considered the effect global policies have on everyone."

"Oh, we've won you over," Kara said in a dry tone. "Looks like everything will get cleared up now."

"I know you're being asinine, but you're giving the U.S. government way too much credit."

"What are you talking about?" she said. "You're one of the people who write the laws. Your country is a member of the Russian Federation, isn't it? If any of you cared about what was right, things like this wouldn't happen."

"Right for who?" Drummond clicked his tongue. "Lieutenant, do you know who actually writes the bills that become laws? It's not legislators like me. When we're in session, these bills get handed to us, literally, by our 'partners' from industry action committees. We're told how to vote by our party leaders and those same action committees. At least, that's how ninety-nine percent of Congress does things. It's a joke. A sham. We don't run our country. Private interest does."

"And you're the lone holdout, is that it?"

Despite the bite in her tone, Drummond actually laughed. "That was the idea. Didn't work out the way I planned. To be honest, I'm not even sure how the party allowed me to be elected. Only thing I can come up with is that they considered me such a longshot they didn't bother fixing the results from my district. Maybe my grandfather had something to do with it. Letting me win just to crush me afterward. Sadistic bastard."

"Whoa," Kara said. "I feel like I'm missing some critical information here. Your grandfather?"

Drummond took a moment, obviously thinking. "You remember when we first went to Vish? Captain Faulkner started spouting off about the Great Calm and some treaty negotiated by Hunter Gilligan?"

"You mean when he tried to lay claim to our fleet?" That got a sardonic smile out of Kara. "Yeah, kind of hard to forget."

"Right," Drummond said. "Hunter Gilligan is my grandfather. He's morally bankrupt, self-righteous, corrupt, and extremely rich because of it. Men like him made a fortune suckling off the post-war government teat. One of his biggest victories was supposedly over the Mariners. Getting your people to sign a treaty he called the Great Calm, which gave the U.S. power over your fleet in times of emergency. It all but stops short of calling your islands and waters our territory."

"How on Earth would anyone believe a load of bilge like that?" Kara's fire burned higher with each of Drummond's words, but she stopped herself long enough for him to go on.

"I'd suspected it was all a sham for some time. To answer your question, I think it's a mix of cunning and willful ignorance. Let's start with this. The last time our nations fought, why did it end? What do your people say?"

For the second time that night, Kara was reminded of her last night at home. "We had a representative, Ollie Dietrich. He went to the U.N. to plead our case. They agreed to sanction the U.S. if they kept up their hostilities."

"Exactly." Drummond brought a finger to his chin. "On our side, history says that we won the fighting, but left with the understanding you'd been taught a lesson. Within government circles, where information is allowed to be a little closer to truth, it's said that we ceased fire because of the U.N. 'aggression' but the fighting didn't completely stop until my grandfather personally sailed to your territory with a small delegation and negotiated the Great Calm."

"I've never even heard of this guy," Kara said.

Drummond shrugged. "Why would you have?

I've suspected for a long while that he never went. Hunter Gilligan was supposed to have parlayed with your people before the fighting even started. When tensions rose after the incident with the F.V. Maria, the President sent my grandfather, who was a junior ambassador, to meet with the Mariners. I'm not sure if he was expected to fail, or what. From what I can piece together, he didn't go at all. He was too scared to enter your waters. So, he sailed around the coast with his 'delegation,' which were his college buddies. They got drunk, did cocaine, hired prostitutes at port towns, that sort of thing. He knew he'd have to face the music eventually. But when the U.N. called off the fighting for him, he saw the scam of a lifetime staring him in the face."

"How so?"

"Reparation payments. By claiming he'd negotiated a treaty with your people, he wrote clauses that required the U.S. to make regular payments to the Mariners for damages caused during the fighting. In return, we'd get your fleet in a time of war if we needed it."

Kara made a sour face. "We've never been given a dime from you people."

"Exactly," Drummond said. "Somebody's been taking that money, though. I'm speculating here, but I'm sure I'm right. Hunter's claim was outlandish and could have easily been debunked. He must have offered a split of the payments with the most influential party leaders of the time. In return, they supported his ridiculous fabrication. They all grew richer. To put a bow on the whole thing, he added a provision in the treaty that we weren't allowed to publicly disclose it, as it would injure the Mariner's national pride."

After a moment of shared silence, Kara shook her head. "That really happened?"

"Back then, after the war, if the party said the sky was red half the people would say they always thought that was the case. The other half would've stayed quiet. It's somewhat better today. Not by much." Drummond turned around and leaned his back against the rail. "I want us to do better, Kara. Sometimes, when I see what I'm up against, I get overwhelmed by how difficult that really is."

"So, your grandfather—"

A shrill alarm whistle shot through the air. Three short blasts, repeating.

"We're under attack," Kara said.

Chapter Eleven: Ambush

"Sailing is dangerous. Living is dangerous. What is danger? The chance you may lose your life? Let me break it to you, that chance is already one hundred percent. If the fleet calls to you, don't let that stop you."
Shannon Meyer, Deckmaster Emeritus

Kara yanked the telescope from its base. With a smooth pivot she scanned the waters around Voyager in a three-sixty arc. No matter where she looked, however, only inky black waters and star-speckled sky came through the lens. How could they possibly be under attack?

"What's going on?" Drummond said. "I don't see anyone else out here. Could the alarm be for one of the other ships?"

"No." Kara made her way to the ladder. "That's a different alarm. You're going to want to get somewhere safe below decks. Follow me, I'll show you where."

With her feet on the outside of the ladder's rails, she nimbly slid down to the deck. As soon as her feet touched down, Kara sensed something very wrong. Muffled shouting rang out from an open deck hatch. Right next to her, the bridge hatch hung open as well. Unlike the portal leading below deck, no sound escaped the bridge at all.

Drawing her weapon and chambering a round, Kara held the barrel down and slipped through the open hatch. Keeping her eyes up, she almost didn't register the small, wet splash the ball of her foot made as it touched down inside the bridge.

Her pulse thrummed through her ears. Time became sticky, small moments adhering to the present longer than others. A thin, wet red line arched gracefully over the bridge's central display, which showed a weather radar map twitching through the next few hours of predicted movement.

Down at her feet, the toe of Kara's boot breached the edge of a deep red puddle. As she followed the liquid pool, she found the toe of a scuffed black boot.

"No," she breathed. "No."

Kara scrambled around the command station. A weak yowl escaped her as she fell to her knees.

Captain Ansari lay dead. Cracks of red marbled her mentor's neck where it had been stretched. His head lay ninety-degrees in relation to the rest of him. A sharp protrusion inside his neck looked as though it was about to break skin, warping his Mariner's Anchor tattoo.

He wasn't alone. Lying prone next to the skipper was Commander Satry. The side of his neck flayed open, one hand uselessly positioned to staunch the blood flow. A brownish smear from the command center keyboard to his other, lifeless hand showed his last act was to warn the crew.

No one else was on the bridge.

Kara shot upright. The noise below decks. The killer was still on board.

"Oh my god." Drummond said from behind her.

Satry's blood stained the knees of Kara's trousers. Swiftly, she knelt, extracted the commander's pistol, charged it, and handed it to Drummond.

"It's loaded, round chambered. Point it at what needs to die. Pull that trigger only if you're one-thousand percent sure you should fire."

He stammered, but took the gun.

Kara hustled to Martin's communication station and picked up his headset. She opened all intercom channels.

"All hands, this your Navigator. We have been boarded. Hostile forces have boarded Voyager. Stand your ground. Response team mobilize. Kill any personnel you do not recognize. Attacker may be heavily augmented or spliced. Do not attempt to capture. I say again, capture risk too high. Kill immediately upon sight."

With a few keystrokes she locked the bridge controls and set the alert to replay every five minutes.

She ran to the open hatch. "Follow me. Keep the barrel of that weapon down and your finger off the trigger until you need it."

"It's one of those mercs, isn't it?" he said. "The spliced ones."

They moved down the deck to the other open hatch. "Has to be." Kara kept her voice low. "No one else could get the drop on two seasoned Mariners like that. No more talking unless necessary."

Drummond gave her a strange look, but accepted what Kara said.

Three steps into the passageway and Kara spotted another victim. She swore softly, stepping over a young deckhand, who lay in a heap on the deck, his weapons still holstered. For the smallest moment, hope bloomed. He could still be alive. But, as Kara checked for a pulse, she found nothing but a stretched neck. Gently, she rested her hand on his head, then moved on.

The oppressive silence from the bridge followed them down below deck. Kara took point. At intersections and hatches she tapped on the bulkhead, warning other Mariners that a friendly was coming. A quick response tap was all she needed before proceeding.

Drummond stayed true to his word, dutifully following with his weapon trained down. His eyes betrayed the fear he must have been feeling, but he didn't back down. Kara swept past an open passageway near the galley. A shadow flashed across the deck.

A glint of steel flew in front of her, Kara reacted on instinct, stepping back and swinging her pistol upward. Her finger pulled the trigger back automatically.

And froze.

Kara stopped herself a hair's breadth from firing. A knife blade halted only centimeters from Kara's belly. The galley mate who held it let out an audible sigh of relief, lowering her blade and slumping backward against the bulkhead. She started to make a hand sign, but Kara caught her in an embrace. Touching her forehead to the young woman's, Kara made the signs for caution, listen, and tap. Visibly shaken, the young mate took her blade and retreated into the shadows.

They crossed the central passage of the ship. A limp, bloody form lay on the other side of the intersection. Kara scanned the three directions the mercenary could have taken.

At once, she understood.

Beckoning Drummond to come close, she whispered in his ear. "He's going to engineering."

First, cut off the head of the snake by killing the

bridge crew. Then, disable the engines. The Mariners would be left leaderless and crippled. Somehow, that mercenary managed to climb onboard while his ship was out of range. All he had to do was get back to them while the Voyager tried to limp away. They'd be overwhelmed within hours.

Another thought gave her pause. Kara considered it, then motioned for Drummond again. "Go back. Find Tren. He's in danger. Take him to the bridge. Lock yourselves in. Remember to tap."

Drummond took a hard swallow. He nodded softly, his eyes wide. Without further comment, he turned around and crept back toward the galley. If he was very lucky, Tren would be waiting for him inside. Otherwise, Drummond would have a trek over to the passenger quarters where Tren had been assigned a room. Both places were well away from engineering, however.

She made her way to the ladder going deeper below, fighting down her worry for Drummond and Tren. They weren't Mariners. What if Drummond forgot to tap? A well meaning crew member could accidentally gut him on instinct alone. What choice did she have? She had to trust them. Well, she had to trust Drummond, at any rate. He'd proven himself so far, hadn't he?

Kara paused at the hatch. Pressing an ear to the metal, she tapped twice. Although she hadn't been expecting it, a single tap answered her. Slowly, she spun the hatch locking wheel. It didn't squeak as she turned it, which was a bit of a relief. Kara pulled open the hatch at a steady speed, not too fast. She didn't want to spook whoever was on the other side. Darkness and a dim red glow waited on the other side of the hatch.

A familiar hand touched the back of Kara's arm. Chief Lambros. She helped Kara get the hatch shut. Standing on the landing, Kara wasted no time flashing hand signs to catch the chief up. It wasn't exact communication, but it sufficed.

Intruder, dangerous, destination, engineering, destroy.

Lambros nodded. Although Kara was the senior officer, Chief Lambros had more combat experience and training. It made her feel more than a little awkward taking the lead, but she knew without a doubt the chief would have her back.

Engineering took up the lowest two decks of the ship. In days long past, when ships burned diesel or other fossil fuels, the internal combustion engines demanded tremendous amounts of space and constant maintenance. Mariner vessels ran electric motors, powered mostly by batteries that stored power from their sun sails. Only a fraction of the space was needed and a third the number of parts for the same power output.

Unfortunately, in this case that meant that fewer Mariners crewed these decks. Kara and Chief Lambros would have less help fighting off the merc. Maybe that wasn't a terrible thing, Kara thought. The way the mercenary cut through their ranks, perhaps it was for the best.

They reached the landing of the first engineering deck. Chief Lambros paused and looked to Kara. Kara signaled for the chief to go down to the lowest deck while Kara would take this one. Chief Lambros motioned to their guns then made the sign for no.

Great. Perfect. Of course.

Kara let out a quick breath. Firing guns below deck was dangerous enough with ricochets and the tight quarters. Down in engineering, with the possibility of puncturing some vital equipment, or exposing battery chemicals to the open air and then causing a fire, it was too great to risk. Kara holstered her pistol and drew her knife. This situation grew worse by the moment. Not only did they have to fight this super soldier, now they had to do it with knives.

Lambros gave her a quick nod, then softly moved down the ladder.

Naturally, it would have been safer to lie in wait and ambush the mercenary on his way out of engineering. But by then he would have carried out his mission, which made that a terrible plan. No matter how she thought it through, Kara had to press on.

Much like the ladder passageway, only dim red light pooled around the engineering deck. Someone must have cut primary power. She hoped it had been Lieutenant Morgenstern, the ship's engineer who made that call and not the intruder.

Kara spotted the first drops of blood just a few meters into the deck. She stepped around them, not wanting to track blood. That plan fell to pieces as she crept forward, the blood covering more and more of the decking. As she approached the first intersection, she spotted the tip of a bayonet on the floor. Getting low, she tapped the bulkhead twice.

No response.

Moving forward, Kara saw the rest of the corridor. An engine mate, Temple, she thought his name was, lay broken and cut. His blue jumpsuit dotted with ragged knife holes, his femur snapped and protruding from a swollen thigh. A long rifle lay just out of his reach, the bayonet fixed on the end coated in blood. Kara reached out to his outstretched hand, gently touching the lightning bolt inked into his skin.

Two taps rang against the bulkhead behind her.

Kara ducked to the side and tapped once in response.

Another blue jumpsuit smoothly took the corner. Kara looked up at the Mariner. Lieutenant

Morgenstern stood shorter than Kara, but he had muscle to him. Thick hands lowered the bayonet-tipped rifle he carried. His face broke, eyes welling with tears as he lowered himself down to Temple.

Kara touched his shoulder and gave him a firm squeeze. Morgenstern wiped his eyes with the back of his hand. Catching his gaze, Kara signaled to the engineer.

Together. Strike, she signed.

Together. Always, he responded.

With two fingers she touched Temple's forehead, thanking him for the weapon and wishing him peace. Sheathing her long knife, Kara picked up Temple's rifle. Holding the bayonet at the ready, she motioned for Morgenstern to follow.

It wasn't difficult to know where to go. Temple must have cut the merc. A steady trail of blood spatters gave them a way forward. Two more corridors passed by without incident. Engine hum grew louder and the air hotter as they crept along, closer to Voyager's stern. At last, Kara caught sight of him.

She signaled for a halt, then pointed down the passageway. There, next to one of the control stations, stood the tall man who had pulled Gary out of the street in Skatch Harbor. He wore a skin-tight wetsuit topped with a waterproof vest and pistol belt. Keeping a K-Bar style knife pinched with the two smallest fingers of his right hand, he tried over and again to gain entry to the engine systems.

Mariner vessels used heavily modified versions of commercial control systems. No one should be able to walk aboard and control one of their ships, that was the whole point. This didn't buy them a ton of time, however. Soon enough the mercenary would grow tired of being clever and resort to physically breaking things.

Down by her feet, Kara spotted the blood trail,

which had been growing fainter. He couldn't have some kind of freakishly fast healing, could he? Kara didn't want to believe that was possible, but given what Tren had told her, she couldn't discount the idea.

Behind the mercenary the decking stopped at a long curved rail. It ended in a sort of balcony overlooking the lower engineering floor, providing space for motor maintenance. Could they somehow knock him over the rail? Doubtful that would do much more than aggravate the man.

No, Kara thought. They only had one choice here. She looked for alternate routes, to see if maybe they could catch him in a pincer. Morgenstern cottoned on, but shook his head no. There was only one way forward unless they backtracked to the lower deck.

She double-checked that the bayonet sat tight on the end of Temple's rifle. Kara and Morgenstern locked eyes. As one, they faced forward, blades front, and charged.

Other fighters may have belted out a war cry. Kara and Morgenstern only breathed harder, trying to move quickly but also keep as much surprise as possible in their attack. For glorious seconds as they ran, blades out, the mercenary kept his eyes glued to the control display. Kara stepped closer and closer still. She gripped the rifle at the joint of the stock and pistol grip with her right, and her left on the hand guard, guiding the bayonet to its target.

With her teeth gritted, she ran the bayonet forward, mere inches from the intruder.

Then he moved.

Before Kara completely understood that he had moved, the man slipped away from her strike. One graceful spin took him out of Kara's path. In that same instant he raised his right leg in a smooth, downward heel kick, smashing Morgenstern's bayonet down to the deck.

The mercenary struck out with both hands. His left held in flat strike, he contacted Morgenstern's forehead, slamming the man backward. With his right, still holding his K-Bar, he made a wild stab for Kara, slicing her right forearm.

A line of fire tore down her arm as the skin split. Only adrenaline kept Kara from crying out. She grunted and staggered against the control console, barely keeping the bayonet in her hands. Without missing a beat, the mercenary brought the knife to bear on Morgenstern. The chief engineer got his bayonet back up, but only just. Morgenstern had an awful position, half sitting on the floor, dazed from the earlier strike to his head.

Kara screamed, thrusting the bayonet again. It didn't matter if it connected, she needed to get the merc off of Morgenstern. As if working on precognition, he sensed Kara's strike. Slipping forward, her bayonet rushed by his back. He slashed out in a wide arc at Kara while keeping his eyes on Morgenstern. Unlike her attacker, Kara couldn't get out of the way. His K-Bar cracked just above her left eye.

Blood sprayed into the air in front of Kara, then splattered to the ground. Without thinking, she reacted, shoving the bayonet down and back at the intruder. To her shock, she felt a wet connection on the other end of the rifle. He had tried to slip her strike again, but must have slipped on some of his own blood that had built up on the floor.

Grunting, he lurched back toward the railing, moving deeper into a puddle of red light. Spots and streaks of his wetsuit shone darker than others. Kara realized he had several cuts, slashes, and stabs. Working his way in, Mariners had taken small pieces of the mercenary along the way.

Good, she thought.

Her own blood ran free and hot down her face. She squinted her left eye, trying to keep her vision clear. Lieutenant Morgenstern recovered, taking his place next to Kara. Keeping their eyes on their attacker, they instinctively spread out, making it harder for him to track their movements.

Kara stabbed. The merc shuffled back, only to move quickly again, out of the way of Morgenstern's incoming strike.

Something in the man's face shifted. His expression went from all-business to hell-with-this. Kara's stomach lurched. Quick as a snake, his left hand blurred down to the waterproof holster on his pistol belt.

Compared to him, she may as well have been wading through hip-deep water. Kara began a thrust, but he already had his pistol out, rising steadily toward her. Kara couldn't have stopped her momentum even if she wanted to. At this point, she was going to charge headlong into his bullets, but damned if he wasn't going to eat some bayonet for it.

Then his eyes widened.

Both of the mercenary's feet flew backward and under the guard rail. His body toppled forward, arms windmilling to regain some balance. He hit chest first with a hollow thump, managing to keep his chin from striking the deck first. Despite the surprise, his reflexes stayed intact. Already he had his hands down in a push-up position, ready to recover.

By then, it was too late. Kara and Morgenstern reached his position. Guiding their bayonets downward, they both struck him in the back. Sickening wet slaps mingled with his grunts and half screams as they stabbed over and again.

Kara wasn't sure who got the fatal strike. She wasn't sure she had the energy to care. At some point tears began streaming from her eyes.

"It's done," Chief Lambros said. She climbed the rest of the way up the ladder leading from the balcony down to the lower deck. Her hands had been the ones to pull the attacker off-balance.

Lieutenant Morgenstern doubled over, hands on knees. "Chief, you saved our lives. I can't ever thank you enough."

Chief Lambros leaned down and checked the mercenary's pulse. "We all did what we had to, Lieutenant."

Kara cleared her throat and stood up straight. She walked over to the blood streaked console where the intruder had been trying to sabotage them. Unlocking the station, she opened the intercom.

"All hands, this is the Navigator. One intruder is down. Every available Mariner is to begin a sweep of your current deck. Ensure no intruders remain. Engagement rules remain unchanged. All wounded report to sick bay."

Morgenstern readied his weapon again. "I think we know we're clear here. Empty down below, Chief?"

Chief Lambros nodded, still staring at the dead man.

Kara blinked. She felt Lambros's hand touch her shoulder and the sting of salt in her eyes as blood ran into them. Gently, Chief Lambros wrapped a gauze bandage around Kara's forehead and wiped blood from her brow.

"God almighty," Morgenstern said. "I've never seen such a thing in all my years. What's the skipper going to do about this?"

The skipper wasn't going to do anything. He was gone. As was Commander Satry. Which meant that burden fell on the next in command.

Her.

Chapter Twelve:
Burdens of Command

"A Captain's greatest commitments are to his crew and the Mariners as a people. Our fleet is the lifeblood of our trade and conservation work. For us, this is a most serious commitment."
Mariner Fleet Training Manual, Chapter XIV

Admiral Kim and Elect Shostakovich both wore grim expressions. Even though the connection pixelated and stuttered, Kara could see that much.

"You and your crew did everything you could," Admiral Kim said. "I'm proud of you all for stopping the attacker. Tell them I said so."

Amber light filled the bridge. Most of the blood had been cleaned, but Kara had told the deckhands to focus on more important work. She hadn't slept, even though she did try to get an hour's nap. Something in her wouldn't allow it. So on top of the throbbing tenderness from the wounds on her forehead and wrist, a dull fuzziness blanketed her thoughts.

"Six lost," Kara said. "Including our Captain and

First Officer. I can't help but feel like I could've done more, sir."

"That's a path you don't want to travel, Lieutenant," the admiral said. "Take it from me. Battles are won in the moment, by working with what you have. Second guessing yourself won't change a single thing that happened. From what I read in your report, it could have been much, much worse."

She wanted to push back, but only nodded. "I understand that the Gallant wasn't attacked?"

"Yes, but the Penitent wasn't as fortunate. The mercenary who attacked them failed to get into their bridge. Two deckhands getting some air spotted him climbing the hull and sounded the alarm."

Kara couldn't help but wonder what would've happened if only she and Drummond had been looking over the other side of the observation deck railing. Could they have had an early warning like the Penitent did?

As if sensing her thoughts, Admiral Kim added, "They still lost four of their crew fighting that mercenary, Lieutenant. Including their navigator. These were opponents the like of which Mariners have never before faced."

"True." Kara couldn't help but wonder if this would be the last time they had to go toe-to-toe with a spliced fighter.

Elect Shostakovich picked up the conversation. "As for the fallen, I expect Chief Lambros will perform their honors?"

"Yes, sir," Kara said.

"You'll need to speak as well," Admiral Kim said. "The crew will look to you. Now, more than ever."

"Admiral," Kara said. "The Penitent is close enough for us to intercept. Captain Grayson's first officer could come take command of Voyager. He must be more qualified."

"Commander Orozco is a fine Mariner with years of salt on him. But your crew needs to see one of Voyager's own rise up and lead them through this. Besides, how much time will you lose with that docking maneuver? I hate to say it, but if that attack shows us anything, it's that your mission is more critical now than ever."

"Aye, Admiral," Kara said.

Admiral Kim paused and then spoke earnestly. "We're confident you can do this. We have faith in you and your abilities. Now get out there and lead these Mariners. We're counting on you, Skipper."

The call cut out. Kara's stomach jumped into her throat at the Admiral's last words.

Ensign Martin stood from the communication station. Despite the chill morning, he wore his light vest and trousers, as did Kara. Showing their tattoos showed what bonded them. Martin stood on his tiptoes and looked through a porthole facing the deck.

"They're all gathered, Skipper."

Funny. Kara had spent her whole life dreaming of the day another Mariner would call her that. Now that it was here, she wished it were anyone else in her shoes. Captain Ansari should be standing at the command station, immovable and resolute. Not her. Between him and Commander Satry, with his annoyingly precise countenance, they would've known exactly what to do and how. Unlike her. She felt like a child playing dress up. Holding her mother's knife, covered in homemade tattoos she'd drawn on with a pen.

Kara took a steadying breath and tried to shake off her doubts. The promotion was temporary, but that didn't make the responsibility any less real. Truth was truth. The crew would be counting on her to lead them.

All remaining twenty-four crew stood on the deck. Some wore a little finery beyond their normal shell-and-bone—polished boots here, a family necklace there—but every mariner exposed their arms and shoulders. Loose vests flapping in the chill wind showed marks of merit inked onto chests and backs, skin pebbled in the cold.

She stepped from the bridge to the sound of two notes, high and low. Deckmate Garrison, one of the deckhands who'd been with her during the squall, dropped the whistle from his lips and saluted her, fist to heart. As one, every Mariner stood tall and echoed the motion.

Sea air stung the freshly stitched wounds on her wrist and face. Kara faced the Mariners at the position of attention and returned their salute. "At ease," she said.

Did her voice sound weak? Had she spoken loud enough?

Fatigue, anxiety, and doubt swirled together inside her as she walked down to the deck and over to where Chief Lambros stood, a simple length of white cloth draped around the chief's neck and shoulders. Summoning all the internal strength she had, Kara approached the bow. Rising sunlight painted six long bundles wrapped in white cloth in golden-amber light. The fallen Mariners lay with their heads facing east, toward the rising sun.

Taking her place next to Chief Lambros, Kara ensured the chief stood in front of her by a step or so. This morning the chief wouldn't be speaking from her role as deckmaster. She'd be addressing the crew as a teacher of the Core.

Chief Lambros held a thick charcoal pencil in her right hand. Walking slowly behind the first body, she knelt by the head, and carefully drew a cross on the shrouded forehead, then lightly touched the cheek.

"Deck Mate Jason Morrison," she said loud enough for all to hear. "Christian. Once, I caught him way too drunk at a port bar down Vancouver way and had to tell him off. He told me to mind my own business." The corners of her mouth twitched up. A couple people chuckled. "Turned out he was having some troubles. Talked to me about it. Next month, on my birthday, he gave me a hand-carved flute. He was thoughtful that way."

Lambros moved to the next body. Kneeling, she drew a cross on his head. "Engine Mate Earnest Temple, who fought his killer with all he had. Christian. Sort of." Chief Lambros smiled wistfully, holding his head in both her hands. "Couldn't name more than two books in the Bible, but got the gist of it. Never treated anyone in ways he wouldn't want to be treated. Unless it was his turn cooking in the galley, in which case we all had to endure a little pain. He was really homesick his first month at sea. It got better for him, though."

She moved in this way to the next two fallen. Giving them their mark and speaking a few words of truth. As the breeze shuffled through her hair, Kara let Chief Lambros's words wash over her as well.

Ship Mate Jeanine Taneva. Atheist. Knew the Voyager back to front and used that knowledge to find spots to nap while she was supposed to be on duty. Always fed Chief Rocket from her ration.

Ship Mate Boris Goldman. Jewish. Fancied himself a boxer but hated getting punched. Bought a ring of silver down Gane way and hoped to propose to his partner.

"Commander Arlo Satry. Atheist." Chief Lambros drew on his forehead a mark of the Core. A circle breached by three equally spaced arrows pointing inward. "Our first officer was the human embodiment of a clock. Precise, and unyielding. Yet, an officer with the fairest hand I've served under. Never played favorites. Always acted in the crew's best interest."

Last, Chief Lambros came to their skipper. On his head, she drew a graceful mark of Om. "Captain Pranav Ansari. Hindu. We used to talk for hours about Vedanta. I'd heard people say he was a social climber driven by ambition, but I never found that to be true. He cared deeply, not only for the ship and the crew, but for all Mariners. Pranav shared that dream with so many of us."

She moved to stand centered behind the fallen. "Death reminds us of our impermanence. For many of us, it's an uncomfortable subject. One filled with fear. It doesn't have to be that way. Khalil Gibran wrote that life and death are one, even as the river and sea are one. This oneness is important. It comes up over and over in all aspects of life. There, if we only look for it. As Mariners, we respect nature and our interdependence with all. When we reflect deeply on interdependence, we question where we end and where everything else truly begins.

"*Tat Tvam Asi.* That thou art. A phrase that Captain Ansari and I spoke of often. Our essence is the universal essence. Separation is an illusion. These Mariners believed different things. Saw the world though unique eyes. Sought truth in their own ways. And yet, a part of them is a part of us. The same air passed between our lungs. The same sea water soaked our skin. The same smiles warmed our hearts.

"They return to eternity not alone, but with a part of us. Just as we, one day, will return with a part of them."

Chief Lambros inclined her head to Kara. Slowly, Kara walked to the feet of the bodies and faced them. Deckmate Garrison sounded the captain's whistle again. Kara led the Mariners in a final salute for their fallen. With fists to hearts, Chief Lambros raised her voice and began the song of Journey, to honor those souls returning to the Core.

I thought I was alone,
But you are a part of me.
I thought I was a wave,
'Til I became the sea.

Kara lent her strength to the pallbearers as they lifted and tipped each shrouded Mariner into the ocean. Despite the fire burning in her wrist with every grip, she wouldn't let anyone take her place. One by one, they placed each body on a smooth, varnished plank. As one, the pallbearers lifted the plank, set the far end on the railing, then tipped the other side skyward. A part of her tried to flinch with each splash, but Kara forced herself to remain open-eyed and steady.

When, after moments that stretched like warm dough, Kara helped tip Captain Ansari into his final resting place, a surge of panic flared up in her. What were they going to do? What was she going to do? The urge to scream and run all at once threatened to overwhelm her.

She returned the board to the deck, then gave her attention to Chief Lambros. A few heavy seconds of silence passed while Kara waited. Lambros strolled over to Kara and gently touched her elbow. Leaning toward Kara, she said, "They're waiting for you."

An electric jolt shot through her guts.

Kara's mouth went dry. She scanned the assembled Mariners, where every single eye held on to her. Why didn't she think about something to say ahead of time? Had she? There was no point in trying to jog her sluggish mind. Anything she had planned to say had evaporated. An awkward cough came from within their ranks.

No matter what sentences she tried to form, her

thoughts kept flashing back to last night. To her journey through the ship. Blood. Fallen. The spliced mercenary standing in dim red light, weapon held at the ready.

Kara caught sight of Lieutenant Morgenstern. Red eyed, but standing tall. A fresh bandage wrapped around his chest.

The spliced mercenary standing in blood red light. His wetsuit torn.

Morgenstern at her side.

Temple on the ground, his rifle bloody.

A shudder ran down Kara's neck. She looked to the deck and inhaled the chill air. When she looked up again, she found not only her Mariners, but the black sails rippling above them, absorbing the sun. Chief Rocket lay on a boom, his black tail swishing. Lapping waves and engine hum gently filled her ears.

"Last night," Kara said, "could be one of the worst nights any of us have faced. A single enemy did what no one has managed to do for years, decades, even. He boarded a Mariner ship. He killed those of our blood and hearts. I can't stop thinking about what I saw and those who fell. Morrison. Temple. Taneva. Goldman. Satry. Ansari."

She paused for breath, willing her racing thoughts to slow.

"Do you know what else I saw? When I, shoulder to shoulder with Lieutenant Morgenstern, finally caught the bastard? You know what I saw?"

No one moved. Every eye stayed on her.

"I saw him. Cut and bleeding. I saw the pieces every Mariner took from him. No matter how spliced he was, how amazing, how supposedly perfect, he could not break us! Every Mariner, knowing they couldn't win, fought to the last to wear him down for the next one of us, so that no matter what, one of us would make that final cut. With Commander Satry's last breath, he didn't pray, he didn't beg, he lifted his arm and hit the alarm. We will survive because we survive for each other. We will win because we live for something greater than ourselves. That is what we should take from last night. It doesn't matter what we face, so long as we face it together, as Mariners. And when we find the tub that bastard merc came from, we'll scatter her parts across the deep in a shower of fire and pain."

Crew members called out their support, fists raised and eyes filled with pride. Raw energy coursed through them all, flowing from body to body.

She dismissed the assembled group and remained standing by chief Lambros. Focus and lightness filled her. The words seemed to have come on their own accord. Kara's first action as captain, and she had done well.

But when she turned to look at Chief Lambros, the deckmaster wasn't smiling. She regarded Kara with something like concern, as if watching a wounded animal.

Captain Grayson sat at his command station, heavy with the weight of the decision in front of him. His bridge carried the somber mood from the morning when they'd bid farewell to their fallen. Sometimes, after a funeral, a little gallows humor would lighten the mood here and there. Without Bilby, their chief supplier of inappropriate jokes, the senior officers stayed subdued throughout the day.

He tapped his thumb softly on the hard plastic of his workstation keyboard, reading one of Bilby's final reports for the dozenth time. Grayson ran a hand over the prickly short hair budding from his scalp. Would he bother his staff with this again? Get their opinions one more time? Too much of that made a captain look indecisive. In their situation, that was a non-starter.

Did last night change his decision? When Ansari sent over that warning about spliced mercenaries, Grayson wondered if the man wasn't losing his nerve. And now? Captain Ansari dead, along with his first officer. Their young navigator was acting captain of Voyager, God help them. He supposed it did change his decision. Before last night, he might have sought out Ansari and used the old man as a sounding board. Felt him out. Gotten a sense for how willing he was to toe the line for Admiral Kim and his gutless leadership.

No, it was up to Grayson. Every sign on this path had shown him that. Within his grasp was the power to truly help the Mariners weather this newest storm. He only needed the courage to do the right thing, no matter what. Standing, he asked his senior officers to give him twenty minutes alone on the bridge.

Commander Orozco must have known what this was about. Rather than commenting, he snarled at the others to hurry up and give the skipper his space. Grayson walked over to Chief Fen's communications station, and tapped out some commands.

After a moment of connection buffering, Captain Faulkner blinked into life on the main display.

"Did we have a conference scheduled?" he said in a bored voice.

"No. I wanted a word."

Faulkner made a noise. "To what do I owe the pleasure?"

"Let's speak plainly, Captain." Grayson leaned back against the vacant navigator's station and crossed his arms. "We don't like each other. We don't have to. Let's put our cards on the table. No lies, no half-truths. If we can do that, I think our working relationship can improve."

"What on earth are you talking about, Grayson? Is this your way of calling me out for fisticuffs so we can bond like men, or something?"

Captain Grayson let a few seconds of silence stretch between them. "I'll go first. The night our crews had a dust up with Big Madrid in Skatch Harbor, I sent my navigator back to Big Madrid's apartment after we returned to our ship."

Faulkner cocked an eyebrow and turned up his palms.

"I see. You need more before you'll come clean. Bilby found a drive hidden under the floor. Not a lock drive, just a storage device. It was encrypted, but yesterday, Bilby managed to break it before...before we were attacked. Among other files, Big Madrid had backed up his correspondence. Are you willing to guess who's name came up?"

"Is this supposed to be blackmail of some kind?" Faulkner went back to looking bored. "Yes, I had already contacted Big Madrid before we set out for Skatch Harbor. Yes, I offered to buy the data. Maybe I didn't share that knowledge with the rest of you, but I'm not so convinced I can trust you all. Had it worked, I would have saved us all some trouble. As you saw, the thief had different plans. I swung and I missed. What's the problem?"

A curl set on Grayson's lip. "All true, but you're leaving out the part where you and Big Madrid chatted, and he offered to sell some stolen goods for you. I can provide specifics if you'd like. This merchandise is incredibly specialized. To be frank, I'm surprised a dockside fence like Big could move it."

Captain Faulkner went very still.

"It wasn't only text messages on that drive, Faulkner. I don't claim to be a genius. Lucky for me, doesn't take one to figure out what your plans are."

"What is it you want, exactly? If you wanted to stop me you'd already be doing it."

This was his last chance to back out. Images of the fishing vessel on fire filled his mind.

"If I wanted to stop you, your ship would already be in pieces. No, Faulkner, I want my due," Grayson said. "And some truth."

On average, Mariners didn't consume entertainment the way the rest of the world did. Even though Kara had been born elsewhere, she grew up on Vish, where satellite connections weren't always reliable or available. Only so much money was allotted to it by the Vish Council, so it tended to be used for more serious business like staying in contact with the fleet. Sure, they'd get together and watch the occasional video, but they didn't hunger for it the way people on the mainland did. It may have been that the business of maintaining the islands and the waters took up enough of their time that little was left for such things.

But people had to get their entertainment somewhere. Which meant that despite how cohesive Mariners were as a people, everyone had an opinion and everyone needed to express it. As the lifeblood of the Mariners, ships were also the lifeblood of their gossip. Whispering in the passageways and galleys was nothing new, and the few days since the attack had been no different.

So why did it bother her so much?

Ensign Martin twisted his knit cap between both hands. Only the two of them were on the bridge. Helm control was on auto, Voyager piloting herself as usual. Night had just fallen, which meant Lieutenant

Morgenstern and Chief Lambros would be joining them soon for a meeting. "It's not like they were talking mutiny, Skipper. Just blowing off steam. You know how it is."

"No, I don't," she said firmly.

He had the air of a man who'd decided minutes ago that he'd dug himself into a deep hole and now needed to do everything in his power to get out.

Kara forced herself to change her posture. Uncrossed her arms, softened her face. "Of course I do," she admitted. "I'm worried, Ensign. This isn't the best time for people to lose faith in their captain. You might have noticed we're in a tight spot. What is it, exactly, they think I should be doing?"

Martin relaxed a bit. "They want us to go after Big Madrid, not the American bunker. They want revenge for the fallen."

"That's the stupidest thing I've ever heard." Some of the bite found its way back into Kara's voice. "Big Madrid is going after the bunker. We get there, we get to Big Madrid. What's the problem?"

The hatch swung open. Kara twisted, one hand going to her sidearm. A blast of cold air tightened up her skin, making the slash on her forehead burn.

Chief Lambros eyed Kara's hand, then continued her way into the bridge. "The problem is that they are in pain. Losing their friends is a situation they can't control, so they want to control something. Their passions were hot to begin with, but have been stoked, so they focus on that instead of their grief. Revenge is insidious that way. Logic only works on people who are ready to listen."

The hatch swung open again. Drummond, Goldi, Tren, and Morgenstern piled in as a group. Sensing the tension hanging in the air, none of them spoke.

"Right." Kara stepped over to her navigation station and pulled a map of their target location up.

"I suppose that's all my fault, is it? For trying to lift people's spirits?"

Chief Lambros returned Kara's cold stare with a neutral one. "I've shared my thoughts already, Captain. I'm not blaming you. You want to know why people are fixated on revenge. Well, you planted that seed."

"Tell me what to say, then. If you've got this all figured out, what do I need to tell these people to get them back on course. Because I cannot have the crew turning against me," Kara said.

"They aren't," Chief Lambros said. "You have a few loudmouths. That's all. This will blow over, but only if you stop overreacting."

"Overreacting?" Kara's jaw set firm. "What makes you so sure of that? How are you so confident that I'm not right, and you shouldn't be worried more about this?"

"Because I've actually slept during the past few days, Skipper." Chief Lambros didn't raise her voice or change her tone. She stayed in that annoyingly calm posture and went on. "You're running on fumes. You need rest. I'm not going to pretend this is a problem to placate you. You need to hear only the truth from your staff. I'm the deckmaster, not the comfort-master."

Her gut roiled. Acid stung the back of her throat while her wounds throbbed. Kara needed to lash out, to tell Chief Lambros to get off of her bridge. As she looked at the others, though, her predicament closed around her like a trap. Tell Lambros off, and she'd only be proving the stubborn woman's point. Finally, she ignored the whole thing and motioned for the crew to gather around the display.

Kara started the meeting without ceremony, her voice thick with impatience. "It's obvious that we need to find a way to tighten up security in a smarter way.

We can't keep running extra guard shifts on deck. It's wearing the crew down. Lieutenant Morgenstern had an idea on that, but to do it we're going to need some help. Lieutenant, would you like to take us through your plan?"

"Sure, Skipper." Morgenstern ducked over to a corner of the bridge and came back with what looked like a large, silvery salmon. Tren backed away from the fish as Morgenstern came back to the group with it in both arms. With a heavy thump, he dropped it on to the navigation table, it's glassy eyes staring blankly.

"This is one of our swimmers." He focused more on Tren than anyone else. Tren seemed to find the attention disconcerting, shuffling around behind Goldi and avoiding Morgenstern's eye. "More or less, it's an underwater probe disguised as a salmon. Swims like one and everything. We make them over Gane way. Normally, we use them to spy on other fish and ocean life. Get an idea of their numbers and all that. What I'd like to do is repurpose the two we have aboard. Instead of watching marine life, they can patrol the ship, keep an eye out for any divers trying to sneak over to us underwater like that bastard merc did."

"Huh," Tren said, all traces of his earlier hesitation gone. "I'm guessing they aren't remote controlled, or this wouldn't be an issue. Autonomous?"

"Indeed." Morgenstern nodded. "Programmed to watch and record all on their own. Makes them much more effective. Trouble is, anyone who knows how to reprogram one of these is on Gane island."

"Do you have access to the source code?" Tren said.

"Aye, we'll get it for you. This mean you can do it?"

"Can I?" Tren scoffed. "It's a question of time,

not ability. You want this fast, right? Hell, I want it fast, forget what you need. If this fishy can keep us from getting attacked again you have my undivided attention. I'm only saying that something like this could take a while to finish."

"Tren," Kara said. "I don't need to tell you the kind of trust we're putting in you. Mariners don't let outsiders into our secrets. This is a trust you do not breach. Do you understand me?"

"Perfectly," Tren said, a little coldly. "Don't forget Big Madrid will want me dead just as much as you. Maybe even more."

"Lieutenant Morgenstern will set you up with a workstation down on the engineering deck. Goldi, you're to stay with him." Kara stood up straighter and addressed the whole team. "We're about three days out from our coordinates. At any moment we could run into Big Madrid's ship and we have no idea what other surprises they have in store. Or, for all we know, they could be waiting for us at the site. We need to be ready. I cannot stress this enough."

Kara dismissed the team and went back to her navigation display. Ensign Martin couldn't wait to get out of the bridge. The rest weren't far behind him. Once she heard the hatch swing shut, she breathed out a sigh.

"Everything okay with you and Chief Lambros?"

Drummond's voice sent Kara reaching for her gun for the second time that night.

"Jesus, Kara!" Drummond said. He had his hands raised. "I didn't sneak up on you, for God's sake."

"No," she sputtered, "But you...I thought you left!"

Drummond gave her a moment. "Look, I just wanted to talk to you. I heard part of your argument with the chief. I don't want to pry—"

"So don't." Kara went back to tapping commands, bringing up different maps.

He shook his head and made to leave, but stopped short of the hatch. "You know what? No. I'm saying this. Whether or not you listen is up to you. I respect the hell out of you, Kara. Everyone on this ship does. You want to know what people say about you when you're not around? That's basically it. But if you keep acting like you have been, the people closest to you are going to reach their limit with your attitude. The chief is right, you're running on empty. Pissed off about crap that doesn't matter and jumping at shadows. I'm not saying it isn't understandable; you've been through hell. I'm saying that you need to eat, rest, and trust the people who trust you. Because everyone on this ship is rooting for you and will help you if you let them. Take it from a guy who lives a life where ninety-nine percent of the people he works with are actively plotting his failure. That isn't what's happening here."

With that, Drummond let himself out.

Chapter Thirteen:
Concern

"To be beneath the notice of so many may hurt the fragile ego. But, it is a tactical advantage which should not be ignored."
Mariner Fleet Training Manual, Chapter II

Several days had passed since Nakamura's 'security professionals' had failed to return to the DCV Verne. Big Madrid had been against their plan from the start. As if their harebrained scheme were his fault! Big Madrid said let's pull up alongside the bastards and shoot them. No? Fine, let's send Gill and Gary over there, see how the shipsies like that. Gary's been itching for some payback. But, no. Had to do it their way.

Not that he was against the spirit of the plan, of course. It was he who had asked for those shipsies to get a good kicking to begin with. No, it was the plan itself he took issue with. The one the blokes from Vasco Tactical Solutions, Ltd. had hatched. Swim to the bleeding shipsy boats? Were they daft?

How long, exactly, can you hold you breath, sweetheart? He had asked the blond one. And what was that all about anyway? No names? Couldn't even use a code name, or a street moniker, or a term of endearment?

Well, see where their superior attitudes got them. Mad. Absolutely mad. Big tried to tell them, but, oh no. Just stood there out in the cold, wrapped up tight in wetsuits and weapons, holding those ridiculous little diving motors.

Hubris. That's what it was. Now look where it got them. Probably drowned halfway to the shipsies. Naturally, because they had the discourtesy to die, it was Big Madrid himself answering for it. Standing tall in the orange conference room, set to atone for his sins.

"We're very concerned, partner. I won't lie about that." Nakamura had abandoned his golf clubs for this meeting. He took the call from his desk, but still had that fantastic view in the background. Cloudy skies looked right about to dump some rain. Fitting.

"It's like I said, Mister Nakamura. These men have great abilities, but these seas may have just been too rough. Heard from the crew here that the farther north you get, the more unpredictable the water. If they would've made it to the shipsies, we woulda come across their boats by now. Poor blokes must have drowned. Or, and I hate to say it"—Big Madrid paused to make a solemn face and a sign of the cross—"but they tell me there's all sorts in these shipsy, er, Mariner, waters. Sharks and killer whales and the like. What if the boys got on the wrong side of one of them, eh?"

"Unfortunately, partner, we don't have any way of knowing. What we do know, is the loss of these men, the tragic, tragic loss, also comes with a hefty price tag to our little operation. Now, I've been talking to the big brains at Vasco and they're telling me something different. They're saying their guys are too well trained and they wouldn't have gone aquatic unless they knew they could make it. In fact, their people are saying they think the Mariners fought them off."

Nakamura sat back in his chair, the leather (was that real hide?) giving a little squeal. As impressive as his upholstery was, Nakamura had no idea what he was saying.

"Mister Nakamura," Big Madrid began in his best let's-be-reasonable voice, "I saw one of those lads in action at Skatch Harbor. Saved Gary's life, you may well remember. I know shipsies. Seen one or two win a brawl on occasion, I'll grant you. But to take on one of your Vasco blokes? I don't care if there were a hundred of them on that ship. There's no bloody way. He'd cut through them like hot butter."

Nakamura's brow rose a bit in the middle. He breathed deep. "Dunno, Big. From what their guys are saying, these Mariners are a surprisingly tough little bunch. They've got a history of fighting with the U.S. and, not to mention, ships do go missing in their territory. That's what I'm hearing from Vasco."

"With all respect to Vasco, sailors sink their ships all the bloody time. Mostly on account of them being drunken numpties. Maybe a shipsy boat took out a fishing ship or a smuggler. What of it? Was your Vasco man a fisher? I think not. Odds those shipsies won a fight against one of your Vasco fighters are slim, but, maybe it could happen, I'll grant you. But both of them? Can't be. They hit a squall or something, Mister Nakamura. You mark me."

Nakamura spent a moment rubbing his chin. Big Madrid felt like he was being sized up for sale.

"You know what," Nakamura said, dropping his

hand. "I agree with you. I do! Partner, I can't see how two highly-trained Vasco specialists could've both been taken out. No way, right? I'll tell you what it is, and this is just me talking to you and no one else, okay? Contract rates. If their guys died during an engagement, we have to pay a ton more than if they died in some non-combat accident en route. Money! Right? It's always money."

In Big Madrid's mind, Clouds parted overhead, letting the sun through once more. For a few moments there, he could almost feel Nakamura considering whether or not this operation was worth pursuing.

"I'm going to toss this one over to the lawyers, 'cause that's what they're good for." Nakamura chuckled. "Now, I realize we still have a situation to take care of. Remember that Vasco support ship that I said was coming your way?"

"I surely do, partner."

"Well, I'm going to have them make a little detour. We don't need our operation getting any more complicated. When I ask for them to take care of our problem, I'm going to ask for a very straightforward solution. None of this secret agent business. You feel me?"

Big Madrid grinned a toothy, metal grin. "I believe I do, partner."

"A wise man once said"—Tren raised a single finger in the air—"that what one programmer can do in one week, two programmers can do in two weeks."

"What does that even mean, Tren?" Kara, the acting captain of the ship squinted one eye at him. "Is it done, or not?"

Goldi, his ever present chaperone, leaned back in her thin aluminum chair, gently rubbing her broken arm. She kept her eyes on Kara, which meant she wasn't staring at him for a change. So, small victories did happen here and there.

"No." Tren gestured helplessly to the workstation and the fake salmon, now wired up to the computer. "Not yet, I'm working as fast I can, you have to believe me. But I had to add in a lot of code for these new features. Now you can use the swimmers for any kind of search, they can even act as signal relays for your radio. I mean, they had the hardware, so why not?"

Kara blinked at him. Something about the captain, could've been the dark circles under her eyes or the bright red knife wound held together by stitches on her forehead, but something about her was brooking no nonsense these days. Or was that just his imagination?

"Nobody asked you to do that. I don't give a gram of bilge how hard you're working, it's not enough," she said.

No, definitely not his imagination.

"We need every possible warning system we can get," she said. "Save the other stuff for later. You saw what happened last time we got attacked. I can't allow that to happen again. I won't. Get it together, Tren."

With that, Kara stormed off down the engineering deck passageway. Tren watched her exit. Once she disappeared behind a hatch, he counted a few more seconds for good measure, then exhaled.

"She used to be nicer."

Goldi snorted. "She didn't used to be captain. You do the work. You'll be fine. I watch. I know you try hard."

He went back to the workstation with its multiple open code files and muttered, "I could get done faster if she wasn't interrupting me ten times a day."

"Ha!" Goldi slapped his back. It kind of stung. "When I was child, back in Yakutsk, my father is well respected carpenter. He had client, very impatient. Father said to me, 'Goldi, this is kind of man who think three women together can make one new baby in three months.'"

Tren, still staring at his code, let a genuine chuckle pass his lips. "You're all right, Goldi."

"Of course I am," she smiled. "Now hurry up with the damn fish."

✦ ✦ ✦

A little over a day.

That's all they had left until they reached the coordinates. Barring any kind of unforeseen disaster, of course. Which described the whole voyage pretty accurately, when Kara thought about it. But nothing on the weather reports looked like a squall was brewing on their path. Nothing in Kara's gut told her so, either. Which meant that they were going to be attacked within the next day, before they got there, or they'd be attacked once they got there. She wasn't the only one able to reason that out, thankfully.

Captain Grayson stood on one side of the split screen while Captain Faulkner had the other. Kara shared the bridge with Ensign Martin and Lieutenant Morgenstern, whom she had appointed as acting first officer.

"We'll send you our approach vector." Grayson said. "Long as we don't come in from either side..."

He didn't need to finish the thought. Kara heard him loud and clear. The last thing they needed was to end up at opposite ends of the site where they'd be in each other's line of fire. "Understood. If we stay on our approach it'll make a nice flanking maneuver."

"Do you even have guns on those ships of yours?"

Faulkner interrupted.

Neither Kara nor Grayson answered.

"Whatever," Faulkner said. "Better you than us if you want to take the lead."

Grayson scoffed. "Oh? You'd like to take point? Going to launch your hot tubs at them, are you?"

Captain Faulkner rolled his eyes dramatically. "Just stay in contact. Faulkner out."

Kara tried to get Grayson's attention, but the man had already killed the call from his end. She rubbed her eyes. If she ever needed advice from a seasoned captain, now was the time. But Grayson hadn't been all that available lately. He hadn't even had the heart to argue with Faulkner as much as he normally did. Could've been that Bilby's death still weighed on him. Kara could definitely understand that.

"Uh," Martin tried to speak, coughed, then tried again. "Skipper, we got something on radar."

Kara bolted past Morgenstern and slid over to the radar display. Clear as day, she could see the blip closing in on their position. On a cold, clear day like this one, they'd be in visual range soon enough. Ringing slowly built in her ears. Starting with a low whine and rising steadily with each passing second.

It's happening again, it's happening again, it's happening—

"Skipper?" Morgenstern said. "Orders?"

Kara swallowed. "Martin, relay our status to the fleet. Morgenstern, sound the alarm. Set Voyager's helm for a tactical approach. All hands, weapons hot. Full deck crew ready."

Morgenstern nodded. He tried to turn to go execute her orders, but Kara stopped him with a hand. "Rick," she said. "Get the guns ready."

He hesitated. "Are you sure? It's a clear day and if the Gallant gets close and Faulkner's people see..."

"We're way past that," Kara shook her head. "If

this is who I think it is, we can't take the chance. Warm them up. Blame it on me. I'm in charge."

"Aye, Captain," Morgenstern said. "I'll get down there right away."

"Martin," Kara interrupted the ensign as he worked at sending messages. "Any radio contact from the bogey?"

"None." Martin gave his equipment another grim once over. "I've tried most all commercial band channels. They're ignoring us."

"Not for much longer, I think." Kara pulled on her jacket, her wrist screaming as the sleeve slid over her wound. Quickly, she buttoned up and buckled her pistol belt on over it. She grabbed a handheld radio and walked stiffly to the hatch.

"Keep an eye on that radar, Ensign. You have the bridge until I'm back. Be ready on the helm. I'll tell you when I want a full turn to approach."

Moving stiffly down the ladder and to the port side, close to stern, Kara squinted into the distance. A thunder of footsteps rang on the deck behind her. Chief Lambros and four of her deckhands crowded her at the railing.

"What do you think, Chief?" Kara gripped the rail with her bare hands. Cold ate at her split knuckles.

The chief lowered a set of binoculars. "They'll be on us in minutes. She's built for speed. Put her at about thirty meters long. No big artillery, but there's something mounted on the foredeck. Probably a fifty cal."

Kara accepted the binoculars from the chief. Everything through the lenses shook with her hands. She could see well enough, though. Low slung, sleek, angled prow pointed knife sharp, with two rooster tails of water spraying from her stern.

"So." Kara lowered the binoculars. "They'll run in straight, gun blazing, is that it?"

"That'd be my guess. Not much other choice with the speed she's traveling." Chief Lambros said. Her voice stayed calm as ever. For a small moment, a painful twinge reminded her of the last time she'd spoken to the chief in any personal sense. She had to make it up to her. Soon, she promised herself.

"Chief," Kara said. "Get your crew to the stern. We're coming about and giving her the guns."

Chief Lambros eyed Kara for a second, but didn't argue. Instead, she turned around and barked the movement orders to all of her deckhands. Immediately, they rushed to the rear of the ship. Which, currently, was the area of the deck closest to the incoming attacker.

Cold air washed over the wound on Kara's forehead. Carefully, she brought the radio up to her mouth. "Martin. Bring us about relative to the bogey, full."

Warning whistles sounded from the deck speakers. A second later, the ship lurched, rolling hard to port as she changed position. Icy water sprayed from Voyager's back end, misting everyone on deck. Each and every crew member held on to the rails or each other.

What Kara hadn't counted on was the other ship's velocity. Voyager was surprisingly agile for her size, but Chief Lambros hadn't joked when she said the other craft looked built for speed.

"Captain," Martin's voice buzzed through the radio, "Gallant and Penitent are both inbound. Gallant will be in visual range any second now."

Kara held fast to the rails. Letting the Gallant see their next move could be disastrous. Mariners thrived through intelligence and cunning. If a Captain in the U.S. Navy saw their next move, one of their few trump cards would be laid bare for all to see.

Voyager righted herself, engines cutting out,

then quickly reversing. Her stern fishtailed for a few meters, overcorrecting their position. Kara stumbled forward, away from the rear and toward Voyager's bow. A quick glance to starboard had her swearing. The tall, narrow, bleached white profile of the Gallant headed their way. She still had some distance to close between them.

"Morgenstern," Kara said into the radio. "Are you dialed in?"

"As soon as Martin quits moving the damn ship!" He shot back.

A staccato beat filled the air.

As one, all Mariner's hit the deck. Sparks flew as hammers pounded Voyager's hull. A porthole on the bridge shattered, more sparks burst from the forward mast. Holes ripped through the black sails, clouds of static shocks erupting from the broken solar material. She looked forward and up.

Their attacker bore down on them, close enough for her to make out the two black-clad figures on her deck. Skin-tight wetsuits. Waterproof gun belts. Her heart thrummed. Fire filled her belly.

Morgenstern's panicked voice crackled through the radio. A faint alarm came from his end. "Dialed in!"

Kara jerked the radio to her mouth. "Fire."

Barely audible over the barking gunfire, two hydraulic pumps quickly shot the gun covers open on Voyager's prow. From her spot lying on the deck, she could only see the tips of the two covers, one port, one starboard, barely peeking up over the deck.

An electric hum overpowered all other sounds on the ship. Electricity crackled from the open holes on the sun sails. A short chirp broke through all ship's speakers.

Every Mariner held on to whatever lay nearest to them.

Voyager rocked backward, sending Kara's stomach into her throat.

And again. Again.

Again.

Each thrust came with a rush of screaming air. Not an explosion, like a cannon, but a thrum; a bowstring in flight, air rushing over an open bottle. Arcs of smooth, yellow-orange fire shot from Voyager, destined for the attacking ship.

Deadly clang of metal on metal. Twisting groans, screams, the rush of fire drinking in the cold sea air. Kara slowly rose, first getting on one knee, then lifting herself the rest of the way up. The air over Voyager's deck stood deadly quiet now. Not a Mariner said a word. Slowly, they made their way to the bow, all eyes on the ship in the distance.

Their attackers, that sleek, insectile craft, listed in the water. Absolutely wrecked. Her front half wasn't simply mangled, it looked chewed by some mythic beast. Great gashes and tears opened her forward hull to such an extent that the bow couldn't be said to exist anymore. Fire roared from one of the torn openings. Whatever fuel she used would be catching now.

An arm dangled over one of the rent pieces of the foredeck, clad in skin-tight wetsuit. Blood ran freely down off of the pale hand and into the ocean below.

A tap on her arm. Kara turned to her left. Chief Lambros pointed to the wreck. "Look stern ways."

She brought her binoculars back up. There, cutting wake in a rubber raft from the sinking ship, was another one of the spliced mercenaries. He didn't bother stopping to pick up any of the sailors abandoning ship. One hand on the tiller, he deftly moved away from the wreck without looking back. Unlike the professional soldier, the sailors had no wetsuits, only uniforms of tan trousers topped with blue and white striped shirts. About half had life vests. The others clung to floating debris.

Chief Lambros didn't have to ask the question. Kara already knew what she was going to say. Before answering, Kara looked again to the Gallant. She was still a ways away, but there wasn't a chance in hell she wouldn't have seen Voyager use her railguns. Her shoulders slacked, heavy and light all at once.

"No," Kara said. "We're not pursuing. Let him go. Let's come about on the wreck. Keep the weapons free and let's sweep up some of these sailors. Any who surrender peacefully are to be treated fairly."

For the first time in days, Chief Lambros gave her the smallest of smiles. "Aye, Captain," she said, fist to heart.

Kara lifted the radio to relay her orders to Martin. Before she could thumb the button, the hatch nearest her flung open. Tren burst out from below decks, tottering with the massive sliver salmon in both hands and Goldi on his heels.

"I've got it, I've got it!" he cried out. "Captain Nkosi, the swimmer is ready!"

Kara mouthed words that wouldn't come.

Beaming, Tren looked to the wreck, then gave a start of surprise. "What the hell happened there? Is that a ship? Where did they come from? What have you all been doing up here? What was all that shaking, anyway? Are they on fire? How did that happen?"

From behind Tren, Goldi just gave a half-shrug.

Kara decided to give Martin her orders in person.

"Where are you going?" Tren said. "What about this?"

Goldi stood next to Tren and gave him a consoling pat on the shoulder. As Kara walked back to the bridge, she heard a great splash off the port side deck, followed closely by Tren's exasperated voice.

"You're welcome!"

Chapter Fourteen: Recovery

"A navigator guides the ship on the water, and guides her next mission from the land. You must learn to read people as well as the stars and weather."
Mariner Fleet Training Manual, Chapter VII

Fifty caliber machine guns, while not rail guns, could wreck a ship pretty effectively as well, it turned out. Lieutenant Morgenstern had all his engineers and most of the deckhands conscripted into repair work. As it was, they didn't have enough material on board to completely get back to running order. With that, and the four prisoners they pulled from the icy waters, Admiral Kim's next order didn't come as much of a shock to Kara.

"Captain Grayson and the Penitent will be happy to have you aboard," the admiral said. Their connection wasn't too bad this time, but they'd lose signal in a few hours all the same.

Kara stood at the part of the bridge that had

become hers over the past several days. Both Martin and Morgenstern stayed quiet. As did Chief Lambros who stood out of view of the camera. Drummond lurked by her navigation station, staying uncharacteristically in the background.

"I understand, sir," Kara said.

"You've done a fine job as acting Captain, Lieutenant. You were challenged and rose to the occasion. But, under the circumstances, we need to get Voyager repaired and those sailors to a safe harbor. They requested Skatch, you said?"

"Aye, sir." Most of the fight she'd had earlier in the day had ebbed away. A deep fatigue set into her bones. Sensing the admiral wanted a little more she added, "I interviewed them all personally. Separately. They're merchant sailors, simple as that. Hired to crew a rich person's toy. They say they had no idea who the mercenaries were or what they planned on doing. Their stories are mostly the same. The mercs told them they needed to find some Mariner ships, but said nothing about an attack. It wasn't until one of them took the helm and they started their approach that the crew realized what was going on. Or so they say. Either way, they've abided by their surrender."

On the screen, the video buffered a bit, then Admiral Kim nodded. "Then Captain Grayson will be expecting you and Chief Lambros. Congressman Drummond will join you. Are you sure you want to take the other prisoner as well?"

"Tren has proven his worth. He wants to see the end of Big Madrid more than we do, I think. Not like he's asked The Question or anything, but I think he still wants to prove useful. Truth is, if we take him back to Skatch before dealing with Big Madrid, he's as good as dead anyway."

"And you're positive Madrid wasn't on that ship?"

Kara grimaced, but nodded. "As sure as I can be. We sent the swimmer to investigate the wreck. Nothing. None of the crew recognized the description, and Big Madrid sticks out. It's bad enough that he's still out there and could attack again. But it's the bigger implication of him not being there that bothers me."

"Explain," Admiral Kim said.

"Somehow, Madrid convinces TXM to finance his salvage operation. Fine. I can see them hiring a deep-sea wrecker and some divers to come pull cargo from the ocean floor. But this? Spliced mercenaries? Multiple ships? There's no way this was a completely new crew trying to get to the same pot of gold. They attacked us, specifically. What corporation would sink this kind of money into simple salvage? Someone at TXM, or the company that pulls their strings, knows what's really down there, Admiral. Or at the very least they suspect enough to dump this kind of money into their operation. That's the only explanation."

After a moment of his image stuttering on the pixelated screen, Admiral Kim responded. "I'm inclined to agree. We need to act with caution now more than ever."

Before he could end the call, Kara stopped him. "Sir, I haven't had a chance to read the reports from the latest burst. Have there been any developments since the trade agreement?"

"Yes," he said carefully. "You'll see in the reports. We've had one fishing vessel we chased out of the waters down Ordina way. Then a container ship blasting its way through the waters near Gane tore through farming platforms. Extensive damage to the kelp and gold-wheat crops, not to mention the windbreaks surrounding them. It's all there in the reports."

"What about the ships," Kara's brow furrowed. "We just let them go? Did those fishers manage to fill their nets first? What's to stop them from—"

"That's enough, Navigator." The Admiral's tone brooked no nonsense. "We are working on a response. You need to stick to your mission. You have your orders. Command out."

On the main display of the bridge, the call closed, leaving only a map of the Bering Strait in its place. Despite the nature of the call, the bridge crew remained solemn. Drummond stood and walked over to the main display. He pointed to the map.

"You know, I don't think I've actually seen the spot where we're headed. Is it on here?"

Thankful for the excuse to get out of her thoughts, Kara nodded. "It is. Northeast of the Bering Strait, right off of Lopp Lagoon. See that break in the land mass there?"

"It's certainly out of the way," he said. "Your territory doesn't go this far north, does it?"

Chief Lambros joined them in front of the map. "No. We have ships who've sailed her often enough, though. Our closest island to here is Gane. That's much too far south to be of any help to us out here."

"The Penitent is out from Gane way, isn't she?" Martin said.

"She is," Kara said. "Wonder if Captain Grayson's gotten the latest about that container ship."

Chief Lambros picked up on Kara's train of thought. "We can only deal with what's in front of us, Kara. You'll make sure Grayson knows. You're about to be his navigator, after all. But we have to see this through first."

"Even so, there's not much more comfort in that. We can't send Voyager away," Kara said. "Not now. Big Madrid still hasn't shown himself. That ship of his is going to be waiting for us, I swear it."

"Respectfully, Lieutenant," Morgenstern said. "What good could we do? We've used every bit of patching material we had to plug up the bullet holes. Not to mention the damage to our sun sails. If we get into another scrap, we won't be able to fully power our engines, much less the railguns. Voyager would be a sitting duck. If we get hit below our water line, with nothing reliable to stem the leaks we'd be in serious trouble."

Kara leaned against the command station. A tiny plastic statue of Ganesha still sat by the keyboard, a relic of Captain Ansari's.

"Stop making sense, Morgenstern," she said with a wan smile. "Tell the skipper what she wants to hear."

"Ah," Morgenstern countered with a raised finger, "technically, I'm the acting captain now. So, scrape off and get packing, Lieutenant."

Laughter burst from Kara. "You're lucky I'm in no shape to fight, Morgenstern."

Rendezvous with the Penitent took less than half an hour, since they were already nearby after the attack. Chief Lambros's deck crew hurried to make fast the gangway between the ships. As the waters were blessedly calm, they didn't need to use a dinghy to get from ship to ship. Still, the day had slipped by quickly with the preparations for departure.

Kara, Drummond, and Tren all stood near the gangway, readying themselves to leave Voyager. Time grew shorter as the sun began to touch down with the sea on the western horizon. It would be more dangerous to keep the gangway between them as they lost daylight. Kara's simple canvas duffle lay only half full. Mariners travelled light and generally didn't hoard possessions. It seemed that Drummond also wasn't bringing much along with him. Perhaps he had a bigger bag aboard the Gallant somewhere? He did sail in with them.

Next to Tren, another bag of Mariner canvas sat on the deck, mostly empty. Goldi had seen to helping him get his clothes washed and took a collection from the crew to get him a pair of boat shoes and another change of clothes. She stood by his side, chiding him before they parted ways.

"Not every Mariner is as kind or generous of spirit as Goldi, yes?" She said. "When you ask your questions what will you watch for?"

Tren sighed, and replied robotically, "If they don't answer, or squint at me, or otherwise look angry."

"And what do we do?"

"We don't ask more questions."

"Why?"

"Because it's rude," Tren said.

Goldi gave him an affectionate pat on the side of his face. "You are good boy. You will miss Goldi."

Choking back a laugh, Kara watched Goldi move over to Drummond. Lazily, she draped her good arm around his neck. "*Kotyonok*," she purred at him. "You have been so brave. Knowing we are about to part ways, maybe for all of times, yet you shed no tear. Strong man. This, I have always known."

Two deckhands snickered, turning Drummond's cheeks a deep red. Goldi had all the fuel she needed. Louder, she went on. "I cannot accept your diamonds, *moi horoshiy*, nor your gold or gifts of furs. Even the big house on the Oregon coast. I have told you, a Mariner craves not these things. No, the engagement is off. I have said it, do not make me repeat! If you are helpless without me, then you must be helpless. My mind is set."

With gales of laughter from the deckhands, Goldi

leaned forward and kissed his cheek. Much softer, she said, "You have my thanks. Always."

"Anytime," he said somewhat lamely.

Her performance over, Goldi stepped back to join the other deckhands at their work. Kara spotted her with a knot of crew members surrounding Chief Lambros. Her canvas bag draped over her left shoulder as one by one, her deckhands came to speak with her. She had words for all of them, each of whom would then salute her, heart to fist, before making way for their fellows.

Kara couldn't help the twinge in her gut at the respect being shown the deckmaster. Hadn't she been their captain?

"Not jealous, are you?" Drummond said from her right.

"You don't have..." Kara trailed off as she turned and saw his face, grinning. "You know, I liked you better when I didn't like you."

Drummond puzzled over that for a few seconds. "I'm sure that will make sense at some point. Anyway, time for goodbyes is up."

She saw what he was talking about. Over at the gangway, the deckhands called out they were ready. Chief Lambros made her way over and, in a single line, they crossed the metal bridge to their sister ship. Lambros had to walk behind Tren, gently pushing his shoulders to keep him moving over the bridge. The man looked straight ahead, eyes wide as saucers, and shuffled forward without once picking up his feet.

In no time at all, they were across and the gangway was lifted back over to Voyager. Funny, how in such a short time she'd come to regard the ship as her home. Now, as they prepared to separate, a piece of her would be leaving. She took in the deck of the Penitent; a little more careworn than Voyager, but clean and well maintained. Among the new faces, she spotted a familiar one coming their way.

Kara and Chief Lambros rendered salutes to their new captain.

Grayson returned the gesture and welcomed them aboard. As he called over his first officer, Orozco, to go through the details of their stay, Kara kept glancing over at the growing space between them and Voyager. Then, frightfully soon, Voyager began to come about, drastically changing her course southward.

Turning her attention inward, Kara couldn't help but wonder why, when she was on a Mariner ship, crewed by those of her blood and heart, did she have this nagging feeling of being in hostile territory?

"That's *Doctor* Wantanabe," Kara said. "She doesn't have a rank because she's not technically part of the sailing fleet. Doesn't mean she can't be part of the crew, though."

"Not all Mariners sail, then?" Drummond asked. "Kind of wondered about that."

They kept their voices a little lower than strictly necessary as they sat in Penitent's galley. The dinner crowd had waned a bit, which was more than fine with Kara. She'd been meeting the crew by ones and twos all day, leaving her more than full of social interactions. Drummond seemed unusually subdued as well, although she wasn't sure what he'd been up to.

"Of course not," Kara said. "Not everyone has the stomach for it, or even likes it. Sailing is a big part of our culture, but we have plenty of tradespeople and even educated types who stay on the islands for the most part. Otherwise, who would do the farming, or teach the kids, or handle the plastics recycling?"

"Or build the railguns?" he added flatly.

"Or that." Kara didn't bother sounding abashed. "Which, by the way, I'd appreciate your silence about."

"It's Faulkner you should have that talk with, not me. Anyway, I'm impressed, is all. I don't think anyone else has been able to make those work. Not in any reliable sense, anyway."

Chief Lambros slid down on to the bench next to Kara with a steaming bowl of thick stew and a slice of brown bread. "Talking about the railguns? Well, think about who came together to form the first Mariners. You had folks from all walks of life uprooted after the war for being on the losing side. Property seized, citizenship revoked. In that group were some well respected scientists and engineers. Without them contributing, along with everyone else, the plan to start a new society would've failed."

"We value people pitching however they can," Kara said. "Some people are good sailors. Other people have an aptitude for ecology, like Doctor Wantanabe."

"But where did she go to school?" Drummond leaned forward a little. "Do you have your own university?"

"We have access to educational materials," Kara said. "We're not savages."

He gave her a bored expression. "That's not what I meant and you know it."

Chief Lambros interrupted. "Those who wish to attend a university somewhere else are welcome to do so. It's a bit tricky, though. Since we aren't internationally recognized as a sovereign nation it complicates things when it comes to citizenship and visas. It can be done though."

"Like for Doctor Wantanabe," Drummond said.

"Why don't you ask her all this crap?" Kara

scraped the last of the stew from her bowl.

"I would, but..." Drummond trailed off, making a non-committal gesture with his hands.

Kara looked around the galley, noting how distinctly empty their table was compared to the others. "Oh," she said. "I see."

"Bit like starting over, eh?" Lambros said. "Don't worry too much about it. You're a good man. Even if you are a soulless American locust."

Drummond snorted into his bowl. "Thanks, Chief. You know how to cheer a guy up."

Kara felt a bit foolish now that she thought about it. On Voyager, Drummond had proven himself to the crew during the squall when he'd saved Goldi's life and helped them protect the ship. Of course, Goldi also encouraged the crew to give him a chance. Here, he was back to square one with the Mariners on the Penitent. They didn't know about his other deeds, and might not care if told. To them, he was an American politician. Certainly not a person to be trusted.

Kara gave him a playful tap with the back of her hand. "Come on. I thought you'd already be on the bridge, working your charm like you did on Voyager."

He made a rueful grunt. "That would imply I'm allowed on the bridge."

"Huh?" That took Kara back. "Wait, Captain Grayson isn't letting you on the bridge. At all?"

He looked reluctant to talk about it. "The captain said that if there was a conference call, I'd be told ahead of time and invited in. Otherwise, he said the room was cramped and he needed to keep his crew focused."

"Penitent's bridge is a bit tight," Kara admitted. "Still. How are you supposed to do your job?"

"He...had some thoughts on that as well." Drummond tapped his spoon against his bowl.

"Apparently, my job, according to the terms of our agreement, is to be a hostage. So. No wandering around into the bridge. Or engineering. Or the top deck, if the crew is busy. Pretty much, I'm to stay on this deck, where my quarters and the galley are. Don't worry about me, though. I won't be bored. I'm bunking with Tren."

"Until we reach the bunker, right?" Kara said.

Drummond shrugged. "He didn't say."

Before she could press him for more information, Chief Lambros slid her empty bowl forward. "I wonder. Kara, what sort of responsibilities are you taking up so far? I saw you topside more often than not today."

"Oh," she said absently. "It's all been pretty routine, actually. They're behind on some work since they lost Bilby. I looked through the weather and ecology reports for anomalies, checked in with engineering. Had some questions for Doctor Wantanabe, actually."

"And?" Chief Lambros said when Kara trailed off.

"I don't want to make anything of it, but now that you mention it, it did seem like Captain Grayson was much more interested in me catching up on all of that rather than gathering intel on our destination or coordinating our excursion with the Gallant."

"Maybe," Drummond said with a hopeful look, "Maybe he's easing you into the job. You know?"

Now that Kara had started talking to them about it, the sense of unease and isolation she'd felt the night before sank back in. "That's not how Mariners work. A Navigator should be effective their first day on board. Catching up on work, I get. But why keep me from working with the Gallant?"

"Maybe he wants to deal with Faulkner personally," Lambros offered. "There's something definitely untrustworthy about the man."

"Only something?" Drummond deadpanned. "That all?"

"Fair enough." Lambros made an attempt at a smile.

"That could be it," Kara said. Then, a seed of doubt planted itself. Hadn't she been noticing how much less hostile Grayson had been with Faulkner? If it was, as she thought, the result of the man's grief, wouldn't he be all too happy to pawn off dealing with the Faulkner on to Kara? Why else the change in behavior?

"Maybe you should spend some time in meditation. Clear your mind. Then come back to your thoughts," Lambros told her. "You might find you're more open to possibilities after that."

Easy for her to say. Kara didn't need to clear her head to see what was possible here.

There were possibilities, all right. She just didn't like them.

Grayson walked the perimeter of the submersible craft along with Lieutenant Tilden, his chief engineer. Commander Orozco stalked behind them. While the aft deck had enough room to carry it, the A-diver was still a strange sight on his ship. They'd only brought it aboard for the mission. Tilden traced features of the craft with a thin LED light, necessary in the full dark of night.

"Just as last reported, Skipper. She's in fine shape and ready to dive. It's the best of luck she didn't get punctured when we had that firefight." Tilden had a slight, short build, and the curious eyes most who took up engineering seemed to have.

"Luck," Grayson said. "Aye."

But it wasn't. He knew it, deep in the well of

his soul. Everything, absolutely everything since they took that fishing vessel had come together as if preordained. Why else would he have been given the intelligence about the wreck? Why else would dear Bilby have found the one bargaining chip they needed to get a thumb over Faulkner? How else could he explain the attack on Voyager, the tragic attacks, plural, that led to the ship getting recalled back to port?

There was no other way to explain it. Grayson had been shown a sign. Bright as Polaris, guiding the way. While the Mariner's sworn leaders did nothing to protect them, he was being shown the way to do it for them. If they wouldn't act to save their own people, fine. He didn't need them to.

"Ever piloted one of these, Skipper?" Tilden said.

"Aye," he said, taken from his ruminations. "Used to help pick apart wrecks as a young crewman. I still say this work would go faster if we took Voyager's A-Diver as well."

Tilden shrugged. "Might've been more trouble than it was worth, Skipper. Deck can hardly support this one. And if it's close-quarters down at the wreck site, they'd just get in each other's way. Besides, there's a chance Voyager might need it."

"There's also a chance that it could've made all the difference on the most important job we've done." Grayson's expression darkened, his words trailing off as if he wasn't speaking to her any longer.

Tilden and Orozco shared a glance. She cocked an eyebrow, then cleared her throat. "Captain, you asked about the hold size. I used the measurements you gave me. It's tight, but you could load four of whatever they are at a time. Might be better towing them on the outside if that's possible. Of course, that's without knowing what the cargo is, Skipper. If it's some kind of hazmat you'll want to check with

Chief Lambros. As a deckmaster, she'd be able to steer you right as to how to handle it. Could be you shouldn't squeeze them in together or tow them. I wouldn't know."

Grayson sharpened his words before he spoke them. "Why do you say that? What makes you think this is hazardous material we're talking about?"

"Well, I…" Tilden sputtered. "Uh, our destination, Skipper. We all know the mission. If there's dangerous material down there, I thought we might get charged with securing it."

He dialed down the intensity of his stare, but kept an eye on the engineer. "Right."

From behind them came Commander Orozco's gravelly tones. "Thank you, Lieutenant. You're dismissed."

As she quickly skittered away from the submersible, Captain Grayson went back to examining the vehicle.

"You think I was too harsh?" Grayson said in a clipped voice. "That it?"

Unfazed, Orozco approached, leading with his nose in that doglike way of his. "Don't matter what I think, Skipper."

Grayson tensed his jaw. "Just say it, man."

"You plan on going against the Admiral's word, you may want the crew's hearts with you as much as possible. That's all."

"And what is that supposed to mean, Commander?" Grayson turned fully toward his first officer, his sheer size towering over the man. "Do you have reason to believe they won't follow me, or have you already decided that you won't be helping me when it comes time to do the right thing for our people?"

Orozco craned his neck to look directly up and meet Grayson's eye. "You want your people to obey you, while you disobey your superior. Not an easy thing to pull off, Skipper. I'm your first officer. Supposed to advise you. This is advice."

Grayson could have snarled at the insolent little man. "How can you be so narrow minded, Orozco? So short-sighted? We let Admiral Kim and the Elect and the Council go on as they have, then we are going to be standing here with our dicks in our hands while all of our work is destroyed. Our water will be overfished, our crops will be wrecked, the waters will go oxygen dead like all those spots in the Atlantic. Mark me, within weeks we'll have landing parties on our shores laying claim to our islands. Our survival is at stake. What does it matter if I have to disobey the word of an ineffective coward?"

"Coward or no," Orozco said simply. "Wrong or right. He's still your admiral. Plan accordingly."

Captain Grayson spun on his heel and headed back to the bridge, gnashing his teeth all the way.

Chapter Fifteen: Arrival

"It is necessary and right that this government be given the broad powers it needs to protect this great nation. This is how we preserve individual freedom and protect law-abiding citizens."
Aiden Spencer, 53rd President of the United States of America

Normally, a Mariner tried to limit their attachment to material things. A habit ingrained in their culture. Little things mattered more because of it. Which was why Kara knew she shouldn't clean out any of the small drawers at the navigation station on the bridge. It wasn't hers to use permanently in any case. But as she'd been sitting there most of the day, opening a drawer or two was inevitable. Kara just made sure to be respectful of any personal possessions she came across. Bilby hadn't been gone long. His friends might still want to poke around and be reminded of him. By opening the drawers, she got a bit of a sense of him, too. The ticket stub from a kick-boxing match in Mexico—natural only, no augmented fighters competing. A printed pic, sun-bleached, of a blond and tanned Mariner girl with the marks of a sail-seamstress inked into her hands. In the next drawer down, a broken length of red string and a small medallion shaped like a hand with an eye in the palm.

"Weren't much for religion, Bilby," said Chief Fen. Kara gave a guilty start.

Fen's communication station sat next to the navigation station on the bridge. He leaned back slightly in his chair, pointing to the medallion. "It's called a hamza. His mum gave it to him. Now, she were properly religious. But Bilby used to say he was only Jew-*ish*. Still don't feel right, him being returned to the sea."

"Sorry." Kara gently slid the drawer shut. "I wasn't trying to pry. I was just...prying."

A wide grin split Fen's round face. Short black hair grew short from his round head. She caught a speck or two of gray mixed in.

"No worries," he said. "Bilby wouldn't have minded anyway. Good man. Sharp. Almost scary, like. Figured things out faster than a person has a right to. Damn good shipmate. You met him, didn't you? Over Skatch way?"

She bobbed her head. "Just the once. But it turned out to be a memorable night."

"Ah," Fen said. "Bilby told us you had that augmented programmer begging for mercy in record time."

"Tren?" Kara laughed. "He's harmless enough. Poor guy just wanted—"

"That's quite enough." Grayson's chill voice cut through their chatter.

Fen instantly clammed up and turned back to the communication station. "Right you are, Skipper."

"Skipper." Kara tried to catch the captain's eye.

Reluctantly, Grayson pulled himself from what he was doing. "Yes, Navigator?"

"It's about the destination. We're close enough now for radar and something's amiss."

"What did you find?" He said quickly.

"Well, it's what I don't see, Captain. There's no sign of any other ships in the area. By all accounts, Big Madrid should have beaten us here by at least a day. We know he wasn't on the ship we sank the other day. So, where is he? I'm concerned about an ambush."

"Oh," Grayson said. Some of the interest leaked out of his expression. "We can't get hung up on that. Big Madrid is a dock criminal. I'd love to see him skinned for what he did to us, believe that. As we've got work to do here, let's set that concern aside. He may have realized he was in over his head after you gave that other ship both guns. Might have tailed it."

"It's possible," Kara said. Although, given what she'd seen from Madrid, giving up didn't seem his style. Surely, Grayson could see that, too.

"Speaking of," the captain said. "I commend your gumption, blasting that ship the way you did. Given our standing orders about use of the railguns, I was a little surprised you did it. What did the Admiral have to say about it?"

"I could tell he wasn't thrilled. Especially when I had to report that it's possible Faulkner's crew saw. Still, not like I had much of a choice. Admiral Kim is reasonable."

"Oh?" Grayson said.

"I know how he comes across," Kara said. "I served under him when he was captain of the Water Lily. He really does have the Mariners' best interest at heart."

"Hmm." Another slip downward in interest from Grayson.

"Sir," she tried to hold his attention before he left. "I have some plans I put together for the excursion to the bunker. Of course, I wrote them with Voyager in mind. But, if you have a minute, I can go over them with you."

"No," Grayson said, although not unkindly. "Bilby drew up some extensive plans for us. We're using those, so no need. In fact, Doctor Wantanabe was asking this morning for your help cataloging storm activity. Something to do with phytoplankton. If you're caught up with the day's intel, look into that. Unless..." he paused.

"Yes?" Kara looked hopeful.

"Any new reports of incursions since the last two? Any more fishers or container ships?" he said, words bitter.

"No, sir. Nothing new today."

"Well." Grayson left it at that and went back to his command station.

Across the deck, the crew waited with a tense sense of anticipation. Like a drawn gun with a finger on the trigger, or a diver about to leap, something would happen soon. Kara stood at the bow, staying out of the deckhands' way. With elbows on the forward railing, she watched the land masses off to the starboard side of the ship. Dark black rock, ground smooth over millennia by glaciers. Towering walls of ice, once impenetrable, they had melted completely away by the time she was born. Left in their wake were these barren fields and clifftops, scraped down to the hardest rock.

In the waters off the coast, no sign of Big Madrid.

A small fishing boat trolled along the coast. The fisher-pilot knew well enough to steer clear of them. Could've been their larger size, or the fact that fishers tended to steer clear of Mariners. With one mittened hand on his tiller, he puttered ahead, his nets flapping in the breeze. Their reputation wasn't completely fair. Mariners had no issue with fishers like the man in his little boat. Large commercial ships that overfished and killed off entire species through greed—that was their problem.

Despite the late afternoon hour, the sun warmed her from above as though it were midday. Kara looked around at the land features, mentally checking their location again. Almost there. And yet, no signs of any ships that would be capable of an underwater salvage or extraction. Where was he?

"No sign of him?" Chief Lambros caught up to Kara at the railing.

"Doesn't make any sense," Kara said. "Why go through all he's gone through just to give up now? He's still planning something. We can't let our guard down."

"You tell the skipper this?"

Kara made a soft grunt.

"Sounds like that went well," Chief Lambros deadpanned. "Could be he's preoccupied with the excursion. God knows the deck crew have been on knife's edge about the whole thing."

"Why?" Kara cocked an eyebrow. "I mean, I get that this is a sensitive mission. But for a seasoned deck crew, what's the problem? We get there, you make ready the submersible and bust out the gantry. It's work, sure. These Mariners must have done it a hundred times, though."

"I gave them similar reassurances this morning. None of them have said it outright, but my impression is that they're all worried about upsetting the captain. After some gentle questions, it seems as though his mood has been growing darker for some time."

Kara took a second to think back on her first meeting with Grayson. He had seemed a much different person then, even though it wasn't that long ago. Back in Skatch he had been roguish, boisterous, even.

"At first," the chief went on, "I assumed he must be feeling the pressures of the mission. You of all people know what that's like. When I probed a little deeper, though, it seems his attitude has been changing for some time. Even before this mission and the deaths of his crew. You heard about the scrape they had with a fishing vessel?"

"Oh, right." Kara had almost forgotten about it. That report had come right before they'd intercepted the Gallant at the start of this whole mess. "You hear something about that?"

"Not in detail. What I did hear suggests that Captain Grayson may have been impatient, and quick to violence. Which isn't how he's operated, historically. That's all I could find out without damaging trust."

"Hmm." Kara sucked her teeth. "He's had a reputation as a bit of a maverick, true. Nothing that would suggest he'd break peace without real cause. If it's true, then..."

"This change in attitude isn't sudden and can't be attributed to grief or mission stress alone."

They stood in silence for a moment, listening to the waves and the scattered cries of gulls along the far away shore. Kara raised a hand and pointed out Gallant's tall, narrow profile as she made to come up alongside them. While they watched the approach, a deck speaker crackled to life with a short announcement from Chief Fen that they had reached their destination.

Chief Lambros bumped her shoulder against Kara's. "You come up here to brood, or are you avoiding the bridge?"

"Both." Kara snorted. "Actually, I'm saving a spot for Tren and Drummond. They're allowed to come up once we reach the excursion site. Captain says that Faulkner is supposed to be able to see Drummond once he gets here. It's part of the whole 'hostage' part of the agreement. Proof of life. Make sure his congressman is unharmed."

"That's only going to disappoint him, trust me," Drummond said. Grinning, he strolled over with Tren at his side. They both sucked in the fresh air.

"I can't believe we're in the arctic!" Tren said. "The sun won't set until almost midnight tonight, isn't that amazing? I've never been this far north. I thought it would be colder. Well, it is summer, I suppose. Does the temperature drop much at night, Kara? What's the solar forecast, will we see any Aurora Borealis? I've always wanted to see that! How cold is the water? I've heard that when people fall in, they drown because their muscles lock up, not because they can't swim. Is that true? Or is that only in winter? Are there really polar bears left, or was that a hoax?"

"Well," Kara said with a helpless expression. "Where, exactly, would you like me to begin, Tren?"

Drummond let out a throaty laugh.

"I better get back to it." Chief Lambros motioned with her head to the bridge, where the Captain stepped out on deck. She moved over to her crew and began directing them to unstrap the submersible and ready the gantry. In the meantime, two deckhands secured a ladder to the starboard railing. Kara looked over and spotted a sleek white dinghy that must've come from the Gallant. Faulkner, his tech man Glen, and one other sailor worked at tying their boat lines to the Penitent.

"Think they're going to launch the A-diver today?"

Drummond asked her.

Kara watched the gantry being swung over the submersible. "Looks like it. I haven't exactly been kept in the loop though."

Climbing up the ladder from the port side, Captain Faulkner and his team made their way on deck. The junior sailor traveling with them boarded first and helped Faulkner with the last couple of steps.

"Looks like it's my time to shine." With a grand flourish, Drummond waved to Faulkner, who gave him a simple nod in return. Drummond slumped with mock exhaustion. "God, I'm glad that's over. Well, mission accomplished, everyone. I've done my part."

"Quiet," Kara said. "Captain's about to speak."

Standing mid-deck, Captain Grayson had finished greeting the new arrivals. He motioned for silence, then brought a radio up to his mouth. All the ship's speakers chirped to life.

"Mariners, guests. Thank you for your determination so far. We've arrived at our destination." There was some scattered cheering, but the skipper bulldozed right over it. "Our mission is far from over. We still have much to do. In fact, now may be when the work really begins. In more ways than one. Today, we will embark on an excursion to scout the area. Beginning tomorrow morning, we will start our operations in earnest. The scouting team will consist of myself, Captain Faulkner, and Lieutenant Grant. Given the sensitivity of what's down there, our agreement with the U.S. team is to limit the personnel going down to the site to essential hands only. Thank you for your dedication."

Grayson cut the radio and went back to supervising the prep of the submersible.

"This is insane," Kara muttered. She hurried over to Captain Grayson, stepping around and squeezing between people on the crowded deck.

"Captain," she called out. Grayson paused. Kara saw a flutter of irritation cross his face. Still, she steadied herself to face him. "Sir, this is incredibly risky. If something happens down there, it could have a serious impact to the chain of command. Please, send someone else. I'm the navigator, this should be my responsibility."

Kara trailed off at the end of her pitch. Grayson's eyes bored holes straight through her. Mariners took notice, giving them a wide berth.

"You mean to tell me," he said soft and deadly, "what I can do on my own ship? Is that it, Lieutenant? You give the orders now?"

"No." She tried to diffuse his anger with a lighter voice. "Sir, of course not. This is standard procedure, that's all. I'm thinking about the ship."

"And I'm not?" Grayson let a bit of silence follow his words. "Everything I do is for this ship, and for our people, Lieutenant. Never forget that. If I'm not following ordinary procedure, it's because this is not an ordinary mission and these are not ordinary times. Now, get back to your regular duties, Navigator."

As he swept away to the aft deck and the submersible, Kara stood in the same spot, stunned. A zone of dead space followed the Captain as he went, a roughly circular area in which no Mariners dared walk.

Drummond appeared at her side, Tren in tow. "Back home," Drummond said, "one of the ways people in government hide their grifts is through compartmentalization. If the left hand doesn't know what the right is doing, then neither hand can snitch on the other when they dip into the community chest."

"That's not what's happening here," Kara said, but couldn't find the conviction to put to her words.

Drummond didn't respond. She mulled over what he said, despite her protests. Grayson may be moody, or going through a dark spot that he was taking out on the crew. Losing his touch, even. But that didn't make him corrupt, or indicate something shady was going on. Mariner captains were better than that.

Weren't they?

Chapter Sixteen:
Big Moves

"[...] so we left them to themselves. To their culture of intrigue, lies, and blood-thirst."
James Keeling, Reborn at Sea: Mariner History 2041-2063

Where, exactly, in the ice-cold hell were they now?

As far as Big Madrid knew, which is what the bloody captain chose to tell him, they could be next door to Father Christmas. The man, who Big was paying (well, Nakamura was paying him, but never mind semantics), could be excruciatingly tight lipped about these things. Why-oh-bloody-why had they arrived at their blessed coordinates, begun readying to drop down for some delectable deep-sea treasure, then suddenly pissed off without so much as a word to their employer?

The matter burned Big Madrid something fierce, as he was wont to tell anyone who would give him the time of day to listen. Which meant Gill and the freshly healing Gary, of course. Stunning conversationalists though they were, Big Madrid still hadn't gotten any closer to answers.

Finally. Finally he had an open link to some real information since the crew of the DCV Verne had seen fit to stonewall him. Standing once again in his favorite waterborne conference room, Big Madrid turned his eye-lined and metal-toothed visage to the central display.

"Where is this, then?" he said to Nakamura.

"It's called Lopp Lagoon," Nakamura told him. "You're on the inland side of it now."

Nakamura spoke in a distracted manner, as if something else held his attention. From behind Big, the hatch to the room opened, and Mister Grint let himself in. The stocky, gray-haired steward glided in, a short towel draped over his left arm.

"Excuse me," Big Madrid flicked the annoyed words over his shoulder. "Private conversation."

"Don't worry about Mister Grint," Nakamura said quickly. "He's here to help you get squared away after the call. Listen, Big, buddy, we've had some developments and that's why you're parked where you are. Vasco sent their support ship over to catch up with the Mariners. Bad times. Bad times. We had some video feed make it over to us. Long and short of it? Looks like you and I were wrong about the Mariners. Their ships have some sort of, what are they calling it? Rail guns? No idea. I'm not a gun guy. Anyway, the support ship got shredded like cabbage, so we're down another troop and in a lot more debt to Vasco."

"Well, that's..." Big Madrid rarely found himself at a loss for words. "Right. A big man can admit when he's wrong, and I'm Big-bleeding-Madrid after all. Listen, partner, we got the wrong end of it. We can still salvage this salvage, am I right? We're already in place. The shipsies don't know we're here. We can sneak up on them, can't we?"

Nakamura didn't look convinced.

"No, no, listen, we sweep in, middle of the night, right? Me, Gill, Gary, and any sailors on this ship with minerals in their jockeys, we board their ships and take what's ours, right?"

Sweat beaded on Big's forehead.

Nakamura let him stew for a moment, the man's attention wandering over to something offscreen again. It sounded like he was tapping something out on a keyboard.

"Sure, that sounds great, buddy," he said.

"Really?" Big Madrid's brow furrowed.

"Of course!" Nakamura's full attention was back to Big Madrid. "Tell you what. We still need you to stay put for bit, because I think we can build on your plan. Make it even better. Get you the tools you need to succeed. Only this is going to take a bit more planning, so I'll need you to work with Mister Grint, okay? He's got my full trust on this. Now, I've gotta run, but thank you so much for being patient, all right? I know this was frustrating, but good things are ahead."

"Excellent, sir, I think so, too..." Big started, but Nakamura had already signed off.

The display screen flipped back to black. Big Madrid stared at the empty display, a deep sense of dread setting alarms off in his head.

"If you're ready, sir," Mister Grint said in that dolorous voice of his.

Big caught sight of the steward's reflection in the glare of the display. A flicker of motion caught Big's eye. He froze for a second, willing himself to see it again. A flutter of the tea towel, caused by the air rushing through the room's vents. It wasn't just the towel moving, though. Something narrow, something hard, it hid behind the towel draped over Mister Grint's left arm.

Cheeky, cheeky bastard.

For a man like Big, to whom promises came and went with the tide, the betrayal was of no consequence, really. Survival instincts, which had served him well, kicked in, mandating that he pay no mind to what lay beyond the room where he could possibly take his last breaths.

Smoothly, he turned around, fixing on his most congenial face. "You know what, Grinty? I owe you an apology."

"Oh," the man said.

Suddenly, the few steps between the men may as well have been a chasm. How could Big possibly cover that distance before Grint fired? How could he possibly keep the steward from noticing if got too close?

As a wise street magician once told a cockney street rat, *misdirection.*

Big slumped his shoulders and made an overly large swing of the thumb back toward the display. As planned, Grint's eyes flicked up to Big's thumb, giving him leave for the smallest of steps forward. He covered the motion by leaning into the room's table to take a pen from a cup in the middle.

"Great man, that Nakamura," Big said as he rolled off the table casually, closing a little more ground. "I know I've been a bit of an arsehole, I can own up to that. I'm sorry, Mister Grint. You've got Nakamura's confidence. That should've been enough for me. Oh, wait a sec."

Covering another slide forward, Big leaned back into the table to snatch a notepad. Holding the notepad between thumb and forefinger, he hid the pen now curled in his left hand, the point facing down.

Big sighed. His next expression was earnestness. He waved a finger with his right as he made his point. "You know, back in Skatch, I'm something of a fixture. Well known for competence, you could say. Truth is, I've never done this kind of work before. You know, being on the sea. Always work the land side of these deals. Well, seems I have feet of clay after all. Didn't think it would be this difficult, you know? But here we are. I fear I've disappointed Mister Nakamura, after all the man has done for me. But I won't let him down this time, Grinty.

"Suppose what I'm saying," Big went on, "is I'm in new territory. Should've been more accommodating to you, as you're only trying to help. Well, I want to get started, Grinty. Let's win this one for the team, yeah?"

Big, now a single step away from Mister Grint, held out his right hand for a shake.

Mister Grint opened his mouth, but didn't extend his own hand.

That was all Big needed. With his enhanced reflexes, he could move his whole arm as fast as Grint could squeeze a finger. In a single moment, he thrust his body to the right and forward, bringing his left fist up, letting the notepad flutter away. A sharp crack, like a thick plank breaking in two, burst from behind Grint's tea towel. Raw heat blasted across the left side of Big's stomach. He kept his left fist moving, the tip of the pen now connecting perfectly with Grint's temple.

A moist snap vibrated through Big's fist. He pushed them both to the ground, Grint's body spasming in great convulsions. Big Madrid thrust the pen in deeper, deeper into Grint's brain.

"Die, you sodding bastard," Big whispered.

Grint stopped kicking.

Only then did Big notice the spatter of blood

running down his own face. Stupidly, he touched it, realizing he had smeared it around more. Untangling Grint's tea towel from behind his knee, Big used it to wipe off some of the blood. The scorched fibers scratched his skin.

Pausing to pick up Grint's discarded pistol, Big stood up straight and checked himself for wounds. A bit of the faux fur on the left of his stole was singed.

"Bastard!" Big said to the dead man. He stopped short of kicking the corpse, his instincts telling him that all was not rosy, yet.

Surveying the situation, Big realized this to be true. The crew worked for Nakamura, just like Grint. Grint had tried to kill him, presumably for Nakamura. They were out in the middle of the blasted Arctic Circle for all he knew, with no way back to civilization. Even with his mercenaries, they'd have no chance of taking the ship. The bridge was a fortress, locked at all times. They could shoot their way in the second someone opened the door, sure, but the crew would just lock them out of the controls.

He made a frustrated noise, then found the control box for the display. Big dialed up Gary's room and the mercenary answered.

"Big?" he said. "Where are you? Why isn't your video on?"

"Never mind that, my friend." Big put a load of false cheer in his voice. "We've got big things to plan, we do. Be a lamb, grab Gill and meet me and Mister Grint in the orange conference room."

Good, he thought as he hung up. If the numpties on the bridge were keeping watch on the ship's communications, they'd think Grint hadn't done the deed yet.

Big's calculations led him to his next move. One he didn't like. Not one bit. Looking back at the body of Mister Grint, however, gave Big the resolve he was lacking. Taking the phone from his pocket, Big connected with the ship's network and went through all of his standard masking routines. Taking a breath, he found an address and entered it.

After a few moments, the call was accepted.

On the other side of the call, a clean white conference room dotted with plush furniture and a narrow black table winked into view.

"Can't say I'm not surprised to hear from you," Captain Faulkner said. With a curious knot in between his brows, Faulkner lifted himself off his seat as if getting a closer look at Big Madrid. "Oh, my. Someone's in a pickle, aren't they?"

"Never mind that," Madrid said. "You're a shrewd one, so I suppose we can dispense with the apologies? I've got a proposition for you."

Chapter Seventeen:
An Attempt

"This new alliance, this partnership of freedom, with our former adversaries in the Russian Federation will strengthen America in the new age to come as we rebuild in the aftermath of this failed insurrection."
Aiden Spencer, 53rd President of the United States of America

An A-Type submersible, also called an A-diver, came equipped with grabbing and cutting appendages with fine motor control, had an extendible soft airlock, and could provide up to four hours of breathable air with four people inside. Kara knew this, as the Mariners only owned a few of them, one of which had been with Voyager. Eager to know every inch of that new equipment, she'd committed those facts to memory, among others. With her understanding of the environmental tolerances, Captains Grayson and Faulkner must have been close to dizzy by the time they emerged from underwater and called for the crew to bring them back on board.

Even though she stood present as they returned

and disembarked from the craft, the captain gave her no opportunity to speak with him again before he bid the American officers farewell and stomped off to his cabin. Kara had watched until Faulkner's team left on their dinghy before turning in herself.

She wouldn't be thwarted this morning, however. Kara rose early and waited by the one piece of equipment she was positive the captain would eventually make his way back to.

"Don't touch that." Unfortunately, she also had to bring Tren with her.

"I was only looking." Tren stood on his tip-toes to try and look through the fore porthole on the submersible. "They really go deep underwater in that?"

"Deep is relative," Kara said. "There's a shoal right next to us. Around the area the depth could change from as shallow as four fathoms then drop off down to twenty-one. It will make finding this bunker even more difficult. Obviously, it would be easier to place such a structure in shallower water. That would also make it easier to find, though."

"How deep is a fathom?" Tren asked.

"Two meters-ish. Hang on, here comes the captain."

She stood taller, ensuring he couldn't pretend to not see her. Tren seemed to melt behind her. He'd protested when she'd asked him to come with her, not wanting to stir up trouble for himself.

Grayson rubbed his hands together in the cool morning air. He spotted Kara immediately, but resigned himself to speaking with her. "Lieutenant," he said simply.

"Sir." Kara had thought about what strategy to take when she did catch him. She opted for simple and straightforward. "I have an idea as to how we can improve our defenses. It may be possible that

Big Madrid isn't a concern anymore. That doesn't mean that anyone else the Ionova brothers sold this location to won't pop up. We need to be ready."

He watched her. Mostly unreadable. "Go on."

"Back on Voyager, Tren reprogrammed one of our swimmers. Instead of observing ecology, it could also patrol around the ship and watch for intruders, alerting us if anything out of the ordinary occurred. Especially intruders approaching from underwater. You heard my report about TXM. If other companies with deep pockets think they know what we're sitting on here..."

Captain Grayson raised a hand to steady her. He took a great breath in and watched the waves for a few seconds. "How long will this process take? What guarantees do we have that he won't interfere with our other ship systems?"

Kara looked over her shoulder at Tren, who slunk into view.

"Depends," Tren said. "Since I've done it once before, I can write the code faster this time. Couple hours to a day, I guess. As for guarantees, I dunno." When Kara shot him a look he went on the defensive. "I'm being honest! Last time you had Goldi watch me. Guess that's about the best you can do, right? Unless you have any other programmers on board who can review my work?"

A spark of inspiration came into Grayson's eye. "Yes. Yes. Now that you've explained it properly, I see the benefit. I want this done immediately. In fact, Lieutenant, you'll supervise Tren personally. I won't trust anyone else to do it. Make this your top priority and report back when the swimmer is in the water."

Captain Grayson didn't wait for any sort of response before continuing on to the bridge. Kara stood, almost stunned, while Tren nattered on about where he was going to set up a workstation. How was it possible, she wondered, that she could get what she wanted and still somehow lose? Of course she wanted the swimmer operational. But it couldn't have been more obvious that Grayson didn't care about the early warning system. He just wanted Kara out of his hair.

Why?

At least the searching portion of this excursion was done and over with. Grayson deftly piloted the submersible deeper under the water. Past four and a half fathoms, they crossed the continental shelf that separated the shoal from the real depths. Their intense spotlight illuminated the sheer cliff face in front of the submersible as it sank down.

It had taken hours to find the damn place the night before. Hours of sniping comments from Faulkner, inane suggestions from his toady, Grant. Hours of smelling their farts and enduring their ceaseless speculation. Never did he lose faith, though. He knew that he'd be the one to spot it. So it was.

Pumps hummed as water rushed into the submersible's tubes, increasing her weight kilo by kilo. Seeing the depth move to ten fathoms, and the pressure move to two atmospheres, he slowed their descent. Their vessel was well within its tolerances. Two atmospheres of pressure would do nothing to a craft designed to operate at thirty. No, the brilliance of where this bunker lay hidden wasn't in its depth. After all, at some point it became impractical to put the storage deeper. Getting weapons and personnel in and out would be a logistical nightmare.

This? Not too deep. But very well hidden.

Crews must have carved a hole right into the side of the shelf, or else made use of a preexisting one.

Either way, ships could sail overhead for the rest of time and never notice this place. They had, in fact. The builders went to great lengths to camouflage it, despite how out of the way it was. Bright lights washed over kelp and sea grass that gave way to red algae growing in tufts and spots along the rocky wall. The shelf took a bit of an inward turn, the spotty foliage waving off like curtains.

Grayson, however, wasn't fooled by the bunker's concealment for long. Unlike passersby, he had set out to find the bunker, coming armed with metal detection equipment and radar in his vessel, which had been built specifically to find shipwrecks.

Placing his right hand on the claw control, Grayson slowly maneuvered them forward. It felt good to be at a helm again, in a way. After years of command he forgot how simple and thrilling it could be.

"Easy does it," Faulkner said.

Grayson resisted the urge to reach back and slap Faulkner's narrow face. It wasn't easy.

Brushing aside a length of fake kelp, Grayson brought them directly in front of a large, circular door. A much larger submersible than their own could have fit through. One of those incredible submarines the richest navies had could make its way inside, dock, and conduct their underwater business.

"Holding position," Grayson said. "Now, let's get inside the damn thing."

Grant shuffled a thin tablet on his lap. "Working on it. Signal received. Give me some time."

"How did you realize this was the entrance?" Faulkner said. For once he asked a genuine question instead of a cleverly disguised insult.

"Kelp." Grayson flicked his chin toward the ship's monitor. "Green kelp can grow this deep, but it won't flourish. Not enough sun. Long strands like that are near impossible."

"Huh." Faulkner made an impressed sound and settled back into his seat. "I'll be damned."

"I only dabble," Chief Fen said. He squinted at the code streaming across Tren's workstation, looking suitably impressed. "Can't wrap my head around a single thing you're doing though, mate."

"Oh." Tren perked up. "I'd be happy to walk you through it."

"Er," Fen said. "Maybe some other time, eh? You've got enough to be getting on with."

Kara smirked as Fen drew over a thin chair and took a seat next to them. Overall, Kara liked the guy. Easy smile, fun to talk to. Given the tense climate on the Penitent he was a refreshing change.

"Where's your American congressman at, eh? Thought he'd be palling around with you two, as usual."

"He's not allowed off the passenger deck." Kara did her best to keep her tone even. "Captain's orders."

"Ah." Fen tilted his chair back with a knowing tilt of his head. "Well, it's not forever, is it? Seems a decent chap. Hope he's not too put out by it."

"Gotta admit, I'm surprised you're so easy going about him. Took him saving a deckhand's life to get the crew on the Voyager to stop hating him on principle."

"Well, as you may have noticed from my cultured and melodious dialect, I'm not born into the blood. Nor was I adopted. I asked The Question and became one of the blood and heart of my own sweet accord. As such, I completely understand why we hate the yanks as we do, but it's not as intensely personal. Know what I mean?"

"I can see that. It took me a bit to start trusting him. As much as it pains me to say it, I think he's throwing straight dice with us. Just wish I could get the skipper to see it." Kara tossed a glance over to Tren, but the man was completely lost in what he was doing. She'd most likely have to poke him a few times if she needed his attention.

"Ah, the skipper." Fen's voice took an apologetic tone. "Actually, that's why I came down to find you. Heard you were on a, er, supervisory assignment. This, right after the row you had with him yesterday. Look, I don't want you thinking this is what Captain Grayson is usually like. He's a damn good leader."

The Navigator in Kara lifted its head. "What's he usually like?"

"Cares about his crew. Truly. Give you the shirt off his back if you were cold. That's the God's honest. You get into a brawl at a dockside pub? Well, the skipper would stand back to back with you and swing with the best of them. Then, when you get back to the ship, that's when he'd call you to task. Fair, he is. Spent his whole life dedicated to the Mariners. As true a believer as they come."

Kara put a couple of pieces together. "He brought you in."

"Right in one." Fen smiled his huge smile again. "Pulled me from a wreck off the southern horn of Africa. Damned cheap corporation I sailed for cut every corner they could find on their ship maintenance. As we went down, even the damn emergency radio broke. If not for him, well. A few days aboard with the Mariners, I felt more like my own man than ever before in my life. You know how it is."

"I do." Kara felt a warmth inside her. Thoughts of her mother's face buoyed it along.

My ship needs an experienced cat wrangler. God

help me, but I can't find a one worth their salt.

"With all that's happened"—Fen's words snapped Kara back to the room—"it's understandable the skipper would show some cracks, eh? That's why we're giving him his space."

She could read between the lines well enough: He's our captain, cut him some slack. He's earned it.

"I get it," Kara said. "On Voyager, we lost six of our blood. Including our skipper and first officer. I admit, when I took command I found it to be more trying than I expected. My temper may have been...a little short."

Tren snorted.

"Quiet, you. I guess you are still with us? Anyway, this mission has been beyond stressful enough as it is. I won't add it to if can avoid it. Fair?"

"Don't misunderstand me," Fen said. "Do what you believe is best for the ship and crew. I only wanted to give you the other side of things, yeah? That night, Jesus, that night when we got attacked, it was...See, I think the skipper took Bilby's death extra hard. Not just 'cause they were mates, see, but it came at the worst time. As if these things come at good times."

"What do you mean?"

"Well..." Fen looked around. "Don't go spreading it around or nothing, but Captain Grayson and Bilby, they'd been arguing something fierce that day. Then all that happened. I think the skipper blames himself for what happened."

"Why? I mean, I can understand how leaving things on bad terms would hurt. Absolutely. How would he figure any of that was his fault, though?"

Fen shook his head sadly. "Timing, is why. They had this row on the bridge. I couldn't tell what it was about, they were speaking in generalities, you know? Next thing I know, Grayson up and orders

Bilby off the bridge in a big huff. So, Bilby storms out, slamming the hatch behind him and all."

"Oh, no," Kara said. "Don't tell me."

"Right in one. That's exactly when that spliced-up locust snuck his way on board. Some crew shouted an alarm, but it was too late. Bilby's was the first throat to get cut."

Every bit of sympathy Kara showed was genuine. Still, beneath the waves of pain she shared with Fen, a new question nibbled at her from below.

What had they been arguing about?

Grayson checked the time. Again. Checked the O2 gauge. Again. Unnecessary chatter would only use up their breathable air faster, so he refrained from asking Grant the burning question on his mind:

What the hell was taking so long?

For as impatient a man as Faulkner normally was, he could be surprisingly still. It seemed the man was full of surprises today. His only concession to boredom was the occasional fiddling around with the seat restraints. Other than that, he was about as busy as a barnacle.

"Got it," Grant said.

"Thank God," Grayson breathed.

Faulkner gestured to the row of displays ahead of them. The monitors showed the front camera, side views, and rear camera. Absolutely nothing happened on any of them. "Slow down, Grant, how will I ever keep pace with all this progress?"

Grant grimaced. "I meant that I found the door control code. At least, I think it is. Give me a second, I'm trying to run an opening routine."

Grayson shot upright. On the central display, a halo of water quickly burst from the perimeter of the door. Its two sides slowly split down the middle. Surprisingly, the audio sensors picked up very little vibration from the movements.

"That's ominous," Faulkner said.

He wasn't wrong. Grayson adjusted the ship's depth, moving their search light to point directly into the open portal. The light disappeared into what looked like a long tunnel with a definite end. It squared up with his submarine theory.

"That's it?" Grant said, his head poking around to look at the display.

"No." Grayson readied the thrusters. "I'll take us in, then we'll need to rise until we reach an inner dock. Air pressure and locks will keep the water from flooding in."

"Right." Grant's face looked paler than it had.

Grayson eyed the young sailor. "What's wrong?"

"Uh, nothing, Captain. Only, I haven't found anything for dock controls, yet."

"Let's go in and see what we're dealing with," Faulkner said reasonably. "If it takes poor Grant here another two hours to find the dock control, then so be it. No good sitting out here, though."

"Agreed." Grayson eased on the forward thrusters and brought them in.

While their small submersible had room to maneuver a bit, it would've been a hell of a squeeze for a submarine. Then again, everything involving submarines was a tight fit. When entering the place legally there was probably some sort of auto docking feature to guide the vessels in.

The side and rear monitors darkened. As Grayson brought her inside, even the meager light from outside got snuffed out. On the rear display, the ring of blue-green light that was the entrance grew smaller. Every animal instinct screamed and assaulted him with a sudden bout of claustrophobia. Sweat leaked from his palms as he gripped the controls tighter.

He took them forward.

"Okay," Grant said. "I'm still looking for any sort of docking protocol, but—"

Flashing red light filled the tunnel. All three men froze.

"Grant," Faulkner said. "What did you do?"

"Nothing! I mean, I haven't run a single command yet!"

Swiftly, Grayson pointed a camera up. He could see the crest of the water! Just above them! But through the red light, he saw oblong shapes appear overhead. Bubbles erupted from up top.

Grayson didn't have time to swear. With the instincts of a seasoned wrecker pilot, he flipped the thrusters into reverse and gunned it. Faulkner and Grant cried out in surprise, but Grayson paid them no mind.

The vessel fishtailed a little, veering dangerously close to the tunnel wall. Moving backward at full speed, Grayson had to keep his eye on the rear camera. As he feared, the two doors were already closing. With a quick glance to the forward camera, he caught the two bubbling streaks heading right toward them.

"Watch it!" Faulkner yelled.

Grayson let them veer too far to port. Tunnel wall scraped dangerously close to the backside of the submersible. A quick, angry squeal sounded through the cabin as they bounced off. Struggling to regain control, the submersible spun completely around in a hundred and eighty degree turn. Instinctively, Grayson twisted the thrusters.

One of the small torpedoes pegged the wall where they had scraped by only seconds before. A shockwave from the blast tipped the submersible again, threatening to send them out of control once more.

Up ahead, the doors were more than halfway closed now. The second torpedo gained on them. Grayson added extra thruster, and gunned it harder. Even as they sped forward, the doors threatened to clamp down and wreck the vessel completely. At the last second, eyeballing the distance, Grayson twisted the craft on its axis, shooting sideways through the closing portal.

Blue-green light expanded around them as they burst past the fake kelp.

A dull thud rolled through the water. It came from the direction of the doors, which sealed shut again.

As the vessel slowed, both Grayson and Faulkner twisted in their seats to stare at Grant.

Sweat rolled freely down his reddened face. "Sorry?"

No, it wasn't usual to have a christening or a sendoff when launching a swimmer. Since absolutely nothing about this voyage had been normal so far, Kara figured what was the harm in a little more strangeness. At least this oddity didn't have any violence attached to it.

Tren held the swimmer in both arms. This model had been molded to look like a Pacific Halibut. Large, round, flat and brown. The man stared at it almost lovingly.

"And now we...?" Drummond didn't finish the question. He stood, hands in pockets, giving unsure looks to both Kara and Chief Lambros. They had nothing to add at the moment. Behind them, Doctor Wantanabe looked through her glasses at the horizon.

"Still so bright. I never get used to these polar seasons, no matter how many times I come here."

She stepped carefully over the deck to stand next to Tren. Despite him not being a large man by any means, Doctor Wantanabe only came up to his shoulder. "You ready to send him off?"

"Him?" Kara said.

"Yes, him." Tren came off a little indignant. "Harry Halibut."

Drummond coughed rather conspicuously. "I thought scientists needed to remain detached and impartial to their subjects?"

"Detached?" the doctor said. "If this thing keeps another mercenary from creeping onto this ship, I'll marry it. Forget detached. That was the scariest night of my goddamn life. Launch it, Tren."

Tren made a solemn face. "Farewell, young Harry. Godspeed!"

Harry Halibut landed with an anticlimactic splash. They all watched the waves for a moment, as if expecting the swimmer to surface and say a proper goodbye. In that respect, Harry left them disappointed. At last, Doctor Wantanabe broke the spell.

"What other possibilities can you see with this sort of targeted behavior programming?"

"Doctor," Tren said seriously, "What can't we do is the question. Now, let's say for example you are studying your phytoplankton. Not entirely sure what that is? Is it dangerous? Regardless. We can condition Harry to specifically follow any that he sees rather than just doing a general search as he has been. I also have a way of extending his search range by stacking communication relays with other swimmers."

As both the doctor and Tren headed below decks, Drummond stepped closer to Kara and Chief Lambros. "Better her than me," he said. "I bet they're headed to the galley. Too bad, I'm hungry."

Chief Lambros nudged him with her elbow. "Come on, I'll go with you. I can bore you with more tales of the Core while they talk about robofish. Coming, Kara?"

She looked toward the aft deck and the submersible. Engineering mates scrambled over every inch of its surface, looking for damage and making repairs. Apparently there was some kind of incident today. An incident Kara had been kept completely unaware of.

"Not yet," Kara said. "I have to note the swimmer's launch in the ship's log. It's not glamorous, but it's honest work."

Chief Lambros gave her an appraising smirk. "Funny."

"Meh," Drummond added. "What? I've heard better jokes. Even from her."

Kara showed him a hand sign even non-Mariners understood. Their laughter followed them as they disappeared below decks. She walked across the deck in no particular hurry, watching the buzz around the submersible. At first glance she couldn't see anything wrong with it. But with craft that had to dive, the damage you didn't see could be the most deadly. A hairline crack that gets missed in an inspection could be what springs a leak when you get to more than a few atmospheres of pressure.

Like most of the crew, the engineering mates stuck to their work and didn't dawdle. Even though her conversation with Fen had shown her that Captain Grayson had better days with his people, there was no denying that his crew was terrified of him now. Most of them would occasionally cast quick glances over at the bridge. No doubt checking to see if the Captain's face appeared in one of the high portholes, keeping a watchful eye on their group.

But he hadn't. Something else kept him occupied.

Kara approached the bridge at that same slow pace. Since none of the deck crew were talking much, voices echoed out from an open porthole.

"None of us had any clue," that sounded like Faulkner. "How could we? Not like we can drop by and ask what sort of defenses they have active."

"If I hadn't gotten us out of there, we'd've been blast to pieces, still locked in that damn chamber!"

Oh, Kara thought. *Definitely Grayson.*

"Yes, yes, and what a hero pilot you were," Faulkner said. "Let's focus on what's in front of us, gentlemen, please? How do we penetrate these defenses? We've come too far to quit."

Kara couldn't stand there and listen, one of the engineering crew working on the A-diver would certainly notice her. So she settled for walking nice and slow, trying to drink in as much of the conversation as possible before she entered the bridge.

"It's not that simple. I expected the software in the facility to be less advanced than it is. There's some kind of overarching security mechanism. Getting the door open is one thing." That sounded like Grant. Although he was missing that edge of self-satisfaction his voice normally carried. Must have been a bad day.

Kara stood only steps away from the door. *Come on,* she thought. *Give me something to work with here!*

"The locking and opening protocol is being monitored somehow, and I can't figure it out. I need more time, but the only way I can connect to their systems is to get next to the door like we have been. The range of their acoustic signal receiver is too short to do it from the surface."

Kara stepped up to the bridge's hatch, as slowly as she reasonably could.

"We aren't going to be stopped by a computer problem!" Grayson thundered.

The hatch flung open. Kara stood, lamely, only a step away from the entrance. Grayson's bulk filled the portal. His burning eyes zeroed in on her. Kara's thoughts kicked into high gear. She hadn't heard anything incriminating. Not that she recognized as incriminating. Obviously, Grayson felt differently. She only had one way to play it.

Kara stepped up to the open hatch, a wan smile on her face. "Evening, Skipper. You heading out? I was going in. Unless you need the bridge, of course. I can come back."

"How long were you out here?"

"Just got here, Captain." Kara flicked a chin to the open porthole. "Sure you're not busy? I heard talking as I walked up."

"Did you?" Grayson left it at that.

"Sure." She shrugged as if it were the least important thing in the world. "I only came by to log the swimmer launch before I forget."

Wordlessly, Grayson stepped to one side.

Not good, Kara thought.

If she had any sense, she'd get far away from this man. She had no idea what secret she was supposed to have stumbled on, but Grayson had the look of a man who could chew rocks and spit fire.

As she stepped inside the musty bridge, she noticed only Grayson's inner circle from the submersible were present. He swung the hatch shut.

Don't break character. Not now.

Countless hours of training kicked in. Practicing faces in the mirror, conditioning herself not to give away any tells. These were the greatest tools a Navigator had when working with people. She never thought she'd need it against a superior officer.

"You should see what Tren's done with that

swimmer," she nattered on. Kara made for her station and pulled up the log page. As she tapped her keys, she worked fast to keep from showing how her fingers shook.

From the corner of her eye she saw Grayson touched his gun holster.

"I've already set some alerts on it," she said. "Tren showed me how. If this works right, we'll have at least several minutes to prepare if we get another incursion. Hey, by the way, why don't you just ask Tren?"

Captain Grayson blinked. Faulkner stayed as still as snake about to strike.

"Ask him what?" Grayson said carefully.

"When I walked up"—Kara paused to close her log screen—"you said you weren't going to be stopped by a computer problem, or something like that? Whatever's going on, why not ask Tren about it? He's happy to help. You saw the job he did on the Ionova, Grant."

"Right." Grant's eyes lit up. He spun to face Faulkner. "Captain, that's the same guy that cracked the systems on that ship. I'd never seen anything like it. Let's get him!"

"Anyway," Kara said. "I'll leave you to it. But, Captain, my offer stands. Anything you need just ask. And if you're looking for Tren, he's in the galley with Doctor Wantanabe right now. I'm actually headed that way. Want me to send him up?"

Grayson's fingers left his holster. "Yes. Please do that, Lieutenant. Keep in mind, anything you overheard is confidential."

"Naturally," Kara said. "Count on me, Skipper."

Leaving the bridge, Kara wrestled down the urge to run. What in the hell could've made the captain react like that? Would he have honestly pulled his weapon on her?

No. No Mariner captain would do that.

Kara repeated that assurance to herself as she went to find Tren. By the time she caught up with him, she'd almost started to believe it.

Chapter Eighteen:
Second Chances

"Think about every bad choice you made. Be honest. Why did you do it? When you look deeply enough, I'll bet fear had a lot to do with it."
Alan Schwab, The Tao of the Core

It took hours for the bridge to clear. As she had promised, Kara had sent Tren over to see the captain. When she'd found him, however, she couldn't help but feel she had sold him out somehow. It could've just been how the man blanched at having to talk to the captain. That made her feel bad enough. Especially, when she told him she wouldn't be accompanying him.

There shouldn't have been any reason that Kara needed to wait at the foredeck to make sure Tren came out of the meeting okay. He was a guest, after all, and didn't their traditions mean everything to them? Wasn't honoring the tradition of truce what got them into this mess in the first place? Still. She did worry. After assuring herself that Tren was as healthy and nervous as ever, she double-checked that the Gallant crew had left on their dinghy and Captain Grayson had gone below decks to brood in his cabin before she entered the bridge.

Chief Fen had beat her there. He'd been kept out as long as she had and needed to catch up on work as well. Despite the late hour, the sun still showed a crack of light over the western horizon. Twilight pushed through the portholes. Solemnly, they both pushed through their tasks, neither speaking to the other.

"Why the skipper won't let me deal with it, I have not a clue..." Chief Fen muttered. "They'll be sending carrier pigeons before long."

That caught her attention, but Kara had to ignore it and focus. Her thoughts kept pulling her back into the same circles.

What had Grayson and Bilby been fighting about?

What did Grayson say in that meeting he was so afraid of people hearing?

Why were those two captains, polar opposites, suddenly thick as thieves? Especially with the temper Grayson had lately, he should've throttled the man during that meeting.

Why did they need Tren? Wasn't this old American military tech? How could Faulkner's own computer systems officer not be equipped for this?

And what was with all of these secrets? Mariners didn't do the state secret thing. Council meetings were held in the open. Anyone on board could ask the Navigator about their missions. How was Grayson okay with—

A shrill whine from Kara's workstation sent her tumbling backward in her seat. The flexible phone in her pocket picked up the buzz as well.

"Jesus Christ!" Fen cried. "Nearly did me in with

that! Shut it off, will you?"

"Sorry, sorry..." Kara muttered while checking her workstation for the alarm window. It was the swimmer. Already? She acknowledged the alarm and checked the message.

From: Harry Halibut (M.V. Penitent)

Subject: Alarm "Suspicious Activity" Has Been Triggered

Message: <u>View attached video and location data</u>.

"Not again," Kara said aloud.

"What is it?" Fen perked up. "What's happening?"

"Harry, I mean, the swimmer's picked something up. Video's coming in now." Kara motioned for Fen to come to her station.

He rushed over, banging his knee on his desk in the process.

Harry's cameras were surprisingly clear. Although, given the low light, the image came back in grayscale.

"This just happen?" Fen said.

Kara nodded. "Look at the time stamp. One-and-a-half minutes ago. It's still feeding, this is happening now."

"Should we sound the alarm?" Genuine concern came through Fen's voice.

"Let's see what we're dealing with, first." Kara set the playback rate to double speed. A small area map on the lower right showed Harry's location, which put him close to the Gallant. Kara tapped the screen to show what had caught Harry's attention. "That's the underside of a small boat."

"Oh." Fen relaxed. He rapped her shoulder. "Well that's only Faulkner's dinghy, isn't it?"

Harry switched up his position, moving to swim alongside the boat.

"Then why's it heading away from the Gallant?"

"Eh?" Fen leaned in closer.

Kara tapped the map for emphasis. "Watch."

Sure enough, the dinghy puttered through the calm waters, away from her mothership.

"Maybe they're just..."

Kara gave Fen a flat look.

"Yeah, I know," he said. "Let's see where the tricky bastards get off to."

Upping the playback speed again, they watched the boat travel even farther. Over into the waters over the shoal, too shallow for any of their ships.

"They going sight-seeing?" Fen gestured to the map. Harry had made it almost to the rocky shore.

"I hope he's smart enough to stay out of the really shallow water. He's too big, he might be spotted."

"Who?" Fen said.

"Harry! Who else?"

Fen gave a surprised blink but kept watching. As it turned out, they didn't have long to wait. After only a minute of the boat resting near the rocky shore, it bobbed in the water, waves splashing around from side to side. Almost immediately, it pushed off and the dinghy's motor took over again. Kara and Fen watched the seconds on the timestamp tick by while the boat picked up speed.

Kara leaned back, rubbing her chin.

In less time than it had taken for the boat to get to the shore, it was back by the Gallant. At which point, the bottom of the boat lifted out of the water, and Harry lost interest.

"Well what was that all about?" Fen said. "They head to shore just to have a lovely dump on the dry land? Mini vacation from the rigors of ship life?"

"No." Kara moved the video playback marker. Images jerked backward by tens of seconds to the time before the dinghy pushed off from shore. "There. See it?"

"Let's pretend I don't have the finely tuned senses

of a navigator."

"When they leave shore, the waterline of the dinghy is higher. Much higher. They picked someone up. Maybe multiple someones."

"How do you know it's not cargo?"

"Too much movement on the boat. See how it rolls there? People are getting in and moving around."

"Now those people are on the Gallant," Fen said.

Kara had no idea to what to make of this development. "Looks like."

Add one more log to the mystery fire, she thought. *Super.*

There were windows on the submersible. Small, though. One in front. One in back. Couldn't see much through them. But the displays? Oh, brilliant. Tren watched, enthralled, as they descended, the ocean floor lit by the powerful searchlight. To think he'd been seconds from having a panic attack when they'd boarded. Well, in truth, he was generally seconds away from a panic attack regardless of the situation.

It's not like the merry band he was cooped up with had made things any easier. First off, that Grayson captain guy always looked ready to take a bite out of the nearest person's face. And was he ever pissed off at that Faulkner guy? Even Tren could spot that.

Better him than me, he thought.

Tren had showed up, exactly when he was supposed to, and waited by the submersible. Then those two thundered across the deck, Grayson yelling about something, Faulkner coming back with, *Well, how else do you plan on moving these things?*

Maybe the Mariner captain was mad that they always had to use his equipment. Seemed like a fair criticism. It's not like the Gallant got attacked like everyone else, or contributed their own little submarine thing. Tren decided he was on the Mariners' side. Even if Grayson could be intimidating, most of the Mariners seemed like decent people to him. What kind of fish was that? Are those tube things plants or animals? Doctor Wantanabe would know.

Tren ached with the need to get his questions answered. But, as Goldi would have told him:

Hey, professor. Read the room.

He missed Goldi. She reminded him a little of his old bodyguard.

"Lieutenant Nkosi said you used to work for AssureGen?" Grant said.

Tren pulled his eyes off the display. "Yes. Until recently."

"I heard"—Grant's eyes lit up—"that if you get hired for one of their professional jobs, they give cars as sign-on bonuses."

"I can't say for certain without knowing all the data," Tren said. "In my experience, they do."

Grant showed him an incredulous smile. "What? No way."

Why was he so surprised? Hadn't he come to Tren for confirmation? People were so odd.

"Yes," Tren said. "They gave me a Tesla Model W."

"What? A model W!" Grant's eyes went wide. "Well, where is it now?"

"Seized with the rest of my assets, I suppose. I was pretty upset about it. But now..." Tren shrugged.

"If you children are done wasting our oxygen," Faulkner said from his seat, "it's time to get to work."

Grant didn't respond, but he watched Tren out of the corner of his eye as though the man had a transmittable form of insanity. It made no difference to Tren. In fact, speaking about the past gave him a sticky feeling, as though he had done something wrong and would be discovered at any time. He contented himself with watching the display. Captain Grayson took them over the edge of some underwater cliff, turned the little submarine around and just like that, Tren felt lighter in his seat as they sank even lower. Some of his earlier giddiness faded. How deep were they going to take this thing? How far could it dive before things started popping and cracking like in the movies?

Turned out they didn't have much farther to go. Grayson slowed them down, Tren's body pressing harder on his chair this time. In front of them drifted a great curtain of seaweed. Beads of sweat popped on Tren's forehead as they pushed closer. They were going to crash! What was Grayson thinking? They'd be crushed against the, wait, okay, looks like there was space behind the plants.

He let out an audible gasp. Faulkner narrowed his eyes at Tren. Before the man could say anything, Grayson guided them to what was obviously the entrance to the facility.

"Uh, Tren," Grant chanced the words, watching Faulkner to make sure it was safe to speak. When his captain didn't unleash hell on him, Grant went on. "There's a network signal that won't allow unsecure connections. I can send you over the credentials I cracked last time."

"No need." Tren had his fingers already contacted with the slimline deck sitting on his thigh. "I found another entry point. There's a second hidden signal. I found it by manually scanning the frequency range. It had protection, but I broke it fairly easy."

Tren thought about asking Captain Grayson if he could commandeer one of the ship's displays to do his work, but a glance over the man's way told Tren that might not be the best idea. He kept using his in-eye display.

"Oh, here's that door protocol you told me about. Exactly where you said it was, Grant."

Grant perked up. "Nice! Okay, trouble is, that was the only control protocol I could find. That directory has a bunch of binaries in it, but I couldn't tell what they do."

"Hey, a light!" Tren said. "Neat."

A light blue glowing ring blinked into life around the circular door.

"Where did you find that?"

"Around." Tren waved a hand dismissively. "Get it? Around? Because it's...I'll keep looking."

Tren shut the light off.

For the next few minutes, the only sound from Grant's seat was frustrated tapping.

Grant let out a grunt. "I hate to say it, Captain, but this may take a lot longer than we planned. Even with two of us working on it. There's just no way to know where to even begin. We're working with nothing here. Security on this system is crazy tight. We might need to plan to do this in shifts."

"I think I found it," Tren said.

"Found what?" Grayson shot back.

Tren pulled his attention away just long enough to respond. "Uh, the control plane. The master system that controls everything else. Look."

Blinking back to life, the circular light came on as the doorway halves slid apart from each other.

"How did you do that?" Grant sat up taller, looking between Tren and the display.

"More importantly," Faulkner said. "Is it safe now?"

"Yes," Tren said. "It should be. I think so. Probably."

"What does that mean?" Grayson roared.

"It means..." Tren flapped helplessly at Grant.

"What he said. There are too many unknowns. The way this is all put together doesn't make sense for the time period. I've worked with prewar systems before. This is unbelievably advanced for when it was built. For a moment, I almost thought it used a Davies-Expo control lock orchestration system, but that would be impossible. And there's some weird kind of error; most of these servers had their operating systems defaulted to Russian. They could be infected with a virus. I've had to run a translation shell on top of everything else."

Grayson practically growled, "Can we go in?"

"Y-yes, I think so." Tren hurried up to add, "I found the security measure that fires the torpedoes. It won't go off if we enter. I can guarantee that. If we use this control plane to enter instead of manipulating things directly, then they won't be set off."

Faulkner considered him for a moment. He spoke directly to Grayson. "If we still have door control and we know there's no torpedo, at least we can see what else is waiting for us."

"God help us," Grayson muttered.

He pointed the craft at the open entrance, and eased them in.

A trail of sweat ran down Tren's back, right between the shoulder blades. How did he always end up in spots like this?

Keeping the control plane log outputs running in one terminal window he opened a second where he could try new commands, and a third where he could keep poking around their servers. Vaguely he became aware of the craft slowing.

"I'll be," Faulkner said.

Tren checked the ship's display. The interior of the tunnel they entered now had white chaser lights running its length. As they reached the end of the space, the lights changed direction and began to run from down to up.

"Looks like we're supposed to ascend," Faulkner said.

Grayson grunted but didn't move right away. "Tren?"

At least he wasn't yelling anymore. "Yes, I'm not seeing anything indicating we're in trouble."

They went up.

A new log entry, immediately translated into English, printed out in Tren's eye: 4052369311 Now Start Exterior Door Close Together

"The front doors are shutting," Tren said.

"Are they supposed to?" Faulkner shot back.

"How should I know?" Tren fluttered helplessly. "You're the boat people. You tell me if it's normal!"

"If it's, uh," Grant stammered, "acting like a lock system of some kind, the front hatch might have to close."

Captain Grayson's hand hovered over the depth control. Cleary, the choice of whether to keep rising or to retreat had him flummoxed. He moved his hand back down and kept their ascent.

"That's the ticket." Faulkner pointed at the display. "Too late to back out now. Look."

Tren and Grant both looked. A thick metal ring with a gaping opening smoothly passed them by.

"All right!" Grant gave Tren a quick pat on the shoulder. "That's the torpedo problem solved. Knew you'd get us through this."

4052369535 Exterior Door Now Close Lock Engage

"Thanks," Tren said without thinking. Something didn't seem right. The resources on the servers were still showing some load, but there wasn't anything happening around them or getting logged yet.

"There's the top," Grayson said. His display showed another set of doors above them, these long and square. Though they appeared to be just as sturdy as the ones they'd entered through. And just as shut. "Do you need to do something to open them, Tren?"

Around the perimeter of the square doors above lay a light bezel, softly glowing blue.

Tren furrowed his brow. "I shouldn't have to. The control plane should be managing this for us. Unless there's another..."

4052369580 Scan Now Transponder Security Protocol Apple Tau

A blink on the display. Around the overhead door, the lights pulsed yellow.

No. No, no, no!

"What? What?" Grant yelled.

Tren sat up, suddenly realizing he had been vocalizing his thoughts. "This submarine thing, does it have a transponder?"

When no one answered, he shouted, "Quick!"

Grayson snapped back to life. "No, it doesn't."

4052370900 Scan Now Transponder Results None 1 of 5
4052370901 Scan Now Transponder Retry Wait

Seconds. That only bought them seconds.

Think. Think. Think!

"Radio!" Tren fumbled his harness open and wriggled from his seat. "Where radio! Where radio!"

"There!" Grayson pointed to the center instrument cluster, just below the displays.

Both Faulkner and Grayson recoiled, watching Tren as if he were a man possessed. To be fair, Tren was doing a pretty fair impression of it. He climbed over the armrest between the two men, sliding headfirst over Faulkner. With his back half now pressed against Faulkner, legs in the air, Tren flipped over so his shoulder blades were resting on the footwell of Faulkner's seat. When Faulkner tried to move, Tren yelled, "Stay where you are!"

Radio, radio, radio, where were those damn control wires?

4052375900 Scan Now Transponder Results None 2 of 5
4052375901 Scan Now Transponder Retry Wait

"Found it!" Tren jammed his left hand under the console, felt around then ripped out a cluster of wires.

Grayson roared, "What the hell are you doing, Tren!"

"I'm working!" Tren screamed back.

Fumbling the bundle of wires, Tren pulled up some radio schematics for the submersible on his deck. Pages of diagrams swirled through his in-eye display before he found the correct one.

4052380900 Scan Now Transponder Results None 3 of 5
4052380901 Scan Now Transponder Retry Wait

He found it. "Aha!"

With no time to waste, he stripped the two wires with his teeth. Saliva and plastic mixed in his mouth, he tried to spit the pieces out but one stuck in the crack of his bottom lip and oh forget it anyway.

4052385900 Scan Now Transponder Results None 4 of 5
4052385901 Scan Now Transponder Retry Wait

"What the hell is happening? Why did that light turn red?" Grayson shouted at the top of his lungs. The very air shook around Tren.

Pinching the bared wires between the contact pads of his deck and his two fingers, Tren got to work. Grayson's voice faded into a low buzz, along with Faulkner who had not only joined with him, but started to jostle Tren with his knees.

All irrelevant. Jostling, shaking, the odor of Faulkner's shoes. Irrelevant.

Flying through a directory search of the server Tren located a database of hashed values. Must be the transponder code whitelist. Finding a readme file in the source repo he pieced together the hashing algorithm used. Kid stuff. Basic password injection. Command after command filled his terminal window too fast to be read by anyone but him.

```
TrensBigDeck:/sys/var/emulators/$./genId-f/tmptCode
плоскостьуправления:/data/db$./insert/tmp tCode
TrensBigDeck:/sys/var/emulators/$./emco-967-maritime-b
transponder-i /tmptCode
```

Tren's eyes shook from side to side, making all the characters in his inner-eye display vibrate.

```
4052389912 Transponder Found
4052389912 Transponder Code Check Now
```

He couldn't breathe. Somewhere, near his body, he might be getting slapped on his thighs.

```
4052389925 Transponder Code Check Success
4052389925 Inner Entry Hatch Control Engage Open Now
```

"Oh, God..." Tren exhaled at once.

"It's blue again! Now it's white!" Grant whooped from the rear seats. "Yeah!"

"Someone help me up?" Tren said.

With a bit of help from everyone pulling at his legs and arms, Tren managed to slide and bump his way upright. While finger combing his hair away from his sweaty face, he took his seat again.

"What happened?" Grant said. His face held a mix of fear and awe. "The light was yellow, then it went red, did we trip another security measure?"

Tren was going to wave the question away, but the stern looks he had from the captains told him otherwise. Well, he had practically been on Faulkner's lap, so he did owe them some kind of explanation.

"The control plane started scanning for a transponder. I had to hack the acoustic receiver/transmitter unit to broadcast a fake transponder signal, and insert the code into the control plane's white list so it would accept that code as valid."

"Holy crap, you did all that in like, five seconds?" Grant gave him a wide, open mouthed smile. "Wait? Why not just look up one of the valid codes in their white list?"

"Hashed and salted." Tren shook his head. "No one in their right mind would store secure values in clear text."

Grayson cut across them. "Will it happen again?"

Tren swallowed. "Yes. It will undoubtedly scan every time you enter. I can try to change that, but it would be easier to mod your radio to permanently broadcast the code."

"Do it," Grayson said simply. His hand returned to the controls.

Faulkner dusted off his trousers. "Once I'm out of my seat, please."

Thank you, Tren. Is it really that hard to say?

This was exactly the kind of thankless crap that made him run off and... Well, Tren didn't want to think about that too much. Resting his head against the side of his seat, the heavy feeling in his rear told him they'd started heading up again. Watching the display, Tren kept a lazy eye on the log output from the control plane. It noted when the doors had completely opened and when they passed some point, started closing again.

All around them, the display showed only a dull colorless metal with more of the embedded lights guiding them up. At last, they slowed. The submersible suddenly lurched and bobbed.

"We've surfaced," Grayson said. He and Faulkner shared a significant glance.

Grayson turned to Tren. "Anything new?"

Tren checked the control plane logs, then shook his head.

"Let's take a look." Faulkner grinned. It may have been the first time Tren had seen him do that.

Grant and Tren had to go first, as the hatch was nearest to them. A little hesitantly, Grant unlocked the pressure door. With a great hiss, Grant depressurized the hatch and flung it open.

He climbed up the ladder. "Okay, there's a small dock right next to us and another door. We'll need your help with that Tren."

Without waiting for a response, Grant slid up and out of the hatch.

A please might be nice, Tren thought.

His knees didn't want to cooperate. Tren's whole body trembled slightly. Still, he forced himself to clamber up through the hatch after Grant.

Half expecting the air to be toxic, Tren took his breaths in short, shallow bursts. Where was this door, anyway? The sooner he could open it, the sooner they could be done with all of this. He landed a bit awkwardly on the metal dock, the plate ringing loudly and echoing throughout the long concrete room. With the lights still on below the waterline, an eerie blue-white glow danced around the room, cast up from the water.

Ah, the door.

Grant already stood next to it, bouncing with excitement and waving Tren over. Slowly, Tren made his way, vaguely aware of the two captains also exiting the vehicle. Words and arrows had been stenciled out in white and yellow paint throughout the room. Tren squinted and rubbed his eyes. For a moment the characters looked like nonsense. But as he opened them and looked again, he realized his eyes weren't the problem.

The writing was all in Cyrillic characters. Russian.

Oh, God.

Captain Faulkner sauntered up behind them, looking as clean and pressed in his dress whites as ever. Deliberately, he looked at Tren, at the Cyrillic writing, then back at Tren.

"Tren," he said. "It seems you've done us a great service today. Done the impossible, one could say. No doubt, a smart man such as yourself is putting some information together. So. Let's talk about the future, shall we?"

Big Madrid didn't enjoy being in anyone's debt. Who did? A life underneath someone else's thumb was no life, indeed. On the other hand, a man had to admit the circumstances of life as they were. There was a hierarchy. A pecking order. A hill upon which the proverbial feces rolled down. This was nature, simply put. Dog-eating-dog, etcetera.

So as he stood in Captain Faulkner's little conference room aboard the Gallant, Gill and Gary at his side, Big Madrid didn't resent the situation too much. He did what Big Madrid did best: Made the most of it.

Faulkner let himself in, harried and tired. Rubbing at that ridiculous pencil mustache of his, Faulkner motioned for one of his nameless lackeys to go make him a drink. Infuriatingly, the man made a point of ignoring Big until he had his libation in hand.

"So," Faulkner finally said. "We meet at last and all that. This better be worth my while, Madrid."

"Of course it is." Big Madrid adjusted his shoulders. His favorite stole, a little worse for wear, still draped over him. "I bring solutions, Captain. Not problems."

Faulkner scoffed. "That's news to me."

"Listen, darling," Big Madrid said. "Not only have I got a buyer to move your precious cargo, I believe I can do one better. You remember your little problem of having to rely on the shipsies for submersible transportation?"

Slowly, Faulkner lowered his tumbler.

"What if I told you, that I know where you can get one of your very own. Not too far from here, in fact. It's on a ship called the DCV Verne, which I just departed from. If we act now, I think we can procure this little asset for you cheap-cheap-cheap. Know what I mean, love?"

"You're sure they have one on board? You've seen it?"

Big Madrid laughed. "Dearest, what did you think we planned to do when got here, go for a swim? Give me a few guns. Them, me, G and G? You'll be twenty thousand leagues under before you know it."

Setting his glass down, Faulkner gave Big a level stare. "We'll put it together."

"You won't be disappointed," Big Madrid said.

Faulkner swallowed the last of the amber liquid in his tumbler. "Let's hope not."

Chapter Nineteen: A Confession

"Mainlanders may look down on us, but what control do they truly have over their lives? Every luxury they think they possess is at best ephemeral and at worst an illusion."
Karissa Piccato, Second Mariner Elect

As far as cabins aboard Mariner ships went, the passenger quarters were positively roomy. Kara's first several years on ship were spent in shared crew quarters, bunked in with seven others. It took her promotion to Lieutenant to get her own cabin, even though it was roughly the size of a broom closet. The privacy was nice, though.

Which meant that, between her, Chief Lambros, and Drummond, they now had a very tight fit into the guest cabin Tren and Drummond shared. Drummond and the chief sat on the lower bunk while Kara, unable to sit, partially leaned against the room's tiny desk-dresser combo.

"It doesn't mean that anything bad has happened

to Tren," Drummond spoke with his head in his hands. "You said that Grant didn't come back with them either, right? Maybe it's exactly like the captain said."

"You don't understand," Kara snapped. "He didn't even want to tell me where Tren was at first. I practically had to drag it out of him. Trust me, that wasn't my first choice. The guy's a time bomb right now."

"Why do you say that?" Chief Lambros wore a concerned look.

Kara hadn't told her, or anyone, about what had happened when Grayson caught her eavesdropping outside the bridge. In a way, she still wanted to convince herself that she had misinterpreted what she'd seen.

"He's on edge," she said simply. "Everyone on board sees it. Even Chief Fen thinks so, and these guys practically worship their captain."

"How did he react when you asked him?" Drummond brought his face out of his hands and scooted to the edge of the bunk. "Did he yell, or lie, or ignore you?"

Kara bobbed her head. "Grumbled, told me to mind my own business. Then when I pointed out that I'm responsible for logging all crew movements, he finally gave in. Took him a minute. I mean, he really thought about it. Finally, he tells me Tren is still down there along with Grant."

"What would be the alternative, though?" Chief Lambros said. "If you think he could be lying about Tren, what are the other possibilities?"

"I don't know, maybe Tren got hurt, or there was some kind of accident," Kara said.

Chief Lambros's gaze pierced her. "Is that honestly what you're worried about?"

She took a second to gather her thoughts and

courage. "No. If I'm being honest, I'm not worried about that. Something is very wrong on this ship. Captain Grayson is, well, I don't know, exactly. But I'm worried that he might have done something to Tren. Maybe in a temper, maybe to hide some secret."

"All right." Drummond rubbed his eyes. The hour was late and she had woken him up for this. "I don't want anything to happen to Tren, either. So, I'm taking this seriously. I am. Let's look at the facts, though. Why would you have any reason to think Grayson might do something like that? Sure, Tren can get on people's nerves, but he knows his stuff. If Grayson made it back then he did whatever they brought him down there to do, right?"

"That's exactly my point, what if whatever it is that's happening down there needs to be kept secret, to the extent that Captain Grayson might, no, don't look at me like that," Kara said to both of them. Steeling herself, she began to tell them of her suspicions. How Grayson had argued with Bilby over something important before the man was killed. The way he was suddenly getting along with Faulkner. How he now kept secrets from the crew despite Mariner traditions. She told them about the boat she and Fen tracked going from the Gallant to shore and back. Finally, the conversation she overheard and the way the captain reacted.

Both of them watched Kara in various stages of disbelief.

"It comes down to this," Kara said. "A Mariner captain doesn't keep secrets like this from his crew. It isn't done. Whatever he's wrapped up in now is what he and Bilby argued about. Guarantee it. That secret? Has to be down below. There's no other explanation."

Drummond turned up his palms, searching for an answer. "I don't know what that secret could be,

Kara. The mission report I received didn't have any other surprises in it. Everything I told you that first night on Vish is basically it. Maybe there are other reasons he doesn't want anyone else down there. Do you think Captain Grayson is trying to limit the crew's exposure in case there's some kind of weapons containment breach?"

"I hate to say it, but, no." Chief Lambros tapped her chin. "He'd just say so if that were it. Tell me, Drummond, how did you get involved in this mission in the first place? I was never clear on that."

"Oh, that." Drummond gave them a weak smile. "No point in sugar coating it. I'm one of the less, if not the least, popular member of Congress. So, the party made sure I was put on the most pointless and powerless committees possible. One is the post-war reconstruction committee. These days it doesn't do much, but years ago it was concerned with rebuilding after the war. The second committee, and the most pointless, is the oversight committee. Designed for the laughable goal of appearing to fight corruption. I'm getting to the point, Kara. Faulkner's mission was deemed a secret operation. We couldn't make a show of getting to the bunker because we didn't have the resources readily available because of the blockade, and we didn't want anyone to realize what we were doing. Just in case they tried to interfere. You know that part. No matter how secret the mission, though, it needed funding, so it had to go through a congressional approval process."

"The reconstruction committee," Lambros said. "I suppose this could be considered post-war recovery."

Drummond pointed a finger at her. "Exactly. Since I'm the only one young enough to travel by ship and live to tell the tale—or the most expendable, depending on who you ask—I was appointed to come along and supervise. I thought it would be a good opportunity to keep an eye on Faulkner, but you see how well that worked out. He outplayed me early on with his hostage transfer idea."

"Fine, fine," Kara said. "That still doesn't answer the question. What's the big secret? What has Grayson so keyed up he was ready to pull his gun on me?"

"You've mentioned before," Lambros said to Drummond, "that corruption is basically endemic in your government."

Drummond grimaced, but nodded.

"I see," the chief said. "What are the chances that the mission briefing circulating through your committee contained all the facts to begin with? Would it be possible for a group of people, including Captain Faulkner, to coordinate and ensure that only certain facts were shared so they could somehow take advantage of the situation. "

At that, Drummond slowly closed his eyes and sank down on the bunk. "Is it possible? Absolutely, now that I think about it. If you'd have asked me this a few days ago I'd have said no, but it's possible Faulkner could be more well-connected than I gave him credit for."

"What makes you say that?" Lambros said.

"Bits and pieces. I didn't take it seriously before. Things he'd say in passing. Clubs he belonged to, people at high levels of government that he knows socially. At first it sounded like ordinary bragging. People at his level can't breathe without name-dropping. Now that we're talking about it, though... Maybe it wasn't."

"Wait." Kara gave her head a tiny shake. "Who ordered the mission in the first place? If it's one of Faulkner's cronies then we pretty much have our answer."

Drummond groaned. "That information was

classified."

✦ ✦ ✦

It wasn't exactly a roomy place, was it? The submarine dock definitely held the record for largest room in the building so far. Even bigger than the warehouse floor Tren had found. Sure, the other floors had the same square footage as the docking bay, they were right above it, in fact. But unlike the bay, the low ceilings in those rooms made him twitchy, claustrophobic. Which was saying a ton considering his whole life had been spent parked in front of various computers.

It wasn't only the small space, he thought reasonably. The nuclear warheads made him more nervous than anything else. Warheads that captains Grayson and Faulkner were now loading into crates for transport to the surface. Warheads they were shoving around like beer kegs, just beneath his feet.

And there he went.

Tren froze, his heart thumping, sweat breaking out over his face and neck.

"Tren?" Came Grant's voice from somewhere else. "Remember to breathe, man. You're okay."

But he wasn't okay. Heart rate skyrocketing, vision growing red and blurry, mouth getting dry, panting, panting.

You can't let yourself get so caught up, Tren, his dad once told him. At age eight, when he watched a horror movie about demonic possession that scared him so thoroughly he couldn't sleep for days, his dad had sat on the edge of his bed and spoke to him. *I'm gonna teach you a trick. Don't try not to think about the scary movie. That won't work. Think about more than the movie.*

More? Tren had said.

Exactly. More. Think about how hard all those actors worked to make sure they made the right faces. Or how many hours the set builders spent getting everything just right, so it would scare you. I bet it took almost a whole year for them to get it all perfect.

Tren spent the next hour or so thinking about all of it. When his dad went to bed, Tren pulled out his tablet and spent hours looking up facts about movie making. Special effects, famous directors, how they were shot, scored, produced.

Afterward, he slept like a rock.

So far, they'd uncovered three floors in the underground (underwater? Technically, both) facility. Tren had been able to hack access to almost every room except for the space on the third floor off on the area he'd dubbed the Command Deck. It sounded very Naval. The others must have agreed, as the name quickly stuck. The second floor was dedicated exclusively to weapons storage. Naturally. It looked to be the primary purpose of the facility.

Oddly, the locked room off of the Command Deck had tighter security than the room with the warheads. Or at least it had a type of security he wasn't familiar with. It amounted to the same thing, which was him getting stuck in the facility overnight with Grant as they tried to work the problem.

"See, you're all right!" Grant said.

So he was. Tren gave Grant a small smile. People need that kind of acknowledgement. Otherwise they'll think you aren't listening. Tren hadn't thought of his dad in a long time.

"Look." Grant lowered his tablet and rubbed his eyes. Both men had taken places at the unused, empty desks in the office that led to the locked door. "We may have to admit defeat on this one. Captain Faulkner and Grayson are almost done with the load."

"I don't think either of them will like that suggestion." Tren kept his focus on his terminal windows.

Grant sighed. "Don't tell me you're worried about upsetting the captain? Come on, Faulkner loves you, man. You're already in, trust me. He's kind of an asshole, I get it, but if he says he's gonna get you off the party blacklist, then he's going to do it. You're going to stick to the deal, right?"

"Of course." Tren rubbed his shoulders. "We made an agreement."

Captain Faulkner's deal. His parting words before they left him and Grant stuck in the facility overnight.

I'm a man of my word, Tren. Stick with the plan. Stick with me. I'll get you home.

"Then you don't have anything to worry about. Even if we don't crack this door, you can still get your life back. This time next month you're going to be letting me drive your Model W. Bet on it."

"I'm not sure I want to take chances."

"Maybe you'll change your tune when you see this. Check out what I found." Grant tapped and swiped over his tablet, sending a file over to the room's large display, which he had commandeered. Tren still worked on his in-eye display. No matter how tempting it was to have the bigger view, he didn't trust the foreign hardware as easily as Grant did.

Tren hid his terminal windows so he could better see Grant's document.

"It's in Russian," Tren said.

"Oops, sorry." Grant rapidly tapped his tablet.

"No matter, I'll run an overlay."

Flipping his in-eye display back on, Tren restarted his translation routine. Looking back at the monitor, the document, complete with official Russian Federation seals and a neat, bulleted list, faded somewhat as black lettering overlaid it. Actually a pretty slick interface. Tren made a little sound of approval. He'd done pretty well with it.

"Well if you got it, then take a look at the text," Grant said. "See if you can catch what I'm throwing here."

Tren skimmed through the text. Looked like a memorandum scheduling a time to deliver furniture? He gave Grant a sidelong look, then went back to reading.

Priority is given to first tier furniture necessary to begin operations.

Makes sense. *Ah.*

"It's a server room. Very clever, Grant. What gave you the idea to check correspondence for clues?"

"Pure desperation." Grant chuckled. "When I saw they were taking delivery on a bunch of server racks, I did the math and they'd need most all that space behind the door to house them."

"Don't sell yourself short," Tren said. "Desperate or not, that was smart. I didn't find it. Well, it still begs the question as to why they need so much computer power in here. It's overkill even for this place. I can't find any comms to the outside world, so what gives? A bunch of expensive servers sitting here, doing nothing?"

"Well, I mean, redundancies?" Grant offered. Although his expression said that even he wasn't completely buying it. "You know, gotta protect the nukes, right? Double, triple redundant systems."

A weak smile found its way to Tren's face. "Triple redundant systems we cracked like glass?"

"That was all you, man. I bow before your superior skills. Okay, okay. What if they're quantum rigs? No, seriously, you know how much space that kind of hardware takes."

Tren opened his mouth to debate another point,

after all, argument was the true language of the engineer. But Grant's eyes darted from side to side before he lowered his voice.

"Tren," he said, "do you want to be stuck in this place for the foreseeable future? Because I sure as hell don't. That's exactly what's going to happen if the captains think there is even a possibility that there are more goodies hiding back there."

"Point taken," Tren said quickly. "Quantum. Got to be quantum hardware. No other explanation. Let's show them the damn memo."

A crew of four handpicked deckhands carefully used the Penitent's gantry to move a large, dripping crate over to the cargo hold hatch. Kara didn't know what was in it. No one did, save for the Captain and Commander Orozco. At least as far as Kara could tell. All the deckhands knew was that the contents were delicate, dangerous, and to be handled with care. Even Chief Lambros had been kept in the dark. Which, as deckmaster, she was none too pleased about.

Kara stuck to the bow, watching as unobtrusively as possible. Every internal alarm bell she had was going off. A case just like this one had been dropped off to float in the waters by the Gallant, where Captain Faulkner's crew immediately took action to retrieve it. How in the world was that stabilizing or containing anything? True, they could make the argument that the supposed containment systems for the weapons were failing and needed to be removed. So why split them between ships?

She couldn't stop obsessing over it. This, on top of every other damn thing that had happened, it all stank. Kara hadn't meant to spend so long up top, staring at the cargo as if she could x-ray it. Initially, she had rushed to the deck when she heard the submersible was back to wait for Tren. Once the submersible had been brought aboard and she'd checked in on the sleep deprived engineer, Kara had planned on leaving. She didn't, though. A sense of raw anger kept her rooted. Anger at the secrets and deception, anger at Grayson and his failure to uphold his role as captain.

From the stern of the ship, where he supervised the security of their new, precious cargo, Captain Grayson looked her way. Kara pushed off from the railing and headed below decks. The last thing she needed was more scrutiny from the captain. Given how touchy he'd been, watching the deckhands work would've surely sent him into a rage. Besides, it was beyond late. Late enough for the sun to finally retreat below the horizon for its few hours of rest.

She stopped short of the hatch to her cabin. The door stood ajar by a few centimeters. Kara stopped. Had someone been through her room? Were they in there now? She touched the hilt of her knife with one hand, then nudged the door open with the toe of her boot.

"Shh!" Drummond held a finger to his lips. From inside her room, he motioned for her to enter.

Kara squeezed in and closed the door behind her. "Thanks for inviting me in to my own bunk?"

"It was necessary," Chief Lambros said.

Tren stood, nervous as ever, pushed against her thin chest of drawers. With the four of them in the tiny room, it didn't leave much room for maneuvering.

"Necessary because?" Kara said.

"We couldn't all come over at once. It would look suspicious," Drummond said. "We needed to talk, though. Without anyone else hearing."

"What do you want to talk about?" Kara asked.

"Not me." Drummond pointed to Tren.

Tren looked as though he had swallowed something awful and didn't know if he would chuck it back up. From one second to the next, he would start toward the door, stop, then shift back to his spot by the drawers.

"Take your time," Chief Lambros told him gently. "Put your thoughts together."

Oddly, her words had the opposite effect on Tren. Rather than waiting, he seemed to finally find determination.

"This place isn't what you think it is. I got...I got them into the underwater facility. Spent last night there."

"What's down there?" Drummond asked.

Kara shushed him.

Tren seemed to appreciate the assist. "It's not an American storage facility. It's not pre-war. It's Russian, and relatively new. Faulkner and Grayson are robbing the place blind."

"What's in those crates?" Kara's voice felt like ice.

"Warheads," Tren said. "Nuclear. I don't know how many in each crate or any other details. Grayson and Faulkner personally loaded them. Grant and I weren't there. There were rocket motors, too, but they left those. For now, anyway."

"Wait, wait." Drummond ran a hand over his head. "Faulkner is a captain in the U.S. Navy. We're a part of the Russian Federation. Stealing from them is just about the stupidest thing he could do. He'd have no protections at all if he were caught. Raiding other nation's facilities, stealing from independent operators—sure. He'll get away with that. This? There won't be any hiding for him. How does this make any sense?"

The puzzle snapped into place, piece by piece, as if the right curves and edges had suddenly become magnetically drawn to one another. Kara leaned back against her door.

"That's where we come in," she said.

Chief Lambros clasped her hands in front of her. "Can you please explain that?"

"Faulkner—or whoever came up with this 'mission' in the first place—never needed our help. Sure, we did travel through a lot of Mariner water. They are short on ships. These things are all true. But he could've gone this alone. Think about it. He came in a civilian craft and sailed with Mariners. Why? When we went looking for intel at Skatch Harbor, who did all the work? More importantly, who was seen doing the work?"

"Us." Drummond blanched. "And if word does get back to the RF about who was nosing in these waters around the time they got robbed, everyone will point their fingers at a Mariner ship. Jesus."

"Why would Captain Grayson go along with this?" Chief Lambros's normally calm exterior cracked. "What possible reason could he have? Russia could wipe us out. Unlike the U.S. they don't give a damn about worldwide condemnation or sanctions from the U.N. Especially when they can say that we struck first."

But Kara understood. The fishing vessel. Bilby.

"Strength," she said. "The Penitent had that scrape with the fishing vessel around the time this all started, remember? I've got the impression from the some of the crew that Captain Grayson went right to the gun, rather than trying to scare them off. He's... well, let's face it...we're all worried about our future. With this new trade agreement, we'll be overrun by ships. We could lose our islands. Even I've been mad about how little the admiralty and council are doing, but I think Grayson decided to take matters into his own hands. We can't fight off every ship that comes our way. We can't fight the militaries that will come looking for payback if we do."

"But if you were a nuclear-armed nation, maybe you'd have something to bargain with." Drummond shrank. "That's got to be the stupidest plan I've ever heard."

"No, it's not," Kara said. "Desperate, maybe. Not stupid. It's leverage. Something we have none of at the moment. It's a bad option, but it's looking more and more like our only option."

"So you agree with him?" Chief Lambros said.

"No, I..." Kara made a frustrated grunt. "I'm just saying I get it. But he's acting against orders. There's no way he got this approved by Admiral Kim or the council. They'd never agree to stealing from Russia or threatening anyone with nuclear weapons. This must be what Grayson and Bilby we're fighting about. Bilby was an excellent navigator. He must've found out what Faulkner was really up to and told his captain."

"Then Captain Grayson got the idea to strike a deal with Faulkner, rather than calling the mission off. What were the terms? Nukes in exchange for going along with his plan?" Drummond folded his arms over his chest.

"That's what it looks like," Chief Lambros said. "Considering there are a load of them in the cargo hold. He's guaranteeing us one of the most powerful enemies in the world in exchange for token weapons."

"Token?" Kara scoffed. "I hardly think nuclear warheads are token weapons."

"They're token if they're unused," Drummond said. "You better hope they stay that way."

"Regardless," Chief Lambros said. "Here we are. This is our situation. What do we do about it?"

"Can we just put everything back and leave?" Tren said hopefully.

Kara gave a small cough of a laugh. No one else bothered to respond.

After a few moments, Kara spoke. "Captain Grayson is set in his path. That much is clear. I have to go over his head and talk to Admiral Kim. But I'll need proof."

"What other proof do you need?" Drummond said. "You've been talking about how everything he's done goes against the Mariners' traditions, or way of life, shouldn't that be enough? That and the load of nuclear warheads on this ship?"

"We can't take any chances. If it comes down to our word against his, this thing will drag out and Grayson will have all the time he needs to finish whatever plans he has for those nukes. If we get proof of what's in that facility, of who really owns it, that will be more than enough."

"But what then?" Drummond swallowed. "I'm not saying we don't do everything we can. Cat's out of the bag, though. Do we even have the capability to recover the nukes from Faulkner? His crew is just as large as ours and they are armed over there."

"One step at a time," Chief Lambros said reasonably. "Even the brightest lamp only lights the path so far. We need to get proof of what's happening first. We can trust the council and Admiral Kim to do everything they can to support us once they're aware of what's happening here."

Tren, who had been listening with a thumbnail clamped between his teeth, spoke up. "What is Faulkner planning on doing with those nukes? Don't we have enough of our own already?"

"Probably sell them," Drummond said offhand. "There are literally thousands of warlords and tin-pot dictators who would love to get their hands on them and do exactly what Grayson is planning on doing. Make a name for themselves. Carve out some respect."

Kara bit her tongue. That was not what was happening here. Grayson's choice was terrible, yes, but the world was forcing their hand.

"Tren." Chief Lambros lightly put a hand on his shoulder. Since she stood taller than him, she looked down into his eyes. "Thank you. You've been a real friend to us. I don't know what your plans are after all of this blows over, but I got the impression that your life hasn't been stable lately. You're welcome to sail with us, or come stay on Vish."

He blinked, then met her gaze. "You want me to join you?"

"I'm offering shelter and friendship. We don't ask people to join us. People should make that choice on their own. I'm asking if you want to be my guest."

Tren took a moment, but didn't say anything. He nodded, and gave her a weak smile.

"All right," Kara said to the group. "The submersible is tied to the port side. They didn't bring her aboard tonight since the Captain is planning on making another run in the morning. Chief, can we get a clear moment on the deck to sneak aboard?"

"Wait." Tren bit his lip. "Before you go down there, I need to tell you the rest. Or you won't know what you're walking into."

Chapter Twenty:
Red Handed

"In the end what we strive for is freedom from fear. To lose those shackles and soar through each moment of life."
Alan Schwab, The Tao of the Core

"I've asked Heather to come relieve you," Chief Lambros said. Kara and Drummond stayed out of sight, hiding around the other side of the hatch from below deck. "No sense in waiting, I'll keep watch. I'm sure it will only be a few minutes."

"I don't mind waiting, Chief," the deckhand said. "You've got more important things to do. You could be sleeping," he joked.

"No," she said seriously. "I think we've both seen how on edge the skipper is about this cargo? I'm not taking chances, and I've already lost sleep. Go ahead and get down there. Avoiding the old man's ire is worth a few minutes of fresh air."

Kara couldn't see the man, but he must have done

as he was told. Chief Lambros tapped the hatch a moment later. Gently, Kara pushed it open and crept on deck. A touch of a chill had settled in the air in the short time since the sun had set.

Using hand signals to coordinate, Kara and Chief Lambros dropped a rope over the port side rail and secured it to a cargo strap eyelet on the deck.

Moving first, Kara nimbly swung a leg over the rail and readied herself for a descent down the side of the hull. With a firm grip on the rope she walked herself down, lower and lower, until she could push off and swing onto the top of the submersible.

"I can't do that!" Drummond whispered.

Chief Lambros gave him a look that said otherwise and led him to the rope. "Kara will help you get to the submersible. Just hang on and go slow. I'll help lower you. It's not that far down."

If he fell, Drummond would be fine, in a manner of speaking. Although cold, the waters were more or less calm, and Kara would pull him out right away. No, the danger here was in being caught. Every sailor knew the telltale splash of a body hitting the water. A "crew overboard" alarm would awaken every Mariner on the ship.

To his credit, Drummond did show courage. He didn't dawdle on the railing, knowing that time was in short supply. Picking up the rope, he wrapped it around his right hand and positioned himself on the outer side of the railing.

An errant wave slapped the side of the Penitent, rolling the ship just enough to send Drummond slipping. Both of his feet went wide off of the ship's hull. Kara gasped. Chief Lambros held fast to the line, however. A deep, ringing gong-like sound rolled through the plating as Drummond accidentally kicked the hull. Kara winced.

True to her word, Chief Lambros lowered

Drummond, hand over hand on the rope, her feet solidly braced up top. As soon as his legs came within reach, Kara grabbed hold of the back of his pants. In less than a few seconds, she had him on board, an arm around his midsection to stabilize him.

Drummond released the rope and cleared his throat. Kara gave an awkward start and let go of him, then turned back to the chief. Her face felt a little warmer than usual. Nerves, that was all.

Under her feet, the submersible bobbed with the waves. Although it was stable, the movement could be unnerving without a large deck or railing to give the feeling of safety. Seeing Chief Lambros deftly move herself onto the hull, Kara eased open the hatch. She waved Drummond in just as Lambros stepped foot onboard.

A giddy thrill surged through her. They hadn't been spotted yet. Chief Lambros's distraction had worked. Of course their deception wouldn't last long. At some point, they'd be discovered. That was simply a given. Either they'd get pinged by the Gallant or the Penitent's sonar, or the next deckhand on watch would spot the submersible was gone. No matter what, the chances of them making it there and back undetected were slim to none. They all understood that.

The goal, Kara reiterated as she slid into the A-diver and strapped into the pilot's seat, was to get the evidence. If Grayson wanted to cause a scene when they got back, all the better. She'd give the crew a scene, all right. Show them exactly what their captain had been keeping from them.

"You've piloted one of these before?" Drummond said from the rear seat.

"No," Kara said. "Thought I'd just give it my best shot."

"Ah." Drummond waved a finger at her. "Funny."

She took them down.

At first she kept the headlamps on low, red light, preferring to use instruments for navigation as much as possible. A drifting spot of light under the waves would be visible this close to the ships and while she understood they'd eventually be caught, there was no sense in rushing things.

"You have Tren's instructions ready?" Kara asked Chief Lambros, who was gazing dreamily at the monitors.

"Of course. He said the transmitter would activate automatically, but I'll keep an eye on things."

Kara tossed a couple more glances Chief Lambros's way. Kara's blood pumped strong and fast. While she felt as under control as one could hope to be after stealing their boss's submarine, Chief Lambros looked positively at peace. Way more than her usual calm demeanor, which was saying something.

"Chief, are you okay?" Kara asked.

"Just enjoying things," Chief Lambros said. "We've made a difference, you know. Us Mariners. I love being a part of that."

"Yeah, I guess we have." Kara eyed the chief again, her brow furrowed.

Kara brought them over the edge of the shoal and descended again. Drummond grabbed onto the nearest hand straps. If she were honest, Kara was a much better navigator than she was a pilot, but she wasn't going to give Drummond the satisfaction of admitting that. She kicked the lights on brighter and set them to white as they brushed past the curtain of fake seaweed and toward the vault entrance.

True to Tren's word, the center console beeped. A small black window with text streaming across it appeared on the bottom display. Within seconds, a ring of blue light around the vault entrance pulsed. The doors slid open.

"Holy, spooky hell," Kara said, breathlessly.

"Yeah," Drummond agreed.

"This is where it happens," Chief Lambros said wistfully.

Slowly, Kara sent them forward and into the open maw. Guidance lights kicked on, showing them the way. Thankfully, with Tren's modifications to the vehicle, they didn't have to go through any of the trial and error that Grayson's team did. Nice and easy, they ascended to the top and crested the water of the docking bay.

Kara was the last to disembark from the submersible. As she touched down on the deck, her footsteps ringing on metal, a sense of deep foreboding seeped into her all at once. Even Chief Lambros had lost some of her earlier serenity.

"All right, Lieutenant," Chief Lambros said. "Where do we go from here?"

Slipping the thin, flexible phone from her pocket, Kara turned on the camera. She motioned for Drummond to do the same. "We make a sweep. Capture the same areas so we have two different videos showing the same evidence. Start here, then work our way up to the command level. Get as much of the weapons storage area as we can. Show what was taken. Make sure you get the Russian writing everywhere. There can be no doubt who owns this place when Admiral Kim sees this."

As they readied their cameras, Kara gave them a few more words of advice. "I know it feels like we need to rush, but we don't. We all know that we're most likely going to get caught when we get back. Since we've got the only submersible, though, we're free to do what we need to while we're here."

Chief Lambros looked upward, hands on hips, a serious, straight expression on her face. For a moment, Kara thought she might say something.

Instead, she gave them both a piercing look and a small smile. "I've got your back," she said.

"This is Congressman Arnold Drummond, representing Oregon's fourth district. I'm filming as part of a top-secret mission I was assigned to supervise, which I have discovered is nothing more than a corrupt cash grab on the part of a Naval Captain and unknown others, who are putting our nation at risk for their own gain."

Kara let Drummond jabber as she silently swept her camera around the docking bay. Pausing only to ensure that she got the stenciled writing on the floors and walls. Chief Lambros stepped confidently in front, opening the bay's only door, which led to a bleak, narrow stairwell. Pipes ran alongside the metal steps, which were little more than skeletal plates anchored around a central column. She led the way up to the next floor's landing, then held the door open for them there.

Drummond, in full political mode, kept droning on about theft of taxpayer money while he ascended the stairs, metal bouncing and groaning with each step.

Pausing on the second floor landing, Kara examined a hefty locking mechanism that sat inert on the steel door. Tren had left them all open. What would be the point of locking them again, after all? By the time anyone from the Russian military came through here again it would be obvious they'd been robbed. No sense in putting things back nice and neat.

Slowly, she worked her way around the floor. Just as Tren had described it, the whole level spread out in front of her. No individual rooms. Low ceiling, LED strip lighting casting dull pools of light on the bare cement floors, with painted yellow and red stripes to mark off different storage areas.

"This must be where the warheads were," Kara said while moving her camera. Blank spaces on the bare floor, cordoned off with red lines took up half the room. Cables with some kind of shiny, black balls on the end hung above each space. Maybe sensors? Tren hadn't mentioned them. She covered every meter of space, methodically, square by square. Only then did she move on to the other side of the floor. Drummond already busied himself walking up and down a row of headless missile bodies.

"We are looking at a way station of some kind, built and owned by Russia, off the United States coast in a clear violation of our treaty," Drummond continued his narration as he walked. "Intended purpose would be to arm nuclear launch capable subs. Why this was allowed to be built on our coast, and why Captain Faulkner decided to rob it, is unknown."

Kara let him get on with it. Maybe the talking helped his nerves. Tren could be rubbing off on him. Despite the tense situation, the thought made her mouth twitch. Drummond wrapped up his monologue when he saw her and Chief Lambros gathered at the door.

"What were you smiling about over there?" Chief Lambros gave her a friendly nudge.

"Something stupid," Kara said.

Chief Lambros stopped before going through the door. "Well. Make sure to think about stupid things every now and then. Life's serious enough."

She stopped herself short of asking the chief if she was feeling all right again. Who would be? If dispensing wisdom made the chief feel better, who was Kara to burst that bubble?

"Why don't you two go ahead this time," Chief Lambros said. "I'll watch your six."

Kara took point. A strange, electric sensation ran

278

over her skin. Her skin pebbled and the hair on her arms stood on end.

"Go on," Lambros softly urged her.

Without dwelling on the feeling, or the nerves that must have caused it, Kara forced herself to trudge up the steps to the top floor of the facility. Again, as she swung the door open she found it more or less as Tren had described. More cement floors, but filled with desks and monitors. Two smaller rooms flanked off the sides of this space, and the door Tren couldn't get open stood opposite the entrance.

"I'll start this way." Drummond, still holding his camera up, motioned to the left with his head. Speaking again into his phone, he walked on. "I'm entering what looks to be simple crew living quarters."

His voice faded and echoed as he disappeared through the open door. Kara took the other side. There wasn't much to see. She scanned a Spartan looking latrine with her camera. A couple of toilets without cubicle dividers (that wouldn't be awkward at all) two shower heads, two sinks. Topped off with a chrome drain on the gently sloped floor. Light from her phone flashed her as she passed the simple mirrors set over the sinks.

Kara walked back into the main entry way. "Well, that was a little bit of a—"

Her voice trailed away as the sound of clanging metal rang out from the stairwell. Dumbly, Kara turned her head toward the noise. In disbelief, she watched the metal door flung open, a bright beam of light entering with the thundering sound. Kara's hand automatically went for her sidearm, her phone dropped and forgotten.

As she reached, Chief Lambros standing closest to the door, spun around to face it. In horror, Kara saw her lift her pistol, pointing toward the open door. A single bark. A gutter of flame.

Chief Lambros flew backward, folding in half as if hammered in the gut.

"Stop!" Grayson's voice roared over all else. "Hold your fire!"

Out of the corner of her eye, Kara caught sight of Grayson physically wrestling the barrel of the man's rifle upward. From behind the struggling pair, Captain Faulkner appeared, holding a revolver.

Kara cared for none of it. All else forgotten, she dropped her weapon as easily as she had dropped her phone, and ran to Chief Lambros's side.

Lying, legs splayed on the bare cement, the chief clutched at her belly. Dark red wetness spread from under her trembling hands and from behind her back. Her eyes fluttered while the color drained from her face.

"Kara," she whispered. "Kara."

From behind her, Kara barely registered the sound of Drummond surrendering. Snips of Grayson yelling about not giving the order to fire. Meaningless.

She fell to her knees, thrust a hand down to help the chief put pressure on her wound. "It's okay, Chief, we're going to get you help."

But Kara's words shook worse than her knees.

"Kara," Chief Lambros's words came softer. Kara had to put her ear next to Chief Lambros's mouth to hear her amidst the chaos of the room. "Tren. Run with...Tren. Run with..."

"What are you talking about? Tren's not here, Chief. You're going to be fine. They have to have first aid here. Captain Grayson won't deny—"

A soft tug on her shirt. Kara looked down. A finger and thumb, slick with blood held on to her shirt. Kara realized the chief had pulled her hands away from the wound, as well as Kara's. Blood flowed freely.

Chief Lambros's lips moved softly. Tears streaking

her vision, Kara leaned to her again, desperate to hear her.

"We are...Ocean. Not. Wave."

Her breath slowed into a faint sigh.

And she was gone.

Lambros's hand went slack, releasing Kara's shirt, a bloody handprint left in its place.

The world lurched and darkened. Her lip curled into a sneer. Kara moved her head slowly, to look at the entrance.

Grayson had stopped wrestling with the rifleman. One of Faulkner's men, by his uniform. Faulkner himself kept his weapon trained on her, while his subordinate kept his weapon on Drummond.

"Give him your phone, Congressman," Faulkner said to Drummond. He pointed to the rifleman. Drummond may have complied, but Kara only had eyes for Grayson. If she could have bored holes in him with her vision, she would have.

Her chief. Dead.

Her teacher. Dead.

Her friend. Dead.

"A worthy plan," Faulkner began. "Too bad you didn't think things through. Didn't even consider we could get here another way? What was your end game? You had to come back at some point."

"You bastard," Kara said.

"Oh, what a wonderful retort!" Faulkner said.

"Not you, you arrogant prick. You. *Captain.*" Kara kept her gaze on Grayson, baring her top teeth. As she spoke, each word picked up momentum from the last, amplifying in volume and hate. "You don't deserve that eagle. Or that anchor. Or your breath. You stand next to him? You did this! You murdered her! She was your heart and your blood. Now, for you, and your greed, she's dead!"

"I did this for her!" Grayson shot back.

"The hell you did!" Kara's words tore her throat. "You did this for your own glory. So you could be the brave Captain Grayson who saved all the Mariners too stupid and worthless to save themselves. She was worth ten of you, Grayson! You've betrayed your oath, betrayed your blood."

"Touching," Faulkner said, dry as ever. "Well, let's add one more before we get this done with. Off you go."

From behind Faulkner, feet shuffled from the stairwell.

Tren.

Kara's breath caught. She looked back to her fallen friend, who lay as still as the floor she bled on.

He came slowly, shoulders slumped, hands in pockets. Tren looked over at her, a small needlepoint of light shining from his left eye. Impatiently, Faulkner waved his gun again, hastening Tren's approach. As Tren settled in to Kara's left, she made sure to position herself within arm's distance of Drummond.

"Very good," Faulkner said. "Already in a neat row. Thank you for saving us from anymore pointless distractions. Grayson, if you're not going to participate, at least do us the courtesy of not glaring at those of us with the will to do what must be done."

Tren nervously cleared his throat.

Kara caught his eye.

Tren, the Chief had said. *Run with.*

Kara gave Tren the slightest of nods.

At once, the lights went out. An alarm blared in discordant pulses, alternating from different speakers throughout the room. Kara ducked, grabbing both Tren and Drummond as she moved. Gunfire barked in front of them. Hot shrapnel bit into her from below as Kara twisted herself around.

Suddenly the lights clicked back on at an insane

brightness. Just as fast they were off again. She fell to her knees, hard, as the disorienting flashing and the noises danced around them, both blinding and deafening everyone in the room.

A hand pulled at Kara.

More gunfire. Or was it?

Kara kept her grip on Drummond. In a ragged line they stumbled as quickly as they could. With no idea where they were going or how quickly, Kara felt another blast of cement flakes burn her face. Suddenly a hammer struck the back of her hip and she flew forward. Hard flooring smacked against her face, sending stars through her vision.

A strong set of hands dragged her for what felt like two meters.

Then it stopped. A door must have shut, sealing out the din. In the dim light of this new room, the cacophony of the third floor was reduced to a dull rumble. Kara looked up from where she lay, on her belly. Dark spots corrupted her vision, but it cleared enough for her to see racks of computer servers humming away. Long thin drives protruded from their faces while soft LEDs blinked in a strange rhythm.

Three dull thumps came from the door.

Drummond's face jerked that way. Tren panted, then spoke. "They can't shoot their way in. Door's too strong."

"Kara," Drummond said, "I can't, there's no other way..."

"What are you babbling about?" She gritted her teeth against the dull pain in her hip.

"You've been shot, I need to put some pressure on it."

Her ass. Shot in the ass. Of course. Kara grit her teeth. "Don't worry about being a gentlemen, Arnold, slow the bleeding!"

"Right, right," he said. Quickly, he pulled off his shirt, grabbed Kara's knife and cut a strip off the bottom. He folded it and held it against her wound.

"Tren," Drummond said. "When they get in here to finish us off, can you pull that trick again? It might give us just the time we need. Why are you shaking your head?"

"Because they're leaving," Tren said. He looked up, that tiny light still sparkling in his left eye. "And they're taking both submarines with them. They don't have to kill us. We're stuck."

Chapter Twenty-One: Marooned

*"After Sailing Day it was different. We still had enemies.
We had problems. But we had a fresh start. We had each
other's backs. No question."*
James Keeling, Reborn at Sea: Mariner History 2041-2063

They waited, keeping the server room locked until
Tren confirmed the outer bay doors had shut behind
Grayson and Faulkner. Drummond then tore out
of the server room, looking for a first aid kit. Kara
called after him, suggesting he check the latrine and
the living quarters first.

Of course, Drummond leaving meant that Tren
had the awkward duty of holding the bandage on
her left cheek. Thankfully, Tren's mind seemed to
be somewhere else completely. He stared blankly at
the server racks, his head slightly tilted. They sat in
silence for a moment while Drummond presumably
rifled through the living spaces.

"What happened back there, Tren?" Kara said.

Tren slumped. "I didn't know about the other submarine, Kara, I swear. Everything happened pretty much like you and Chief Lambros said it would." He let his gaze float out of the door. When Tren looked her way again, his eyes had filled with tears.

"Except," he said, "Grayson didn't wait for you guys to get back. He made Chief Fen call the Gallant. Next thing I knew, he dragged me into that other submarine. He knew I had helped you I didn't have to say a word. I'm so sorry, Kara."

Chief Lambros.

Kara's heart tore open again. While she lay on her stomach, waiting for help, her friend and mentor grew cold.

"She knew," Kara said breathlessly.

"She knew what?"

"Right after...She told me..." Kara's voice caught. "You wouldn't believe me. I guess she wouldn't need you to believe her. But, she warned me, Tren. She told me to run with you. Thing is, we hadn't seen you yet. You were still in the stairwell."

"Hmm," Tren said. "I don't know what to make of that. Possibly she saw me when you didn't? Doesn't matter. If it helped, then she used her final words to save us."

Drummond appeared in the doorway. "For how long, though?"

He settled down next to Kara, thumping a large black case down by his side.

"My wound isn't that bad," Kara said.

"It's bad," Drummond said in an offhand way. He opened the case. "You're in shock. That's not what I meant, though. You might have noticed were stuck here with no way out. Tren, can you translate any of this stuff?"

Tren nodded. Drummond slid the case around so

Tren could see the contents. One by one, Drummond showed him items in their thick, plastic packages.

"Gauze bandages. Pressure dressings. I don't know which stuff we actually need, Arnold. Wait! Go back. Yes, that. It's a diagnosis machine? I have no clue what that is but it sounds promising. Here, switch with me."

Not commenting on how nonchalantly they were treating her wounded backside, Kara shivered. Somehow the floor felt like it was getting colder by the minute. While Drummond held the makeshift bandage on her wound, Tren tore open the package and went to work. Kara had seen devices similar to it. Doc Angus had one aboard Voyager.

Holding the bulky device a few centimeters over the wound, Tren ran it in small circles around the wound site. Drummond had to maneuver out of Tren's way.

"Oh, boy," Tren said. "Oh, boy."

"Well don't keep us in suspense!" Kara's teeth chattered.

Tren's voice shook along with his hands. "The, uh, according to this, the bullet is lodged into her hip bone. We need to get it out. There's a bone shard that needs to come out, too. And she's going into shock."

"Everyone, calm down." Drummond made a cutting motion with his free hand. "Tren, you'll read me the instructions, I'll do the work. My hands are steadier than yours."

"Gladly," Tren said.

"What's the first step?"

Tren fumbled a thin packet over to Drummond. "We need to give her that. You need to, I mean. It says to inject it here and here, see?"

Kara couldn't see, but she could hear the package tearing open. "What are you two chuckle-heads doing back there?"

They both ignored her. Tren went on, "That will numb the area. But it says there will still be pain."

A sharp tug at her belt and clatter of metal. Her knife lay on the ground. Tren handed her the leather sheath.

"Bite down on that, Kara," Drummond said.

"Is it supposed to hurt that bad?"

"Maybe," Drummond shot back. "But I really just need you to shut up for a bit."

Before she could stop it, a thick peal of laughter burst from her chest. Kara grabbed the sheath. "If I make it through this you better not be within arm's reach, Arnold."

Drummond paused. Two tiny bites of pain into her muscle. Insignificant compared to everything else. After a moment, a fuzzy numbness spread across her backside.

"Better?" Tren said.

"Little bit."

More package tearing. Drummond's voice started in again. "Okay, I've got the grabber things, Tren. Keep the screen in front of both of us so I can see what I'm doing here. Put your elbow on your knee, buddy. It'll keep the shakes down."

"The 'grabber things?'" Kara muttered. "Medical school, here you come."

"Try to stay still, Kara," Drummond said.

She had a prime comeback for that, but her words were quickly enveloped by a scream.

While the pain at the surface was numbed away, it suddenly felt as though Drummond had taken hammer and chisel to her bone. Stuffing the knife sheath into her mouth, Kara bit hard, tears streaming down her cheeks.

"One down!" Metal tapped onto the floor.

Another explosion of pain. Kara clenched so hard

her teeth were in danger of cracking or peeling away from her gums. A hot knife wrenched around inside her gluteal muscle, tearing and shredding everything in it's path.

A tiny click. "Got it. Damn it, more blood, what do we do? Tren, come on, buddy."

"Get, get, get that gun looking thing. Yes, yes. Put the end into the wound, like that. See?"

"But if I nicked a blood vessel—"

"You didn't! It says right, oh, yeah, it says it here. The bleeding is from the muscle. Just do the thing with that other thing like it says. Hurry!"

A warm, soft pressure filled the gaping hole rent into her backside. Kara let the sheath fall from her mouth, sighing at the same time.

"Grab that one. No, that one. It's an auto-stitcher. See what's happening here? Do that."

"Oh, just do that," Drummond muttered.

"No, no," Tren insisted. "You push the button when it gets to that spot on her. That's what the red dot means."

"Tren, I can't read the damn Russian! You have to tell me this stuff."

"Sorry, sorry, but do it, okay?"

Drummond mumbled.

A sort of quick, snappy pressure, like the flick of a rubber band against her numb skin told her that whatever was going on back there was working.

"Good, good," Tren said. "All we have to do is clean the outside, around the wound with those disinfectant pads. You do that and I'll clean up around here. How are you feeling, Kara?"

"Like I was just operated on by a Russian computer and the village idiot."

A low chuckle echoed through the room. Drummond finished with his task. "Guess Tren's the computer, right?"

"You have to stay put for an hour," Tren said. "That's what the computer's telling me. I'm going to get you a pillow and blanket from one of the beds."

After he got back and helped shove the bedding underneath her, Kara started feeling considerably warmer.

"Is this one of those things," she said thickly. "Like, when you get a concussion and you're not allowed to sleep?"

Tren checked the medical computer again. "No."

"Good." She closed her eyes.

She might have dreamed, but if she did, it came and went quickly, in shattered images of molten fire and towering waves.

Kara came to, still lying prone on the floor. With arms down at her sides, and legs straight, she wondered if she should just stay there a bit longer. All at once, the day came flooding back on her. Everything she wanted to duck and hide from refused to be ignored.

Chief Lambros.

Her heart sank all over again.

Drummond and Tren spoke softly to each other. They couldn't have been too far away from her makeshift bed on the floor.

"Air won't be our problem," Tren said. "I can see the system diagnostics. There's something called a rebreather system. I have to guess that's a kind of air scrubber, a device that can pull oxygen from carbon dioxide. Anyway, it's working fine. Environmental controls aren't giving any warning about that."

"Well," Drummond said. "We've got about a month's worth of rations for two people in the kitchen storage. Since I can't read Russian I have no idea what it is, but we've got some time before we starve."

Kara opened her eyes. Tren and Drummond sat against the nearest server rack. A large gray case had been closed up neatly next to them.

"Am I allowed to move now?" she said. Her voice cracked.

Tren swallowed. "You should be fine. It'll probably hurt though. Anesthetic would've worn off by now."

He wasn't wrong. Every muscle in her ass and down her thigh felt stiff as brick. Slowly, she rocked herself onto her uninjured side and made to bend her leg. A low growl rumbled in her throat.

"Let me help you." Drummond leaned over her, hand out.

She took his hand. Gently, he gave her a stable base to lift herself on to her feet. Once standing, Kara looked through the open doorway to the command floor.

"Where is she?" Kara said.

"Come on," Drummond said gently.

Kara tried to take a step, but collapsed when her injured leg touched down. Drummond jerked forward, grabbing her arm and keeping her upright.

"Let me help. We'll find you a walking stick out here."

Resigned, she nodded and let Drummond prop up her injured side.

Together, they walked back into the command room. A long, thick bundle of white cloth lay next to the wall that held the room's large display. She didn't know what to say. Tren and Drummond had moved Chief Lambros's body. Bound her in what looked like a bedsheet in a close approximation of a Mariner burial shroud.

"We, uh..." Tren's voice broke a bit. "Didn't know exactly how to do it. But we did our best. For her."

Kara could see that the knots were wrong. They

forgot the strip of cloth around the knees.

They'd done their best. Because they cared.

"It's perfect. She would have been very happy with it. Tren, do you know if there are pens, grease pencils, or anything I can use to mark her?"

"I'll look." He rummaged though the desks in the room, even the ones that had been turned over and broken during their battle with Grayson and Faulkner. While he searched, Kara hobbled over to the chief. With Drummond's help, she knelt down, trying to keep her mending leg straight. Every time it bent a wild shock of pain ran up through her backside.

"Here, Lieutenant." Tren passed a thick black marking pen to her.

"Thanks." She held the marker in her hand, thinking. Finally, she looked to the others.

"It would mean a lot to me if you could stand witness. I want to do this right. She deserves that."

"Of course," Drummond said. "Wait a sec."

Jogging over to the side of the room, he took the Russian Federation flag off of the wall. Kara wanted to ask him what he was doing, but couldn't muscle up the will for it. Drummond removed the flag and left it lying flat over one of the desks. As he walked back, he held the short flag staff up and eyed Kara's height.

"It's a little tall," he said. "But it'll make for a decent enough walking stick."

Kara assessed the brass-colored pole as he laid it down next to her. Made of thin metal but stout. A fist-sized ball at the top. She thanked him. Drummond moved off to stand next to Tren.

Still holding the marker, Kara used the walking stick to get back to her feet. The round metal knob at the end made for a good hand hold. She cleared her throat.

"Chief Athena Lambros," she began. "Student of every religion she found. But she held allegiance to the Core, most of all."

Stiffly, Kara brought herself back down far enough to bring the tip of the marker to the cloth over Chief Lambros' forehead. There, she drew the circle and three inward arrows of the Core.

"I've seen you reduce a deckhand to tears. Only to comfort them later. When I first got assigned to the Water Lily and saw you were my chief, I almost pissed myself. You stood there, tall, solid, indestructible. I knew I better watch myself around you. And I was right, you were a tyrant. Everything had to be perfect, all the time. But...You never asked me, or anyone else to do anything you didn't ask of yourself. A ship has to run according to the best of our abilities, or it sinks. You told me that. You were also our Core Teacher aboard the Water Lily. I learned so much from you. You made me want to be the best version of myself. Beneath your demanding exterior, was the kindest, most loving soul I've ever met.

"You knew, Chief. I know you did. You knew what was coming for you in here. And yet you walked bravely. Your last words on this earth were not a plea for mercy. They were to help your friends. Your dying act was to keep us safe and less afraid."

Kara had to take a moment. While she let herself cry, she looked down. When she looked up, both Drummond and Tren had come to her. They each draped an arm over her shoulders.

"Will you sing with me?" She asked them.

They agreed. True to their words, Kara led them in the Song of Journey. Voices cracked, tired, and breaking, they lifted the words in song all the same.
I thought I was alone,
But you are a part of me.
I thought I was a wave,

'Til I became the sea.

After some discussion, they decided to take Lambros down to the docking bay. Eventually, they'd need to take her for a proper release to the sea. By no means was it a perfect plan, but it felt more right to let her rest by the waves and the sparkling, ethereal light of the bay than to leave her to rot in the command center. It was nominally cooler down there, which would help, given they had no idea how long they would be stuck inside the Russian facility.

Kara half sat on the edge of a desk, keeping her bad leg straight. Tren sat in a desk chair while Drummond paced a slow circuit around the room. "Are you sure about the schedule, Tren?"

"Sure as I can be." Tren shrugged. "The days vary a little, but they always send a two man crew here once every quarter of the year. They're due any day now. That's going off the last logged visitor time."

"We don't have much choice," Drummond said. "If they get here on a fully staffed submarine, there's no way we'd be able to fight them and somehow steal their ship. We'll need to surrender. God, help us."

"Will your political ties help you?" Kara said. There wasn't any bite in the question. She genuinely wanted to know if it could protect him.

"Doubtful." Drummond picked a squishy ball out of a desk drawer and began tossing and catching it as he walked. "Any other congressman? Maybe the other members of government might negotiate a release or an extradition or something. Me? I think the Federal government will throw in some cash if the Russians keep me longer."

Kara did a double take. "Why are you nodding, Tren?"

"Because it's true," he said baldly. "You didn't know? People really hate him."

"Thanks, buddy," Drummond said.

"No, really." Tren pressed the issue to Kara. "I never agreed with them. I liked the idea of better government oversight and all that. All the major news sites say he's leading a dangerous return to pre-war socialism, and that all his talk about fighting corruption is just a ploy to get his subversive hooks into the business of hard-working statesmen."

"Seriously?" Kara said. "This guy? You're famous?"

Drummond took a bow. "In the worst sense of the word, yes."

"Honestly, it's disturbing how much attention the major news sites give him," Tren said. "It's safe to say that none of us will be welcomed with open arms. Especially, with, you know, the warheads being stolen."

"Is there any way we can"—Drummond searched— "I don't know, get out on our own steam? Kara, you're a strong swimmer."

"No one," she said, "could hold their breath that long. Even if you did, you're up topside. Now what? It's another seven kilometers to shore. Depending on the tides, it's a death sentence. There's a reason they put this thing where they did. Is there any way we can call for help?" Kara scooted a little, trying to shift to a better position on the desk.

"No, Faulkner took my phone," Drummond said. "That was a joke, Tren, of course I know we can't call from here. Oh, before I forget. Happy birthday."

Kara stayed put while Drummond handed her a thin, flexible phone. "They got mine, but I found yours in the latrine. Doesn't look broken. I mean, fat lot of good that does us if the Russians pinch us. It's the thought that counts, though."

"Spirit of the idea isn't bad though," Kara looked

over the phone. "If there was some way to send a message to Voyager they could rescue us. They still have an A-diver on board. If anyone can find this place and get in, it's them. Obviously a phone is out of the question but do we have any other options? There has to be some kind of signal or communication system in here. In fact, we know there is."

Tren added his two cents. "The type of acoustic wave antenna this place uses is very short range and has to be used in line of sight. That's a limit of the technology, there's no way to extend it."

"Wait," Kara said. "How did the Ionova get the distress call, then?"

Tren waved her away. "Different hardware. Somewhere around here the station has a broadcast only transmitter, separate from the receiver we used by the main door. If you're passing overhead, sure, you can pick something up. That's how the Ionova got wind of this bunker in the first place. I could hack that with a message, but someone would need to pass directly overhead to receive it like the Ionova did."

Gingerly, Kara brought over a desk chair and slowly settled herself down into it. "That's something else I don't get about this whole mess. At first I thought that the distress call was just something Faulkner and his cronies cooked up to justify coming here. That can't be right, though. The Ionova got the signal. And they didn't have any connection to Faulkner that I know of."

"No, that was real," Tren mumbled. He had his fingers planted on the contacts of his deck, the light in his left eye flickering. "When Big Madrid first had me try to decrypt it, I couldn't. Very frustrating. I was working on bad assumptions. We all thought the signal came from some kind of old wreck. As we know now, it came from a very modern, secure facility. I underestimated its sophistication."

"Can you get it now?" Drummond asked.

"I've been playing with it off and on. Finally cracked it earlier when we were keeping an eye on Kara. It's a series of codes relating to server failures." He jerked a thumb to the server room.

"Huh?" Kara sat up straighter, groaned, then slid back down. "Why? I mean, what would be the point of risking detection of this facility because a computer's messed up. There's a ton of them back there. Something must have corrected itself, right? Everything seems fine in here."

"But it's not." Tren's attention stayed on whatever he was watching. "All primary systems are working, yes. One of the servers back there, however, is having a hardware failure."

"And that's worth risking someone finding this place?" Drummond raised his brow. "I'm with Kara, that makes no sense."

"No, there has to be a logical explanation. No one would plan this carefully only to make a mistake like that. I still don't know what most of those servers are for. Only a few of them are needed for primary facility operations. The rest are a mystery. Interestingly enough, they all have lock drives sticking out of them. Which suggests some kind of long-term data storage. But this place isn't networked with anything else."

"Fascinating." Drummond tossed the ball again.

"Fine," Kara said. "Let's forget about the mystery servers for a minute. Those aren't going to help us get out of here. I know it's a short range transmitter, but is there any possible way we can change that? Make the transmitter, bigger, somehow? Or build a new one, or extend the range?"

Tren stopped, the light winking out in his eye. "Well, I don't know if we can get to the transmitter from in here. There might be a way to rig a new one, though."

"Seriously?" Drummond let his latest toss bounce to the ground. "That could work?"

"Maybe," Tren said. "Well, let's think this through. Conventional radio signals don't go through sea water very well at all. This short-range transmission from base to surface we have here is a different animal altogether. However, we could use the primary acoustic transmitter as the source, and create a secondary that would act as a kind of signal repeater that would be long range. If we could create a floating platform of some kind with the second antenna attached, get it up to the surface, it could bounce our signal. Then again, everyone would get our broadcast, including the Russians..."

"Could we use one of our Mariner encryption protocols?" Kara asked.

Tren shook his head. "Guarantee you Russian intelligence can already break it. And they'll be monitoring this area close. If only there were a way to physically run a message, oh my God, I have it, Harry!"

Exploding in a flurry of action, Tren ran into the server room and zipped back out. He fumbled through a tool box, grabbed two tools that Kara couldn't identify before sprinting back into the server room.

Drummond gave her a helpless expression. "Who the hell is Harry?"

Kara motioned for him to help her up. Limping behind Tren, Kara remembered.

"Harry Halibut?"

"Exactly!" The light in his eye glowed brighter. Tren had a cable pulled from the wall and a length of it stripped of its insulation. Expertly he grafted another segment of wire to the spot and ran it to his control deck.

"Listen," he said with some difficulty. "Would Grayson have stopped to pick up Harry before they left the area? Doubtful. Would he still be in the area? I don't know. If Harry is here, though, I can reach out to him."

"Your, your, thing." Kara waved a finger at him, bouncing on her good leg. "The signal repeater thing you were talking about!"

"What's this?" Drummond said. "Come on, Tren, you know I wasn't listening the first time."

Tren waved them both away. "It's simple. I send an encrypted message meant for Harry using the short-range transmitter. Where we are, how to get in, everything Voyager needs to know. Maybe he's close enough to receive it. Then, God willing, he'll find his way back to the Penitent, or if he can manage it, another Mariner ship. He knows what to look for."

As Kara put together all of the variables—if Harry was even around, if he could find another Mariner in the wide ocean, if his programming was even good enough for him to not get lost chasing phytoplankton—it all felt like an incredible longshot. Adding to that how long it would take him to do any of those things.

Tren paused. He must have seen her face. "I know, Kara. It might be our only shot."

Chapter Twenty-Two: Rescue

"Mariners stand together. That is our strength. That sets us apart. Want to see what happens to a people who don't? Go to any harbor on the mainland."
Aisha Warner, Founding Mariner

An entire day passed, minutes grinding like a mythical glacier over black rock plains. Waiting, in itself, normally wasn't difficult for Kara. Waiting in this situation, however, was a beast of a different stripe. Every moment they spent sitting around the facility was a moment that brought them closer to being discovered by the Russians. It was a moment that brought Grayson closer to his goal of using his newfound weapons to hold the seas hostage, supposedly for the good all Mariners.

Even now, Faulkner sailed away, drinking in the sea air, tasting freedom. To what end he would put his share of the theft, Kara didn't know. But it killed her all the same. Kara had no way to stop them, no agency at all. Hell, she couldn't even help herself.

Periodically, Tren and Drummond would lapse back into a discussion about how to create Tren's floating antenna, as a back up plan. They even went so far as to raid the facility for supplies, but found that they were far short on the cabling they'd need to get the repeater above the waves and anchor it in place.

Could they strip rope or wiring from someplace else in the facility and use that?

Could they chance it and hope that it didn't float away too quickly?

Could they just let it float away, broadcasting their location until its batteries died?

As their options drained like a ship's battery on a cloudy day, they each fell to their own distractions. Kara felt it, as she was sure they did, too. That moment when their optimism buckled under the weight of their catastrophic situation, breaking open a dam of wildly oscillating emotion. She sought out a quiet space in the sleeping quarters and sat (as well she could) for a long meditation session. Tren retreated into the server room, investigating the first and last mystery of their doomed adventure, what was the deal with the servers and the distress signal?

Drummond found a bottle of vodka hidden among the rations and proceeded to drink. Which would've been harmless enough, but he turned out to be a loud drunk.

She would've forgiven him, given the hopelessness of it all. But he was being so damn noisy and all she wanted was a few minutes of inner peace, goddamn it. "For the love of God, Arnold, shut the hell up!" She hollered.

Hoisting herself up with her walking stick, Kara grunted and hobbled into the command center.

"No, no, no, you guys." Drummond's cheeks

burned red as apples. "You guys. I've got it. I know it. The answer. Everything's cool. It's under control. Announcement. I have an announcement to make."

Tren poked his head out of the server room. "What is this?"

"The answer, my friend. And it's blowing in the wind. Literally!" With a great flourish, Drummond leapt to the side of the desk holding the RF flag. Still managing to keep the vodka bottle in his hand, he dramatically swept the Russian colors over his shoulders like a cape, and tied the ends around his neck.

Kara watched, open mouthed. "What fresh hell is this?"

"Acting Captain," Drummond shouted. "It's the only way. Listen, there's only one flag, and obviously, as the inventor of this genius plan, *I* will wear it. However, the plan goes as thusly. We, using every stitch of cunning we possess, shall pose as Russian Federation agents. No, no, hear me out!"

Drummond stumbled forward, bleary eyed, sloshing the bottle out in front of him for attention. "It's perfect because of its beautiful simpli-simplicity. They'll never expect it. Okay, our cover story, we have to get this straight. We were assigned here by, I don't know, Oleg. Get it? Oleg, he's our guy. We're just here, doing our jobses, and then bang! We get attacked by the dirty Americans! We barely made it out with our lives, Comrades!"

Kara couldn't help it. She leaned forward on her walking stick, bellowing laughter until her eyes streamed.

"Don't laugh! It's perfect. Listen to how good my accent is." Drummond loudly cleared his throat and took another swig. "*Greetings, Comrade. We drink so much vodka on Putin Day, did we not? Americans are stupid. Potatoes are great. Can I offer you some* borscht?"

Wiping her eyes, Kara braced herself against a wall.

"That is..." A female voice, thick with a Russian accent, rang out from the stairwell behind Kara. The door squealed and sealed shut. "The worst impression I have ever heard."

Kara froze. Slowly, she stood up straight. Her pulse hammered through the artery in her neck. Her brow flushed, prickling with sweat.

Heavy heeled boots clopped from the doorway into the corridor.

"*Kotyonok,*" Goldi said. "Put down the bottle, hmm? You embarrass me in front of our guests."

Goldi found herself overrun by the three of them. They poured questions over her, but Goldi brushed them off. Gently, she undid the knotted flag around Drummond's neck. She patted his face.

"Go put the bottle back. It is time to leave."

"I can't take it?" he said.

Goldi gave him an appraising look. "I would say not. There's my good boy."

"You got the message," Kara said breathlessly. "We hoped, but we didn't think it would really work."

"It is very strange." Goldi gave Tren a light punch to the shoulder. "To get a message from a robot fish. We must talk fast. We have little time if your message is right. You expect my former countrymen to be here soon, no?"

She nodded. "We have to catch up to Grayson. Goldi, he's the one who left us here."

Goldi stepped back. "What? No. No, surely, no."

Tren confirmed it, as did an unsteady Drummond as he wavered in from the kitchen.

"How did Harry find you?" Tren's eye light still flickered.

"We stop at Skatch Harbor to unload the survivors

from the gunboat. While we are there, Admiral Kim called. Said he had not heard from Captain Grayson in days and wanted us to check on him. So we come back. Now we are here, I see how it makes sense. He has turned on his own blood and heart."

"We have to catch him, Goldi. He's going to start attacking any ships that come into our waters. He wants to threaten any groups that do with nuclear retaliation."

Goldi swore in Russian. "Kara, would that we could, but Voyager still has flimsy patches over big bullet holes. We move too fast and we are sucking in water."

"Could you use any of the material here to patch the hull?" Tren said.

Kara gave him an exasperated glance.

"Why not?" Tren said a little indignantly. "We've stolen everything else. In for a penny, in for a pound. I'm going to steal stuff from the server room."

Kara rolled her eyes and went back Goldi. "Who else is here?"

"Morgenstern," Goldi answered, then paused. "Kara, downstairs. Who...Who of our blood and heart is shrouded?"

Kara choked up, her wounds still terribly fresh. "That's Chief Lambros."

Goldi's face fell. "No, sister. No. It's not her."

Kara embraced Goldi, wrapping herself around the woman's thin, strong frame. Goldi sniffed as she pulled away.

"This is because of him?" Goldi asked. "He is why my teacher has returned home?"

"Yes." Kara swallowed down everything else she wanted to say.

"Then we have no time to waste, Skipper," Goldi said.

✦ ✦ ✦

Downstairs in the entry bay, Morgenstern waited by the docked A-diver. At seeing them following Goldi through the door, he rushed over and greeted them, relief clearly showing on his face. As good as it was to see him and their way out of the facility, Kara's relief quickly became overshadowed by what lie ahead, and the scope of what they had already lost.

Morgenstern grabbed Goldi and a rapidly sobering Drummond to help him gather any supplies that could help him patch up Voyager. While they worked, Tren brazenly found an unused duffle bag in a wall locker which he used to load items from the server room. Kara made him swear that nothing he was doing would lock them in or shut the place down. In true "Tren" form, he barely paid her any attention.

Step by step, Kara limped down the narrow stairs, still using her makeshift walking stick. As she reached the deck of the docking bay, she found Voyager's submersible still docked, her top cargo door open. All else had been loaded, save for one critical passenger.

The rest of their small crew waited by Chief Lambros's shrouded body. Goldi stepped forward to meet Kara.

"I see you have given her a mark," Goldi said. "Did you speak for her?"

Kara nodded.

"Sang for her journey?"

"We did," Kara said.

"Then it is done. We will take her back to Voyager for her final salute." Goldi walked with Kara over to the rest of the group.

With her bad leg, Kara couldn't help. So she stood in vigil as Goldi, Morgenstern, Tren, and Drummond picked Lambros up and moved her into the cargo hold. After a short, stiff climb and help from her friends, Kara found herself strapping into the submersible. Morgenstern took the pilot's seat. There wasn't much room to spare in the little A-diver, but they managed.

The engines hummed to life. Kara closed her eyes, feeling the smooth vibration and relishing the moment of their escape. Tren walked Morgenstern through the procedure to leave. As a measure to delay discovery of their crime, he was going to 'jam the locks' behind them.

A hand touched her arm. Kara opened her eyes. Goldi had leaned over her seat and reached out to her.

"Thank you," Kara said.

"You never have to thank me, sister," Goldi said seriously. Then, with a sly grin, she motioned to Drummond, who snored in his seat. "Him, though? Owes me big time."

The craft shook gently from side to side as Morgenstern guided them out of the Russian facility. Kara vowed to spend the rest of her days top-side of the waves.

Chapter Twenty-Three: Pursuit

"In a large society it's easy to lose sight of an individual's contribution. A Mariner has no such luxury. Duty isn't an ideal, it's a necessity."
James Keeling, Reborn at Sea: Mariner History 2041-2063

"I expect this is the end of our partnership," Faulkner said. His voice ringing tinny from the small speakers on the central display in the Penitent's bridge. "Mission complete, and all that."

Every muscle in Grayson's neck and shoulders knotted like rocks the second he saw the other man on Faulkner's display. As they spoke, the Gallant shoveled more distance between the two of them. Grayson seriously and honestly debated the merits of following them and giving them both railguns.

"And if you find yourself needing to unload that treasure," Big Madrid said. "You come look me up, eh?"

From on screen, the man smiled with a mouth

full of chrome teeth, the bottom of his eyelids lined by tattoos. That smile. That blasted smile.

Grayson's voice came out in a growl, "If you ever see me, you'll want to run the other way, Madrid. And fast. I've got a score to settle with you."

"Ooh," Big Madrid gave a playful little jump, flipping up the ends of his stole. "That's me chastened. I'll never do bad again, mummy, I swear it, I do."

Faulkner let out a little hiccup of a laugh. "Lighten up, Grayson. I don't know where this moral superiority of yours comes from, but it's tiring. Well done, and all that. Toodles."

The screen went blank.

Yet, Grayson stood, facing the blank display, his fists balled with impotent rage. How dare he? How dare that fraud of a captain, that travesty of a human? The thick, inky silence which had taken up residence on the ship since he'd come back from the facility without their wayward crew seemed to follow Grayson wherever he went. Now it puddled around his ankles in the bridge, moving everyone it touched into fearful muteness.

They'll see, he told himself. Sacrifices had to be made. For their future. They'll all see.

See.

A shadow of a thought brushed against his mind: A salute and a firm shake of the hand.

I see your third eye mark, he had said to her. *Have you really Seen?*

I have, Chief Lambros said with a small, easy smile. *It's overrated.*

Grayson shook his head, holding back a snarl. It didn't matter. Nonsense. It wasn't his fault. Nonsense.

"Well," he shouted at Orozco, who just stood there like a lump. "You have our new course, Commander. Let's make way."

But Commander Orozco didn't budge.

"What is it now, man?"

Slowly, Orozco turned his way, his eyes narrowed. "Him. Madrid. You were working with him? This whole time?"

"I didn't know Faulkner was keeping him onboard like some kind of pet!" Grayson roared.

"And when you found out, what did you do then, sir? What did you do about the fact that your new business partner sheltered the man who sent ten of our blood and heart to the deep?"

They stood nose to nose. The air inside the bridge burned.

"I'm doing what needs to be done for this ship and for all Mariners, Commander!" Grayson shouted in Orozco's face.

"Well." Orozco backed up a step, his voice dropping low. "I'm sure that'll be great comfort to Bilby's family."

Without thinking, Grayson stepped forward, his fist flying straight into Orozco's face. A wet snap met his knuckles as Orozco spilled backward onto the deck, clutching his bleeding nose.

"Captain!" Chief Fen ran between the men, arms out to either side like a human blocking dummy. "That's enough!"

"That is enough," Grayson raged. "Get off my bridge and report to the deck. You're demoted to general crew, Orozco."

The former commander stood. He dropped his hand, blood pattering down to the deck with it. His voice thick and nasal, he spoke, "Better yet. Find me in the brig. I won't obey a traitor. Save us both the trouble of you throwing me in."

Chief Fen froze on the spot. In Grayson's chest, the fire guttered and then burned hotter. He made to rage back at the insubordinate little nitwit, but

Orozco had stormed out, the hatch to the bridge swinging open in his wake.

"Fen," Grayson snapped. "You're first officer now. Get our course set. I'll be in the cargo hold."

Unsteady, Chief Fen nodded. "Aye. Captain."

Grayson swept out of the bridge, making sure to close the hatch securely. He'd make a little stop off at the ship's tiny brig to make sure Orozco stayed true to his word, then he'd forbid anyone to speak to him. This cancer had to be rooted out now. It was a stern measure, but necessary for their survival.

As he stomped on to the deck, a pair of deckhands saluted him. Grayson could tell by the way they held his gaze they wanted to talk. Did they have some opinions they needed to share as well? So be it. Grayson had enough teeth for everyone.

"Sir," the closer of the two, Berens was his name, spoke first. "Sir, me and some of the crew, we just wanted to say it's about time we took the fight to these trespassers. We're with you one hundred percent, Skipper."

Grayson had to pause for a moment while the pleasant surprise soaked in. He thanked the men for their loyalty, and went back to his walk around the deck. Well. Didn't look like everyone on the ship was a weak-willed traitor, after all. As for the others?

They'll see.

I see your third eye mark, he had said to her. *Have you really Seen?*

I have, Chief Lambros said with a small, easy smile. *It's overrated.*

The highs and lows of the past few days didn't get left behind in the Russian facility. Unfortunately, as Kara found out, they followed her group back to

Voyager. When they first disembarked from the craft, helped along by the others inside, shouts and cries of welcome from the crew blasted over them. Even Tren and Drummond were brought happily back into the fold. Smiles and laughter rang over the deck.

Until Kara called them to attention.

Some of the Mariners tossed confused glances her way, but did as they were told. Then she called them to salute. Some, she thought, some understood then. When their small team carried Chief Lambros's shrouded remains out and on to the deck, the whispers spread like fire.

Every Mariner aboard Voyager took their turn on deck, wanting to say goodbye to their deckmaster, teacher, and friend. At that moment it stuck Kara how many lives Chief Lambros had touched. She never strived for achievement or rank. But she was mourned as greatly as any Mariner Kara had ever seen.

When they returned her home, to the sea, the crew sang for her again. Then slowly, in disbelief, they returned to their day alone and in groups. Despite how much her leg pained her, or how badly she wanted a rest, Kara made her way to the bridge.

As she limped in through the hatch, she refused help from Ensign Martin but thanked him all the same.

"Just in time, Skipper," Morgenstern said.

"I'm not the acting Captain, you are. Anyway, in time for what?"

Morgenstern pointed to the main display.

"Ah," Admiral Kim said. "Good to see you, Kara. Lieutenant Morgenstern has been filling me in. You have my deepest condolences."

Kara leaned against her walking stick and nodded. In the glare of the display she caught sight of herself. Her eye, blackened by her fall in the command center, complemented the reddened knife wound on her forehead, which, all things considered still hurt like a bastard. The one on her wrist wasn't much better. God, she was a mess.

From the screen, Admiral Kim's expression went grim. "Lieutenant Nkosi, it sounds like we're up against the clock. So let's get to it."

✦ ✦ ✦

Kara called an all hands meeting once the ship got underway. Of course some would have to remain at their stations, but they could listen over the ship's speakers. She hobbled out of the hatch while Morgenstern stepped behind her, light as a feather.

"Would you quit gloating?" she said.

"Not gloating," he added quickly. "Just, better you than me, that's all."

Kara stopped and gave him a look.

His mirth faded. "But, honestly, I want you in charge, Kara. There's no other Mariner on this ship I trust more to lead us right now."

Bracing the walking stick under the crook of her arm, Kara raised her hands and flashed him two signs.

Together. Strong.

Morgenstern gave her a wan smile.

Together. Always, he responded.

He followed her across the deck, as they moved through the thick groups of assembled crew. As she approached the bow, Kara caught sight of Goldi standing close to Tren and Drummond.

"You know," she said to Goldi, "you don't have to watch Tren anymore. He's more than earned our trust."

Before Goldi could respond, Tren jumped in. "Are you sure? I could be up to anything, you know."

Goldi gave him a little shake. "He could! You do not know how tricky this one is, no?"

Declining comment, Kara finished her walk to the raised forward section of the bow. Facing the crew, she accepted a radio from Morgenstern. Ensign Martin had already routed it to play through the ship's speakers.

Taking in the assembled crew, Kara felt the apprehension running through them. Chill air brushed through their hair and tugged at their clothes. In a way, they were heading both home and into new territory all at once.

"Two Mariner ships have never fought," she said without preamble. "I know that's what's on everyone's mind. We try not to keep secrets about our missions or what our goals are. So, many of you already know what our orders are. I'm confirming it now, with everyone, instead of letting word come through normal channels. We are pursuing the Penitent. She's running dark, so we don't have a location. But I have an idea of where they're headed. Captain Grayson is looking to sink any ships trespassing in our waters. There are only a couple of hot spots near enough that would be of value to him. We can find him."

A couple of the crew clapped and cheered. Kara saw a hand raised and called on the crew member.

Collin, the young deckhand who had boarded the Ionova with her spoke. "Are we really going to cross guns with the Penitent? Is that what our plan is?"

A chill tickled the back of her neck. In that instant, Kara's focus on the crew sharpened. Chief Lambros's words after the attack came floating back to her. She needed to be careful.

"You know what happened to Chief Lambros," she said.

Flickers of anger touched faces in the crew. A few

spat their anger and curses into the wind.

"Captain Grayson didn't pull the trigger. He was complicit in her death, though. Had Tren not intervened, I am positive the three of us would have been murdered as well." Kara gave Tren a small nod. He looked down at his feet, embarrassed. All at once the crew looked torn between gratitude at the skinny man and rage that one of their own could do such a thing.

"Hey," Drummond yelled. "What about me? I pulled a bullet out of your ass!"

Scattered laughter rolled through the crew. Watching his broad grin, Kara caught his drift. Drummond could read people just as well as she. Better, maybe. That little joke of his helped break apart the swiftly congealing anger.

"We're proud of you, too, Congressman." Kara rolled her eyes dramatically. "Incidentally, he was pretty eager for the job."

She let the catcalls and chatter die down. A small moment passed where the only sounds were the flapping sun sails and the passing wind.

"I know you want revenge. Because a big part of me does, too. Trust me. Then I think of the chief. I remember that the only time she argued with me was after we were attacked, when I swore revenge in front of all of you. 'Holding that anger,' she told me, 'is like drinking poison and expecting someone else to die.' As much as I wanted to ignore her, she eventually proved herself right. As always. What I wouldn't give for her to be with us now. But that's not possible. All I can do to honor her is to remember what she taught me."

Thumping her walking stick on the deck, Kara tread a slow pace across the bow. "Fighting the Penitent will only cause more misery. Her crew didn't know about any of this. Do we punish them for Grayson's acts? I hope not. There are damn fine Mariners on that ship. So, we find them. And if Grayson can't be made to see reason and come back to be held accountable for his actions, then, and only then, we must resolve ourselves to fight and win. This is not in service of revenge. This is done in the name of justice and accountability. To the laws that we all hold sacred. We are being tested, Mariners. Do we devolve into bloodthirsty savages? Or do we carry forward the society our ancestors strived to build?"

There were no cheers, no bloodthirsty shouts. This group couldn't have been more different than the one she'd spoken to after that mass funeral. Kara saw the steel in their eyes, the set in their jaws, and the pride in their shoulders.

They weren't some mob. They were Mariners.

Chapter Twenty-Four:
Mending Fences

"No matter how battered a sun-sail is, you can repair or repurpose it. Maybe it's not the same, but that doesn't mean it isn't valuable."
Lizzy Hernandez, Sail Apprentice, Gane Island

It took a bit of convincing on Big's part to get Faulkner to take the stick out of his arse and see the opportunity.

"He tried to kill you," Faulkner said.

"Don't be such a mincer. He tried to have me killed, there's a difference. Anyway, if I refused to do business with every punter who's sent the occasional bullet my way, I wouldn't have a client list." Big Madrid ultimately got Faulkner's concession, but not his blessing.

When the conference screen lit up, Captain Faulkner made sure he wasn't in view of the camera. Self preservation and all that. For a big tough Navy Captain he was a bit of a Nancy.

Big rubbed his battered faux fur against one cheek, hoping to register at least some surprise from Nakamura.

"Darling," Big drawled.

"Mister Madrid!" Nakamura embodied perfection. Huge smile, not a trace of guilt. A master. A true master.

Big let himself fill with a little envy at that marvelous office the man possessed. "You don't seem surprised to see me," Big teased.

"Should I be?" Nakamura half sat on the edge of his desk, arms relaxed. "I got some reports about the DCV Verne. Nasty business. Don't tell me you're still mad? You don't seem like the type."

"Me?" Big laughed easily. "Oh, Mister Nakamura, surely you're pulling my tit. Of course, I'm not angry. It's in the past, eh? I feel I compensated myself well from the holdings of the Verne by way of restitution. No, no, this isn't about revenge or gloating. This is about business."

"Oh?" Nakamura's brow raised, his mouth pulled in an exaggerated moue. "Unfortunately, Big, our last partnership went a little off the rails."

"Well, now..." Big raised a finger. "If we're being honest, I think you knew a little more about my job than you were letting on. I think you had some fairly accurate suspicions about what we were going to find down there, did you not?"

A flicker. Not much. But enough.

Casually, Nakamura plucked a golf ball off his desk and began juggling with one hand. "You actually made it to the site? I'm impressed. Find anything of value?"

"Oh, I think you know what we found."

Nakamura kept juggling. "Don't make me guess, buddy. I'm bad at it. Lowers my self-esteem when I'm wrong."

Big chuckled. "Well, it happens that I'm sitting on a cache of seeds."

"Seeds, huh?" Nakamura snatched the ball from the air and held it. "And what do these magic seeds of yours grow? Beanstalks?"

Big grinned with all his chrome teeth. "Not beanstalks. They will grow you some clouds though. Of the mushroom variety."

"Hmm." Nakamura considered Big, tapping the golf ball on his chin. "You think I'm interested in such things?"

"Oh, Mister Nakamura," Big chided. "I think you are, and have been, very interested from the start."

Taking a short walk from his desk, Nakamura found his putter and set his ball carefully on his putting green. "I'm not saying I'm not interested. We can talk."

"Just one thing," Big said.

"Naturally, there's something else. Go on."

"We are of course, looking for an exclusive arrangement. If you happen to hear from other prospective sellers, we would, of course, like to be made aware."

Nakamura laughed. "Exclusivity? What is this? Are we going steady now, Big? You've gotta give me something else for that kind of VIP treatment."

"How about this?" Captain Faulkner swept into view, thoroughly throwing Big Madrid off his game. So now the poncy bastard wanted a bit of time in the spotlight?

Par for the course, Nakamura didn't miss a tick. Easy as you please, he looked over Faulkner, his eyes sweeping the man's uniform once, and said, "Captain Faulkner, Pacific Fleet, is it? Can't say we've had the pleasure yet."

"Apologies, Mister Nakamura. I felt that I could add some value to this, er, exchange. I can offer you a little something extra. For free. If you decide it's worth your time, then do think more on our proposal."

Nakamura stood fully, one hand resting on his club. "I'm listening."

"You have two container ships crossing through Mariner territory soon, do you not? They'd be TXM vessels sailing along the new trade route."

"I have many such ships," he said coolly.

"These would be sailing dangerously close to a speck of an island they call Gane. They'll be attacked by the shipsies. And I'm going to tell you how to beat them."

"Well," Nakamura's smile returned. "As our mutual friend Big Madrid would say, 'I'm all ears, darling.'"

✦ ✦ ✦

Gane.

Captain Grayson's home island. Hub of plastics recycling and some of the Mariner's largest saltwater crop farming. They grew out on platforms that extended kilometers from the island. Winds out Gane way weren't as harsh as they were on the other islands, including Vish. No need for artificial windbreaks. It also made Gane susceptible to attack and vandalism. Mariners were already unpopular, especially among the Americans that their islands lay closest to.

For the past generation, since the last failed invasion by the U.S., it was understood internationally that travelers were to leave Mariners alone. Respect the work the Mariners did for ocean conservation and not disturb their homes. Even if the Americans didn't completely obey that edict, they'd toned down some of their torment.

The trade agreement thumbed its nose at all of that, calling out routes through waters the Mariners had been protecting and conserving, and which brushed against their home islands. It was deliberate and unnecessary.

So, Kara understood where Grayson came from. Partially. Over time, the routes would destroy what they had worked for. Pollution from the ships that still ran on fossils would kill their crops and poison sea life. In a matter of months commercial fishers would destroy the sea life Kara's people had spent decades replenishing. She understood the anger. Hell, she'd argued for methods close to Grayson's before she'd left home.

No, she hadn't. Had she? Kara knew where to draw lines. Never would she have gone to the lengths he had. Then again, a part of Kara believed that Admiral Kim, Elect Shostakovich, and the Council would find a better solution to all of this. Despite all evidence to the contrary. Perhaps for Grayson, being older and more jaded, the lack of faith that a better way existed was what drove him.

Perhaps.

She folded her arms over her chest, watching the main viewer. Voyager's cameras were on max zoom, so the images had their share of pixelation. The scene looked plain enough, however.

"Looks like she was a trawler of some kind," Ensign Martin said quietly. "Markings on her hull look Japanese."

The image came into sharper focus. She had almost completely submerged, but the poles sticking off her stern still had a net line fixed to them. Listing hard to the bow, she only had a few minutes left.

"Steady on," Kara said. "Any signs of life? Martin, are you getting any distress signals?"

"No, Skipper," he said. "All quiet."

"Can't be right," she said. "They'd have about eight crewing a ship like her. Tell the helm to get us closer and do a circuit. Keep us well clear of suction as she goes down. We're looking for any survivors."

On the display, the view tilted and turned as Voyager altered course to circumnavigate the wreckage. Still, no matter where she looked or how Martin scanned, there were no signs of survivors. Not on lifeboats, not bobbing in the waves with vests on, not clinging to flotsam.

"Captain..." Martin hesitated.

"Survivors?"

"No. It's, well, take a look." On the display, the camera jerked and panned upward, focusing in on a darkened shape in the sky. As Martin adjusted the focus, large, quadcopter blades and a slim body came into view.

Kara's mouth dried. "Morgenstern, get us back on course. We're done here."

As the first officer gave a quick affirmation, Kara put her focus on Martin. "I need Admiral Kim on a call. Immediately."

Ensign Martin's eyes went wide. "Skipper, he's calling us."

"Put him on."

Admiral Kim dispensed with any pleasantries. "Since I can see Voyager on four news networks, I assume you found Grayson's latest exploit?"

She nodded. "Aye, Admiral. We're pursuing as fast as possible. It looks like he sank them with his railgun. We couldn't find any survivors in the wreck."

He waved her away. "You won't find any. Grayson took them aboard his ship as prisoners before he left. As for his guns, that was on that damn news as well. So much for our secret weapons. I'm going to kill that man!" Kim raged, losing his temper for the one and only time Kara had ever witnessed.

"Sir, we can still catch up to him," Kara said. But she knew it wasn't enough. Not now.

"Any goodwill the Mariners had from the international community is gone now. Gone. The Elect and I were about to get underway to meet with the E.U. and the U.N. about revising their trade routes. Now? They're talking about sanctioning us. That fishing vessel was out of Japan. The Japanese, who have always been our allies, are now forming a response. A response that could include military action."

Every voice on the bridge grew still. Kilo by kilo, the weight of it settled over them. Grayson's actions were already irreparable. The man knew exactly what he was doing. Every action he took forced the Mariners' hands. With no allies and an angry international community, they'd have to rely on his nukes and brute force to assert their independence.

On screen, Admiral Kim regained some of his composure. "Lieutenant, I don't know what happens tomorrow. But what happens now is you getting control of Grayson. One way or the other. Find our wayward blood and heart. Bring him back by any means necessary. At this point, he need not be breathing."

The display winked out.

In the few minutes it took to validate all of Admiral Kim's claims, Kara's heart grew colder. The situation, it seemed, was every bit as dire as he predicted. Already, on social sites throughout Japan, citizens were calling for extreme measures against the Mariners for attacking a peaceful fishing vessel. Kara could argue the finer points of that claim, but knew it would be lost.

Already the E.U. had released a statement condemning their actions, 'regardless of the reasons behind them.' In the space of minutes, Grayson had all but sealed their fate.

Needing some air and the chance to move her leg, Kara took a walk on the deck. Before long, she found herself with company. Drummond, Goldi, and Tren stood by the central mast. In seconds they beckoned her over. Strange, how she found herself so relieved to see them.

"Skipper," Goldi greeted her.

"Deckmaster," Kara said in return.

"Ah, that," Goldi said. "You give me entirely too much to do. And when my little kitten is visiting, no less."

She managed a weak smile for Goldi. "You've been doing great."

"Perhaps," Goldi said. "Still. Big shoes to fill. Skipper, we saw the news reports."

"Yeah." Kara swallowed. "Came out here to get away from that for a minute."

"He's got everyone where he wants them," Drummond said. "I hate to admit it, but it's simple and clever. He's almost guaranteed to get his way at this point. All he needs is a minimal amount of support from your people and his plan is going to be your only option."

"Thanks, Arnold," Kara said hotly. "For recounting every terrible detail of that to me. Tell me something I don't know."

"I figured it out," Tren said in a small voice. "The signal thing. I came to get Arnold to tell him about it when we saw all the, well, news."

A flash of annoyance ran through her. Kara found herself a second away from ignoring Tren and getting back to the bridge. But then, a small, persistent voice that sounded an awful lot like Chief Lambros prodded her.

He saved your life, Kara.

"I'll bite." Kara let out a weak laugh. "Might be

nice if we can solve at least one mystery out of this whole debacle. What was it?"

Heartened, Tren raised both hands. "It's actually very interesting. It was the servers! If things were different, we could've made some money off of this. As it is...Well. It turns out, there was a communication line into that facility."

"You mean we could've called for help?" Drummond sputtered. "Without relying on fake fish or trying to build a floating antenna?"

"No, no," Tren said. "This was a quantum tunnel between a server in the facility and one somewhere else. Probably in Russia. Actually, it could be anywhere. A satellite, even. Jamaica. Another facility? Now that would be an interesting idea. A whole network of these—"

"Tren." Goldi said.

"Right. Totally unusable for us, unless we wanted to call the Russians direct. They, however, had been beaming data into all those lock drives in the servers. An expensive operation, but now I understand all the security on that room."

As he went on, Kara didn't find herself tuning him out. Even when he wouldn't stop elaborating on technical details. In fact, the tiny pieces of his explanation began to click together. Although she wasn't entirely sure what to do with the information yet, she filed it away for later.

"Why would they go to such lengths to hide whatever this data is?" Drummond said. "And in lock drives? Isn't the point of those things to ensure no one can copy it?"

"That's the idea, but...You remember the Ionova brothers. It doesn't always work." Tren sighed. "Well, I suppose if the Russians were mad before they'll be doubly so now."

Kara gave him a flat stare. "Thanks, Tren. For

reminding me about that. I was worried that someone in the world might not be pissed off at us right now."

As he looked down at the deck, Kara felt a guilty pinch in her stomach. "See if you can figure out what's on the drives, will you? Without corrupting the data. It has to be important to someone."

Tren perked up. "I can do that. Do you think it will help?"

She didn't.

"You never know," Kara said. "If anyone can figure it out, you can."

As she limped back to the bridge, her walking stick clanking on the deck, she hoped Chief Lambros would be proud of her. What would the chief have thought of all this? She wasn't the person to go to for help with strategy, necessarily. But her advice never fell short. Even when Kara had been too stubborn to take it.

One step at a time, she'd say. *Even the brightest lamp only lights the path so far.*

Chapter Twenty-Five: Intercept

"We fought to survive after the war. We fought our way off of the continent. We fought to keep our islands. We fight to save our waters. My greatest fear is that future Mariners will know nothing but violence and struggle."
James Keeling, *Reborn at Sea: Mariner History 2041-2063*

"There's two of them, Captain. We've no idea what they're packing. Are you sure you want—"

Captain Grayson broke Chief Fen off mid-sentence with a look that could cut glass.

Chief Fen faltered. Then, picking up the intercom, he called to engineering. "Ready the guns."

Grayson kept his voice low as he brought his hands to the helm control. "Moving us into firing position."

The Penitent had been traveling at close to top speed in order to intercept the two intruders. To get the firing solution right, the computers would need her to reduce speed. Fine. He had enough gun for the both of them. No need to rush.

Engines cut off, then reversed, hard, to slow them down without giving the other ships time to react. By now they would've seen his exploits, thanks to the drones spying on their battle with the fishing vessel. No matter. Two container ships, one fishing trawler, what was the difference? They weren't outfitted for real battle. He was.

"Where's that firing solution?" he barked at Chief Fen.

"Aye, almost there, Captain," Chief Fen answered. Beads of sweat speckled the man's round face.

Did he not have the gumption for this? Grayson wondered. Any Mariner who didn't have the stomach for battle would have to find one. And soon. It was the only way.

"Sir," Fen shouted.

"Are those guns finally ready?"

"No, sir, it's the container ships. One's peeled off from the other. They're splitting too far apart. We'll need to reposition for the second volley."

"Bah," Grayson spat. "Bother me with that after we've shot the first one. Where are my guns?"

"Wait," Chief Fen waved his arms. The man was becoming a real nuisance. "We've got a small boat, some kind of speeder. She's launched from behind the second container ship and closing fast. Can't tell if she's armed, Captain."

"Well, get the small gun on deck trained on her. Now!"

Fen went to the intercom, relaying the orders to the deckmaster. Why was it so hard for them to just do what he said?

Grayson worked his jaw, gritting his teeth while the bridge crew rushed and Penitent finally slowed enough.

"Guns are hot, sir!"

"About damn time," Grayson said. "Fi—"

✦ ✦ ✦

Kara knew that Morgenstern and the engineering crew were pushing Voyager as hard as they could. But with her damage from the gunboat barely repaired, every extra knot she pushed brought those makeshift patches on the hull closer to shaking loose and strained the hastily repaired battery and power gen systems.

However, Kara didn't have a choice. As they pressed on, the waves grew choppy while a roll of heavy gray clouds pressed them from overhead. It didn't look like a squall yet, but it could turn into one in the blink of an eye. With a bit of luck, the low steely clouds would inconvenience any drones that might be following the Penitent. The last thing the Mariners needed was more publicity courtesy of Grayson.

In the back of her mind, she hoped the prisoners he took were still alive. Killing them would have gone against all Mariner traditions, but Grayson hadn't exactly been holding their beliefs sacred lately.

"There," Ensign Martin said. "Check the viewer, Skipper. We're just about in range. I've been sweeping the area, and I've got something. Can't tell what yet. We'll need a few more knots before, oh, holy hell."

She had expected wreckage.

"Steady on, helm." Kara's voice cracked. "Don't let up now."

But she hadn't expected this.

The Penitent floated dead in the water. As the pixelated image sharpened and the shapes in the murky gray horizon cleared, the scene looked even more grim. Off Penitent's stern, a small, narrow dinghy with a large outboard motor drifted in a lazy circle. A dead man in plain blue coveralls lay slumped over her side, a smear of blood on the hull beneath him. Kara held a thumb up between her eye and the Penitent on the screen.

"Look like she's listing to you, Martin?" Kara said.

He gave it a few seconds. "Aye. To starboard, toward us. Getting worse, too. Skipper, look."

Martin didn't have to say what he meant. Two container ships, that must've been Grayson's targets, closed in on him. They had a ways to go, sure, but there didn't appear to be a spot of damage on them.

"What happened here?" Kara whispered. Her eyes scanned over Penitent, again and again. As the resolution improved and they got closer, the details materialized. A cluster of dark holes and shredded metal bored into Penitent's hull.

But only in one area.

Over on the small boat, Kara spotted the flash suppressor on the barrel of a thick machine gun. Fifty cal, probably. Something that could pierce a ship hull anyway. Details be damned.

"No, no." Kara shook her head. "Look where they concentrated fire. Most attacks would go for common targets. The bridge, engines, fuel tanks. Hitting that exact spot on the Penitent? That can't be random."

Morgenstern put his intercom down. He craned his neck to look at the screen. "That's her batteries. Penitent's main batteries are on the other side of that exact spot, I'd swear it. My first post was on The Lancer, one of three Keeling class ships, her sister."

"How could anyone know where..." Kara's mind reeled, flashing back to that near miss in the Penitent's bridge. Walking in on Grayson, Faulkner, and Grant.

Grant.

"Seven spooky hells! That locust was on the bridge!" Kara spat. After a confused look from Martin, she quickly explained. "Faulkner's tech guy,

Grant. He was on the Penitent's bridge a bunch of times. He's integrated with an enhancement like Tren's. He'd only need to access a workstation and he could've stolen everything on her computers. They'd know exactly where her batteries were from the engineering schematics. That's the single best way to prevent one of our ships from using their railguns. No power, no guns."

Morgenstern grunted. "Looks like word must have got around."

"Skipper," Ensign Martin said. "We're getting closer. If the Penitent is taking on water, what do we do?"

"Do we..." Morgenstern gave them a guilty look. "Do we let them? Sink? I mean, come on, Skipper. Grayson's the whole reason for all this mess. We may have had to do it anyway, if we're being real."

Kara closed her eyes. Adrenaline surged through her, making her fingers shake. Every sound, every image, every bit of stimulus demanded her focus. She forced a slow, steady breath. Then another. And another.

"No," Kara said. "We can't let them. Don't forget, Lieutenant, it's not only Grayson on that ship. It's his crew. The prisoners. And an unknown number of nuclear warheads."

Morgenstern sniffed. "Well, there is that, right."

"Like it or not, we've got only one option here. We need to get the Penitent to safety. Or get her crew and cargo to safety at the very least."

"Captain." Ensign Martin's voice grew increasingly agitated. "Look at those ships. There's no time for any of that. They'll be on top of her before we could get even half the crew out. No way we could patch her up that fast, either."

Kara bent her leg, wincing against the heat and pain as she did. She clanked over to Martin and gave him a pat on the shoulder.

"You're right," she said. "That's why we have to finish Grayson's job."

"You want to fight both of them?" Morgenstern's raised brow spoke volumes. "Skipper, we can try and take them, but look what happened to the Penitent."

"No," Kara said. "I want them to go away."

"Skipper, it amounts to the same thing. Maybe we could lead the ships away, then come back for the crew and the nukes?"

Kara squared her shoulders and shook her head. "Even if leaving our blood and heart here in the wreckage were an option, our A-diver can't take the pressure at the bottom of this patch of sea. It's too deep. We'd never be able to recover the nukes quick enough. This is what we have to work with. Get our guns warmed up. Ensign Martin, call the deckmaster and tell her to ready the short guns on deck. Morgenstern, set a course for the container ship closest to us, then come close around her far side, and I mean close. I want to scrape the barnacles off her hull."

"Her far side?" Morgenstern said. "How do you plan on getting both targets that way?"

"Lieutenant," Kara said. "The guns."

"Ah, right you are, Skipper," Morgenstern said.

But the truth was, she wasn't entirely sure. In her head, a hasty plan had been sketched, but that's really all it was. As a Navigator she knew ships. She knew those container ships were small for their class but still slow, even though they had powerful engines and thick hulls that wouldn't be pierced nearly as easily as the gunboat had been. Her only advantage in facing them was that Voyager's technical data hadn't been stolen by Grant and his magic fingertips.

Magic fingertips. Tren.

Kara swore. She moved to the nearest intercom

and called the deck. "Goldi," she said into the device. "Get Tren and bring him up topside with you. Yes, you have to. We're going to fire the rails, if he's too close to the guns the EM discharge will fry his integration circuits. Just get him up top and tell him to stay low!"

"Captain!" Ensign Martin shouted. "We've got a bogey! Another dinghy, it's heading right for us. Looks like she's—"

Glass exploded from the forward portholes. Instinctively, Kara ducked. Tiny cubes of glass pelted her neck and chest.

Kara brushed the shrapnel away. "Return fire!"

"No time, Tren!" Drummond yelled to be heard over the loudspeaker announcements coming in bursts over the ship's intercom. "We have to go up top!"

"Where the shooting is?" Tren could have cried. "You must have heard Goldi wrong."

The deck rolled under Tren's feet. Before he could compensate, he stumbled sideways, against the metal wall of the corridor. At least he didn't have far to fall before he smacked against it. Small blessings, and all that.

"No." Drummond righted himself. "She said, clearly, that I had to get you up to the deck. Tren, this is serious. You know she wouldn't have said that if it wasn't important."

Red lights pulsed throughout the deck. Drummond's point sounded reasonable, but Tren's fear made arguing it seem very, very attractive.

All he wanted to do was eat something, but no. Drummond had to accost him on his way to the Galley. A celebratory snack, was that too much to ask? He'd cracked the case, done the deed, climbed the mountain. And then? Now there was some kind of attack. Of course. Perfect. Is this all these people did? Sail around and shoot things?

"But, why?" Tren pressed. "What's so dangerous about being here? She normally tells me to go hide down here!"

"I didn't," Drummond fought to get the words out. "She didn't say, exactly. We were on the phone and then she had to start, well, shooting back."

"What!"

"But, Tren," he added hurriedly, "It sounded really important. She said it wasn't safe for you, specifically, you."

"Oh." Tren snapped his fingers and pointed. "It's the railguns, right? It's fine, Arnold. I was on this deck last time when she fired them against that other boat. I was okay. This is far enough from the coils that the shielding in my implants can handle it. Like I told you, very advanced stuff. Although, Voyager has good shielding on her computers, too. She'd have to, right? But any other electronics too close would be completely ruined. I hope you don't have a tablet or anything in your room. I don't think you do, though. Do you? Well, really a lot of devices would be susceptible. Watches, glasses, drives."

Tren's wayward train of thought found its way back on to the rails.

Lock drives.

"Arnold! We have to get to engineering! Come on, come on!"

Tren spun on his heel and tore down the corridor, sliding into another wall as the ship took another sharp roll. From behind him, he heard Drummond swearing.

"That is the exact opposite way we're supposed to be going!"

✦ ✦ ✦

"They're coming about again!" Martin shouted from his station.

Glass sparkled red and orange over the decking. Kara stayed on her feet, using her walking stick for balance when her leg threatened to give way from under her.

Martin shouted orders to the engine room from his intercom. "Guns are hot, but we need a target, Skipper."

On the main display, their target containership filled almost the entire screen. Voyager sat much lower than her, so they looked up at the black and red behemoth. The container ship's dinghy dogged them with every knot Voyager traveled, buzzing around like a wasp. They'd tried to concentrate fire the way they had on Penitent, but Goldi and her team were waiting with Voyager's own 7.62 machine gun. Deck crew used their sidearms and rifles to shoot back, as well. Two passes taught the dinghy crew to keep their distance and move fast, creating a stalemate of sorts.

Now, pushed by desperation and Voyager's gaining on the first container ship, they gunned their motor and came in for another strike.

Kara ripped the intercom receiver up to her mouth. "Mariners, designated gunners to starboard, now!"

She couldn't see or hear it. But she knew that below her, on the passenger and crew deck, Mariners rushed to the starboard side of the ship.

Martin changed the video on the main display. He split the screen in two, the left half showing their destination, and the right showing their attackers. Their pilot was decent, Kara would give them that.

He didn't charge them on a straight course. He juked and moved in random patterns, even fishtailing from side to side, throwing up spray just to keep Kara's crew from getting an easy target.

"Morgenstern, ready the engines!" Kara said.

"Aye, Skipper, ready." Morgenstern stayed on the intercom with the engine room.

On screen, the brown and white hull of the dinghy grew ever larger, zig zagging their way toward Voyager. Gutters of flame burst from their gun.

"Now, Morgenstern!"

On Morgenstern's orders, the engines suddenly changed direction. At once, Voyager gave a violent lurch to port. Deck and bulkheads alike groaned with the sudden strain, but they held fast just the same. Kara's knuckles whitened against the edge of the command station.

She brought the intercom back to her lips. "All gunners, fire!"

Every porthole on the starboard side of the ship flung open. Gun barrels pushed through negative space, setting bristles along Voyager's side. Every Mariner opened fire.

Water around the dinghy churned and sprayed. Kara took no pleasure in watching the small boat fly apart in chunks as her gunner jerked over and again, riddled with bullets.

Voyager slowed, righting herself after that great lurch.

Kara opened the intercom again. "Ceasefire."

Without ceremony, Martin cut that part of the video feed off. Only the huge container ship remained. And somewhere behind her, mostly likely moving toward Penitent, the container ship's sister.

Normally, she would've asked for their position after a maneuver like that, but Kara could see well enough how they were oriented toward their target.

It would have to do.

"Deck crew," Kara said into the intercom. "Ready the bumpers!"

"How about that target, Captain?" Morgenstern said. "Guns still ready."

"We'll see it soon enough, Lieutenant," Kara said. "Just a few more seconds."

"This is what you came back for?" Drummond gave Tren a helpless look. "Seriously?"

He waved his arm at the tiny workstation Tren had been using on the engineering deck. An engine mate shouted, "Hard to port!" And the ship ran out from under Tren's feet.

"No!" Tren flailed at the desk, where stacks of the plastic lock drives, all about the size of a deck of playing cards, toppled and clattered down to the decking. "Help me!" He pleaded with Drummond.

Muttering, Drummond picked himself back up and stumbled over to the desk. Snatching up Tren's green canvas bag, he shoveled the drives in as fast as he could.

"Careful with those," Tren cautioned.

"Careful with you!" Drummond shouted. He pointed up at the pulsing red and orange lights.

All around them engine mates shouted as they worked their stations and dashed about the lowest deck of the ship.

Tren gently placed a stack of the drives in the bag, deliberately trying to show Drummond how it was done.

"Hurry up, Tren," Drummond said. "They're about to charge the rail guns! Come on, man, just go, I'll get the rest of these."

"No, we can't, they'll get wiped!" Tren didn't even

look up when he spoke. Under the desk, he spotted the edge of a drive and dove in to retrieve it.

"Fine," Drummond said.

Tren shuddered as the sound of more drives clattering into the duffle bag reached him under the desk.

"Charge sequence!" an engine mate shouted, his voice ringing around the deck.

"Come on!" Drummond grabbed Tren's ankle and pulled. Hard.

With the last drive in hand, the two men scrambled upright, the bag firmly in Drummond's grip.

"Was that all of them?" Tren asked.

Drummond didn't bother to answer. He shoved Tren forward.

A low whine started. It came from the tubes and coils running the length of the hull.

"Faster!" Drummond prodded them on, pushing Tren to move even faster to the main ladder. He practically flung Tren into the stairwell, and jammed the hatch shut behind them.

"That won't stop an EM field," Tren scoffed.

"Then climb, you idiot!" Drummond shouted.

Huffing, Tren slapped his free hand on the railing and ran upward using the combined strength of all his limbs. Drummond didn't have to start with the name calling. Tren would've started up the stairs. And he didn't need the man poking and prodding him to go faster. He was going as fast as he could.

The whine from below decks raised in pitch, vibrating the handrail Tren held on to. Did his vision just get a little blurry?

Maybe he could move faster.

High-stepping and flinging himself around the stairs, Tren raced to beat the building, invisible EM field before it could scramble the drives, or, well, him. A Mariner stepped out of the hatch, almost moving in their way before Tren let out a scream of, "I'm sorry!" And plowed his way onward.

At last, daylight beckoned as Drummond raced by Tren and flung open the hatch to the top deck.

"Oh, thank God," Tren breathed.

The sense of relief didn't last long.

Gunfire burst all around them, hammering Tren's ears.

Drummond pulled him down to the deck. Together they crawled away from the bow of the ship, where Goldi and her deck crew stood, manning a machine gun that barked like thunder, drowning out all other sound on the deck.

Some sort of order rang out over the ship's speakers. Tren couldn't understand it, though. His ears were full of cotton and a dull ringing. Hunched over, Drummond pointed out a spot by the central mast. Tren agreed that would be their safest bet. Only, as soon as lifted a foot to walk, Voyager decided to run out from under him again.

Gray and white clouds spun into the fore of his vision. Tren fell backwards, smacking hard against the deck. Stars exploded in his eyes while heat spread over the back of his head. In his hand, he still gripped the lock drive. He still had it.

Wait.

The others!

Tren scuffled with the deck, trying to get himself upright while gravity tugged him the opposite way. Before he found Drummond, something green and lumpy slid past him.

He froze. Eyes widening, Tren watched as his green duffle skidded across the deck, nearing ever closer to the rails and the large gaps between the rails that would easily let his bag through.

Move!

"Gaaah!" Tren choked out his war cry, stumbling

in great, dizzy steps toward the sliding bag. He reached out, fingers extended. The bag touched the edge of the deck and held there for an excruciating moment, like a cartoon animal running off a cliff.

Voyager rocked back the other way.

A spray of salt water and foam crested over the rails, knocking against the bag. Tren almost lost his footing again. His hand fell short, but blessedly, the motion slowed the bag's momentum just enough.

Tren gripped a handful of the canvas and yanked it back toward him.

"Aha!" He cried in triumph. "Arnold, I got it! Arnold?"

Lying motionless a couple meters away, Arnold must have been knocked out cold by his fall. Guiltily, Tren ran to give him first aid.

All forward cameras on the bridge showed on the main display. Goldi's deck crew threw thick rubber bumpers down over the rails with only centimeters to spare. Voyager's multicolored hull moved against the black and red of the container ship. Kara could see every crack and mar in her paint. Above her, in large, block lettering read, "Rosario."

"Easy does it, helm. Let's touch down and give her a push."

A deep, bass gong rang through the ship. Everyone on the bridge lurched forward, but recovered quick enough.

"Give me those engines, Morgenstern!" Kara yelled. "Let's spin this beast around!"

Voyager's engines shook the deck. She'd never had them running this hot before. But with the massive size of the container ship, she had to count on all of her engine's torque to get Rosario spun off her current course, away from the Penitent.

"We've got her, Skipper," Morgenstern called out.

On the viewer Kara watched the behemoth turn. Rosario was small for a containership but she dwarfed Voyager. It put the "large" transport vessels in perspective. From the starboard side of the screen, sea and sky revealed itself as Voyager, grappling with Rosario, forced her along an axis she wasn't prepared to fight against.

"Deck crew," Kara shouted into her intercom. "Get ready to target her bridge. I want clappers as soon as she's visible. Blow out her glass."

Intercom down, Kara raised a finger. "Railguns ready. Four volleys. Target the other vessel. Aim high and blast her hull close to the top deck."

Morgenstern flicked her a glance. It was a non-critical target. Would it damage the ship? Sure. Would it keep her from sailing? No.

But Kara had a choice to make. Two paths split in front of her. One path with a clear way forward, stained in blood. The other shrouded in uncertainty. She took a gamble that the words of her mother and Chief Lambros weren't wasted on her. She hoped it would work out.

"Aye, Skipper," Morgenstern called back. "Ready."

At last, Voyager spun Rosario around far enough that the other ship's red and black hull crested into view.

"Fire." Kara said.

Tren clutched the duffel bag in both arms. Sitting down next to Drummond, who had awakened only when Voyager slammed into the other ship (what was that about?), Tren gasped as Voyager stepped backward in two huge leaps. Molten fire shot from somewhere under her bow in two great streaks from either side. He watched as the projectiles flew in a graceful arc, only to slam into the other container ship which sailed half a kilometer from the Penitent.

His breath froze. Fire broke out over the ship's hull. Even as far away as he was, he could see a smoking hole torn away from it.

Suddenly, Goldi started calling to her crew. A Mariner with a long green tube—it wasn't a rocket launcher, it couldn't have been a rocket launcher—sent a streak of fire upward, toward the top of the huge ship next to him.

Okay, Tren admitted, it was a rocket launcher.

Smoke guttered and blasted from the end of the rocket, propelling itself in a spiraling trajectory up and away.

On the display, the angles were terrible. But Kara could see enough of the bridge that sat high up on the container ship, higher than any other point, in fact. The clapper screamed with a trail of yellow fire behind it before flying up to the bridge, and exploding. White burned across the display.

A shockwave rang through the bridge. Deadened by the space and the hull, Kara knew the blast she just gave the crew of the Rosario would be ten times as bad. To confirm, she watched the image recover on the main viewer. Only broken, spider-webbed sections of glass remained in the large windows of the Rosario's bridge.

Quiet settled over them. The crew waited for their captain.

"Hail them," Kara said to Ensign Martin.

After a few, tense moments, Martin cleared his throat. "I've got them. Video conference."

"Put them on."

As the image of their bridge winked across the screen, a haughty woman took front and center. Her crew scrambled behind her, trying to move glass or calling out reports. Her dark hair was pulled back in a tight, professional bun, although her makeup was a little heavier than Kara was used to seeing on sailors. An errant lock of her hair twitched in the breeze now pushing through her bridge.

"This is Captain Schwab of the Rosario, you have attacked two TXM vessels. We demand an explanation."

Kara walked closer to the screen. Schwab, perhaps only now fully seeing her, recoiled a bit.

"This is Lieutenant Nkosi, acting Captain of the Mariner Vessel Voyager. You are in our waters. You are at our mercy. I can scuttle the two of you in less than ten minutes. You aren't demanding anything from me."

Schwab opened her mouth for an angry retort, but Kara silenced her with a raised finger.

"That clapper I just sent up to your bridge could just have easily been a grenade. It wasn't, though. Consider that. I understand the M.V. Penitent was going to attack you. You had a right to defend yourself. That right ends at this exact moment. I will take the Penitent into custody, and she will be dealt with by our own people. You will turn about and leave our waters now."

"You've lost the element of surprise. Why should I leave before I have justice?"

Kara brought her walking stick in front of her, setting both hands on its round handgrip. She nodded. "That, of course, is your choice. How many battles have you fought, Captain? Have you and yours had to fight as many pitched battles as my crew? Are you persecuted as much as a Mariner?

Ask yourself these questions. Because once you raise arms to me after this parlay, I will stop at nothing to destroy you. What will happen then? Any of your crew who surrender peacefully will be taken prisoner and treated fairly. That is our way. You, on the other hand, have lost that right. If you are still breathing when I find you—"

"Let me guess"—she rolled a hand in a hurry up gesture—"You'll make it painful."

"I won't have to," Kara said in a calm tone. "As punishment, I will leave you in an unpowered raft, with no supplies, on a stretch of sea that I can guarantee no traders or fishers travel. I won't need to lift a finger. The sun and sea will do all the work for me."

Schwab gave her a serious stare.

"I take no pleasure in violence, Captain Schwab. Justice will be taken against the captain who attacked your ship. But you must leave. Now."

Her screen went dark.

Martin cleared his throat. "Guess it was something you said," he muttered.

"Captain," Morgenstern gave her a harried glance.

"Give them a moment," Kara said.

Silence stretched between them on the bridge. On the deck, Kara knew the crew would be waiting on the balls of their feet, ready for whatever would come next.

Ensign Martin shot to his feet. "Her engines are starting. She's pulling away, Skipper. Rosario just sent a message by text. They're leaving."

Kara fell back against the command desk, sitting on its edge and breathing out hard. "Keep an eye on them. Then, we need to go fetch our wayward captain. I hate to say it, but this was probably the easy part. Morgenstern, I think you'll need to take your old post again for a bit."

"Skipper?" Morgenstern said.

Kara rubbed her eyes. "Let me explain."

Chapter Twenty-Six:
In A Handbasket

"The most damning idea of the old world was freedom without consequence. Every action creates reactions. That's not philosophy, it's physics."
Karissa Piccato, Second Mariner Elect

Kara breathed. In, then out. In, out. Not forcing. Only breathing. It wasn't a meditation, exactly, but it kept her from boiling over with rage as she listened to the man's wretched voice over the bridge's display. Working her bad leg a little helped. All that stiffness and pain, it called her thoughts away from pointless fantasies of revenge. In her head, this movie kept playing, unbidden, where she marched herself on deck and put two in his chest, then kicked him over the rail for good measure.

And what would that do? A voice inside her said.

She might feel better. But then... You know. Mutiny from his crew. A massive battle and two ships in flames. Endless guilt. Pointless death and suffering.

"You did swoop in like true heroes," Grayson said. "What brought you out our way?"

Tren and Drummond both sat in the bridge with her. Over the past few minutes, the deck crews had been at work, setting up a gangway between the two ships. Morgenstern had gone out to greet Grayson. No mention of Kara had been made.

Both Tren and Drummond stared daggers at the screen. God, but she knew how they felt. She gave them a reassuring smile. Tren held onto a duffle bag like he was planning to run away from home. Kara hoped he had a little more confidence in her than that.

On screen, the hulking man with his short dark hair passed neatly on to Voyager. Morgenstern answered Grayson.

"In truth," Morgenstern said, "Admiral Kim sent us after you. Seems you've been out of contact for days. He's worried."

You can't outright lie to him, Kara had told Morgenstern. *He's more observant than he lets on. He'll immediately know something is wrong.*

"Did he now?" Grayson said on the viewer. "Well, unfortunately we may have a change in plans, Lieutenant."

Ensign Martin stood up. "I can go with you, Skipper."

"So can we," Drummond added.

Tren didn't say anything, which made the corner of her mouth twitch upward. No dummy, that one.

"No," she said. "I need you to crew the bridge in case everything goes to hell. Your job is to get us out of here. You two need to stay put. If this goes tits up, we could have a full scale firefight on our hands."

Back on the screen, she heard Morgenstern's voice grow uneasy. "What kind of change, sir?"

"That's my cue," Kara whispered. Clutching her walking stick, she moved to the hatch, and let herself out. When she turned around, Drummond and Tren stood right behind her on the other side of the portal.

Wordlessly, she gave them a nod. With a grimace, Drummond shut the hatch.

Wind filled her ears. In a short moment it was gone. Steeling herself, Kara leaned on her walking stick, and clanked her way over to the port side of the deck. Never had the deck of the ship felt so small. Within seconds she could see the gathered deck crews from Voyager, and only meters away, Penitent.

Across that short space of water, a set of eyes locked with hers. Chief Fen. Standing with arms crossed, his eyes went big as saucers. Kara looked away and continued her journey, the end of her stolen walking stick clanking with every other step.

"It's simple enough, Lieutenant," Captain Grayson went on. He towered over Morgenstern, using his size as well as his authority to cow the engineer. "You have a ship without a Captain. I am a Captain. I will be taking command. Leave communication with the Admiral to me. First, I need—"

"You are wrong." Goldi's heavily accented voice drifted across the deck. She caught Kara's eye. "We have a Captain. She's right there."

"What is this?" Grayson turned on the spot.

His face turned to stone.

More wind fluttered over Kara's ears. Briefly, she looked over to the starboard railing, close to the bow. The place where they'd laid to rest seven of their own since this voyage began. Fire consumed her belly from within. Kara used all her will to tamp it down.

"Lieutenant Nkosi," Grayson said softly. "I see you made it back."

"Grayson," Kara said curtly. Mutters went through the assembled crew on both ships. The lack of title didn't go unnoticed. "If by 'made it back,' you mean escaped from the Russian bunker you marooned me in after trying to execute me, then, yes. I did."

Among the Mariners on Voyager this came as no surprise. But for the Mariners on board Penitent, this was clearly a new development. Kara tried to stay cool, to keep from letting her temper get the better of her. For this to work, she needed to be the better leader, the one more deserving of trust.

"I see you aren't asking about Chief Lambros." Kara said. She took a few steps closer, her stick ringing on the deck. "She's just as dead as she was when you left us."

Grayson fumed. But... Beyond the anger, something else hid in his face. A wrinkle of the chin, maybe? Did he actually feel guilt about it? Was there still room for that with all of his mania?

"We sang for her, there in the facility," Kara said to him. "If that matters to you."

Nothing.

"I spoke for her." Kara kept her voice low now. But it didn't matter. Every ear was hers. "I spoke for your blood and heart. And drew her mark. If that still means anything at all to you."

"Enough!" Grayson spat the words, slicing his hand through the air between them like a knife. "Of course, it matters to me. Our ways mean everything to me!"

"But not enough to keep your business partners from killing your own. Is that where your dedication ends?"

"Don't test me, Kara!" Grayson's face burned red. He stomped toward her, hands going threateningly down to his gun belt.

Kara stood her ground. "Did you tell them? Did you tell your crew what you did? How you partnered with a man who killed our sister? How you sold your soul for some nuclear weapons?"

A buzz rose over the crew of the Penitent. Kara couldn't look. She had to keep her focus on Grayson, but some of their people milled about, presumably to go check the contents of Grayson's precious cargo. She wasn't sure, but Kara thought she spied Chief Fen among them. Someone was missing in Grayson's normal retinue, though.

"You think you've got the right to lecture me, do you?" Grayson took a single step back, some modicum of control returning to his face. "Come here to do Admiral Kim's dirty work, have you? Gonna lock me up? Take me back to Vish for being a bad boy, eh?"

Kara sighed and leaned heavier on her walking stick. "Where's Commander Orozco?"

The question took Grayson off guard. "What?"

"Where is your first officer? Did you kill him, too?"

"No! I didn't. He's in the brig!" Grayson crossed his thick arms.

"You jailed him?" Kara squinted. "What for? For disagreeing with you? For pointing out how insane this plan of yours is? Because it is, Grayson. Sounds like Orozco knew it. I know it. Bilby did, too. Didn't he?"

Grayson grew still. Even the crew on both sides picked up on it. No one moved. Suddenly, the whole scene had become charged with tension.

"You want to be very careful with what you say next, Lieutenant." Grayson said through gritted teeth.

"I'm done with your threats. I'm done with your intimidation." She pulled her phone from her pocket. "Forgot to pick this up when you and your friends left us to die. Do you think your crew would like to hear a recording of how you let your friends try to execute us? How you let them kill the chief? All to keep your precious secret?"

Now Kara did look at the Mariners behind Grayson. Some remained defiant. Most, though, looked uncertain. A few wore anger plainly on their faces, but it wasn't directed at Kara. They could've burned holes in Grayson's back.

One such, was Chief Fen.

"That true, Skipper?" Fen's cockney accent came through strong, even from on the Penitent's deck.

Spinning on his heel, Grayson roared at the chief, "Who cares if it's true! I did what none of your other so-called leaders have had the courage to do. I've found a way to get all of these trespassers and killers out of our lands, away from our waters. What have they done, eh? Nothing. Not a damn thing!"

His chest heaved in great gasps. Grayson turned back to Kara as if the matter was settled.

It was not.

From dozens of points on the Penitent's deck, metal scraped across leather and plastic. Blinking, Grayson faced his crew again. The majority had pulled their sidearms. Unfortunately, weapons were being pointed in all directions.

Kara's heart thumped. She closed her eyes for a single second, trying to find a shred of focus. When she opened them, the scene hadn't improved one bit. Groups started to form, a small knot of Mariners on the Penitent's deck looked to be supporting Grayson while others simply shouted at their shipmates to put their guns down. That knot of Grayson's loyalists tried to shoulder their way through the deck to get to their captain.

Tempers flared. A scuffle broke out on the Penitent.

Grayson watched. With his back turned, Kara couldn't see his face. But if there were even a hope that she could end this without blood, then she only had one choice.

Stepping closer to his side, Kara spoke just loud enough for Grayson to hear.

"Is this what you want? Mariner crossing steel with Mariner?" She said.

Grayson said nothing.

"What does this get us, Grayson? Haven't you done what you came to do?"

He didn't respond. But he wasn't fighting her, either. Kara hoped above all else that her instincts were right about him. That Grayson still had some decency left.

Grayson filled his lungs with air. "At ease!" He roared at his crew.

Within seconds the grappling on the deck of the Penitent settled. Crew detached themselves from each other and went back to their groups, still glaring.

"That's enough," Grayson said for all to hear. "Let's settle this. I'll come willingly. Admiral Kim will see sense or we'll all die. That's all there is to it. Let's stop wasting daylight."

In that tiny span of time, the climate on both decks shifted. Grayson's loyal few stayed, watching sullenly as their Captain began his surrender. Some Mariners simply walked away from the scene, turning their back on him. Kara caught Chief Fen's eye. The communication's officer waved his pistol at Grayson.

Slowly, Grayson raised his hands. One of Kara's crew moved forward, she held out a hand to stop them.

"No," she said. "He's their captain."

Chief Fen made a small gesture of thanks. Crossing the gangway, he walked up to his former captain, and snatched the weapons from his belt. "Hands behind your head," he said.

Jaw clenched, Grayson complied.

Kara put her hand down. Two of Goldi's deckhands went to either side of Grayson, and clapped cuffs around his wrists. She gave them a simple nod, and they moved to take him to Voyager's brig.

"It doesn't matter now." Grayson jerked to a stop, looking over his shoulder. "You said it yourself, Lieutenant. It's done. So, fine. Take me in. It's all set in motion anyway. The world will be after our blood, Kara. Mark my words, all of you. Within days you'll be thanking me on bended knee for arming us so we can gain our freedom once and for all."

Kara looked deep inside for the fire, preemptively thinking she'd have to fight that anger back down. Surprisingly, though, she didn't. Staring at the beaten man, she only felt a mix of revulsion and pity. "Go on," she told the deck hands.

Chief Fen came forward, his eyes brimming. "Ah, Kara," he said. "We didn't know. We didn't bloody know. He said your lot had left on the Gallant. It didn't sound right, but..."

"It's been a long few days, Chief," Kara said. "We'll get this all figured out. For now, I think you'd better get Commander Orozco out of the brig. Then we need to get your ship moving under her own power again. We don't have much time."

Kara spent a few moments on deck, greeting those crew from the Penitent who wanted to wish her well and assure her they had no idea what Grayson had really been up to. Perhaps they did. Perhaps they didn't. Kara knew it wasn't so clear cut. Some may have realized and chosen to ignore it because it didn't affect them. Others may have felt he had the right idea. For now, though, it was too much to deal with. Her job, at that moment, was to get Grayson and the Penitent back to Vish.

One step at a time.

Even so, it didn't stop her from worrying.

Grayson had a more than valid point. The proverbial earthquake had already struck undersea, and who could stop the coming tsunami? He might be in custody, but Grayson's plan had worked, regardless. Would the Mariners, true to his prediction, be left with no other choice?

Eventually, Tren and Drummond found their way out on deck.

"You can put your bag down, Tren," she said. "You don't have to run anywhere."

"This?" Tren gave the bag in his arms a gentle shake.

Drummond made a noise. "Don't get me started on that damn thing. Guy almost fried his brain to pull it from engineering."

"What?" Kara's brow raised.

"No, you don't understand, Kara." Tren bounced a little on his feet. "Oh, my head is killing me. You think Doc Angus has time to see me? He always seems a bit annoyed when I come by. Do you know why?"

"Tren."

"Right. These. Yes. Kara, I figured out what they are. I mean, I know what they are. I figured out what kind of data is on them. You won't believe it. I couldn't risk losing a single one."

Kara tilted her head. "I'm listening."

"These are beyond valuable," he said with an almost loving tone. "I've only been able to check a few of them. Every lock drive has a description file and an audit trail. That way you know what's on it without viewing the data, which would, of course, go in the audit trail and could decrease the value."

"So, where does the value kick in?" Drummond said.

"Let me finish, Arnold. The drives I checked contain proprietary data from AssureGen. AssureGen? The genomics company I used to work for before my life went to hell? Come on, I told you both about it a dozen times. Whatever. The data on these lock drives is beyond trade secret. People have been fired, supposedly even killed, for even considering spilling these beans. How these Russians got into our—I mean their—systems to steal it is completely beyond me. They must have help from the inside."

Kara stopped him before he could build up more questions. "Fine, it's a huge secret. Where does the value come in? So, the Russians stole it. What do they do? Ransom it back? Sell to a competitor?"

Tren made an incredulous face. "Where's the... Kara, there are entire trillion-dollar companies who are completely dependent on trade secrets like this. What do you do with it? Whatever you want. Demand your billions from anyone with the money. They'll pay. This data isn't just money. It's power. Imagine what would happen if splicing tech was as freely available as enhancements?"

"Well, who in their right mind would steal something like this?" Drummond eyed the bag like it had grown fangs. "As soon as anyone knows what you have, you may as well put a target on your back."

It might have been a rhetorical question, but Kara answered. "Russian intelligence service felt safe enough stealing it. Who else? Maybe another powerful corporation."

Pieces started clicking together. Big Madrid. The spliced mercenaries. Still, there were pieces she didn't totally understand, but they could wait. An idea germinated in her mind, still half-formed. It might, just might, help the Mariners get out of this mess.

Or it would get Kara murdered.

"Tren," she said. "Do you still have a way to contact the TXM representative Big Madrid was working with?"

"Uh, sure." Tren swallowed. "Why?"

"Yeah," Drummond said. "Weren't you just saying that there were enough people out there trying to kill you?"

She looked at Drummond. "Remember what you said about who really writes the laws in the U.S.? I think Tren may have found the only bargaining chip we have."

"Hang on." Drummond shook his head. "That's insane. Kara, if you even hint to those people at what you have and—"

"What choice do we have, Arnold?" Kara sighed. "It's either that or the nukes."

Tren fiddled with his bag. "Nukes might be less dangerous."

Chapter Twenty-Seven: New Deal

"Yes, the Coast Guard put up a fight, but the full might of the remaining Navy wasn't brought to bear on us that Sailing Day. I knew it. Aisha knew it. Why did they hold back? At home, we were defeated enemies. Our example growing less effective by the day. At large, we could once again be the nefarious scapegoats a government like theirs must have in order to survive. They weren't done with us."
James Keeling, Reborn at Sea: Mariner History 2041-2063

Of course Admiral Kim didn't like her plan. It was either a testament to the trust he had in Kara, or pure desperation, that he grudgingly agreed to it.

Some last minute shuffling took place as a consequence. While the hastily repaired Penitent limped herself back down Vish way, Kara and Voyager found themselves pushing the engines to make a stop before returning to her home island.

Despite the rough conditions of many of the United States' docking facilities, the Port of Portland remained well kept and in order. Mostly due to the amount of commercial shipping and traffic that came through. In years past, some of that traffic would have passed through Los Angeles or San Diego, but those days were long gone for those two cities. Portland and Seattle took most of the respectable west coast sea traffic.

Which meant a couple of things. First, Portland played host to a lot less prostitution, theft, black market enhancement clinics, and the other skullduggery that saturated other ports of call. Second, that on the odd occasion they granted a Mariner ship's request for a dock, the Mariners were told to tie down very, very far away from the respectable folk.

Decades of rising temperatures and sea levels had ruined other parts of the globe. Portland, however, missed the brunt of that pain. According to long time residents, it got warmer, but it still drizzled all the time. Life went on.

Kara limped through such a drizzle now. As far as these things went it wasn't bad. Certainly not as cold as the arctic she had only recently left. Her flagstaff-cum-walking-stick clopped along the sprawling concrete walkway of the business park. Morgenstern's engine mates had been kind enough to put a plastic cap on the bottom end and cut the thing down a bit.

No cab would pick her up. It's not that she would have wasted the money on it, anyway. Still, it might have been nice to have the option. But drivers spotted her, in her rough-woven, off-white vest and her myriad tattoos, and they turned their faces away. The reaction was the same everywhere.

Even now, as she ascended steps, her small leather bag bouncing softly against her side, the suited and uniformed workers in the business park gave her a wide berth. Some gaped openly. Why? That seemed a little extreme. Yes, she was wearing her gun belt, but it only had her knife in it. In keeping with the local law, her sidearm remained back on Voyager.

Kara had done her best to be presentable, wearing her cleanest clothes and even going so far as to ask Goldi to help braid her hair and add a few shells to it.

As she approached the tall, glass doors of the office building where her meeting was to take place, she spotted her reflection.

Maybe that's some of the reason people are keeping their distance, she thought.

She didn't look much better off than she had a couple days ago. Bruising around her eye and cheek had gone from black to purple with a lovely halo of yellow settled in around it. Of course, the slashes on her forehead and wrist were still bright and angry.

But her hair looked great, so she should win them over in no time. Kara stifled a chuckle and pulled open a heavy door.

Immediately, two black-suited security guards stood from their desk to head her off before she could take more than a few steps into the cool, marbled lobby.

Both men looked like the love-children of a professional wrestler and a butcher's block. Their features weren't symmetrical or proportional enough to be spliced, she decided. Even as normal humans, they were intimidating enough. Most likely enhanced.

"You need to leave," the first one said. His voice was surprisingly soft.

Kara craned her neck up to look him in the eye. "I have an appointment with Mister Nakamura from TXM."

The second guard scoffed. "Sure. And I've got lunch with President Anderson right after this. Go away, shipsy. Do it now."

Kara felt some of her old anger slip out before she could catch it. "Or what, exactly?"

"Gentlemen, gentlemen!" A boisterous voice

echoed through the expansive lobby. From the elevator bank walked the man Kara had only seen over video thus far. Solid, well built, unnaturally handsome. In a suit that must have been tailored to fit him to the millimeter, he strode toward them with arms parted wide.

Immediately, the two guards deferred to him.

"Mister Nakamura, we were just escorting her out of here," the first guard said.

"Woah, woah." Nakamura let out an easy laugh. "What are you talking about, Tim? She's my two o'clock. You guys, always pranking the new people. I got it from here. Come on, Lieutenant. Let me show you up."

Even as the guards made themselves scarce, they kept wary eyes on her. Nakamura took Kara's hand and gave it a firm shake. Kara felt more than saw the streams of people parting around them. Surprisingly, after dropping her hand, Nakamura then touched his hand to his heart.

"I pray the seas were calm and the journey safe."

A war broke out inside her. On one side, her spirit raged. This man knew god-damned well her journey had been anything but peaceful. On the other, his inhuman beauty and sparkling smile made her appreciative that he had taken the time to learn a Mariner greeting.

You don't understand, Tren had warned her. *This won't be like negotiating with a thug like Big Madrid. These people can make you sign over the rights to your kidney, smiling the whole time, and you'll beg them to let you throw in a lung, too.*

She understood now. Part of it was biological, she assumed. People like beautiful people. That was a given. No matter who it was, there was always a tendency to believe that the pretty person was really on your side. Part of it was skill. Perhaps this cadre of elites took the ability to manipulate and persuade to the highest levels possible. No matter where the truth lay, Kara had to be on her toes.

Kara thanked him and let Nakamura lead the way to the elevators. As they rode upward, he gave her a sad smile. "I'm sorry about that. When Parker called you the s-word. It's ignorance, you know? Let's be clear, I don't condone that at all."

Was the whole meeting going to be like this? At least until they killed her?

"I've been called much worse," Kara said.

"Oho!" Nakamura let out a booming laugh. "Hey, don't get me wrong, I know you're made from tougher stuff than most."

Yes, you of all people would, Kara thought.

He breezed her through another office lobby. A receptionist with flaming red hair knocked over her mug upon seeing the pair of them. Kara couldn't see the face Nakamura showed her, but the woman instantly looked down as she tried to clean up her mess. They strode down a hall filled with indoor plants and the scent of tea and coffee. A blue suited man with a tablet under his arm spotted Nakamura and Kara, pivoted and walked back the way he had come.

For a moment she wondered if that was because of her, or the man she walked with?

"I hope you don't mind, Kara, but given the unusual circumstances of our meeting, a few colleagues of mine have asked to attend our meeting as well."

Giving her no chance to respond, Nakamura swung open a frosted glass door that led into a long, sweeping conference room. There, next to the floor to ceiling windows, sat a dozen others at a polished black stone table.

Kara tried to play off her near stumble as an

affectation of her injured leg. Leaning heavier than she had to on her stick, she thumped along to the only empty seats at the end of the table. Every single one of those assembled had to be spliced. They had to have been. No matter what their ethnicity, or their particular coloring, or angles of their face, they all somehow looked absolutely perfect. Some of them gave her expressionless looks. Others had warm smiles. None showed open hostility yet.

A seat had been left empty for her at the head of the table. She touched her fingers to the backrest of the chair and looked at those waiting. Her eyes caught on two men in dull gray fatigues she hadn't seen when she'd first walked in. They stood with backs against the far wall, out of sight of the door. One of those beautiful faces looked a little too familiar. Kara stared openly at him.

He met her gaze. After a few seconds, he gave her a tiny nod. Acknowledgement. Nothing more.

"Please, Kara, have a seat," Mister Nakamura said, seating himself to her right.

Kara made a show of stretching her leg. "Apologies. I need to remain standing for a moment. My leg is very stiff."

And I don't want to be sitting down if you send your mercenaries after me.

On her left, a blond woman with her hair arranged in meticulous curls gave her a sympathetic smile. "Oh, that's terrible. Did you have an accident on your ship?"

"No," Kara said. "I was shot."

It was amazing how much she wanted to believe the woman sincerely cared. These feelings weren't going to serve her here. Taking a second, she tried to find a place, somewhere in her mind, where she could observe her feelings more than experience them—a mediation technique Chief Lambros had taught that Kara was painfully bad at.

Thinking of her friend made her smile. This needed to end. Quickly. The longer she stayed in this room, the more danger she was in.

"Thank you for meeting with me, Mister Nakamura. And everyone else," she said with a short incline of the head.

"Well, when I get a meeting mysteriously pop up on my calendar out of nowhere, I do get curious." Nakamura let out his easy laugh.

"Forgive the intrusion, please." Kara kept her voice cordial. "I needed to contact you. It was the only way I knew how. There was no time to plead my way through your staff, you understand. You see the way most upstanding citizens regard my people. The s-word and all that."

"Oh, forget it," he said with an exaggerated slap to the table. "You're here to talk business, I know."

"Too true," Kara said. "Let us get to it. Recently, you funded an expedition headed by Big Madrid, a fence working out of the Skatch Harbor Free Market Zone."

"Allegedly," a man's voice halfway down the table chimed in.

Kara tossed him an irritated glance. "TXM put, what looked to me and my crew, an excessive amount of resources into an expedition that Big Madrid thought was a shipwreck salvage."

"Allegedly," the man tossed in again. Kara noticed he had a tablet lying in front of him, most likely recording the conversation.

Kara tapped a finger on the table. The faces around her remained more or less unchanged. Polite sympathy from the blond, engagement from Nakamura.

"To be fair," Nakamura said, "if TXM International had any involvement, which I am not confirming at this time, it would have been in a purely financial role with no direct involvement of the operations of said recovery mission."

A surge of heat pushed words from her mouth. "So, those weren't your mercenaries that killed ten of my blood and heart? That wasn't your man I bled out in my engine room?"

As a navigator, Kara had negotiated more times then she could remember. That made her something of a connoisseur of charged silences. This one left them all in the dust. Each perfect face gave her an unblinking stare.

"Kara," the blond said in a soft voice. "That's a very dangerous accusation to make. And an admission of murder."

Clearly, this was going well.

"What is your name?" Kara said.

"Annie," the blond answered, favoring her with a smile again.

"Annie," Kara said, "I'm not trying to raise your hackles. Mariners try to speak honestly and plainly. We try. Of course, we fail, too. Maybe we should stop the recording for a bit? I'd like to have a simple discussion with you."

Blond Annie snapped her fingers and pointed at the man recording, who quickly complied. "It's for your protection as much as ours. As I said, you just admitted to killing a man on a recording."

"No," Kara said. "I admitted to defending myself. Frankly, I'm not sure why you're all so worried about protecting yourselves, legally. Don't your people write the bills that become laws? Don't you put the politicians in power? What could you possibly need to be so careful for?"

Some of Annie's veneer cracked. "There's a lot more to it than that, Kara. It's best if you stay on topic."

"I, for one, am absolutely dying to know what Lieutenant Nkosi's got up her sleeve!" Nakamura said. He motioned to her vest. "Figuratively, of course."

"Right. TXM knew, or at least suspected, that there was something much better than a shipwreck down there. Am I right?" Kara said.

Nakamura made a so-so gesture with his hand. "We suspected. I'm sure that we, like you, worked out that the encrypted signal Big Madrid had was of Russian origin, and it was far too new to be a modern wreck. The rest we inferred from other data. If we're speaking plainly."

"I appreciate it." Kara drummed her fingertips on the table. "To be fair, I didn't make the Russian connection. The U.S. envoy that dragged us into this mess had, though. Lovely people. They're the ones that left me with a bullet in the ass."

No one laughed. Even Nakamura only gave her an encouraging look.

"I never wanted anything to do with that damn bunker." Kara sighed.

"You made it in?" Annie said carefully.

"Aye," Kara said. "You know that already, though. I assume Big Madrid and Captain Faulkner contacted you to sell the nuclear warheads they stole."

It wasn't a question, but Nakamura gave her the tiniest of acknowledgements.

"I thought as much. They must have been in touch, seeing as how the Rosario and her sister ship knew exactly how to fight off Grayson."

"About that," Annie said.

Kara waved a hand. "He's in custody. Listen, he shouldn't have attacked your ships. I want to come to terms on that. For now, let's just say that our people are knee deep in it with yours, and I get that. You've had ten of us killed so far. I know you lost people from our attacks."

"How do you want to come to terms, Kara?" Nakamura sounded genuinely curious. "Are you proposing to trade your nuclear warheads for some goodwill, or what's happening here?"

Kara breathed. This was the moment.

"You know very well that the nuclear weapons weren't the most valuable things in that facility."

Nakamura clammed up.

"All right," Kara said. "I'll lead. I'm reaching into my bag. This is not a threatening action."

She made eye contact with the mercenaries in the back, who both gave their permission.

Slowly, she undid the leather and wood clasp on her bag, and pulled out a single lock drive. Gently, she placed it on the table and took a step away.

Steeling herself, Kara turned her back on the room and faced the windows. Leaving her back exposed to a room full of hostiles went against every instinct she had, but Kara needed to show them that she had the upper hand. Even if she had trouble believing it herself.

"That lock drive contains, what I am told, are AssureGen trade secrets." From the translucent glare of the windows, Kara watched as Annie hurriedly slid the drive down the table, where one of the assembled team produced a tablet and touched their integrated fingers to the device.

"It's something about how you change people's eye color. I won't pretend to understand it. Apparently, there is some sort of file that will tell you about the data, where it came from, if it's been read or copied and all that. You need some kind of key to read the data, but I'm told the encryption can be broken with enough time." Kara turned back around as the mercenaries both moved away from the wall.

"Kara." Annie moved away from the commotion

at the table, where those closest to the lock drive traded whispers. "This is awkward. You see, if that lock drive really does contain the information you say it does, this is a problem. For all of us."

Nakamura nodded along. Kara kept half an eye on the mercenaries trying to unobtrusively cover the exit and get closer to her.

"What would that problem be?" Kara kept her voice conversational.

Annie picked her thread back up. "We at AssurGen International and AssureGen North America, Limited, have had a tremendous amount of trust placed in us by our shareholders. If word of this kind of proprietary data breach got out, our stock price could plummet. As the guardians of that trust, we can't let that happen. Anyone who came to us with that kind of proof, well, they wouldn't be allowed to share that information with anyone else. Ever."

Kara stood straighter. She flexed and loosened her muscles quickly to warm them up. "I thank you for the honesty, Annie. In good faith, I have to tell you that I believe I am capable of killing three of you as your mercenaries attempt to murder me. Since you and Nakamura are closest, you are the most likely targets."

Annie blanched. "That's uncalled for!"

"And unnecessary," Kara said. "So, we can both dispense with the threats, then? I'm not here to sell you that one. You can have it."

She had thought it might float by them, but both Annie and Nakamura picked up on Kara's words immediately.

"What do you mean," Nakamura said with a sideways glance at the lock drive, "by 'that one?'"

Finally pulling the chair out from the table and slowly taking a seat, Kara shot a pointed look at the mercenaries.

Annie inclined her head to the back wall. Wordlessly, they retreated.

"TXM," Kara began, "is, by some unfathomably complex chain of ownership, associated with AssureGen. I assumed, based on the mercenaries, your company was interested in this venture because you understood, somehow, that the existence of this data was a possibility."

Annie leaned back in her chair.

"We Mariners are in possession of seventy-odd such drives. I don't know what all is on them. Some of the data is yours, undoubtedly. Some belongs to other companies or governments, I would assume. That's an interesting possibility, isn't it?"

Nakamura steepled his fingers. "Indeed it is."

"Before you dispatch a team of your people to die on our islands, I assure you we are not so stupid as to hide these drives anywhere obvious where they could be stolen. We have an entire ocean to choose from, after all."

For a moment, Annie gave her an appraising stare, all signs of her earlier feigned sympathy gone.

"What are your terms?"

"Leave us alone," Kara said.

"That's it?" Nakamura leaned forward. "Leave you alone?"

"Essentially." Kara made another show of stretching her leg. "We never wanted this. Your navy dragged us in to use us as a scapegoat when the Russians find out they've been robbed. We don't want the nukes. We don't want the drives. What we want, is your ships out of our waters. We want sailors to respect our island territories and conservation efforts. I want your help accomplishing this."

Annie gave Kara a brusque head shake. "I can't do anything about the free trade agreement."

"We both know that's not entirely true," Kara said.

"You control the politicians. You control these laws."

"It's not that direct," Annie said. "They won't do anything that could damage their reelection chances. It's too early for them to change position and support you. I'll need..."

Annie snapped her fingers. A dark haired man down the opposite side of the table piped up. "I'm giving seven point two weeks." He said.

"That long?" Annie made a face.

"I have to factor in the baseline approval rating of Mariners in coastal cities and—"

She cut him off with a wave. "There you have it. Can you wait two months?"

"No," Kara said. "We'll be attacked by then. As we speak, Japan is forming a response to the fishing vessel Grayson sank."

"Japan isn't so much of a challenge," Nakamura said. "We have enough influence there. You'll need to make a formal apology, though. Annie? That sound right to you?"

"Fine," she said. "That still doesn't help her with the EU and the RF."

"Ah," Nakamura said with a raised finger. "Challenge accepted. Try this on. TXM in partnership with, I don't know, what's that small frozen fish company we have? Grandpa Pearsons? We have a public change of heart after an impassioned plea by our girl here, and then we are one-hundred-percent onboard with the Mariner's conservation efforts. We brand the effort: 'Partnership for a greener tomorrow,' or something like that. Get marketing on it. Sure, we lose the better shipping routes, but we get the goodie-goodie points. The Mariners get most of the ships off their backs, and in enough time, you can get those stuffed shirts to do their jobs with the trade agreement."

Annie turned her appraising stare on Nakamura.

For a moment, Kara wondered if they even needed her in the room anymore.

"I see how that could work," Annie conceded. "You'll need to write a more detailed plan, though."

"What about the RF?" Kara said. "If they retaliate—"

"Must we do everything for you?" Annie said. "They won't. They can't. That base of theirs was illegal. Their spying is illegal. It's like one criminal robbing another. Neither one will call the police."

Even though she wasn't sure she liked being compared to a simple crook, Kara had to admit the analogy worked. To a point. Criminals often dispensed that sort of justice on their own, in secret. Perhaps Kara's people would need to find another way to deal with that potential retaliation.

"How are you living up to your end of the deal?" Nakamura made a gimme gesture over the table.

Pure negotiation. Finally, Kara was in her element.

"Two lock drives per year, to be paid on the anniversary of this agreement."

"How sentimental." Annie almost smiled, though. "Seven. At your rate we wouldn't finish this little arrangement for another thirty-five years."

"Which we're fine with," Kara said. "We would very much like to be left alone for a long time. Three per year."

"Make it four and we have a deal," Annie said.

Kara agreed. She traded handshakes with both Annie and Nakamura.

"Hot damn!" Nakamura clapped his hands. "I love a good deal."

As she waited for Annie's subordinates to draw up the legal documents, Kara realized she had signed the Mariners to something akin to a treaty. Their first one, ever. In a sense, it would be the first time they were legally recognized as a sovereign people.

After the formalities completed, Annie held out a hand again. "Thank you, Captain."

"Likewise. However, I'm not a captain," Kara said.

"Apologies. I didn't realize. I thought you were in command of a ship?"

"It's an acting command." In an effort to be hospitable, Kara pointed to her wrist, to the braided ropes interrupted by the great stitched up slash in her skin. "See the four ropes, here? Each one is a rank. Mate, Chief, Ensign, Lieutenant. When you reach Commander, you get a rising sun, here, above the sternum. A captain has a soaring eagle on their left cheek."

Her explanation attracted a small crowd. Traditional ink tattoos had fallen out of fashion many years ago in the United States, in favor of more modern body modifications.

"Do they all mean something? How about the compass on your hand?" Nakamura said.

"The compass means I'm a navigator. Having eight points instead of four means I'm a master navigator."

"And the heart on the inner wrist of your other arm?" Annie had zeroed in on her oldest tattoo. An informal mark, not an official symbol of merit.

Kara faltered, unsure if she should say. But she did. "This means I'm born of the heart. My mother rescued me from the docks of Skatch Harbor as a child. I would have died if she hadn't."

A hush swept over her onlookers. How many of them would have seen such poverty up close?

Nakamura rubbed his hands together. "Lieutenant, can I get you a car to take you back to the docks? I hate to think of you walking alone in the rain with that leg."

While the air had become more jovial since their agreement, Kara wasn't ready to get into a car, alone, with their people quite yet.

"Thank you, but the walking will be good for me."

Nakamura and Annie personally escorted her out of the building. Kara noticed that this time as she passed through the office, the people seemed to have evaporated completely. Nakamura seemed especially light on his feet.

At the front doors to the building, Nakamura placed his hand on his heart again. "Calm waters and peaceful passage."

Still bristling at his use of their greeting, Kara opted for diplomacy. "Calm shores, Mister Nakamura. Annie."

Outside, coated in mist, Kara began her walk. Her hands shaking the whole way back to Voyager.

Chapter Twenty-Eight: Home Again

"There's a reason why everyone from Jesus to Marcus Aurelius tells us to forgive and move on; to be unlike those that harmed us."
Alan Schwab, The Tao of the Core

The LEDs set overhead in the plain steel storage room winked to life. Gary, pulling a pallet jack with a large black crate on top, entered the room first. Bringing the jack to the center of the floor, he kicked the brake on with a foot.

"Leave her where she is, Gary," Big Madrid said. He entered the room after his mercenary, a new, more luxurious fur stole around his shoulders. This one made to look like sable.

Faulkner swept in after Big, his aide Grant and a rifleman for security following close by. "I want this done quickly, Madrid. The Gallant has been seen in too close proximity with all of this nonsense. Let's get paid and then I can get gone."

Always something with this poncy bugger. Big Madrid gently slid a hand over the case that held their goods, then faced Faulkner. Something else, however, caught his eye instead.

From the darkened hallway, a tall silhouette appeared. Before Big could react, the figure blurred and a silenced pistol shot cracked out in the room. From behind him, Big Madrid heard Gary crumple to the floor.

Instinctively, Big raised his hands. Faulkner, no dummy, whatever else he was, followed suit.

Faulkner's rifleman, however, felt he had a chance and took it. The poor sop didn't even get his weapon up before a second shot spilled the bastard's brains against the metal wall of the storage room. Bits and blood ran down the filthy steel.

Two people eased into the room. The first, the gunman, motioned for Faulkner and Big to back up. They complied.

As they stood on either side of the crate, the second man to enter shut the rollaway door.

Dressed in nondescript gray slacks and a white shirt, the man looked more or less normal. Too normal, in fact. If he ran from the room now, Big Madrid would never be able to find him in a crowd of tourists. He looked like a hundred other middle aged, balding bastards with a bit of fat.

Taking in the room, the man absently twisted a ring on his left hand.

"Captain Faulkner," he began in a thick, Russian accent. "Big Madrid. We have much to discuss."

Kara sat on a simple chair of woven bamboo. Her walking stick leaned against one of the inner corrugated steel walls of the shipping container.

Their only light came from the thin air holes cut from the ceiling of the long metal box. Steel bars ran from the wall to the floor, separating her from Grayson. Although still just as large, the hulking man seemed diminished, somehow. Stripped of all but his pants and shirt, he sat on the simple cot welded into the frame of his cell.

"Come to gloat about your big victory, have you?" He grumbled. A few days of beard growth had accumulated on his face and neck. "Me in here, you out there with the eagle and fish. Triumphant, or so you think."

"No," Kara said. "I came to tell you we're safe, for now. That was your original goal, wasn't it? To keep the Mariners safe?"

"Safe," he scoffed. "Kara, that agreement is absolutely worthless. Give them a single opportunity and they will break it. You may have bought us time. Nothing more."

"You act like that's such a terrible thing. Nothing is permanent, Grayson. My teacher taught me that. It's just as true for safety, treaties, our lives, anything. All we can do is keep buying ourselves time."

At the mention of Chief Lambros, Grayson's face twisted through a range of emotions. "Bah," he finally said. "Give it a year. You'll be releasing me with apologies. Those nukes will be getting put on display. Mark me."

Once finished, Grayson refused to speak again. Ghosts of bird chirps and wind filtered into the container through the air holes. Swaying branches overhead sent shadows dancing over them.

Letting out a breath, Kara stood and grabbed her walking stick. Before she could leave, Grayson looked up.

"I didn't mean for her to be killed, Kara. Chief Lambros had nothing but my respect. I didn't mean for any of that. I tried to stop the rifleman. You must have seen it."

Kara closed her eyes. "You may not have meant it, Grayson. I believe that. But what happened, happened. And it happened as a direct result of your actions. You must accept that."

With that, she left.

Midmorning was, in Kara's opinion, one of the best times to walk around Vish. With the sun not quite at its hottest, warming her face, the smells of life lacing the air, and all the activity of the people. Of her people.

Still, something in Grayson's words did bother her. In a way, he was right. This safety of theirs was temporary. Shadows still lurked on the horizon, and she had no guarantee that the corporates from AssureGen would truly honor their arrangement.

But a person could never find peace so long as they tried to control the uncontrollable. Another one of Chief Lambros's chestnuts.

Rows of mismatched shops and dwellings rolled past her in a swell of activity. That smell of warm plastic from the overhead solar canopies settled over her as she walked past the inker, where Omar stood outside chatting with a couple of his neighbors and Kara's mother. Their eyes met and Iminathi said a quick goodbye to the tattooist and hurried over to her daughter.

"Greetings, Skipper." Iminathi gave a fist to heart salute to her.

Kara blushed. "You don't have to do that."

"Yes I do," Iminathi said firmly. "It is proper. You are a captain now. I retired as a commander. I am more proud of you than you can know. So you will accept my salute."

Her eyes misting, Kara stood straight, and pressed her right fist to her heart.

"Ow, don't touch it! It's still fresh." Kara pulled away from her mother's fingers, which had gotten dangerously close to the fresh eagle tattoo on her cheek. Clutched between the talons of the eagle's right foot, a slender fish.

"I can't help it!" Iminathi laughed. "A meritorious promotion. My little cat wrangler."

Linking an arm with her daughter, Iminathi walked with Kara toward Vish Central. At first they didn't talk. They simply walked, greeting friends and letting themselves be part of the community.

At last, Kara found herself at the Bowl. Her leg didn't feel quite as stiff as she navigated the stairs to the bottom. Iminathi hung close by, Kara supposed, in case she needed some help. A small crowd chatted by the base of the stage. Drummond, Tren, Goldi, and Admiral Kim.

She hadn't gone to the council meeting that had just adjourned. Kara already knew what they'd be discussing and had opted instead to speak with Grayson. From the edge of the bowl, on the opposite side, Emeritus Mayer paused to give Kara a haughty stare before moving on. That night before they'd left, when Kara had felt nothing but anger for the woman seemed so long ago.

Elect Shostakovich also gathered there with Kara's friends, although he was on his way out. He made sure to congratulate her again on her promotion. His eyes held more than a small amount of worry, though. Ducking away, he made his excuses and left the Bowl.

"Iminathi." Drummond made a grand show of taking her mother's hand and greeting her.

Kara rolled her eyes.

"*Kotyonok*," Goldi said with a tiny smile, "Tone it down. She is out of your league."

"Sounds like it went all right?" Kara said to

Drummond.

The congressman shrugged. "I can't say the Elect was happy. But, with your backing, he believes my version of things. To be honest, I don't see him rushing into any more agreements with us Americans. At least we avoided open hostilities."

Admiral Kim motioned to Kara. "The captain's endorsement went a long way toward that."

Kara gave Drummond a considering look. "He did pull a bullet out of me, sir."

Admiral Kim smirked. "I have to go. Congressman, the Ram will be underway in two days time. I've made arrangements for you to sail with them to Portland. Tren, Goldi will show you to a place where you can lodge for the time being."

"You decided to stay?" Kara clapped his shoulders. "That's great news, Tren!"

Tren looked down at his feet. "Thanks. Hey, I was kind of wondering. How do you become a Mariner, anyway?"

Goldi's face lit up. She draped an arm around Tren and steered him toward the stone steps leading out of the Bowl. "Tren, my friend. You have asked the only question worth asking. Come, let us speak."

Drummond watched the Admiral leave the bowl in the opposite direction, an unsettled quality on his face as he did.

"Do you think we'll ever get there?" he said.

"Where is that?" Kara asked.

"You know. A place where Americans and Mariners can put the past behind us."

"If you would've asked me that at the beginning of this whole disaster, I would've said no. Unequivocally. Now? I think it's possible. It just goes to show that times change. Maybe this relationship between our people can change, too."

"Nothing is set in stone," Iminathi agreed. "And

even stone wears away."

"What are your plans when you get back?" Kara asked Drummond.

"Oh, the usual. Be universally reviled by the party-approved press. Get ostracized for sticking my nose in where it doesn't belong. Give Captain Faulkner a nice little surprise when he sees I'm still breathing. I've got another year before the party makes sure I lose my seat in the house, so I'll make the most of it." Drummond gave her a wry smile. "What about you, Captain? Any new adventures lined up for the Voyager?"

Kara chuckled. "Me? Oh, sleeping with one eye open in case the RF retaliates. Watching our islands like a hawk in case AssureGen decides they're done with our deal and sends mercenaries to come for our lock drives. The usual."

"Well," Iminathi said. "Before any of that happens, I promised Arnold I'd show him more of Vish. Kara, as a senior officer, you should come along and lend your expertise."

She couldn't say no to that.

As they left the Bowl and walked down the lanes of Vish Central, Iminathi commenting all the while, Kara's thoughts went to the future again and again. There were no easy answers and no certainties. About any of it. This voyage had proven that beyond a doubt.

What it also proved was that none of those things were insurmountable, so long as the right people were by her side. As long as they stood by each other.

Acknowledgements

The paradox of writing a novel is that while it's a solitary task, it somehow requires a lot of people to get it done. However, this time I didn't have to do it alone. Special thanks to Bob and the Brick Cave crew for making this book happen. It's good to be part of the team. As always, many thanks to Kathy, Monica, Cass, and Marlee of the Liberry Punx (we spell good) for reading, sharing, and critiquing. The story you've been getting in sporadic installments is now in its final, coherent form. Many thanks are in order to Sharon Skinner for lending your editorial expertise; I am grateful and the story is stronger for it. Naturally, my gratitude to the virtuoso artist Kyna Tek who created the cover for this book. Last but never least, to my amazing wife, Karissa, for not only putting up with the hours I spent holed up in my office, nights and weekends while I brought this story to life, but for always encouraging me to create more and chase my dreams.

Photo Credit: Karissa Burgess

Adam Marsh is a software engineer, U.S. Army veteran, and author of two science-fiction novels, *The Changed*, and *Survived*. His novels both received five stars from Foreword Clarion, and his work has been called "nearly impossible to put down," by Kirkus. As an engineer and lover of all things fantastic, his work tends to straddle the line between the real and the unknown. Adam has a degree in Computer Systems Engineering and a certificate in Novel Writing, both from Arizona State University.

CPSIA information can be obtained
at www.ICGtesting.com
Printed in the USA
BVHW081444041121
620791BV00015B/628